Mark Munger has crafted an electric edge-of-the-chair fiction that will keep you turning each page. Hollywood will take a good look at this one.

—Barry Reed, author of THE VERDICT and other novels.

Mark Munger has written a wonderful book. Not only is it a page turner — it also is rich with context and texture. I found myself engrossed in the landscapes he so richly described. I also found the characters interesting and compelling. I liked this book a great deal.

—Paul Wellstone, United States Senator

As a native of Northern Minnesota, I was particularly intrigued by Judge Munger's captivating depiction of the links between the present and past. Part historical novel, part contemporary thriller, The Legacy is a very impressive first novel which readers of this genre will enjoy immensely.

—Vincent Bugliosi, famed prosecutor of Charles Manson, author of HELTER SKELTER as well as AND THE SEA WILL TELL.

The Legacy

Savage PRESS
Box 115, Superior, WI 54880 (715) 394-9513

The Legacy

by Mark Munger

First Edition

Printed in 2000

This story is fiction. Places, names, characters, organizations or incidents are product's of the author's imagination and are used ficticiously. Any reference or resemblance to "real" people, places, organizations, living or dead, is used merely as artistic license to facilitate the fictional tale.

ISBN 1-886028-48-6

Library of Congress Catalog Card Number: 00-191482

Published by:
Savage Press
P.O. Box 115, Superior, WI 54880
715-394-9513

e-mail: savpress@spacestar.com

Visit us at: www.savpress.com

Printed in USA

Cover photography by René K. Munger

For My Teachers
Judy and Goldie,
Who Gave Me the Tools;
and
For My Wife René,
Who Gave Me the Courage.

Special Thanks to State Representative
Michael Jaros
for his kind assistance with respect to the
geography and history of Yugoslavia.

BOOK ONE: GHOSTS

The Legacy

Chapter 1

All Saints Day 1942

Hidden by the thick pine forests of the Julian Alps, three hundred Slovene guerrillas gambled that their mountain refuge would not be discovered. There had been no respite, no quiet from the war since the Germans invaded Yugoslavia. It was a foregone conclusion that the Partisans holding the mountains north of Ljubljana would be surrounded. They would fall that day. The combination of Nazi will, Italian numbers and Ustashi treachery was irrepressible. There would be no surrender; only defeat and death.

The guerrillas were to hold the peak at all costs. They were to insure the safe retreat of their comrades, to insure their escape from Ustashi and German forces rapidly closing in on them.

It was fall. The rainy season. To the west of the Partisan encampment, the constant retort of German guns could be heard. It was November 1, 1942 and there was no more Yugoslavia.

"When will the rain end?" a young soldier asked nervously.

The youth strained to focus his eyes. Cold November rain washed bits of native soil from his face as he spoke.

"I don't know," whispered an old man lying next to the boy. Both men shivered, immersed in the mire that defined the Partisan position. The old man did not look up as he spoke. He did not allow his son to see the desperation, the hopelessness in his eyes. Instead, Frederick Kobe stared ahead, in the direction of the enemy.

"Maybe they missed us in the storm," the son offered, speaking their native Slovenian tongue.

"I doubt that. Keep still."

The old man, a veteran of the Great War, turned his good ear to the wind. He strained to hear movement. He heard nothing. Nothing but the dripping of rain through the pine boughs. Nothing but the rumbling of the gale as it traversed through the trees.

His weary eyes surveyed the ragged barrier his men had erected to provide a defense. He bit his lip to ward off a deep, unrelenting feeling of death. A wave of dread began to overwhelm him. He fought against its power. He was their leader. He could not allow himself to become clouded by emotion. If his men perceived fear, they would run and running would guaranty their slaughter.

Perhaps if the Chetniks under Colonel Mihailovich and the Partisans loyal to Josip Broz had united in their resistance to the Germans, Frederick Kobe and his son would not have come to the mountain to die. But there was only hatred between the factions of the Yugoslav resistance.

Waiting for the Germans, Kobe considered the history of the invasion. He knew that Prince Regent Paul signed an agreement with Hitler in a feeble attempt to forestall war. What was the word the English used for Austria? Czechoslovakia?

"Appeasement," he murmured to himself.

Like the English, the fools in Belgrade tried to placate the Germans. For 48 hours, Yugoslavia was part of the Axis. A bloodless coup removed the Prince Regent from power and placed King Peter II a seventeen-year old boy on the throne. Embittered by the betrayal, Hitler ordered the German High Command to invade the Balkans. On April 6, 1941, the German 2nd and 12th Armies attacked Yugoslavia. By April 13, 1941, Zagreb and Belgrade, the country's major cities, were in Nazi hands. King Peter fled to England via Greece. The Yugoslav Army surrendered.

But German thoroughness failed in Yugoslavia. In Serbia, Mihailovich escaped to form the Chetniks, guerrillas loyal to the monarchy. Serbian in nationality, the Chetniks guarded the ethnicity of their organization fiercely. In contrast, Josip Broz (known as Tito) formed a cadre of guerrillas based upon Marxist ideology, not ethnic heritage.

The Chetniks were a known quantity to the West. The Partisans were an unknown. Tito himself was a shadow, an enigma. Under Tito's tutelage, the Partisan guerrillas created havoc for the Axis occupation forces.

And then there were the Ustashi; Croatian fascists who collaborated with the Germans; whose existence complicated the political picture dramatically.

Eli Kobe raised his head and listened to the sound of an airplane flying high above the trees. A splash of silver sliced through the mist. His father did not look up. Frederick knew the sound; the telltale exhaust of a Stuka dive-bomber probing the forest floor, hoping to see through the clouds to pinpoint the Partisan defense. Lost in his memories, the old man ignored the noise.

"Stukas," the father remarked.

"It rains harder."

"So it does. That may make it difficult for the Germans to find us."

The old man leaned his rifle against the wall and placed a raw, callused finger to his lips. Silently, the farmer prayed that the rain would slow the Nazi advance. He hoped the weather would force the Germans and their Ustashi allies to retreat from the muddy incline of the forest slope.

"Crack."

The discharge of a rifle rang out from below, indicating that the battle was joined. Immediately the air filled with a chorus of small arms fire. The sounds of war merged with the natural thunder of the storm to form a massive, onerous symphony of death.

Frederick and his son could not see the battle as it began. But the old man knew the tactics the Partisans would employ. He visualized, in his mind's eye, his countrymen leaping over the logs and stones that served as their breastworks. He heard their terrible Slavic battle cries resounding beneath the dark foliage of the mountain forest. He knew his countrymen were brave. He also knew they were outnumbered. Their brief forays into the advancing enemy would momentarily disorganize the assault but the Partisans on the mountain could not stop the methodical approach of the Germans.

From the beginning of the rains in September, the sun refused to shine. That day, the rain continued to pour down upon the bleakness that had become Yugoslavia. And the Germans continued to advance.

Lying beside Frederick, listening to the chaos of the German assault, Eli Kobe stared at a pool of muddy water forming beneath him. His fear would not allow him to look up, to see the progress of the battle.

"Bless me father, for I have sinned."

The words were Latin, not Slovenian. It was the Feast of All Saints. The thin, sickly form of Father Luba, a Catholic priest, scurried from Partisan to Partisan. Stopping briefly beside each soldier, the holy man heard confessions and served communion.

"Don't fear, my son, for you are now at one with God. May the Father, Son and Holy Ghost be with you."

The priest labored towards them on his hands and knees, his cassock torn by the thistle and brambles of the underbrush. The grease of the Slovenian mud soiled his woolen half cloak. Eli glanced nervously at Frederick. His father was an agnostic who tolerated Catholics because he'd married one. The Slovenian farmer would likely push the little priest away in disgust if Luba got too close. Eli held no such hatred. He was Catholic, like his dead mother.

Frederick Kobe's eyes glared out from beneath the soggy cowl of his canvas poncho. Instead of shoving the intruder away, the farmer merely grunted and slid aside, allowing the priest to kneel next to his son.

"Father, I have no sins to confess other than my fear, my fear of dying."

"Bless you son. But fear of battle is not a sin, it is natural."

A thin, skeletal hand, its fingers devoid of any muscle or fluid, touched Eli's brow. The priest's skin was cold, colder than the rain. Instinctively, the boy recoiled.

"Your sins are forgiven, my son, in the name of the Father, the Son and the Holy Ghost."

Again, ancient Latin echoed in the confines of the hedgerow. The words leaked out of the priest's throat, a throat dry and parched despite the abundance of water around them.

"This is the body of Christ, son. Take and eat it in remembrance that he died for you and feed upon him in thy heart for salvation from all thy sins."

The boy took the host and swallowed it quickly. Whatever the bread's true power, it seemed to warm him as it slid down his throat. Satisfied with his work, Father Luba made the sign of the cross and scurried behind tree stumps and boulders to minister to the next Partisan's soul. Eli returned his attention to the battle and peered over the edge of their makeshift wall.

Kobe was able to make out the forms of his retreating comrades as the first position of defense fell apart. Individual soldiers darted from tree to tree, collapsing towards the protection of the stone wall. Here and there, a Partisan would cry and fall, the victim of the unseen enemy. Slowly, the shapes of the advancing Axis soldiers began to emerge from out of the fog, never fully visible, seeming more like apparitions than flesh and blood. The boy raised his ancient fowling piece to his shoulder and aimed. He felt the strong grip of his father's hand lower the muzzle of the scattergun.

"Too far, Eli. They're too far away to waste your precious shells upon. I'll tell you when."

Frederick didn't take his eyes off the scene before them as he spoke. His eyes remained fixed on the enemy's advance. The boy began to shake uncontrollably in anticipation.

"Wait, son, wait. You'll have chance enough to kill one of those bastards, I promise. You'll have more chances than you want."

On their distant left, Eli watched Father Luba kneel over a badly wounded soldier. The injured man was exposed, having fallen just beyond the protection of the hedgerow. The forms of the holy man and the dying soldier were visible only as shadows. But the boy knew that the stricken Partisan was receiving his Last Rites. Eli Kobe watched as the priest applied the sign of the cross to the man's forehead. Without warning, the mountainside trembled, rocked by a barrage from the German guns. Before Eli could cry out, the priest and the wounded man vanished in an explosion of mud and vegetation.

The youth's eyes grew wide, his lean, innocent face contorted by the suddenness of the carnage. When the dirt settled, there was nothing left of the priest or the dying soldier. Nothing but a shallow crater in the dank earth. The bodies were consumed in the maelstrom, leaving no evidence or trace that the men had ever graced the mountainside.

Shell after shell followed the opening barrage, screaming down upon them, punctuating German proficiency in the art of warfare. 88's. 105's, mortars—they all killed the same. The munitions screeched across the storm's canopy and dropped into the quiet of the forest like hawks upon prey. Each distinct type of round emitted its own unique sound as it fell into the Partisans' lair but the death each caused was identical in its finality.

The boy and his father huddled behind their crude barrier. They could smell the gunpowder. Acrid sulfur singed their nostrils. They heard the moans of their countrymen, the cries of pain, the prayers to Christ ringing out across the wood.

The rain continued. Faint, moist drizzle dripped from the blackened needles of the pines.

Frederick had fought in the Great War against the Austrians. As a young infantryman in the Serbian Army, he'd seen artillery barrages before. He'd seen men die in battle. The space of twenty some years had not changed the way the Germans and their allies wrought death. The space of twenty years had not changed Frederick's hatred for them.

Shivering, cloaked with the mud of the hillside, Eli Kobe wondered how his country had come to be at war with itself, knowing that Yugoslavia had been created out of the dust of the Great War; a forced unity of disparate, warring cultures.

In the North, the Slovenes and the Croatians had long been part of the Austrian Empire. They were predominantly Roman Catholic in their faith. In the South, from the time of the fall of Constantinople on, Serbia, Bosnia and the rest had been under the control, the rule, of the Ottoman Turks, except for isolated periods of their history, when Serbia and Montenegro managed to break free and form their own weak, anemic kingdoms; kingdoms more of myth than reality in terms of historical significance.

The isolation of the South from the North entrenched the Moslem and Orthodox Christian faiths in Serbia, Macedonia and Bosnia. Even after a united Yugoslavian nation emerged out of World War I, binding the North and the South together in an uneasy constitutional monarchy, years of ethnic and religious unrest simmered just beneath the surface of the new nation. The invasion of the Germans and their allies stirred the unrest into a tempest, a tempest that fostered the Ustashi persecution of the Moslems, Serbs, Jews and Gypsies.

It was this history that Eli Kobe thought about as he shook in the bleakness of the damp Slovenian forest, his body shuddering from the cold, from the fear of the rapidly ascending battle. It was a history of foreign invaders driving wedges between the Slavic peoples, wedges that sought to destroy the splintered nation's ability to resist.

From somewhere in front of the Partisan line, the ghost of Milan Balich appeared through the fog, a gray specter suddenly outlined by the light of the incoming missiles.

A logger by trade, Balich was the eyes and ears of their section of the Partisan defense. He spent his days silently watching Nazi troop movements. He spent his nights sabotaging enemy positions. His rifle had slain fifteen or more German officers from a distance, from the safety of the forest's deep silence. He killed with no remorse; the Ustashi having murdered his wife and children as they huddled helplessly in a ditch on the road to Sisak.

Balich was Croatian but loyal to his country. Barrel-chested and thick armed from his years in the woods; he seldom pulled the trigger on his rifle without killing his target. The woodsman addressed his superior in Serbo-Croatian, the universal language of the Partisan forces.

"Frederick, it's bad. There are three divisions of Germans with the traitors. They have heavy armor and artillery. Two more divisions of regular Wermacht mountain infantry came in from Zagreb. I count at least twelve to fourteen thousand men, forty to fifty tanks."

Balich leaned against the log wall and wiped excess moisture from his brow with his sleeve, staining the cloth with the dirt and filth he'd been crawling in for days.

"What's happening to our forward lines?"

Frederick Kobe leaned forward. He kept his voice low. He sought to keep their conversation private, out of the other men's hearing.

"We pushed their lead units back for a bit, then they opened up on us with mortars. We had to give up our position and fall back into the trees."

"I saw. Look."

The farmer pointed.

"You can see them advancing."

Balich pulled himself along with his elbows until he was next to the wall. He raised his head above the edge of the protective cover and looked into the forest below.

"What units are they?"

"I can't tell. Germans, for sure."

"Can you slow them?" the elder Kobe asked.

"I don't think so."

The boy pulled himself up to the wall and stared down the misty hillside.

"I see them too. They are at the edge of the woods a few hundred meters from us."

Frederick crawled next to his son and viewed the battle. He nodded in agreement.

"He's right. They're about to break through. Where's their armor?"

"Advancing up the north logging trail. Their Panzers are supported by an SS unit. They're less than a thousand meters from us. Can you hear the tank engines?"

Balich wiped rainwater from his eyebrows and pulled himself back behind the wall. He spoke in short, halting sentences. His teeth chattered as his body fought off the penetrating cold.

"Their mountain infantry has taken the forest to the east and west of our main line. They're advancing more slowly, more cautiously. But they'll be here within minutes."

Eli Kobe strained to hear every word the Croatian spoke. He was startled by his father's voice. He sensed urgency in his father's words.

"Get to Comrade Doyich. Tell him the Germans are breaking through."

The weight of a callused hand, its grip firm and authoritative, pressed upon the young guerilla's shoulder.

"Yes father." The words leaked out from the boy's blue lips. Cold and lack of sleep showed on Eli Kobe's face. He rose from the mud and left the protection of the barricade. The older men watched as the youth climbed the open slope behind them. In seconds, the boy's form melted into the thin, desperate atmosphere of the mountain.

"It's good you sent him, Frederick. Perhaps he'll reach the camp and escape. He's too young to die here."

Frederick Kobe didn't answer Balich. He spoke softly, to his departing son:

"Live to fight another day. Kill them for me."

The soldiers turned their attention to the battle and waited for the Germans.

From airfields to the east, the Luftwaffe sent three squadrons of Stukas. Within minutes of leaving the front line, Eli heard sharp screams pierce the air. Though the rain and fog made it impossible to see the airplanes, he now knew what made that terrible, horrific sound.

Before Eli made Doyich's command post at the summit, hell was turned loose upon the mountain. Bombs dropped by the German airplanes tore through the trees, splintering old growth conifers, creating gaping holes in the Partisan line.

Dodging falling timber, Eli scrambled towards the peak. By the time he reached the place where Doyich's command bunker once stood, it was no more. No flag waved, no tents remained, no comrades were left to greet him.

The Legacy

Tens of corpses, battered by the Stuka's winged death, bloodied beyond recognition, welcomed him. Wounded soldiers saw his shadow and called to him. He did not answer. He was afraid. The stench of the dead, the smell of the dying made him wretch. His stomach convulsed even after it was emptied. He could think of nothing but running, running away.

He scrambled down the rocky slope, sliding on mud and loose rocks as he retreated. His head grew feint, his legs gave out. Covered with grime, dripping with the sweat of fear, he clawed at the wet earth until he was again standing. His fowling piece was gone, lost in the tangle of the rocks and undergrowth. He left the gun and continued his mad scramble down the slope.

He was lost, in pain. He began to cry. His course downhill became a blur, more an uncontrolled fall than a measured escape. In the dim light of the forest, he could not see those around him, though he heard the voices of other Partisans as the battle rose from the valley below, inching its way up towards his father, his friends. Voices cried out in Serbo-Croatian and Slovenian, their tone pathetic and panicked.

"They're through. There, on the left, they're through. Stefan, come here. Bring men. Stefan..."

A burst of small arm's fire. Then silence. His comrades were dying where they had dug in.

He passed no one. There was no retreat. The mist and fog that made it impossible for him to find his unit also kept him from harm. He stumbled on, his face a mass of cuts and bruises. His woolen pants and jacket were caked in mud. His eyes — his eyes were full of fear.

"Father," he screamed aloud, though there was no one to hear his voice but the enemy, "Father, I'm coming."

But he could not outrun the assault on the hedgerow by the enemy. Frederick Kobe was already dead, his heart punctured by the smooth steel of a German bayonet.

A shadow appeared out of the forest. Then another. And another. Helmeted forms moved through the haze. Germans.

Eli Kobe fell to the ground. He felt for the familiar walnut stock of his shotgun. It was gone, left somewhere up mountain. He was unarmed. He was seventeen.

Mark Munger

"Soon", he thought, "I will be dead."

One of the shadows approached him. A small figure, not much larger than he. An enemy soldier. The man carried his Mauser pointed at the ground. The German advanced without caution, without regard for the Partisan defenders. Other than Eli Kobe, there were no Partisans left. The boy remained still, just as his father taught him when they hunted deer. He controlled his breathing but his heart continued to pound beneath the wet wool of his shirt.

"Surely," he thought, "the German can hear the thump, thump, thump of my heart."

Hidden by a thicket, he watched the soldier. The man's short, thin form was thoroughly covered by a gray storm coat. The edges of the coat scraped the wet soil of the ground as the man advanced. They were alone on the mountainside, the other soldiers having merged with the forest. The German, looking to be nineteen or twenty, walked to within a few feet of the boy's hiding place, his steps noisy and careless. He stopped, as if he suspected something.

"I'm unarmed. He's older and likely stronger," the peasant thought.

Kobe noted the corpse of a Partisan, a huge man he did not recognize, a few feet to his left. The man had no jaw. All that remained of the dead Partisan's face was a small piece of flesh hanging loosely from where the man's chin had been. The skin of the corpse was milky white, beginning to turn gray, the color of the Nazi's coat, the color of the sky.

The corpse had no gun. It did have a knife; a long bladed skinning knife. Eli fixed his eyes on the soldier. The German became more cautious and raised his rifle in anticipation of something.

Kobe held his breath. Reaching across the corpse, he patiently eased the knife from its sheath. Kobe's eyes remained riveted on the slender back of the enemy. The German stopped and placed his Mauser against the wet trunk of a thick spruce tree. The enemy soldier kneeled to the ground and removed his gloves before beginning to dig in the trouser pockets of another corpse.

"Foolish Hun," Eli thought, "Partisans have no money."

The soldier crouched over the dead man, engaged in his search, his rifle two steps away. The boy sprang from the soggy ground. Wet leaves and mud dripped from Kobe's clothing as he rose. The sound of the debris falling called the German's attention to his attacker but it was too late. In an instant, Kobe covered the distance between them. With a severe motion, Eli planted the point of the knife in the center of the German's back. The blade sliced cleanly through the storm coat, hit a rib and deflected into the man's heart. The soldier turned to scream, his eyes bulging, surprised and in terror of death.

Eli clamped his hand over the man's mouth and shoved the blade deeper. The point pierced the front of the storm coat in a font of crimson. The German collapsed to the ground without a sound. Thick, warm blood coated the palm of the young Partisan's hand.

Exhausted, Eli Kobe sat down on the musty carpet of the forest floor and began to cry. He did not look at the German. One arm of the dead man rested across his hips. Kobe did not have the strength to push the German aside.

He sat there for what seemed an eternity, alone in the forest, unwilling to leave the dead man, unwilling to move. Then he realized that the guns had stopped, that all was silent on the hillside.

Gathering courage, Kobe touched the pallid flesh of the dead man, rolled the body away from him and stood up. Using the tattered edge of the German's coat, Eli tried to wipe the blood from his hands but he found that the half-coagulated liquid would only smear.

After collecting his thoughts, the young Partisan gathered up the German's rifle and cartridge belt. Above him, the November sun broke free of the clouds, warming the youth as he began to walk down the mountain.

Chapter 2

November 5, 1942

The Germans secured the City of Ljubljana the day the Partisans were slaughtered on the mountain. Immediately after the victory, General Von Reichs, the German commander, entered the undefended city with his men. For the first time in months, the sun sliced through the skies of the Alps. Its brilliance warmed the wet, devastated fields. Delicate fingers of the sun embraced the silence of the mountain, a mountain where three hundred Partisans lay dead. There had been, according to German intelligence, no prisoners, no survivors.

In truth, a few Partisans tried to surrender to the Axis when their ammunition was exhausted, when their outdated hunting rifles refused to fire. Their capitulation was of no consequence. The prisoners were shot by the enemy. Shot with their backs turned. Shot carrying white flags of surrender. Shot with their arms upraised, left to bloat in the warmth of the winter sun.

Von Reichs' troops marched into the city without contest. There was no one left to fight; only old men, old women, mothers and children. Even the single women were gone, having joined the Partisans. Their corpses were numbered among the dead on the mountain, the young women having fallen alongside the men of Yugoslavia in the defense of their unborn children.

With the Nazi's re-entry into Ljubljana, Damos Tomich, the local Ustashi Commander, became powerful. Very powerful. Tomich held tightly to his power; the power of life and death over his countrymen, the power of the firing squad. It was known that the big Croatian exercised his authority, authority bequeathed to him by the Fascists, with perverse joy.

Tomich was a strong, physical man, his physique hardened by years of backbreaking labor in the foundries of Zagreb. Only twenty-four years old, he'd shoveled coal, carried pig iron since his tenth birthday. Six foot two, one hundred and ninety five pounds, Tomich was as unyielding in his embrace of Fascism as the steel he created out of the raw iron of Yugoslavia.

When the Germans rattled their swords in the late 1930's, Tomich left the mill to join the Yugoslav Army. Though illiterate and uneducated, Tomich made his mark in the Army. His physical strength, unwavering determination and an ability to endure severe hardship without complaint endeared him to his superiors. He was an officer at twenty-two. A traitor at twenty-three, joining the Fascist Ustashi only hours after the Germans invaded.

In the process of occupying Ljubljana, Tomich's thugs scoured the alleys, cellars and warehouses. The quarry was not Partisan soldiers. There were none to be found. No, the quarry was the wives, sons and daughters of the Partisans. They found plenty. Over one hundred in nearby Celje alone. Many of the captives were related to Partisans. Many were not. It made no difference. They were all rounded up, arms slashed with bayonets, heads bruised by the butts of Ustashi rifles, herded together like cattle; crying, afraid, wailing to God, to Jesus. In the darkness they were marched through Ljubljana, along the road which even today follows the Ljubljanica River to the Sava. A distance from the city, Tomich lined up each and every suspected Partisan sympathizer for judgment; his judgment, a judgment from which there was no appeal.

They were all shot in the back, executed on the banks of the rain-swollen Sava River. There was no one to witness the deaths of Anna, Marie, Stefan and Josip Kobe. No one but those who pulled the triggers. Or so Damos Tomich and the SS officers, who supervised the atrocity, believed.

Marta Essen, wife of Lt. Franz Essen of the Nazi SS, saw. She was not supposed to. She was not supposed to be out beyond the gates of the city when the slaughter took place. All civilians, including the families of the German occupation, were under curfew. Marta disregarded the order.

Though it was near dusk, a bright moon rose above the terraced farms around the city. Enjoying the brisk night air, Marta went across the Sava to pick wildflowers in the hayfield of a deserted farm. As she knelt upon the soft, moist ground of the pasture, picking a bunch of delicate flowers, she heard the cries of children, the screams of women. The anguish of their voices caused her to look up and see. See the guns of the traitors cough orange across the river. See the bodies of the civilians crumple to the earth. Hear the moans of those wounded. Here and there a single pistol shot rang out, finishing the deed.

Even in the fading light, she recognized the slight form of her husband, Franz Essen, as he slowly walked past each corpse, searching for signs of life. She watched in silent horror as he kicked the dead with the heels of his jackboots. Wherever he detected a response, he placed his service Luger to the victim's temple and discharged it; systematically insuring the peasant was dead. She watched, trembling in fear as her husband completed his ghastly inventory. Night descended, cloaking the river bottom in horrific silence.

She knew her husband killed the enemy. He was a soldier. Soldiers fought wars, fought to survive. But murder was not the work of soldiers. This was barbarism, savagery. In the silent interval that followed, Marta Essen sat alone on the wet dew of the pasture. Her body began to convulse. Tears streamed down her soft, downy cheek and mingled with the dank Slovenian soil. She fought back a sense of responsibility, of shame, for the killings.

When her tears stopped, she labored to rise from the ground. For reasons she could not quite comprehend, she felt drawn to the place, drawn to the site of their deaths. Her legs were weak, making the walk across the wooden planks of the bridge over the Sava difficult. In her anguish, she dropped the wild flowers she'd picked. In her haste, she trampled the bright yellow flowers beneath her shoes.

The mantle of the November night fell around her. She stumbled towards them. She came upon the first of the dead. Two old people, the ages of her grandparents, were sprawled across the bloody grass. The couple clutched each other in death, their eyes glazed and unfocused.

"What did they think as the guns barked?" she wondered to herself. "Were their last thoughts of each other?"

Scattered among the piles of bodies, she made out the faces of mothers and their children. Bending down, Marta Essen reached out to touch the corpse of a little girl. The child was no more than four-years-old and possessed a remarkable, beautiful face. Touching the hollow of the girl's cheek, she felt the corpse's skin. It was cold, unnatural. Partially coagulated blood oozed out of bullet holes in the girl's chest.

"Why, Franz, why?"

She asked the question out loud. Only the dead were there to hear it. Incapable of further tears, she stared at the faces of two young girls, one beautiful, one ordinary, their arms entwined around each other. Two infant boys appeared to be resting within the protective embrace of the girls. Marta tried to breathe, her chest constricted by sorrow. The River coursed onward, completely oblivious to the evil at rest upon its banks.

Her emotions were confused, imprisoned, their release blocked by the sadness of the place. One of the girls, the ordinary one, grasped her sister so tightly that her fingernails tore the skin of the other child's forearm. The deep, serious wounds evinced the terror the girl must have confronted. What was remarkable to Marta was that there was no sign of pain or terror on the face of the other girl. She bent closer, studying the pretty girl's features by the light of the full moon.

Above her, the first stars of the new evening appeared. Infinite fragments of distant light emerged across the ebony sky. The stars caught her attention for a brief moment. But heaven offered only a fleeting diversion from reality.

"God, if you are listening, take these innocent souls to your kingdom," she prayed in German.

Her words were whispered as she sat amidst the carnage, staring up at the universe. Marta Essen made the sign of the cross, hoping upon hope that her Christianity was based upon truth, not myth. It was difficult for her to be sure of anything after what she had just witnessed.

Pushing her body away from the frigid ground, her eyes focused upon the torn tunics and breeches of the babies. The sight of the two dead boys forced her to leave. Their death masks haunted her as she walked home.

In her room, the reality of what she'd witnessed finally came to bear upon her. She climbed into bed, fully clothed, and hid beneath the blankets. She hoped her husband would never return. She knew that he was out celebrating his latest triumph with his men. She was confident that when he returned, he would be drunk and be in need of her.

Later that evening, unable to sleep, her eyes still wide with fear, she heard the turn of a key. She listened as her husband let himself into the hotel room they shared. A single kerosene lantern illuminated him as he stepped into their room. Feigning sleep, she watched her husband through half-opened eyes. Franz Essen was wearing the uniform of the German SS. His clothing was stained with blood and the greasy soil of the valley of the Sava.

"Marta, are you awake?"

She watched from the security of the blankets as he hung his jacket on a wooden peg, as he removed his muddied boots and dropped them to the bare floor. He walked toward her and clumsily sat down on the edge of the bed. His balance was negligible as he teetered precariously above her. He was drunk. The smell of booze permeated his clothing and nearly caused her to gag. She retreated further into the safety of their bed.

"Come here, my little apple dumpling. I know you're not asleep. Come here where I can touch you. I need you. This is no time for games."

The officer pulled the blankets away from her body, exposing her. She sensed his surprise, his anger, at finding her fully dressed.

"What's this, woman? Why do you befoul our bed with these clothes?"

He reached out with a dirty hand, its palm soiled by the work of the day, and grabbed her blouse. His gesture ripped the garment, exposing her breastbone. Her breathing was quick and frightened. She sensed that her bare flesh made him excited. She knew he was anxious for her. But she could not force her eyes away from the dried blood on his uniform.

Frau Essen's tears welled up as she stared at the blood. Babies' blood, grandmother's blood. She started to sob. Franz Essen did not know why his wife cried. Not knowing what to say, he slapped her across the face. The blow was something she had come to expect from him.

"Why are you crying, bitch? What have I done to harm your fragile ego? Did I forget to bring you flowers? Did I fail to comment on your perfume? What is it, woman?"

He reached out as if to strike her again. His eyes followed hers, and for the first time since he'd left the riverbank, Franz Essen realized that his uniform bore evidence of the day's deed.

The German slowly lowered his hand and placed it on his wife's bare forearm. She looked away from him, towards the wall, to escape the blood.

"No, my love, no. I'm not injured. Is that what you think, that the blood is mine? It's the blood of Partisan soldiers. We ambushed a platoon near town. Killed many, took others prisoner."

Marta watched her husband unbutton the top buttons of his trousers. She knew what was to follow. With his free hand, the officer stroked the soft, pink skin of her cheek. His touch made her wince, as if stung by a bee. She turned away from him, repulsed. She began to shiver uncontrollably.

The Legacy

"Damn it woman, why do you spoil my victory, my celebration? If I want you, damn you, I shall have you. Do you hear me?"

She felt his foot slam into the small of her back. She rolled into a protective ball and tried not to cry out. She prayed that he would give up and leave her to her pain. He kicked her again and again. How many times, she didn't know; she didn't care.

"I'll go now, whore, to drink more, to find a real woman who'll give me what I want. I'll be back, and you'd better be ready to service my needs or you'll feel my belt across that pretty face of yours."

Essen moved off the bed. He held the belt loops of his trousers as he gathered his boots and jacket. He slammed the door behind him. Plaster fell from the ceiling of the room onto the hard oak of the floor. His wife's silence drove the German from the room, from the hotel. She knew he would be back. He would not be refused a second time.

Marta Essen threw off the covers and sat on the corner of the bed. She looked at her face in the dirty glass of a mirror hanging on the wall. In the dim light of the room's single kerosene lamp, she surveyed the bruise on her temple. The damaged skin quickly turned a dark shade of blue, its edges streaked with red.

"The skin isn't broken," she murmured to herself, "Like when he used his belt buckle."

The wounds from the belt buckle had required sutures. She still used make-up to conceal the scar. The belt wounds he'd given her in the past would remain on her face for life.

"I'll not give you another chance to scar me, Franz Essen," she whispered, delicately touching the edges of the new wound.

Lifting her blouse, she pulled the cotton fabric over her head. She undid her camisole, allowing the soft silk of the undergarment to drift to the floor. She stood naked to the waist in front of the mirror. Her thin, gentle hands undid the single button of her wool skirt. She turned to examine her back in the reflection of the glass.

"Oh my God."

Four red purple welts intersected the curve of her back.

"That bastard. That child murdering bastard. What if I had been pregnant? He would have killed the baby. I'll be damned if I'll bear that monster's child."

Mark Munger

She wiped a lingering tear away. Staring at the wounds caused by her husband's anger, hundreds of miles from her home, from the safety of her family, Marta Essen came to a decision. She would leave him, leave him and seek out the first seaport that she could find. If she could get to Italy with her passport, she could find a way back to Germany, back to her family.

In the bleakness of the rented room, the officer's wife pulled a fresh blouse out of the dresser. She slid the garment over her head and snapped the fasteners together, quickly covering the bruises. She wrapped a woolen kerchief around her head in the style of the local peasant women. After packing a small leather valise with personal items, Marta Essen opened the door to the Yugoslavian winter and left her marriage.

Sometime after midnight, Franz Essen staggered back to his empty room. Cursing his wife, the officer fell onto the bed and tried to ignore the pounding in his brain. His pain was self-induced, the result of too much liquor. He found that he was unable to muster the energy to remove his uniform. The blood on his clothing had long since dried and did not stain the quilt. In a voice that was hoarse and hard-edged, Franz Essen screamed out his despair in the solitude of the bedroom:

"I'll find her, that little bitch. And I'll break her lovely neck."

The room began to spin as he tried to think. He resolved that he'd look for his wife in the morning. Fighting vertigo, Essen rolled onto his stomach. The sudden movement caused him to vomit over the edge of the bed. Sour, pungent bile dripped from the corners of the German's mouth onto the floor.

"Tomorrow I'll find her and remind her who is the husband," he said to himself between spasms, "and who is the wife."

His stomach empty, he curled up to sleep off the remaining edge of the alcohol, the events of the day having been long forgotten.

The woman walked south, towards the shores of the Adriatic Sea, towards the port of Susak. She walked over dirt roads and narrow trails in the dead of night. She took to hiding in the forests at daybreak to escape detection. But there were eyes watching her.

High on the northern rim of the forest, a seventeen-year-old boy followed the woman's progress. She walked, he walked. She rested, he rested. To him, a youth of the mountains, her gait was unfamiliar. It did not fit her peasant clothing. He couldn't place it. He knew it was unusual, that was all. For three days and nights he followed her. In that time she covered sixty kilometers, half the distance to the coast. By the third day, she began to slow. She appeared tired. The boy decided that he would confront her, ask if she was from Ljubljana. It was logical; she'd come from that way, by that road. She was obviously in a hurry to leave the city. She would know what had gone on there.

As his eyes followed the woman's progress, Eli Kobe sensed that they were not alone. It was a feeling he had, like the premonitions he'd felt hunting, an ability to detect the presence of an animal long before the prey was seen or heard. Someone else was following the woman. Someone was stalking her.

Despite the dense growth of the forest, he saw them. Two Ustashi. A thin, sickly-appearing man of middle age was in the lead. Wearing a poorly fitting uniform, the thin man was armed with an ancient shotgun. A larger, much older man, walked heavily behind the first Ustashi. The old man's upper body was protected from the elements by a battered storm coat. He wore civilian trousers, woolen shepherd's pants and carried a submachine gun. Several hand grenades hung loose from a rope tied around his ample belly. His clothes were stained with the filth of combat.

Eli watched the two men from a safe distance but remained close enough to insure that he would not lose sight of the enemy. It was obvious that they were tracking the young woman. With each stride, the Ustashi narrowed the distance between themselves and the girl.

At a crossroads in the trail, the woman stopped. She appeared to need rest. It looked to Eli like she was exhausted, done in by the cold and by the pace of her efforts. As she sat alone in the small clearing, her thin coat pulled tightly around her, Kobe watched the Ustashi close in. He contemplated responding but realized he could not show himself too soon. The fat man's machine gun would cut him down. He remained motionless as his father had taught him. She would be the bait to lure the prey into his trap.

Wordlessly, the thin one sprang out from the brush behind the woman. Before she could run, he pushed her down in the dirt.

He straddled her body, grabbed the fabric of her coat and pinned her legs down. Eli marveled at her determination. She clawed viciously at the his face with her fingernails. Fresh blood flowed down the sickly man's cheeks.

"Ich bin ein Deutschen Frau," she screamed into the thin Ustashi's face.

The traitor swore at her in Serbo-Croatian and screamed for his comrade to pin the woman's flailing arms to her side.The fat Ustashi tumbled atop her and used his weight to force the woman's body to the cold ground. Eli watched the thin one.The Ustashi's rage boiled over as the woman screeched louder and spit in his face. He tore at her coat and pulled the garment down around the woman's waist.

The fat man laughed as he tightly held his victim' s wrists. His companion tried to unbutton her sweater. She refused to lie still, frustrating their attempts to undress her. Furious at the woman's defense, the thin one tore her sweater apart at the seams, exposing her blouse, ripping the linen fabric, oblivious to the flow of his own blood as it stained the delicate white lace of the garment.

Kobe raised the Mauser, trained the sights on the fat man's temple and waited for a clear shot. Without warning, the young woman lurched upward and caught the end of the fat man's nose in her teeth. With a vicious twist of her head, she bit off the end of the man's nose, leaving only a bloody stump in the middle of his face.

"Crack."

The bullet caught the fat man square in the center of his forehead. He toppled off the girl onto the dirt. Both the woman and the remaining Ustashi turned their heads in the direction of the Partisan's hiding place. A second round erupted from the rifle and tore into the thin man's throat, causing his head to fall limp upon his shoulders. Before Eli Kobe rose from his position, both men were dead.

"Don't run, Frau," he called out in German. "I'll not harm you."

She reclaimed her coat, the remains of her sweater and a small leather valise and vanished into the trees before he could scramble down the hillside after her.

He knew she was exhausted, defiled and in need of food. He resolved to track her, to follow until she stopped once again to rest.

Leaving the relative protection of the brush, he approached the bodies. Unlike the terror that had swept over him on the mountain when he killed the German soldier, Kobe felt no remorse. As he stared into the chalky white face of the thin man, he felt nothing. The man meant nothing, was nothing. He simply wanted to make sure the pig was dead. The sickly one's heart was still.

As he knelt beside the fat man, Kobe's eyes were drawn to the center of the dead man's face. Only a bloody stump remained where the man's nose had been. There was no question the Ustashi was dead.

Chapter 3

November 5, 1942

On the evening of the fourth day, the woman awoke to the sounds of the forest. A subtle suggestion of trees danced beneath the winter stars. The full moon had passed.

Marta's eyes came into focus. Her heart began to race. She was not alone. A young man sat next to her under the shelter of the pines. He held a rifle loosely in his hands. As her eyes became accustomed to the night, she saw that the weapon was aimed at her. She began to shiver uncontrollably. She knew that she was alone in the wilds of the Yugoslavian hills and she was a prisoner.

"What is your name?" He spoke to her in a quiet voice, calm and without tremor, in a language she knew to be Slovenian. She shook her head.

"Auf Deutsche, bitte."

It seemed that he understood the words. His smile appeared genuine. His manner was not threatening. She felt more at ease.

He spoke to her in broken German, having learned it as a second language, Slovenia having once been a province of the Austrian Empire.

"Where did you come from?"

"Ljubljana."

He lowered the rifle; not completely, just enough to convince her that she was not in immediate danger.

"I'm the one who killed those two, the Ustashi."

She nodded. The movement was but the slight tilt of her head, as if the woman was embarrassed and did not want to acknowledge that the attack had taken place.

"Thank you."

She spoke in a quiet, tired voice. He smiled and lowered the muzzle of the weapon.

"I mean you no harm. Please believe that. I myself am on the run, trying to escape the Ustashi and the Germans."

He studied and tried to make out the details of her face in the relative darkness of the forest.

"You're one of them, aren't you? You're German."

The tone of his question bore no sense of threat. She nodded again. He continued to speak in a calm, reassuring tone of voice.

"Why are you out here alone, away from the city, on the road to the coast?"

She brushed her damp, yellow hair away from her forehead, the customary sheen of her blond hair diminished by the accumulated grit of her journey. She pushed the hair away from her skin, revealing a large, ugly bruise on her temple.

"Did the Ustashi do that to you?"

"No, my husband, a German soldier, an officer, gave me this. It's but one of many. I had to leave or he would've killed me."

Her words were spoken matter-of-factly, without a hint of sadness.

"That's a good reason to leave. A wife shouldn't have to endure brutality."

She noted that it took some effort for him to form the words in German. His comment did not roll gracefully off his tongue. His actions were awkward, like a young schoolboy. She did not know that he had been a schoolboy once, before the Mountain.

The Yugoslav moved his hand through the empty air between them in a slow, deliberate gesture. Sensing that he did not mean to harm her, she allowed him to touch her bare forearm. Kobe's cold fingers came to rest near the place Franz Essen had grabbed her with his bloody hand, in what seemed like another time, another life. The boy's touch caused her to flinch.

"I didn't mean to hurt you. Is it painful?"

She shook her head in the negative.

"It's nothing."

He knew she was lying to him. But he also knew her fear of him was gone. They sat beneath the trees in silence. She allowed his hand to remain on her arm. The warm familiarity of their closeness calmed her.

"What's your name?" she asked. Her eyes looked away, up into the night sky.

"Eli."

"That's a nice name, a strong name for a young man. I'm Marta."

She gathered her coat around her shoulders in a futile attempt to cut the evening chill. They continued sitting in silence, their eyes never making direct contact. Every now and then, they would chance a glance at each other in hopes that the other would not see.

Cloaked in quiet, the German woman and the Partisan slipped in and out of sleep, seeking rest in the uneasy slumber that only the weariness of war can bring.

Chapter 4

November 10, 1942

Marta Essen was not yet eighteen years old that November. Slender, tall and blonde-a boyish grin, a woman's eyes. Her eyes, deep brown and expressive, were Marta's most unique attribute. She was more than merely attractive. She was exceptionally beautiful. High Germanic cheekbones and shoulder length blond hair defined her face.

She had married Franz Essen in Munich. He was a rising star in the SS. She was a waitress in a Rathskeller that his unit frequented. He was the most unusual man she'd ever known, sure of himself, sure of his country's place in history, sure of his own ultimate role in realizing that destiny.

They married with her family's blessing when she was fifteen. It was 1939. She followed him to each duty station, as was the custom with the families of the SS. By 1941 Marta Essen had seen Austria, Poland and Yugoslavia. She'd learned a great deal. She'd learned that Franz Essen liked to drink. She also learned that he liked to make love to her after drinking, no matter how she felt about the subject.

At first, she tried to convince him she had a right to refuse his advances. When words did not work, on those evenings when he was too belligerent or violent, she physically tried to resist him. He broke her cheekbone on such a night. Sometime later, he broke her nose.

"Accidents," he told his comrades when they asked about the ugly wounds on his wife's pretty face. "Accidents."

She learned not to provoke his anger, his wrath. She found it easier to submit. She began to lie beneath him as if dead, allowing him his enjoyment. She did not stir. She did not return his kisses. She simply acquiesced to his demands and nothing more. Though their lovemaking had not started this way, Marta Essen knew it was destined to remain so.

Her knowledge of the world outside Germany before her marriage, her knowledge of French, Latin, and English, was gained through books her father gave her as a child. He was a university educator, a professor of literature in Munich. Her mother was a primary school teacher. Her parents gave her an education few children in Germany could afford. She was to begin her own training at the university the summer she met Franz. She gave up the university for love, or what she felt at the time was love. It was a decision that she lamented as she followed her husband's unit across Europe.

Before the Sava, she'd heard whispers of atrocities. Though Franz was violent towards her, she believed that she was somehow partially at fault for his outbursts. She was young. She had been a virgin when they wed.

"Perhaps," she thought, "it's my ineptitude that stirs his hate."

Marta Essen did not believe her husband or his men were capable of the acts rumored. Though the gossip followed the SS from Austria, to Poland to Yugoslavia, the talk did not concern her.

"My husband," she reasoned, "is a soldier, not a butcher."

Marta Essen's beliefs changed forever on the banks of the Sava River; when she looked up from the bouquet of wildflowers, when she witnessed the massacre, when she saw the traitors and their German allies.

"What did they call the big one?" she asked herself after the killing. "Damos Tomich," she responded to her own inquiry.

She knew him. Everyone in the city knew him, knew he was a viper. But until she saw him at the Sava, standing next the piles of the dead, she did not know the true nature of the man's poison.

The bodies she knelt beside and touched, the blood on Franz Essen's SS uniform, confirmed the rumors. These signs also confirmed Marta's suspicion that her husband's brutality fueled his impatience. The failure of their marriage was not her doing at all. Her recognition of that fact caused her to flee, to leave her husband to fulfill his destiny alone.

"Were you there, in the City?" the young Partisan asked as they walked towards the sea. A cold, bitter wind pushed them south, towards Susak.

"Did you see the killings?"

She nodded affirmatively.

"I can't believe your husband let you leave, knowing that you saw."

"He doesn't know. I've told no one that I was there. I told no one what I saw."

"What did you see?"

"I saw death. Little babies and their mothers and elders shot by the SS and the Ustashi," she murmured, the words barely audible over the sound of the wind.

"Now I think I understand the pain, the sorrow in your eyes," he interjected.

"Do you?" she asked impolitely. "I find that hard to believe."

She turned her face away so that he could not see how close to the truth his comments were. She didn't want to be too open with him. She didn't want to be dependent upon the Partisan the way she had been dependent upon Franz.

"You're too young to hear the whole of it," she remarked under her breath.

She was startled by the strength of his grip as he suddenly grabbed her upper arm. He stopped their progress and turned her body towards him. His eyes flashed in anger.

"Those were my people. Some of them may have been my family. I may be seventeen years old but I've killed men, I've seen death. Don't pretend to know the measure of my abilities, Ms. Essen."

"How can I trust him," she pondered as she looked away from his scorn. "How can I explain the shame I felt as a German, watching my husband and his men?" she wondered.

He released her. She began to walk away.

"Were there any survivors?" he asked in a more gentle tone.

"None," she whispered, considering the nightmare she had left on the banks of the river as she replied.

"I was in that place, alone, for a long time. There were no survivors."

Abruptly, he stopped and pulled a crumpled black and white photograph out of his front trouser pocket. He handed the picture to her. She looked closely at the faces in the photograph.

"Do you recognize any of them?"

"This can't be," she murmured.

"What?"

The faces in the picture were those of the four children she came upon at the Sava. She could not forget them.

"Please sit down," she requested, her voice fighting a cascade of raw emotion.

They stopped and sat next to each other on a decaying fir. She studied the picture, then her companion's face, beneath the lonely, lifeless sky.

"Do you know them?" she asked.

"Yes."

"How?"

"They are my brothers and sisters."

Marta gazed off into the distance, searching for the right words, hoping to find the courage to tell him the truth. She released her grip on her valise and placed her hand on his sleeve. The suitcase tumbled to the frozen ground but did not open.

"I'm sorry. I saw them on the riverbank, with the others."

"Are you sure?" he asked, his German faltering as he fought back the urge to cry.

"Yes," she replied, her voice stripped of its maturity.

"I knelt with them, prayed for them. I will never forget them. They were so beautiful. Your sisters tried to shield the little ones with their bodies. They did everything they could to save them."

Kobe's sobs interrupted her story.

"That would be Anna's doing. I should have been there with them."

"And you would have died. There were twenty or more soldiers with my husband. You could not have stopped them."

She moved closer to the Yugoslavian. Her hand reached out to touch his cheek. He did not protest her familiarity. She pulled his head towards her skirt and let it rest on her pelvis. His head found the deep, soft folds of the fabric and he wept. She stroked the base of his neck, gently braiding and unbraiding his hair. The pace of his breathing became slow and content. The tears abated. She leaned against the rough bark of a birch tree and closed her eyes, trying to shut out the images of the dead children.

Hours later, Eli Kobe sat upright, gathered his rifle and rucksack and motioned for her to follow. As they resumed their walk, their pace was slow and labored. Marta Essen sensed the soldier's heart was as heavy as his steps.

"It' s dangerous for me to trust her," the Yugoslav thought as he negotiated the path up a sharp rise. "She' s German, the enemy."

But in his heart, he knew Marta Essen could be trusted. Her eyes betrayed her soul. And her soul was kind and honest.

They climbed a short distance before he turned and spoke again.

The Legacy

"I don't know what we'll do once we reach the coast. I'll probably find another unit. You should find a way home."

Though an anxious look darted across her face, she didn't answer him. It began to rain. Leaving the wet misery of the forest, they emerged into an idle grain field. The stubble of long-neglected barley waved precariously in the brutal wind. Crossing the damp pasture, they found refuge in an abandoned barn. They were only ten kilometers from the coast.

"We'll be safe up here," Kobe said as they climbed into the hayloft. "We'll be out of the wind."

The loft was bare. There were no bales of straw to cushion their weary limbs as they sought sleep. Storm-driven rain assaulted the rotting exterior of the building as Marta reclined against the damp wooden wall of the rotting barn. She began to shiver beneath the meager protection of her coat. Hunger drove Marta to open her valise. She retrieved a small brick of goat cheese and stale bread from deep within the bag.

"It's not much good but at least it's something," she said, sharing a portion of the food with her companion.

"War cheese," Kobe observed as he broke off a small piece and placed it in his mouth. "Stale and dry."

The woman looked at him with sad, wide eyes.

"I can't return to Germany. If I do, Franz will eventually find me. I don't want to think of what he will do to me."

The Yugoslav listened intently. Marta tried to interpret his reaction by studying his face. The fading light did not allow her to see his expression in detail.

She knew he had small blue eyes and slick, black hair. She knew he had a face that she could trust. Gazing absently at the darkened ceiling, the young woman found solace in the auditory pattern of rain striking against wood. Despite the advancing night, she was able to make out the great cedar beams that spanned the width of the barn and supported the roof. Her ears concentrated upon the sound of rainwater dripping furiously between spaces in the shingles, spaces created by years of severe weather. A lingering odor of livestock permeated the place and reminded her of the building's purpose.

In the midst of her melancholy, she felt his eyes staring at her. When she turned in Kobe's direction, the soldier diverted his gaze. In turn, she averted her glance, uncertain of what more there was to say between them.

The wind began to howl and the rain began to freeze. Rivulets coursing between the fragile shingles solidified, creating miniature stalactites of ice. Kobe watched the German girl sleep. He took comfort in the short, strong breathing of her slumber. His eyes followed her dirty hair from the base of her neck to where the yellow fibers rested on her coat. As the tenacity of the storm increased, her involuntary shivering became more severe. He took off his coat and covered her.

The garment rose and fell to the gentle waltz of her slumber.

He felt tears well up and he fought the urge to cry. Leaning against the unforgiving wood of the loft wall, he considered their situation. After a moment of studied contemplation, the Partisan crawled beneath his coat, keeping an appropriate distance from the woman in his attempt to stay warm.

"What will become of us?"

Kobe directed his question to God as a mantle of fatigue descended over him. The angry dissonance of the storm provided no answer to his question.

Chapter 5

November 11, 1942

"Look there, along the road."

Marta's voice was strained with nervousness as she pointed to a flock of doves rising from just beyond a bend in the road to Susak.

"Someone's coming."

Kobe touched his finger to his lips, signaling their need to maintain silence.

"Germans."

He grasped Marta roughly around the waist and pulled her from the edge the gravel into the protective cover of the woods where they silently anticipated the passage of the enemy. Her observation had saved them. She had been alert. The young man knew he owed her his life.

"Susak must've fallen."

"If we'd have only known," he thought to himself. "Now it's too late. We've come too far to turn back."

He admitted to himself that the young German woman had proven her loyalty, her worth. Her detection of the soldiers prevented the two of them from walking headlong into the Axis soldiers.

"Thank you."

Marta looked at him quizzically. The sound of German leather striking gravel overwhelmed his whispered gratitude.

What he did not tell her was that, if they had taken him, there would have been no trial, no appeal, only a bullet in his head or the scaffold. Probably the scaffold, where a man suffocated under his own weight. He did not disclose these thoughts to her. He held his tongue and watched the enemy in their freshly-laundered gray uniforms march by.

Huddled in the underbrush they could do no more than observe the parade of Axis soldiers on its way to Fiume. Fiume. Another town for the taking. Or had it already been taken? Eli Kobe did not know. All that was clear was that he was helpless to do more than watch.

It took several minutes for the column to clear the road. The departure of the Germans did not make Kobe's decision any easier. They were both fugitives;

one certainly to be sought by an angry SS officer; one clearly marked for death if captured. The Partisan had eight Mauser cartridges, no food and no official papers; papers required by the Ustashi and the Gestapo of every person not in an Axis uniform.

"I'm not certain where we should go."

His eyes betrayed fear. Not the fear of the enemy, but the fear that he would ensnare her in his death. The prospect of her existence weighed heavily upon him. He knew that her fate shouldn't be of consequence to him; she was the enemy, a German. It was foolish, stupid. Yet he couldn't help thinking that her life was in his hands. He was falling in love with her and his acceptance of that emotional bond made him feel responsible for her safety.

"We can't go to Fiume, the Germans are headed there. What's in Susak? Your husband? The SS? I can't see a way out of this."

He reached out to her with his hand. She accepted the gesture and pulled herself up from the dirt by grasping the worn wool of his jacket sleeve.

"This isn't my country. I can't tell you where to hide, where to go, where we will be safe. I can tell you that I trust you. I'll do as you say. I have to, you're my friend."

Her eyes sparkled as she spoke. She wanted to say more but she was too wet, too cold, too tired. Her womb ached. It was close to her time again, the unsettled time of each month. She felt ill—she always felt ill then. Franz hated her for it. His beatings were often delivered during those days. No, her condition was something she kept to herself. She did not tell Eli Kobe about the pain and the nausea. She doubted whether he would understand. In any event, the condition would soon pass.

Lost in thought, Kobe stood next to the German woman. Thick fir branches blocked the midday sun. He tried to anticipate what path his father would take if his father were in the same situation. He tried to remember the sound, the texture of his father's voice. The forest remained mute; no spirits counseled him.

The pain of his father's death was still too close, too real. Kobe found that he couldn't think clearly. He stood dumbfounded, his mind seemingly frozen, unable to determine a plan of action. All the survival lessons he'd learned from his father were lost, suspended in the idle wanderings of his mind.

The Legacy

In desperation, he spoke the first words that came to him.

"It's late. We must find a place to spend the night."

Marta sensed the words lacked confidence. Without complaint, she lifted her valise, muddied and torn from their journey through the rugged terrain. Kobe called out to her as he began to ascend a path leading through the conifers towards the sea. She could scarcely hear him over the gathering wind.

"This is a shepherd's trail. It'll lead us to a farm," he advised in a voice filled with false optimism.

"There may be sympathizers there, perhaps a warm bed and hot water."

Raising the hem of her skirt above her ankles, Marta Essen traversed the tall grass, the blades heavy with evening dew, and followed him. Their path took them across a sharp ridge down into a ravine where they forded a small brook. Immediately beyond the stream, the way began to embrace higher ground until the trail ended abruptly in an open meadow. There was no farm at the end of the path; only the decadent yellow hay of approaching winter greeted them as they emerged from the forest. Dead oat straw danced in time to the passing gusts of winter. The pasture was quiet, empty and abandoned to the war.

"It's late."

Evening was close at hand. Kobe was unable to decide which course to take. His indecision and the retreating daylight compelled them to remain where they were, several kilometers from Susak, concealed in the hills.

"We'll stay here for the night. I don't think the Germans will look for us up here. There's nothing for them up here," he observed.

"I'm tired—tired of walking through damp fields, tired of lifting my aching feet. You'll hear no objection from me," Frau Essen said.

She slipped the strap of the valise off her shoulder. The suitcase dropped heavily. A huge plum tree, its branches bare of leaves, cast shadows across the hayfield. Sitting on the valise, her back wedged against the soft bark of the great tree, she pulled off her shoes, her thin silk stockings, and massaged her feet.

Though she would have chanced Susak in hopes of a warm fire and a hot meal, she understood the likelihood of finding either was remote. It was far more likely they would be stopped, questioned and shot if they were discovered. She did not complain about the choice Kobe made.

Her companion pulled his canvas raincoat off from around his waist. Shaking the water from it, he placed it upon the ground.

"It's going to freeze tonight, Marta. We can use my raincloak for a ground cloth and my coat for a blanket."

Kobe did not wait for her to respond. His hand grasped hers and pulled her off her valise, onto the coat.

"Eli, I'm married. I can't lay with you like some common animal." The Yugoslav detected fear in her voice as she spoke.

He continued to pull her towards him. But aware that force would only frighten her and remind her of the beast she had married, he was subtle in his application of strength.

"I won't harm you. God is my witness I won't," he promised.

Staring at the boy in the dimming light, she believed him.

"Alright."

They lay down together; his arms about her waist, their bodies huddled tightly against the cold. Only the glory of the setting sun, pausing large and yellow over the foothills, hinted that their journey together had meaning, had a chance. The day's waning warmth was replaced by the crispness of evenings' descent. It was not long before they both fell fast asleep.

Later that night, Marta awoke to a hand clasped tightly over her mouth.

"Soldiers," she thought, her heart beating excitedly.

She tried to cry out, to warn Eli, but found that she could not scream. The unwelcome grip prevented any sound from escaping her mouth.

She searched the shadows for him. When her eyes adjusted and she finally found his face, she saw that he was calm. He spoke to her in his own language, a language she did not understand. Eli Kobe discerned, from the stark terror spreading over her face, that she was frightened. He spoke again, this time in German:

"Don't worry. We're among friends."

The rough hand, its skin toughened and worn by a hard life lived outdoors, relaxed. It was then that Marta Essen realized Tito' s Partisans had found them.

The Legacy

Chapter 6

November 20, 1942

Anna Kobe had been fourteen. Her eyes were blue, as blue as the sky above the Slovenian hills. She was always laughing, giggling, never afraid to be in tune with herself. Never, never, did she frown. The only moment of sadness her brief life had known before the Sava was when her mother died giving birth to the twins.

It was hard on Anna, being of marriageable age herself. Her body had blossomed; her newfound femininity attracted the village boys. Rounded breasts and hips appeared overnight, transforming her into a young woman. She was short, barely five feet. But her waist was small, her form lean. Anna was quick to flash a bashful smile at even the most rude and persistent boys of her village.

Momma had been due to give birth in June of that year, the year before Ljubljana. The early summer had been hot, unbearably so. There was no doctor in their village near the Austrian border. The nearest was in Jesenice a day away by horse, a half-day by motor car. The labor pains came so early that no plans for a doctor could be made. Only Marie was there. Frederick was in the forest. Eli was tending to the family's sheep and goats up in the summer pasture. Anna was in the village bringing their cheese to market.

Marie was the black to Anna's white. She was sourful. She rarely laughed. At twelve years old, her outlook on all things was serious. She was plump and not very pretty, though her constant frown made her appear uglier than she really was. The approach of womanhood terrified Marie. No matter how reassuring Momma was, no matter how many times Momma explained the need and reason for her changes, Marie could not accept them. She would not.

Her eyes were a mirror of her soul. They were gray, murky and without spark. But she was a hard worker and dependable. She did not give in to occasional flights of fancy as Anna routinely did. Marie was to be trusted, the one that Momma relied upon.

On the day of the twins' births, Marie was there. Sorrowful, dependable, she held her mother Julianna's hand as Stefen, then Josip were delivered. Marie stood by in utter horror and disbelief as her mother's lifeblood spilled uncontrollably from the womb, staining the bare pine floor of the farmhouse. Witnessing the anguish of childbirth and her mother's cruel death confirmed Marie's beliefs, her fears, her hatred of life.

Anna wept when she returned from the village. She wailed when she found her mother' s corpse, when she found Marie cowering on the floor in a corner, unwilling to look at the twins, unwilling to attend to their cries of hunger. But young Anna realized that there was no time for the sisters to weep, to mourn.

After she consoled Marie, after she kissed the forehead of her departed mother, Anna approached the twins as they wailed in the rough-hewn cradle next to the mother they'd never know. Two beautiful, healthy boys. Strong Slovenian stock. Kobe Stock. Black eyes. Black hair. Brown skin. Anna sat beside Momma's lifeless body and held them both. She wiped away her errant tears and smiled. "Hail Mary's" filled the small bedroom of the house.

"God is gracious. God is good. God has sent the miracle of life to sooth our sorrow."

Then she began to sing. Anna sang in the soft high soprano of a young lady. The tune was one Julianna sang while working in the fields, "Anna. Anna."

Lost in the deep caverns of sleep, Eli Kobe murmured her name. In the fantasy light of dreams he reached out to touch Anna, to console Marie. Though he'd glimpsed them in the distance, beneath the crest of a familiar hill, the knoll rose ever higher, ultimately engulfing the girls in an unyielding avalanche of suffocating earth. The Partisan woke in a start, covered with sweat.

"You had a dream, Eli, a nightmare. Don't be afraid. I'm here."

Marta Essen's soft hand reached across a straw mattress to touch Eli's face. Her index finger stroked his weather-hardened jaw interrupting the route of his tears. She knew the reason. She'd heard bits and pieces of the dream. He'd cried out in Slovenian, a language she was only beginning to learn. She recognized enough of what was said to realize the content of the nightmare. Her delicate fingers stroked the sweat-dampened hair of her companion.

"I'm still here," she said to disrupt the awkward silence.

He listened to her words. It was the first time he had concentrated on the texture of her voice. It was mellow and fluid like fine honey. Its tone soothed his upset. He closed his eyes, trying to bat away the tears.

He was ashamed she was witnessing his weakness.

"You shouldn't see me like this. I'm crying like a baby, a child."

The peasant's words were bitter. The harsh inflection of his depreciating remark was not in his nature. She forced his head upward, up from the straw mat that formed their bed. Her eyes glistened as she fought back her own tears.

"There's no shame in missing your family, in mourning their deaths. It makes you more of a man, not less," she said in a reserved voice. "I know this. I lived with a man who could not cry, whose soul could not be touched. Because of it, he was not a man. He was an animal."

"I feel so helpless. Their frightened faces come swirling back to me and I cannot save them. Their cries engulf me, surround me, begging for me to come. But I don't. They are gone before I can save them."

Marta Essen took a deep breath. Her voice lost a fraction of its strength as she continued.

"If not you to keep their memory alive, Eli, then who? Sleep now. Sleep, and tomorrow you will be strong. Their souls will let you rest because you have remembered."

In the morning, a red sun slowly rose above the forested slopes to the East.

"Wake up."

A familiar hand reached inside the wool blanket covering them and roused the couple from exhaustion. Kobe recognized the voice of George Petrich, leader of the Partisan unit that had found them. They were on their way to the Island of Hvar on the Adriatic Sea.

"The Germans are moving towards us from the valley. We've got to get to the beach by early afternoon."

Kobe pulled the coarse blanket away from his face. He nudged the German woman, waking her.

"Marta, it's time to leave."

"Good morning, Frau Essen." Petrich's greeting in German was perfunctory, without emotion. His accent made the words roll off his tongue thickly. He gave the impression he didn't generally take time to exchange pleasantries.

"The two of you better get ready for a long day. We have to make Split before noon or we'll miss our boat to Hvar."

Mark Munger

"Why Hvar, George?" Kobe inquired.

The young peasant uncoiled from the warmth of the wool and stood naked to the waist before his commander, leaving the woman protected by folds of fabric. Kobe stretched his limbs within the sparse confines of the unheated shed they occupied, a building that had once served as a lamb nursery. There was more than a faint smell of sheep locked within the dry timbers of the building.

"Safety," Petrich replied as he exited the shed. "Hurry."

Kobe nodded. Picking up his rifle and his pack, Eli leaned over and placed his eyes mere millimeters from his companion' s face. Despite the dirt and filth accumulated on their journey, she was beautiful.

"Don't be long, Marta. George is not a patient man," the Partisan whispered.

"I've noticed."

Her reply was defensive.

He caught the full profile of her face in the ascending light of the rising sun and moved to kiss her, to touch the softness of her neck. He stopped short. He recognized that there was no time.

Outside, the sun's pale yellow fingers crept above the low peaks of the foothills. Rounded hillocks bordered the pasture of the farm the Partisans occupied. Seventy-five soldiers rose from bivouac at the sound of Petrich's booming voice. Bones and joints moved agonizingly slow in the cold, still air of the early winter morning. A flock of crows squawked and flew over the remains of an unproductive field. Scarce, fragile stalks of oats strained to be noticed in the acres of wild vegetation. It was clear the land had been a poor farm, but its weak soil had likely provided enough mutton, eggs and bread to feed the owners until the Nazis arrived. All that remained of the abandoned enterprise were decaying buildings and wild, weed-infested fields.

They set out across the wind-hardened land with the gathering warmth of the sun behind them. Marta walked near the rear of the column with two old toothless grandmothers whose usefulness in war had long since passed. Seven young Yugoslav women could be counted among the Partisan soldiers. Each of them carried a rifle. Each was as valued in the field as the men they marched with.

At Split, they were to meet the Helena, a Greek fishing trawler owned by

Mikos Pappas. Pappas was not only old, he was ancient, at least seventy-five or better. Short and stocky, he was built for the sea. Sixty years of pulling nets in the waters around Corfu molded his torso, his arms and legs into anvil-hard muscle.

When Pappas was trapped in Yugoslavia by the Axis invasion, his boat had been commandeered by the Ustashi to transport troops and supplies. But the Partisans had liberated Split and, at least for the moment, Mikos Pappas worked for Petrich. He had his reasons for disliking the Axis.

"The Italians and Germans," he had been heard to say, "drink Greek wine and rape Greek women. Give me a chance and I'll castrate them all. I'll throw their balls to the sharks. Then we will see who's the master race."

Petrich's column followed a well-worn path from the edge of the abandoned farm into the dark twilight of the coastal forest. At every opportunity the guerillas attacked the enemy, disrupting supply lines, destroying truck convoys. Fuel depots were burned; Ustashi traitors, German and Italian soldiers were ambushed at every chance. There were no prisoners, for that was the rule of war imposed upon the Yugoslavian guerrillas by the Axis. Knowing the hills, the forests, they struck. They killed. They vanished. Even the Ustashi, natives of the same land, could not find them, could not stop them.

Kobe's eyes glanced to the left. To the right. As the soldiers made their way down the steady descent of a narrow path, he noted the movement of their Scouts probing the forest's silence. On each flank, a single sentry carefully surveyed the thick forest edge, the undulating line where leafless thistle and brush rose up to meet the mature vegetation of the slope. At the junction of forest and trail, slender silver and white trunks punctured the ground. Hard, clear ice covered the limbs of the trees. Drops of melting water traversed the branches, moving slowly towards the earth as the ice disintegrated under the sun's growing warmth.

The path to the Dalmatian beach became steeper. The trail beneath their boots turned rocky. The route was covered with stones. Temperate pines, coaxed into quick growth by the warm winds off the sea, began to interrupt the thick, confining bramble of the hardwoods, creating a less confining canopy. Boulders punctuated the forest floor. The well-defined path they followed became subtle. Segments of the trail were disturbed by nature's random placement of freshly fallen trees. Brown needles carpeted the ground in thick decay. Ferns struggled to maintain their withered, rust-colored manes against the advance of winter.

Kobe moved towards the head of the column. His legs were tired. Their pace, despite the terrain, remained quicker than Kobe was used to. He felt a deep, unfamiliar burning within his thighs and calves. He needed water but there was no indication from Petrich that the soldiers would stop any time soon. His wineskin was empty. His mind drifted back to the German girl.

"What do I feel for her? Love? Sympathy? Lust? What?" he asked himself as he instinctively placed one foot before the other.

The fatigue made it impossible for him to concentrate. Exhaustion made her vanish from his mind's eye.

A single bullet struck Petrich's hip before anyone heard the muted bark of the enemy rifle.

"I'm hit."

Kobe dove behind the nearest boulder and watched helplessly as Petrich fell. The Partisan leader crumpled to the ground, caught out in the open, his lower extremity trapped beneath his good leg. Another shot rang out. Another scream of agony. Another Partisan fell. The battle was joined.

Instinctively, the column scattered. Each soldier sought the protection of the rocky ground. Kobe slid along his belly to a position to the left of the thin defensive line of the guerrillas. He could see Petrich was totally exposed, could see Ustashi bullets slapping the dirt on each side of the fallen man, spraying Petrich with a shower of brittle needles and dead leaves.

"George, don't move. I' ll get you."

"Stay put. Don't be stupid," the officer replied.

The attackers remained hidden. Kobe could not tell how many there were. He knew that Petrich could not last much longer. It was only a matter of time before another bullet struck the man, killing him.

"Lisa, cover me," Kobe screamed above the pulsating beat of the rifle and light machine gun fire. He looked to the rear, to where he knew Lisa Ursich should be. Ursich didn' t respond. Her temple was torn open by a Ustashi bullet. There was scant flesh left where once, a beautiful, young factory worker's smile had been.

The Legacy

"She's dead. This is Dravich. I'll cover you. Stay low."

"I'm coming George."

There was no response from the fallen commander. Rolling to his right, Kobe cleared the boulder protecting him. He was vulnerable, without cover. Behind him, Dravich opened up with a submachine gun, spraying the woods ahead of the prostrate Petrich with rapid fire. Others took up the assault as Dravich paused to reload. Kobe coiled and vaulted the distance between them. A burst of Ustashi gunfire cut through the gunpowder-filled air. The bullets tore through the thick fabric of Kobe's jacket but did not strike flesh. He landed atop the fallen man, his rifle at the ready.

More enemy bullets struck the ground around the two men.

"Keep down, Kobe," someone screamed.

Eli did not recognize the voice. A Partisan to his left threw a grenade. One on the right threw as well. Two dull thuds could be heard as the explosives landed within the Ustashi ranks. Two simultaneous explosions rocked the forest floor; deafening Kobe as he lay on top of Petrich's body.

From the rear, a rallying cry went up as the Partisans began to advance. Outnumbered, the Ustashi, never having seriously threatened the main body of the guerrillas, withdrew into the mystery of the forest. The Ustashi left behind twelve of their number. The attack killed fourteen Partisans. Five others, including George Petrich, were wounded.

Kobe remained motionless. His hands trembled. Only after the Ustashi vanished into the shadows of the forest did he open his eyes. When he did, he found that he was staring directly into Petrich's face.

"Comrade, would you mind getting off of me? I consider you a friend, but this is a little much."

Petrich' s jest calmed Kobe. The young Partisan smiled and pushed himself away from his commander. Petrich winced as Kobe's weight pressed against the shattered hip. Petrich's agony was lost on Kobe. The Slovene thought only of the girl. He stood up. His eyes searched for her. He called out for her.

"Marta, where are you?"

Kobe screamed the words in Slovenian. And again in German.

Petrich motioned to his soldier from his position on the ground.

"You best not fall in love with her. She's the enemy. You can't trust the

Germans, no matter how pretty or innocent they appear. You, of all people, should know that."

"You don't know her like I do. She saved my life. I saved hers. There is nothing left to say. It's fate. I'll go wherever she goes. I've got no choice. I love her."

From the rear of the column, a cloaked form rose from the ground. A thin, poorly woven hood concealed the figure's face. He knew it was Marta.

Dodging the bodies of the dead, he ran towards the German woman. She stood perfectly still. He could hear her sobs, feel her pain, as he crossed the empty space between them. The roof of the pine forest muted the echo of her angst.

"Are you hurt?"

She nodded negatively. He put his arms around her and pulled her close to his body. His gesture squeezed her thin, delicate frame until she thought his body would absorb hers. He felt the tremendous power of her heart beating strong with excitement. They embraced, without another word, without any movement, for what seemed an eternity. Her upset, her need for him to protect her, stirred a passion deep and primitive within him. She felt the same power, the same primeval connection but could not bear to surrender to its authority in the view of the other soldiers.

Petrich appeared from nowhere. His presence altered the chemistry of the moment. The Partisan leader leaned heavily upon Dravich as he shuffled towards Kobe and the German woman.

"You're right, Kobe. I've been thinking about your friend here. She' s important to us. Yes, us, not just you. We must make sure she's kept alive. You see, I just realized the importance of what you told me. She's God's witness to the sins of that bastard Tomich. She and she alone is credible. No one outside of Yugoslavia believes what we tell them. But the world can't doubt the word of a German on these matters, especially the wife of an SS Officer. She has no cause, no reason to lie."

Kobe studied his commander.

"Where should we go?" Kobe asked, looking away from the German woman and into the eyes of his commander.

"You must go with Pappas to Greece. From there, she can be handed over to the British, from there she can tell the world what she knows."

"I have no desire to run, to leave my country, George," Kobe protested. "Isn't there another way?"

Kobe did not look at Marta Essen as he spoke. He concealed his words from her by speaking Slovenian. He didn't want her to hear him, to hear him profess that he didn't yearn to escape the war, the death, and run away with her.

"Can't you see? I can't rest until Tomich dies. I'm not the one to go to Pygros. Send someone else."

A rare shaft of sunlight cut through the trees, illuminating the younger man's face. A faint breeze stirred the pines, causing the light to parade across Kobe's brow. It had been three weeks since the Sava. His father, his sisters, his brothers, all of them were dead.

"I won't rest until the animals that killed the little ones lie dead on this ground. It may take a lifetime, perhaps more. But I'll find them. I won't let my love for a woman prevent me from doing what must be done."

Kobe's hand was soaked with sweat despite the coolness of the atmosphere. Eli touched Marta's face absently with a finger. He watched Petrich carefully as his commander considered a response.The woman' s skin was warm, dry and soft. In another place, at another time, it would have been soft enough to make him forget. Kobe stood amongst the trees, waiting to hear Petrich's response. His stomach burned at the thought of them. He saw their faces. Anna holding the twins. Marie grasping Anna's arm. How it must have been. Anna never afraid, disbelieving that her own countrymen would harm women and babies. Marie sobbing, believing that it would happen. Knowing that it would happen. Guns erupting. Bullets striking them down. Maybe killing them in the first volley. Maybe not. More likely the bullets of Franz Essen's service pistol methodically executing them as they huddled together, barely breathing, barely hanging on to precious life. Essen murdering the boys in Anna's arms. Anna affording them protection even in death.

Then all swept away. The bodies vanishing before anyone knew what had happened, buried in some common grave, lost to him in some unnamed hollow, covered with the very earth the Partisans sought to save.

Petrich moved across the shadows. The light of the distant sun made him squint. He placed his hand on the boy's shoulder.

"There's something more important than the one, than the individual. If we are to defeat the Ustashi, the Axis, we will need help. We can't do it ourselves. The Germans are too strong, there are too many."

Eli Kobe looked into the man's eyes and carefully took stock of the lines etched around them. Petrich was not much older than the Slovene was. The lines had come with responsibility, not age. Kobe knew the words were true.

"If this woman you profess to love survives to tell her story, maybe the British will listen, maybe they'll take stock as to what is happening here. Maybe not. But she is our best chance to shock them into helping us. We can't be like the Jews, shuffling off to the death camps without a struggle. We must fight. We have always fought. The Austrians, the Turks, the Romans."

Petrich's voice became quiet, authoritative.

"You must stop being selfish, stop worrying about your loss. Start thinking about the good of your people."

Kobe turned away from Petrich. He dared not look at the German girl. His eyes focused upon the stiffening body of a dead Ustashi.

"Where will we go, to do this thing you ask?"

"To London."

The Commander's muddy hand touched Kobe's chin. Petrich noted a faint hint of regret in Kobe's eyes but saw no evidence of defiance.

"We'll go. I'll do as you ask."

The wounded Partisan pounded Kobe on the back and turned away. Somewhere overhead, amidst the deep blue sky of the Dalmatian winter, Eli Kobe thought he heard the voice of his sister Anna. Perhaps it was only the distant cry of a tidal marsh hawk diving upon its prey. Whatever the source of the sound, be it bird or spirit, Kobe believed that Anna was listening, watching, and smiling down upon them.

She would know that Eli was in love. She would know that he would not forget his pledge to avenge her murder. These were two good reasons to smile, one more than Anna Kobe ever needed.

The Legacy

Chapter 7

November 23, 1942

April 6, 1941 had brought the power of the Nazi war machine down upon the infant nation of Yugoslavia. Down also upon the ancient kingdom of Greece. Benito Mussolini invaded the Greek Peninsula from Albania in October of 1940. By early 1941, the Greeks had driven the inept Italian Army back into Albania. El Duce was in danger of losing his entire invasion force. And Greece was not without friends.

At Cape Matapan, the British Navy cornered and destroyed a large segment of the Italian fleet, regaining control of the Mediterranean Sea. Angered by the consistent failure of his Southern allies, Hitler was forced to act. He postponed Operation Barbarossa, his grandiose invasion of Russia, in order to concentrate on extricating Mussolini from destruction. He would return to his fatal Napoleonic vision later that same year, the delay costing his tanks the guaranty of good weather Barbarossa depended upon.

Under cover of a clouded night sky Mikos Pappas guided his sixty-foot fishing trawler, the Helena, through the Straights of Ortranto. Pappas needed few words to command his crew. Quiet cloaked the vessel; every joint in the wooden hull, every seam between the decking had been caulked; every gear of the engine and drive had been lubricated; every light was blackened. Only the steady purr of the big diesel could be discerned, its cylinders purring in perfect unison, its exhaust muffled by the water. They were making a course for the Greek Island of Pyrgos, where three destroyers of the British Navy were laying mines to regain control of the Adriatic shipping lanes. The British Navy was desperate to forge some minor victories at sea in the face of the British Army's disastrous defeat on the Isle of Crete, the site of yet another Nazi triumph.

Eli stood alone at the rail of the Helena. He listened absently to the gentle sound of the vessel passing through the waves and the singing of the wind through the rigging. It was too dark to see the water, too dark to see the shore. There was no moon by which to detect Italian warships.

The utter blackness of nightfall also made it impossible to see enemy aircraft. It was obvious that they were there, flying overhead. Every so often Eli would crane his neck upward to the sound of motors droning through the night sky and he would wonder whether they had been spotted. But then the sound would abate and there was nothing to hear but the waltz of boat and sea.

He had reached his eighteenth birthday on Pappas' boat. November 22, 1942. He told no one. Other than Marta, there had been little joy in his life the past month. Other than her, there'd been only death, the extinction of his family with no opportunity for retribution or revenge.

"How are you?" he asked as the woman appeared on deck. The young German remained a distance away from him, a look of uncertainty emanating from her. Through tired eyes beneath the protective cowl of his canvas raincoat, he studied his companion. The coat made the weather bearable. He knew the journey was not easy for Marta. The voyage across the choppy Adriatic made her seasick.

"I'll make it. The waves are smaller, the upset, less."

It was a lie. She did not feel better, she felt worse. But she would not let him know that. He had enough on his mind, trying to justify to himself that their journey took precedence over revenge. She knew that. He had admitted as much to her when the voyage began.

"That's good. You know how it hurts me to see you in pain."

She walked gingerly to his side and sat down heavily on a wet bench. She reclined awkwardly against a bulkhead to steady herself, to minimize the effect of the swells. He covered her with a well-worn blanket in hopes that she would remain near him. He wanted her to benefit from the fresh sea air.

For her part, she could not stand to be away from him. His absence, even for short periods of time, made the pain worse. Her feelings were not without a mirror. To Eli Kobe, Marta Essen was the sole measure of comfort November had brought him.

"At least," he thought, "it's something. A small flicker of light amidst the blackness."

They had exchanged their first intense, romantic kiss the previous night. She had been feeling better. The waves had been stilled; the surface of the water was like glass. It was not their first kiss. They'd been together for three weeks, often alone. Always in danger. Close to the edge. But this kiss, this kiss was the kiss of a man and a woman. Not a boy and a girl, not a brother and sister. It was a kiss of passion and intensity that Eli Kobe had never experienced before.

Unschooled in love, he was unsure of the path he was expected to take. He was at a loss as to what to do when their lips parted. Marta eased his tension, his uncertainty. She lifted his hand beneath the blanket and placed it on her breast, near her heart. Under her blouse, the palm of his hand met her softness. She wore no brassiere for there had been no time, no need for such finery.

The feel of her skin, the delicate roundness of her breast, exhilarated him. The experience was unlike anything he'd ever known. Her breasts were modest, small, and firm. With his breath quickening, she had unbuttoned her blouse. Her fingers guided him to her nipples, each one excited, erect, standing out from the wondrous curve of her bosom. Because their indiscretion had been cloaked by the darkness of their cabin, he could not see her body.

His blindness made the adventure of it all more exciting. With his hand touching her in sensuous, patient circles, Marta placed her head upon his shoulder. Her thick blond hair had been cut short. Loose fibers brushed his cheek. From memory he knew what her eyes were like. Deep pools of brown. Honest eyes, evincing inner strength and purpose. They had remained together for what seemed to be forever, his hands resting upon her skin, her head resting against him; her breath low and deep, his quick and excited.

After a time, she had removed his hand, buttoned her blouse and kissed him on the cheek. The encounter reminded him of the primitive power of sex that he had first discovered at thirteen. The aboriginal drive remained disquieting in its strength. He felt ashamed he had let it happen.

"Not here, Marta. Not on a stinking fishing boat," he had promised.

"I'm yours Eli, here or whenever you like. I love you," she had responded.

"You deserve more than some brief moment of my time."

"I'll wait for you, Eli Kobe. I will."

After, they had fallen into a gentle, peaceful sleep, the boat swaying slightly in the calmness of the night sea. That had been one night ago. Matters had not changed. As he watched her try to sleep on the damp wood of the bench, he knew he had been right to wait, to curb his desire for her until the proper time.

Dawn brought the boat beyond Corfu. There was no sign of the Italian Navy. A steady gale whipped the Ionian Sea. It was unfit weather for flying. Mikos Pappas thanked the Lord Jesus. Good fortune. The luck of the Greeks. They would find the Brits at Pyrgos, find the warships of the Allies without incident.

Entry into Greek waters by daylight still retained danger, the danger of detection, arrest and execution as spies. Both the Italians and the Germans would not hesitate to shoot Mikos Pappas and his crew for harboring a Partisan, or for transporting the estranged wife of an SS officer.

Eli Kobe's thoughts were interrupted by the sounds of the old fisherman's uneven gait. The Greek dragged his salt-encrusted boots across the wood of the deck. The echo of his labored effort resonated with each heavy step. Pappas stopped next to the Partisan. He stood at the rail, his eyes fixed far out to sea.

"These waters are crawling with the enemy. You and the woman need to be hidden. If you're found, we're all dead," Pappas observed.

Eli studied the Greek. The fisherman did not look at him but kept his eyes riveted on some distant horizon. Kobe could not ask the Greeks to run any more risks than were absolutely necessary.

The Greek pointed to the water-stained deck.

"There. Down in the hold, where we store contraband. A hidden compartment. You'll have fresh air. Both of you must stay hidden there."

Marta uncoiled her lithe form from within the warm confines of the blanket. She stood, holding the wool tightly around her shoulders and shook her limbs, shedding momentary numbness from them.

Opening a concealed hatch, the Greek helped them descend into the confines of the bilge.

"Thud."

The hatch closed noisily above them. As Kobe and Marta lowered themselves into the hiding place, Pappas and his men dragged a heavy generator across the deck and bolted it in place over the trap door. Stifling heat from the engine caused the temperature in the bilge to soar. Limited fresh air, tainted by the fumes of the diesel, made it s way to them through vents concealed from prying eyes.

"How are you?" he asked several hours later, his voice low and discrete.

She coughed. A quiet, restrained cough but noticeable, nonetheless. The exhaust was taking its toll upon her. In the limited light of the hold Marta's face appeared to be chalky white. Her lips, normally red and full, were colorless. They sat alone in the squalor, hidden in the hold, confined to the dry safety of a small wooden platform that kept them out of the bilge water, water tainted heavily with the odor of decaying fish.

"I'm fine. I'll survive. I'm German, remember? We're bred to overcome little annoyances," she offered bleakly.

There was little either of them could do to make their situation tolerable. Eli wiped the perspiration from her forehead as she tried to retain the contents of her stomach. The tossing of the waves made such control impossible. She leaned over the edge of the platform and vomited convulsively into the filthy bilge water.

"Throw out the lines. There are sharks aplenty for us in these waters, boys," Pappas yelled to the crew.

They heard Mikos' commands though the heavy wooden planking of the deck muffled the words.

Passing the Greek Isles, Mikos ordered the trolling lines down. He was not interested in catching fish. But they must appear to be. A Greek trawler out from Corfu to catch shark. Shark to feed the conquerors of Greece.

"Someone is following us," Pappas whispered to them through an air vent.

Kobe noted that the Greek's voice had lost the calm, reflective tone he'd heard earlier in the voyage.

"You must be totally quiet. Don't move. Don't talk. It may be a patrol ship. We can't afford to take chances."

"I understand," Kobe responded.

Marta clutched the fabric of her companion's coat sleeve, her grip tightening with each new spasm in her stomach.

The Helena slowed. They were nearing Zante at trolling pace. The sounds of another vessel, larger, much larger, than the Helena, could be heard building behind them. The steady rhythm of the approaching ship's turbines shook the trawler.

Pappas did not quicken his vessel's pace. That would be too obvious. He continued to troll, hoping that the other vessel would pass.

"Damn," the Greek said under his breath. "It's closing the distance, coming right for us."

A familiar horn blared. It was a warning to stop or be blown out of the water. He pulled back on the throttle and forced the gears of the Helena into neutral.

Out of the fog, silent but for the sound of her powerful engines, the shadow of an Italian destroyer loomed. As it closed, it rose above the Helena like a great silver ghost. She was The Etna. Her thin, oil-belching smokestacks were barely visible through the thickness of the mist. The warship slowed and pulled alongside the trawler. Pappas leaned down from the wheel and muttered to his first mate, Andoras.

"Dead," he mumbled, barely audible, "If the Italian sperm eaters board us, they'll find the Slav and the German girl. We'll be dead."

In Italian, a voice from the deck of the Etna called out:

"Prepare to be boarded, trawler."

A thick hemp line snaked through the close air. A rope ladder followed. Grey-suited forms crept down the ladder onto the rolling deck of the trawler. Five, six, seven Italian Marines. Heavily armed. A young ensign or petty officer, Mikos couldn't tell which, came aboard and approached Pappas.

The officer was a small dark complected man. His black eyebrows hung like pine bows over his nose. The man's nose, its great prominence, resembled a mountain peak turned upside down. His nose sat in the middle of his face, occupying the majority of it, poised over a lipless mouth.

"I'm Ensign Palarmo of the Italian Navy. Let me see your papers." The little man looked at the old Greek with disdain, examining him with nearly nonexistent eyes.

"Pissholes," Mikos thought. "The man has pissholes for eyes."

Palarmo's eyes were a pale, urine-colored green.

"Here most excellent, sir. My papers," Pappas responded obediently.

Mikos pulled a set of weather-stained documents from his leather satchel and handed them to the Italian. They were near-perfect forgeries. Mikos was confident that Pissholes wouldn't be able to tell the difference.

"As you can see, they're up to date. I'm authorized to fish these waters on behalf of the Italian Army Command at Corfu."

Mikos found it difficult to restrain himself from adding insulting adjectives to his remarks. He had nothing but disdain for the Italians. A nation of cowards, the Fascists attacked only defenseless little countries. Albania. Ethiopia. Greece. They were forever begging the Germans to rescue them from their avarice and folly.

The Legacy

As careful as Pappas had been not to antagonize the Italian, the Ensign read something into the Greek's discourse.

"These seem to be in order Greek. But I don't like your insolent tone. Perhaps you'd welcome a few holes in the bottom of your trawler from one of our big guns, no?" Pissholes grinned. His teeth became visible. Most of them were stained black by advancing decay.

"His teeth are like his country," thought Mikos, "rotting from within."

The Greek spoke again, this time in a more conciliatory tone.

"Oh no, most excellent sir. If I appeared insolent, I apologize. I, unlike many of my countrymen, value the trade the invasion has brought. I'll retire a rich man so long as your soldiers continue to enjoy good Greek fish!"

Mikos tried to make his smile appear real as he thought of how pleasant it would feel to strangle the Italian. He daydreamed of spilling Italian blood, this Italian's blood, onto to the deck.

The Greek's joke caused the Marines to laugh. Pappas' own men laughed as well. The humor was lost on the Ensign.

"Search the boat," was his response.

The Italians began their investigation on the bridge. The control tower was cramped, filled with levers, the wheel, gauges, and charts, none of which were of interest to the Italians. Inch by inch they covered the two small cabins beneath the bridge, ripping apart bunks, chests, tossing the crews' belongings on the floor in the process. Planks in the decking were pounded upon, beaten. Searching, they were searching for secret holds where contraband could be kept, looking for weapons and explosives being smuggled to the Greek resistance.

Working their way into the bowels of the vessel, the marines waded through the inert, stinking bodies of dead sharks brought onto the boat to confirm the ruse. They gagged when confronted with the stench. Theirs was foul, disgusting work, an undignified task for the elite of the Italian Navy. It was obvious to Mikos that they hated their work, hated the stinking Greek trawler, hated the fish guts and slime clinging to their starched uniforms. The task had ruined their chances of a good night in port with the local women; they'd never be able to get a dance smelling like fish.

"What's that generator for, old man?"

The ever-diligent Ensign Pissholes gestured towards the inert motor bolted to the stern deck. There were no cables connected to the device, no wiring. It appeared to be an obvious waste of machinery and space. Palermo stared at the generator. He cast a quizzical look at the Greek.

He noted that the skin of the Greek's face was chafed and toughened by years at sea. Pissholes waited for an answer, hoping it would be less than satisfactory.

"Most excellent sir. That generator is an advancement. An improvement for this old trawler. When we're not working at sea, when we have time, I'm going to wire it so we will have additional electrical power when we're away from port. My men will not have to break their backs hauling in my nets in the dark, or by feeble lantern light. Electric lights will save time. And time is money, even for Greeks."

Pappas continued to play the fool. This time, no one laughed.

"And I suppose that if I were to have this unbolted, I'd find nothing but deck? Only planking. No trap door? No hold for weapons or contraband? For those pigs who kill my comrades? You see, I'm puzzled. I found two air vents concealed beneath fish crates. They apparently lead to the bilge. I ask myself, why does an old Greek need air vents to the bilge? He has exhaust fans. He has pumps. Why air vents?"

A pale faced Marine of no more than twenty walked up behind the officer. In his hand, he held a woman's valise.

"I found this hidden behind the maps and charts in the bridge."

The man handed the valise to Palarmo. The Ensign placed the suitcase in front of him and opened it. The Officer smiled as he looked inside. He pulled out one of Marta's peasant blouses and a pair of hose.

"Your choice of wardrobe is unusual, Greek, to say the least. But of course, one might expect such fare from a people that fuck sheep, no?"

Palarmo hardened his gaze. Though, the Greek said nothing, his hand began to tighten on a club secured to the gunwale.

"If he insults me once more," the old man thought to himself," I'll beat the son–of–a–bitch on the head. I'll make those eyes piss with the sharks."

Pappas continued to smile. His crewman tensed. They looked around the deck for weapons. There were none at hand. It would be Mikos Pappas against the most excellent Ensign and his Marines. There was little the Helena's crew could do to help.

"I think not, Captain. I think there is a woman on board. A stowaway, perhaps? Why would you hide a woman from us, Greek, unless perhaps she is someone of value? A Partisan operative? A communist?"

The officer tossed the clothing back into the suitcase with disdain. He moved closer to the Greek; oblivious to the weapon Pappas clutched in his right hand. The Italian opened his mouth as if to say something but the words were forever lost.

Behind the shadow of the Etna, a star shell erupted in the fog, illuminating the Italian vessel's forecastle. The sound of thunder roared over them mere seconds after the flare cast its white glow across the sky. It was not the thunder of God that stole the Ensign's thoughts. It was the thunder of the British Empire.

The first salvo from the English broadside hit the foredeck of the Italian destroyer. Beneath the vessel' s thin steel exterior, an explosion ripped open the Etna, sending sparks and smoke towards heaven. The blast threw Mikos Pappas across the Helena, tossing the Greek headlong into the hold where he landed unharmed among the shark carcasses. His men tumbled about the deck of the Helena like rag dolls. A second salvo from the British destroyer landed nearby, drenching the trawler in seawater.

Their ship in mortal danger, the Italians scurried off the trawler and scrambled up the rope ladder. Palarmo struggled to hold fast to the last rung of the ladder as his ship's engines came to life. The Italian vessel sought to escape. As its propellers franticly spun in reverse, the destroyer began to pull the trawler backward through the water.

"Cut the lines or they'll swamp us," Mikos shouted.

A crewman slammed the dull blade of a rusted ax against the rope. The line between the two vessels snapped, freeing the Helena.

"Quick thinking. Let's get the hell away from those scum before they get a second chance at us," the big fisherman cried.

The old Greek ducked into the relative protection of the bridge and jammed the throttle forward, calling upon the idling diesel to provide instantaneous thrust. The engine did not disappoint.

Water poured over the gunwales and into the bilge. Seawater, dirty and fouled by the wash on the deck, cascaded into the sanctuary.

As the water began to rise, Marta Essen grabbed wildly at Kobe in an attempt to keep her head above water. Eli deflected her blows and turned her so she was facing away from him. He placed his arms across her chest and controlled her fear with his strength.

"Keep your head up," he shouted over the din of the bilge pumps which had been activated by the rising water.

Marta Essen's mouth filled with putrid liquid. She lost her ability to breathe. Her eyes searched wildly in the darkness for salvation. Her limbs remained frozen in the anticipatory horror of death by drowning.

"Kick upward. Keep yourself above the water. They'll come for us."

Kobe tried to sound convincing. He knew his voice betrayed a personal premonition that they were about to perish. His face became momentarily submerged, forcing him to struggle to find oxygen. As he broke the surface, he filled his lungs and, with powerful kicks, he thrust the woman's torso upward, straining to keep her nostrils above the rapidly rising cesspool. The inky black pit of the boat's hold sought to swallow them up, to suffocate them within its innards.

Struggling beneath the water, he could not hear the sounds of the Greeks unbolting the generator. He was unconscious when strong arms reached down into their coffin and pulled them out into the inferno wrought by the HMS Devonshire.

"How are you, Partisan?" Leonidas Bartikas, another member of the crew, asked. Kobe's eyes opened as he disgorged the contents of his stomach.

"I'll live. How's the woman?" the Yugoslav asked in a weak voice.

"She'll be alright as soon as we get her into some warm clothes," the Greek replied.

"Take them to my quarters and get them something warm to drink," Pappas called out from the bridge.

Safe in Pappas' quarters, they clung to each other. Wrapped in a woolen blanket, they tried to follow the battle through the distorted glass of a porthole. They watched as another broadside from the British warship slammed into the fleeing hulk of the Etna. More explosions lit the mist, outlining the failing ship. Screams in Italian echoed across the water.

The Legacy

During the heat of the barrage, Pappas turned the trawler away from the shelling and escaped the deadly circle cast by the English rounds. Satisfied that his boat was out of danger, the Greek turned the Helena to witness the final chapter in the life of the Italian warship.

Pappas watched the fury of the British attack through his binoculars. He gazed at the slowly twisting hulk of the enemy ship. The Etna began to list to port, her top deck shattered; her hull pierced through at the waterline by the deadly accuracy of the British guns. Training his glasses on the remains of the Etna, searching the rails of her unsteady foredeck, Pappas saw him, and the Greek smiled.

"Leonidas, take a look," the Captain said, handing the glasses to his Mate.

"See what happens to Italians who insult Mikos Pappas? See the fear in the man's eyes as he clings to the ladder, holding on like a baby sucking upon a tit?"

Showers of seawater exploded around the Italian destroyer. Despite the commotion, Leonidas had no trouble making out the tormented form of Ensign Palermo hanging from the side of the Etna. The Italian's uniform had been torn to shreds by the fury of the British assault. Each time the Ensign tried to pull himself up a rung on the ladder, another shell rocked the ship, nearly dumping him into the sea.

"I see him, Mikos. I think he's shitting his pants as he swings from the ladder."

Bartikas handed the glasses back to Pappas.

Pappas laughed. Allowing himself one last gaze through the lenses, the Greek swore to himself that he could see the Italian soil his trousers from several hundred meters away. Pappas lowered the binoculars; satisfied that Palarmo's fate had been sealed.

"Let me have another look," the mate demanded.

The old man grinned and handed the glasses to Leonidas. Just as the crewman focused the lenses on the flailing form of the Italian officer, an explosion from deep within the shell magazine of the Etna ripped her open. Instantly, the vessel rolled over and disappeared beneath the green waters of the Adriatic.

Still smiling, the old Greek turned the bow of the trawler to Pyrgos, seeking the protective shadow of the Devonshire. By the time they pulled alongside the destroyer, the most excellent Ensign Palarmo and his multi–ribboned uniform were floating lifeless in the brine.

Chapter 8

November 28, 1942

Captain Atley Morehouse recognized the importance of his new passengers. Once the HMS Devonshire and her two sister ships, the Reluctant and Arcadia, picked up what few survivors there were from the Etna, the British flotilla turned for home, leaving miles upon miles of uncharted mines behind. The narrow sea between Italy and the Balkans was closed to the Axis by a British mine field as effectively as a cork closes a bottle of fine Italian wine. Protected by a rolling shroud of fog, the departing British force remained hidden from the German Luftwafte. Hidden by the mist, the British ships vanished.

After interviewing the German woman, Morehouse decided to steam immediately to Gibraltar. Located nineteen hundred kilometers to the West, the island was the bastion of British sea power in the Mediterranean. The Devonshire and her escort made haste for the sanctuary of Gilbralter. Marta Essen was to be delivered to the island fortress with all due speed. From there, she would go on to England.

The journey west proved to be routine. November 28, 1942 brought more rain, more wind, the constant lashing of nature's fury against the tarnished steel of the destroyers. Captain Morehouse scanned the sea beyond the prow of the Devonshire, the vessel's deck completely awash with seawater. He found he had little ability to discern details beyond the confines of his ship.

"Well, Wiggins, we're somewhere due south of the Baleric Islands, off Spain."

Morehouse studied the compass and his charts as he made idle conversation with his First Mate:

"Further south, in North Africa, Rommel's Afrika Korps and the British 8th Army are having quite a row of it. Tank battles strung between Libya, Tunisia, and Egypt, that sort of thing."

Wiggins was a balding, portly inductee known to be terrified of battle. The Mate looked up from his log and nodded unenthusiastically to his commander. His voice, when he finally chose to speak, betrayed his fear of being killed at sea.

The Legacy

"I trust the Captain is convinced that, what with the Battle of Britain having ended poorly for the Germans, 'Itler ain't going to do something crazy like the Japs and start crashing airplanes into our ships."

The statement was laced with incalculable fear, fear that suicidal Nazi pilots were, at that very moment, drawing a bead on the Devonshire.

"Not a chance, Wiggins. Hitler needs all the airpower he can muster. Stupid one, that Hitler, eh? Folly to risk all his European gains by refusing to learn from Napoleon's gamble. Stalin'll send the Germans packing home sooner or later. It's inevitable, like the winter storms on the Russian Steppe."

Convinced they were on course, Morehouse left the chart table to stand at the helm. He looked out across the water.

There was solace in the fact that not far from their position, across the slender sliver of sea, sporadic bonfires of a land war still raged in France. Though the French armed forces were no longer in existence, pockets of citizen soldiers, soul mates of the Partisans in the Balkans, the French Resistance, continued to fight the Germans. All of Europe, France included, seemed to be holding on by a thread against the Axis, waiting, waiting for the Americans.

"You know Wiggins, the Japanese made the same mistake Hitler did. They chose to rile a sleeping bear."

Wiggins pondered his commander's observation. The Mate placed his pencil down on the table in front of him. As it rolled towards the edge, his plump hand darted out with unexpected quickness and stopped the instrument's retreat.

"Trust me Wiggins, I understand the significance of the Japs perceived need to attack Pearl harbor. *The Times*, you remember, went on and on about the great surprise attack, the fact that there was near complete destruction of the American cruiser and battleship force in the Pacific."

Morehouse sat down hard on a stool near the wheel. He watched the wheelman follow the course provided. The Captain continued to talk idly, not really interested in whether Wiggins was listening.

"The Japs missed the carriers. They were all out of Pearl, on duty. Mark my words, Wiggins, the war in the Pacific, because of the great expanse of open sea; will be won in the air, not on the water. So what did attacking America accomplish? Nothing. Nothing more than to stir up the American's wrath, nothing more than to bring about the total global involvement of the major countries of the world. Japan should have kept this an Asian and European affair. They gambled on taking out the Americans with one punch. Now they have to go fifteen rounds with an angry heavyweight. I don't think Japan has that kind of economic stamina. Understand?"

"Yes sir," Wiggins answered meekly. He had little to offer and had not been paying close attention to the Captain. Morehouse recognized that his Mate was intellectually ill equipped to engage in deep conversation.

"Ensign Walters, keep an eye on things up here for a while, will you? I believe I'll try to get a few nods," Morehouse remarked as he left the bridge for the comfort of his cabin.

"Yes sir," the second in command replied in a tersely obedient tone.

In the quiet of his cabin, Morehouse carefully removed his uniform jacket and, after making certain the garment was placed neatly on its hanger, he sat on the edge of his bunk and removed his shoes. Morehouse placed his footwear at the foot of the bed, the heels perfectly aligned with the profile of the bunk. The Captain had realized long ago that he was a creature of habit. Though he did not generally adhere to the precept of form over substance, Morehouse found solace in the sameness of the daily routine of being at sea.

Atley Morehouse never wished to go to war. He was nearly fifty-two and close to pension when the conflict broke out. Thin, razor cheeked, he had no hair left atop his head. Sparse, gray wisps of what was once hair remained behind each ear. The son of Lord Morehouse, a prominent financier in Liverpool, the Captain grew up in privilege until the crash of 1929. The Depression engulfed and swallowed his father's wealth, leaving only a title to nobility, a run-down country estate and little else as the family legacy. The estate consisted of two hundred acres located to the southeast of Liverpool's grime. The land become Atley's after his father's fatal heart attack. There were no other children and his mother had vanished years before, after talk of a mistress and bastard children became the whispered gossip of old women in town.

Thinking about England, about home, placed the man at peace. He reclined heavily in his bunk and closed his eyes. Within minutes, he was coaxed into slumber by the familiar pitching of the ship beneath him.

"Looks like the fog is closing in, eh Wiggins?" Morehouse remarked.

Well rested and back on the bridge of his ship, Morehouse watched the

Devonshire's hull slice through heavy seas. Low clouds and mist socked in the ship. The gathering weather made it difficult to locate the other vessels under his command but Morehouse knew that they were out there; impressive, distinctly British, and undefeated in naval warfare since Lord Nelson destroyed the French at Trafalgar. Morehouse felt the imperious pride of Nelson flow through his veins. He first felt the arrogance of his calling when he was stationed aboard the dreadnought King Richard during the Great War at the Dardanelles. The battle was a minor set back for the British Navy, but not for his career. He and his ship had done their job. The King Richard sent two German cruisers to the bottom while other British ships turned and ran. He would send more Germans to their graves if he had to.

"Yes sir. Looks like we're in for a bit of a blow," Wiggins offered.

The mate stared out through a plate-glass window at the rapidly accelerating storm. Every hair on Wiggin's head stood on end. Morehouse chuckled at the sight and wondered what the timid First Mate would do after the war, if the man survived the war.

Below deck, Kobe played cards with an assortment of British sailors. Marta remained confined to her cabin. Two Ensigns had been moved to give her privacy. A British marine stood guard at her door, Enfield rifle at the port. No one but the Captain was allowed to disturb her.

Unable to speak English, Kobe used gestures to bid his poker hand. He was trying to learn the language but it was difficult. English seemed to him to be an odd assortment of sounds that ventured close to German at times, closer to French at others.

Morehouse knew enough German to communicate with Marta. With Eli it was more difficult. Morehouse' s German was rudimentary, as was Kobe's, and Serbo–Croatian was not routinely taught in English schools. Empires of history did not learn such languages. Empires forced their language on their conquests and did not stoop to assimilate the culture of the vanquished.

"Two? The bloody bloke only wants two cards again, mates. All right, two it is."

The game was five-card draw. A skinny, pale-complected sailor dealt the cards. There were six of them playing. Kobe held three fives. He discarded a six and a queen and drew two cards.

"What'll it be, mate?"

A large man, black-haired, a boson' s mate, glared at Kobe. The mate took one card. They were playing for money, though Kobe had only a silver watch, a gift from his father, as his sole possession of value. The sailors came to an accord that the watch was worth two pounds. It was worth substantially more. It didn't matter. Kobe was taking their money. The watch was not in jeopardy.

Kobe raised three fingers.

"He says three, mate. He's betting three pounds. Right Kobe?"

Eli raised three fingers again and nodded. The boson' s mate called and raised two pounds. The others folded.

"You's bluffin'. I knows it. I can smells it," the big man grunted.

Eli pushed a two-pound note into the pile, then raised another three. Black-hair, the one called "Johnny," picked his nose, wiping loose mucus on his white uniform with a deliberate sweep of his arm. He looked nervous.

"I'll see yer three and raise you two more. Let's see if you got the guts!"

"He's calling your two, Johnny. Looks like there's twenty or more pounds in the pot."

The skinny one, Andrew, leaned over and looked at the Yugoslav's cards as Kobe held them close to his chest.

"Read'em and weep, Mr. Slav," the big Englishman challenged. He placed three tens and two jacks on the table.

"Full house."

The mate had picked up the third ten on the draw. A puffy, discolored hand reached across the table to gather in the winnings. Andrew stopped him short.

"He's got you beat."

Kobe revealed three fives, then a six. He held the last card, the fifth card, for an additional second. Another five.

"Four-of-a-kind," the crowd roared in unison.

The sailors hooted and howled as they reveled in the embarrassment of the big man. Johnny's face reddened in fury. He rose to his feet and swatted the skinny man, knocking him to the deck. Johnny turned to say something to Kobe about the money, but the Partisan had disappeared.

"You may be big, Johnny. But I'll wager you that the lad's a good deal quicker at cards and on his feet than you'll ever be," one of the other sailors remarked. Johnny swung around to see who was tormenting him but the sailors stood in unison. Outnumbered, the big Englishman retreated, swearing loudly, to search for the Yugoslav and his money.

Later in the day, the sun finally broke through the sky, revealing the brilliant green of the Spanish coast to the North. The sun's warmth suspended the card games and brought the crew to the rails.

In their haste to make Gibraltar and liberty, none of the crew saw the danger. The deadly missile was nearly upon them before anyone sounded the alarm.

"Torpedo off the port side at five hundred meters," a crewmember shrieked.

Sirens blared as Morehouse took command of the vessel.

"Come about!" he screamed to the wheelman. "Come about hard! Turn this bitch on her side if you have to."

Wiggins' worst nightmares were realized. The ship was doomed, doomed to be hit broadside by a German torpedo. They were all going to die. He started to cry. The fat man wept plainly and openly. Tears poured out. The moisture dropped rhythmically upon the pages of Wiggins' logbooks.

"Sailor, get the bloody hell off this bridge. Go below if you're going to carry on," Morehouse raged at the frightened Mate.

Morehouse's temple was streaked with sweat. He was no less in fear than Wiggins. He was simply trained not to externalize it. Ashamed, Wiggins sheepishly retreated to his hammock below deck.

"Get this ton of shit turned away from that torpedo, Mr. Stephens, or we'll all be joining Wiggins in a pity-party, and very soon, I'd wager."

"Aye, Aye, sir."

Stephens strained at the wheel, forcing the ship into an unnaturally tight turn. Morehouse wanted to present the ship' s narrow stern as a target. But there was not enough time. The Devonshire's rudder could not respond fast enough, even under full steam, to avoid the torpedo.

"It's no use sir, I can't turn'er any faster. She's gonna take a direct hit," Stephens said, his voice calm and matter-of-fact.

Halfway through the turn, a dull "thud" resonated from below the waterline where the Nazi torpedo struck the plated steel of the hull. Within seconds of impact, a thunderous explosion erupted from deep beneath the bridge.

Morehouse knew it to be a solid hit in the midsection, a fatal blow. He watched as another torpedo passed ineffectively by the stern. But the second missile was no longer needed. The damage to the Devonshire had already been done.

The explosion threw Marta from her bunk. The force of the detonation caused her head to strike a steel support beam. A thin streak of crimson dripped from her head onto the starched sheets of the bed. Blood trickled onto the deck, pooling at her feet. The aftershock of the explosion threw her from the rack onto her knees. Nearly instantaneously, the destroyer pitched to starboard. She heard the steel skeleton of the vessel emit a massive groan.

"Eli, where are you?" she screamed out in German.

There was no answer. To Marta, the noises of the stricken ship reminded her of the sounds made by the fat Ustashi, his brains torn apart by Eli's bullet; the groans emanating from the ship were like those of a dying man. She crawled to the door and opened it.

"Eli!" she screamed again in terror.

"Eli, where are you?"

Her words were quickly replaced by sobs. In the hall, the Marine guard was sprawled across the deck, bleeding from a fatal head wound. A huge chunk of twisted steel pinned the man to the floor. It was obvious the man was dead. The main lights were out. Only the surreal glow of a distant emergency lamp provided illumination.

"Follow the light," she told herself, desperate to control her emotions.

She was convinced she was the only one left alive on the ship. As she crawled across the cold metallic floor towards the pale halo of the emergency lamp, Marta heard voices. She detected the muffled screams of British sailors and Marines in trouble. Thick pungent vapors curled upward through the ventilation shafts, rising from the inferno raging below. She began to feel the fire's heat through the floor. She sensed its power was growing, overtaking the ship. The metal began to turn hot, to sear the tender skin of the soles of her bare feet and the palms of her hands.

"I'm going to burn to death. Lord Jesus, please help me live."

Her voice was nearly gone. Her words were reduced to a feeble whisper. Acrid smoke imposed itself upon her lungs. The heat intensified. The paint on the heated surfaces began to bubble, to liquefy. Risking the noxious fumes of the burning chemicals, she rose to her feet and staggered forward in a desperate gamble to escape. Through the smoke, she detected the shadows of panicked sailors running up the stairs.

"Help me," Marta Essen called out in English. But her words did not deter the specters.

Reaching for the safety of the stairway, she stumbled. The fire's power proved to be too much. Thick, choking smoke billowed up from the decks below, seeking the same fresh air Marta Essen did. The smell of burning paint and compounds overwhelmed her. She collapsed onto the metal floor, coughing, incoherent.

"Take me Christ, take me before the fire burns," she mouthed in a near-silent missive.

Only the motion of her lips, parched and aching in the dry heat of the approaching conflagration, betrayed her words.

"Don't worry, I have you. You'll be all right, you'll see. Hold on now, hold on girl," a youthful voice commanded.

Though she would remember nothing of it, a young officer racing towards open air discovered her crumpled body and reached out to save her as flames lapped at the hem of her dress. Coughing and struggling to breathe, the sailor dragged her onto the stairs, placed her limp form over a strong shoulder and carried Marta Essen to safety.

"Find that damn submarine. Sink the assholes. Don't worry about us, we'll get off. Just see to it that the bloody Germans pay for this," Morehouse commanded from atop the HMS Devonshire's bridge. He spoke to the Reluctant and the Arcadia by wireless.

"Harrison, get Gibraltar. See we can get some air support to find that damn U-boat."

The radio operator dialed up the naval air station at Gibraltar.

"Too far away, Captain. Admiral Orley says by the time the seaplanes get here with torps and depth charges, the U-boat will be long gone. The Admiral says to salvage what you can, save her if you can."

"Save her? Hell, she's about to go down while we're having this little chitchat. She's listing ten degrees. Where the hell is Wiggins?"

"Wiggins is dead. A steam valve exploded, burned him in his bunk," a

Marine guard reported without prompting.

"I was down as far as the engine rooms, Captain. They're as flooded as the Thames. No one's left alive down there. Water's nearly to the boilers. The fires will be out in a few minutes," the marine continued.

Morehouse nodded.

"Can we do anything more to save them?" he questioned, his voice growing reflective.

"Everyone that can get out, is out, Sir. There's no more to be done."

"What about the girl?"

"She made it. She's safe, Captain."

"Good. That'll be all, sergeant."

"Aye, aye, Sir."

The soldier turned on his heels and was gone.

It was obvious to those on the bridge that the situation was anything but good. Morehouse's face was drawn in anguish. He said nothing. The officers waited for their orders. Morehouse surveyed the billowing smoke engulfing the vessel. He knew that the fire would soon make escape impossible.

"McAuley, prepare to abandon ship. Get the wounded to the boats. And be quick about it. Let's get cracking before the devil drags us down with 'er."

It was the first time that he'd ever given the order to take to the boats. His crew knew that the words were uttered reluctantly. Despair colored the intonation of his voice.

McAuley nodded.

"You heard the man, lads, lets get everyone off without a panic."

The command was repeated throughout the survivors. As the first lifeboat was being launched, the Devonshire shuddered like a great whale in the grips of a harpooner's barb.

"Not much time, now, McAuley," the Captain whispered.

Both men knew the obvious. The vibration was likely to be the ship's death tremor. There was no time to search further for the wounded. Their bodies would have to rest with the destroyer on the bottom.

"Sir, we've lowered the boats. They're all away but one. It's time for us to leave."

McAuley squinted intently at his superior as he spoke. The glare of the sun made it difficult for the officer to focus his eyes, though occasionally black smoke, curling upwards behind the captain, blocked out the power of the sun. Morehouse stared past McAuley; his gaze riveted on the heart of the inferno. The fire was quickly weakening the superstructure of the ship. Soon, nothing would remain of the vessel but charred and twisted metal.

Morehouse did not answer. He did not move. He simply stared vacantly at the fire.

"Sir, its time to go."

McAuley grasped the Captain's arm and lead him away from the bridge. There was no emotion apparent upon Atley Morehouse's face.The Captain was ensnared in the guilt of losing his ship, caught in the shame that she'd been lost without ever returning fire.

In a matter of seconds, Morehouse was safely aboard the last lifeboat and the craft was lowered to the water where the crew leaned heavily into the oars. Powerful strokes pulled the survivors away from the burning hulk of the ship as their Captain continued to stare at the funeral pyre that had been his command.

"She's gone, Captain. Best not to watch her die," one of the sailors remarked in kindness.

But Morehouse did not avert his eyes. Like a voyeur riveted upon forbidden entertainment, the Captain could not tear his gaze away. He watched the ship's stern raise high into the air, climbing to a near-vertical line. Standing upward in the water, silhouetted against the azure Mediterranean sky, the ship emitted a screech, as if she knew the fate awaiting her in the gloomy depths, and vanished beneath the oil-stained surface of the sea.

A search by the Arcadia and the Reluctant for the enemy proved fruitless. Somewhere below, U-127 rested motionlessly on the bottom, its crewmembers sweating in the poor air and stifling heat of the silent vessel.The Germans left no trail for their hunters, no hope for retribution, as they waited in their private purgatory for the British to depart.

The survivors were taken aboard the two remaining destroyers. A count of the missing from the Devonshire revealed seventy-five sailors and marines were missing. McAuley tried to keep this information from Morehouse. But the Captain knew. He'd heard the numbers whispered about in the lifeboats. On board the Reluctant he shivered desperately in a bunk:

"All those men dead. My fault, my fault."

Attempts at reassurance by his officers went unheeded. To Morehouse, such talk was only empty words, lost on a man plunged into madness by events he could not control.

Gibraltar loomed into view, its dark, singular mass rising above the flat expanse of the green sea to a great height. On the deck of the Reluctant, Eli Kobe leaned wordlessly against the ship's rail. Enthralled by the power of the place, the Partisan watched gulls circle the island's rocky shore.

"We're nearly there, Marta," he said in German. He did not turn to face his companion as he spoke.

Inhaling deeply, the woman drew in the fresh air. Her seasickness had finally abated; the choking acid of the ship's fire was finally purged from her lungs.

"What is there, Eli, in London, that is so important that God would spare our lives?"

She wasn't being coy. The inquiry was sincere. She was skeptical that Kobe would have an answer.

But Eli Kobe knew the reason, or at least, one reason, that God had allowed them to survive.

"You're that important," he replied softly.

Kobe placed his arms around the woman and pulled her tightly against him. Nothing protected them from the cold but the warmth of their hearts. He looked into her eyes. She smiled her first smile since the Devonshire had been attacked. The Yugoslavian turned back to look at the Rock.

Chapter 9

February 15, 1943

In the reception hall of Barrington Castle, they waited. They were thoroughly refreshed, in love—love forged through personal triumph, through tragedy. In the dim light of the great hall, they held each other's hand and whispered softly of what had been, what would be.

"Who will we be meeting today?" Kobe asked.

"I don't know. The English wouldn't tell me who would be here, what would be asked of us. I'm not even sure why we're here. Not sure at all. I would have thought your King would want to hear the truth about the Sava, about the Ustashi. Apparently, he does not."

Marta's voice maintained a curt, deliberate tone. The words were spoken barely loud enough for the Partisan to distinguish in the cavernous echo of the keep.

They sat quietly on an oak bench in uncomfortable cold. The bench appeared to have been carved from a single great tree. Its rigid, perfectly straight back was not meant to lessen their discomfort or make them feel at ease.

"Don't call him my King. Remember, I'm a Partisan and a Slovene, not a Serb," Kobe replied in equally curt German.

"Sorry, I forgot. Do you really dislike him so much?"

"I don't dislike the King. He's not much older than I am and he's trying to do what he thinks is best for the country. But he's in bed with the Chetniks and they're worthless scum. The English are wasting their time sending Mihailovich weapons. He just uses them to make war on us."

The Partisan sighed and held Marta's cold dry hand.

"I wish they'd get on with it. I'm not used to being cooped up indoors, waiting, always waiting. Do the English think I've nothing better to do than sit and wait on their bidding?"

"Patience, Eli. These things are likely delicate, take a great deal of thought. They'll see us. We must be patient."

She moved slightly towards him, parted her lips and left a light kiss upon his cool skin. Her movement was graceful, like that of a swan bending its neck in a reflecting pool. He smiled.

"I'm a creature of the mountains, the water, the sky. Sitting in this dank, dingy old place, is not my idea of excitement. But I'll mind my manners, be patient, as you say."

"There is much the English need to consider, Eli. They are not optimistic about their chances. Hong Kong has surrendered; the Japanese have taken Manila from the Americans, Singapore has fallen, India is threatened, Rommel still rules Africa. Is it any wonder it has taken them months to get to us?"

It was true, of course. Eli had to admit her observations about the British and the state of the conflict were accurate. There was also invasion of the Soviet Union to consider. The German Army had plunged into the heart of Soviet Russia, advancing to within miles of Moscow. Leningrad and Stalingrad seemed certain to fall. No effective governments remained in France, Poland, Norway, Denmark, the Netherlands or Greece. Governments in exile from each of the defeated nations had been established in London to lobby for Allied intervention and arms. They were governments without lands, without peoples to govern, without armies to fight.

Peter II of Yugoslavia maintained his government in exile in London as well, another deposed ruler without a country. He continued to press the British to aid the Chetniks, a force the King viewed to be the legitimate protectors of his throne. He received little solace and sparse support from the Allies. France, Africa, Russia, Italy were the focus of the Allies' strategy for defeating the Axis in Europe. Whatever resistance occurred in the Balkans was a minor distraction to the Germans. The Balkans was not looked upon by the English as a serious theater in the war. The demise of Yugoslavia was nothing for the British Empire to lose sleep over.

What King Peter, what the country of Yugoslavia needed, to galvanize Allied support for their struggle, was a symbol. A flame to light the fire and compel the Allies to listen, to fund the resistance; something so vibrant and graphic, it would compel London to act.

"We've been held here, virtually prisoners, for more than a month. That's about as much patience as I can muster."

The observation was accurate. Once the British flotilla reached the safety of Gibraltar harbor, the woman and Kobe had been flown over Spain under the cover of darkness, past the silent German guns bristling along the coast of occupied France. The unescorted transport plane had come in low, nearly brushing the trees of the English Coast. They had landed at a RAF field in the South of England nearly a month ago.

"I know, Eli. I know you expected we'd be rushed to an audience with the King, to the press, to Parliament. To tell our story. In truth, it disappoints me as well. We've been sequestered, forced to wait. For what reason? To allow my memory to fade? But we have no control over these people, their politics. We can only wait, tell what we know. That is the best we can hope to do."

He smiled at her again. Of course she was right. Venting his frustration would accomplish nothing.

"Yes, I see your point. I'm an unschooled peasant. What can I possibly know of the politics involved? I don't even fully understand the politics involved with Tito, the Partisans. Communism? What the hell is that to me?" the Yugoslavian said, a hard kernel of bitterness edging his words.

He took a deep breath before he continued.

"All I know, all that I care to know, is that the Germans invaded my home, took my family's land, killed its children. Politics? I don't need to discuss the finer, metaphysical points of dogma when faced with reality."

A cold, chilling hatred framed Kobe's words. Marta had seen the same emotion in his eyes, detected it in his speech, when they talked in private about what she'd seen at the Sava. She knew he was right. What did it matter whether one was a Republican, a Monarchist or a Marxist when all you had known, all that you had loved, was consumed by a fire you could not hope to quench? She released his hand and noted that her palm was lined with his sweat. She wiped the excess moisture on her skirt.

Massive planked doors leading to the manor hall began to open.

"They're ready for you now."

A tall distinguished-looking soldier addressed them in Serbo-Croatian. The man wore a freshly pressed uniform, the dress uniform of the Yugoslavian Army. He motioned for them to enter the inner sanctum of the castle. Kobe and the German woman stood and began to walk behind the soldier.

"This is beautiful, unbelievably beautiful," Marta whispered as they crossed the stone threshold into the room.

The young guerilla scanned the interior, his eyes taking in the man-made artistry of the immense chamber.

"Yes, it is," Kobe replied in a similarly subdued voice.

The room's importance was defined by a high ceiling. Heavy timbers intersected the vaulted space above their heads. Their shoes clacked against the finely polished slate floor. Narrow windows, crossed with delicate lead muttons, allowed only a meager penetration of natural light. Most of the illumination came from three massive wrought iron chandeliers suspended above them. Sunlight did not easily intrude upon the room through the rust–stained muttons and the clouded glass of the windows.

They walked with nervous hesitation across the floor. There was no one inside. The doors swung shut behind them. Their escort vanished. After a brief moment, a small man appeared in front of them. It was difficult to see where he came from because a large ebony table, oval in shape with matching chairs, blocked their view. Three exquisitely dressed military officers entered the chamber from the left. Again, the guests were unable to discern how the men came into the room. Kobe recognized two of the military men as officers in the Yugoslav Army. The third man appeared to be a foreign officer, perhaps British or American. All three men wore their hair closely cropped and marched to position in cadence, as if on parade. Kobe and his companion watched the men take positions behind the table. Unexpectedly, King Peter appeared from behind his escort.

He was not an imposing man. Chronologically, the monarch wasn't much older than Eli Kobe. But despite his lack of physical stature and age, the King was obviously different from the others assembled in the room. One could tell he was an aristocrat by the way he carried himself. His uniform contained so much gold braid and so many honors that it looked like he'd fought in and been decorated for every war ever waged in Europe even though the king was too young to have fought in any war at all.

The five men stood in silence behind the black expanse of the table; the formality of the moment conveyed the impression of an impending inquisition or trial. The air was heavy and uneasy with tension. One of the Yugoslav officers stepped out from behind the table and approached.

"Please be seated," he said, gesturing to a small black table and two chairs.

Another of the officers approached and helped the young lady into her seat.

The Legacy

Both men returned to their comrades. All of the men sat in unison. The King continued to stand, staring across the sea of polished wood at the strangers. He appeared to be gauging them, weighing their presence. After minutes of strained scrutiny, the young monarch sat with determination upon the bare wood of his chair.

One of the Yugoslav officers, round-faced, his mustache hanging down below his chin like a walrus, the whiskers dripped of perspiration, spoke to them in Serbo-Croatian. A small man sitting beside him, the one who had accompanied the German woman and the young Partisan into the room, transcribed what was being said in laborious longhand.

"Little Brother, we've waited long to meet you, to hear the news of our home, to hear the truth from one we can trust. I am Christian Toyostoff, a Major in his majesty's army. To my right is Captain Ruzich. The scribe is Michael Dustich, the King's personal attaché. He will take down our every word so there is no mistaking what is said here today. The other officer is General Fitzroy Maclean of the British Army. He has been asked to attend this meeting by the English Prime Minister, Mr. Churchill. Maclean's here to assess the importance of the news you bring,"

Toyostoff took a breath before continuing, his voice loud and powerful.

"At the center of the table, is his Excellency, King Peter II. We're hear to listen, to hear what it is that you have to say."

Eli Kobe, barely eighteen years old, orphaned Partisan guerilla, looked out over the void between himself and the powerful men as he considered his response.

The atmosphere of the meeting was tense enough without revealing that he was not loyal to King Peter. If he was candid and disclosed his true allegiance, his words would be suspect. He determined that he would not speak of politics unless asked. That being decided, Kobe hesitated. What would these creatures of privilege believe? What did they wish to hear? What part of his journey from the mountains of Slovenia to the shores of Gibraltar was important and what was not? He plunged directly into the matter.

"I'm Eli Kobe, a peasant of the province of Slovenia. I lived, before the Germans came, near the Austrian border. When they came, my family left, seeking refuge in other villages. My father and I joined the Resistance. The

Army had been defeated and the resistance was the only force fighting the enemy. My father died, not far from Ljubljana, in the battle. I escaped."

His mouth was parched. He was nervous. Ruzich stood up. Reaching across the table in front of the dignitaries, the officer poured a glass of water. The water appeared dull and muted due in the reluctant light. Ruzich brought the glass to the young shepherd.

"Thank you," Kobe said, emptying the contents of the tumbler in one swallow.

The young guerilla continued:

"I left the mountains in search of my sisters, my brothers. They were little children, left in the care of relatives not far from Celje. I never made it to that place. I found Mrs. Essen. She'd seen the murders on the Sava River, seen the dead bodies of my family. There was no reason to go there."

His voice cracked, heavy with the pain of loss. He fought back tears. The German woman sat quietly beside him, her long blonde hair braided up, swirled in a knot of honey-colored softness. Her hair had grown back, full and thick, once they came to England. A sense of calm entered him. Her presence satisfied some portion of his longing. She made him strong without doing anything more than being there. He avoided making direct eye contact with her. She fixed her eyes demurely on the stones of the floor.

He told them of the bravery of Mikos Pappas. He described in detail the sinking of the HMS Devonshire. He told it all, slowly, deliberately, without emotion or emphasis, like a soldier reporting to his superiors. He didn't tell them the details of the Sava. He left that for Marta. She alone was God's witness. Only she could tell them of the Sava.

She sat rigidly during her companion's narrative, never looking at him, never taking her eyes off the polished surface of the table or the roughly cobbled floor. As King Peter listened to the shepherd's tale, he watched the German woman with a curious intensity. When Kobe finished, Ruzich began to ask a question. King Peter raised his hand, silencing the officer in mid-sentence.

"And Frau Essen, we understand that you, a citizen of Nazi Germany, have something of interest to relate as well," Peter said, addressing her in thick, guttural German.

Peter's eyebrows drew together as he stared at the young woman.

The Legacy

"Tell us, Frau Essen, what you saw at Ljubljana that is of interest to a King."

Marta's brown eyes filled with tears. She discerned from the monarch's tone, his manner, that he was skeptical of her motives. But her tears were not due to the King's disbelief. Kobe grasped her hand under the table. She drew herself up, took a deep, cleansing breath and wiped the tears away with the sleeve of her blouse. Silence filled the chamber; seconds drew into minutes as she sought to compose herself. Then she began.

"I was outside the city. The sun was just beginning to set. I was not far from the banks of the Sava River, beyond where the Ljubljanica meets the Sava. I saw them. The peasants, the old men, the women, the children. Some, I found out later, were Eli's relatives. They were all herded together like so many cattle. Their backs were turned. They were defenseless civilians. They were all were shot, shot in the back. They were murdered."

A great weight descended over the hall as she spoke. Her words became nearly inaudible as her disclosure echoed off the stone walls. She stopped speaking and stared at her hands. Relating the truth of what she saw reminded her that she was still married to one of them, one of the murderers.

"How do you know this was the work of the Ustashi, the Germans, Frau Essen? I find it odd that a German citizen would risk capture, torture, even death, to escape a country occupied by your own army, a country where you have nothing to fear. How do you answer this charge, Mrs. Essen?" the King asked.

Everything was silent as the tribunal waited for the woman to respond. Marta Essen felt a draft steal over her. She began to shiver.

"The chill of winter? A chill caused by a vision of Franz Essen's soul?" she wondered.

"My husband," she responded, her voice tinged with exhaustion, its tone flat and plain, as if her own life-force had been exterminated by a mere fleeting thought of Franz Essen.

"I saw my husband, Lt. Franz Essen of the SS, and a Ustashi, Damos Tomich. I saw them just as clearly as I see you sitting there. They walked among bodies, laughing, talking, killing those that showed any residual signs of life. I'm not mistaken. There is no other truth."

For Eli, whose nightmares of the deaths had retreated to the mist of memory, her words rekindled his nightmares. As he sat in the sterile confines of the castle, he viewed the atrocity over and over in his mind, replaying images that he had witnessed through Marta's eyes.

"This story should be presented to our press corps at once, to be released to the world just as Frau Essen has told it. Politics or diplomatic considerations should not color the truth. It should be allowed to stand on its own merit," General Maclean said, after a long, uncomfortable silence.

There was a nodding of agreement from the military men. Peter sat limply in his chair, his aristocratic posture having deserted him once he learned the horrible truth of the butchery wrecked by the Croatian Ustashi upon their own countrymen. The young King rose slowly and walked around the great table, his face sullen and bleak.

Peter approached them at a slow pace. His walk was that of someone much older, his gait having been slowed by the weight of responsibility. King Peter' s hand found Kobe's shoulder. The peasant silently noted the skin of the monarch to be fresh, new and youthful. The King pressed his slight weight down upon the boy, staring at the German woman as he whispered:

"Your courage, Frau Essen, may be the light that slices through the dark clouds overshadowing our country. Your act of bravery, in telling of the Sava and the slaughter of the innocents there by the Germans and the Ustashi, will compel the Allies to listen. Your words will be the spark that lights the flame of our victory, a flame that will consume our enemies."

The young King removed his hand from Kobe's shoulder and gently touched the woman' s neck. His movement was light and tender, the touch of a brother to a sister. His effeminate finger followed the curve of her jaw. She felt that the monarch was about to kiss her, a gesture she would have considered awkward, but he simply turned and left the room. In an instant, the soldiers and the attaché followed, their boots marking time in unison against the harshness of the floor.

Alone in the chamber, Eli Kobe embraced the German woman. He absently studied the cold stones supporting the castle's ceiling. His people now knew the truth about Damos Tomich and the Ustashi traitors. Soon the whole world would know.

Chapter 10

February 15, 1943

Others might have thought it remarkable, even unthinkable, that Eli Kobe had not made love to Marta Essen. He had not even attempted the task. She had been his constant companion, his friend. They were in love, and yet, he had not pressed the issue.

That night, after the audience with King Peter, he knocked on her door, each blow on the wooden door no more than a faint tap.

"Marta, its Eli."

His words tripped over one another as he sought to communicate in her language. He knocked again, with less restraint.

"Marta, its me."

She opened the door by drawing it inward in a deliberate movement. She remained in the dark, partially hidden by the slowly opening door.

"Yes?"

"May I come in?"

"Eli, it's late. Is it important?"

Though he was too nervous to notice, her words bore an inflection of humor. She was teasing him. She knew full well why he was knocking on her door in the middle of the night. Kobe's nervousness did not allow him to see past her words, to uncover the mirth.

"I...," he stammered. He wanted to tell her how much he loved her, how much he owed her but the words spun round and round in his brain, unable to make their way out.

She reached out from the shadows and pulled him into the room with surprising strength. She stood next to him, nearly his equal in height, though distinctly more slender and feminine. Tufts of blonde hair touched his face, teasing him as her words had.

He fully expected her to ask why he was there, waking her in the middle of the night. She did not. She knew. Her alabaster hand touched his arm and drew him into the center of the room. Her bare foot pushed the door closed, the hinges squeaking noisily from the effort. The only other sound in the room was the sound of their rapid, excited breathing.

Her bedroom was nearly dark. A small reading lamp beside her bed cast a pallid glow over cotton sheets pulled neat and smooth. A thick down comforter was folded half way down the bed, revealing a depression in the sheets and mattress where she had been. In the face of such intimacy, he felt ashamed of his intentions.

"Don't worry, I'll lead," she said directly, noting the uncertainty in his eyes. "It's all right, I'll show you the way," she murmured.

"But I've never... I'm so lost, feel so foolish. Can't control myself. This isn't how I wanted it. I wanted to be so strong, so perfect," he replied, not daring to look into her eyes.

She pulled him tightly to her body, her perfume wrapping them both in its bouquet.

"Sssshhhh, now Eli. We'll have no more talk of imperfection. Love is perfect. We're perfect, at least at this moment in time. That's all that matters," she whispered.

As she tried to assuage him, her hand extended slowly towards his face. Her fingers touched his weathered, chapped lips with deft tenderness.

He didn't know what she was wearing. He kept his head down; eyes riveted on the floor as they moved towards the edge of her bed.

"Eli, look at me," she urged, using her hand to tilt his chin upwards, towards her.

Her yellow hair, clean and smelling of sweet oils, shone in the pale light. Her skin was soft, even more perfumed than her hair. She wore a simple white blouse, high necked, closed by buttons from her waist to her chin. The first two buttons were undone. The tail of the shirt barely covered the curve of her girlish hips. Her skirt lay upon the nightstand, neatly folded, as if she'd known Kobe would visit long before the thought entered his mind. She hummed the melody of an old Strauss waltz. There were no words, or at least, she did not sing them, but her voice was clear and melodic.

Her thin, slight body moved in time to the beat of the song. She moved the two of them around room in a slow, enchanting embrace dictated by time and music. It was an unfamiliar dance, one Eli Kobe did not yet know. But Marta Essen did.

The Legacy

Her lips parted. She leaned forward to kiss him, her tongue darting. The organ's moist texture probed the confines of his mouth for acceptance. He grimaced. She held him closer. A moan escaped from deep within her throat as she moved them to the center of the room, slowly twirling in the amber of the reading lamp. Their silhouettes danced across the faded paisley wallpaper and the water-stained plaster of the bedroom, until she brought them beside her bed once again.

The bed was soft and bore her fragrance; a sweet, distinct mixture of perfume and musk. She pulled him down alongside her. Her long fingers undid her blouse, a button at a time. His breath quickened as she taunted his patience with delay. Though he tried to control it, the excitement was so novel, so all encompassing, he began to shake in a storm of shuddering anticipation. She stopped.

"Slow down, my love, slow down. We have all night, all tomorrow. And the next day, and the next," she said in a soothing tone, her words controlling his urgency.

He could not believe the time it took for Marta to unbutton her blouse. Each pale bone disc became seemingly reluctant and stubborn; each movement of her fingers so deliberate. When the last button was undone, the edges of the garment fell away to expose the wondrous curve of her belly, the sensuousness of her navel. He hesitantly placed a hand on her stomach and began to stroke the soft skin of her belly. Wordlessly, she directed his hand to follow her body's contours. With her guidance, his fingers touched a wisp of golden hair that delineated the intimacy of her heat.

"Oh, Eli. Yes. That's it. Slow. We must be slow. And soft. A lighter touch," she whispered, watching Kobe's face marvel at the discovery of her body.

The roundness of her breasts remained concealed beneath the loose fabric of the blouse, her nipples outlined as mere suggestions. She pulled the blouse over her arms, exposing the entirety of her body to him. Clumsily, he tried to undo his own trousers. She giggled. His face flushed.

"Don't be embarrassed, Eli. It will get easier, I promise."

As she spoke, she lay before him, gently massaging her pubis as it strained against the white sheen of her cotton underwear. He removed his own undershorts and shirt. She slid hers off with a foot, tossing them off the bed with a flourish of her toes. He sought to close, to press in on her. She held him off her body, away from her, with arms that were far stronger than he'd realized.

"Not yet," she murmured in German, "We must learn from each other."

A fierce wind rattled the shutters. Within Marta Essen's room, the young German woman brought Kobe closer and closer to heaven. Time after time, she led him to the brink of orgasm, only to retract her power in order to sustain their lovemaking. She refused to allow him to take control. She refused to allow him to simply crawl on top of her for she had no interest in having sex; she wanted to make love, to stir the passion of her partner to heights he'd never scaled before, heights she herself had seldom reached with her own husband.

Finally, after countless rushes towards the summit, she climbed upon him and placed her naked body, her torso lean and quick, against his. She began to writhe in pleasure. An ancient, near-sacred rhythm was established. He sucked her breasts, gently biting each erect nipple as her bosom heaved in anticipatory desire. She moved lower on his body so as to allow her mound to become exposed to his erection.

Without losing cadence, she encompassed him. She lifted her body, supporting her weight by the strength of her arms, so that the passion of the dance could fly unburdened.

Then, at the ultimate moment, at the instant of release, they soared towards the sun, becoming lost amongst the blue, nothing but blue; thereafter their souls plummeting from heaven in the catastrophic free fall of resolution.

Eli Kobe could not believe the deepness of his sleep. When he finally opened his eyes, he was alone in her bed. The primitive smell of femininity together with the faint aspect of her perfume lingered over him as if she were still there.

She sat naked on the soft leather of an easy chair next to the window, smoking a cigarette. The outline of her body was framed by rare sunlight. Kobe raised his head to look at her.

As Marta noted him stirring, she turned her face. A faint smile crossed her mouth.

"Why Herr Kobe, you're not dead at all. I feared I killed you last night," she said in a light, airy voice.

She spoke softly, in German. He understood her and returned the smile. She stood up and walked across the wooden floor, her bare feet squeaking against the oak as she walked. Her small, delicate breasts were carried high on her chest and bounced slightly with each step. Her nipples, honey-colored and erect from the cold, demanded his attention as she moved. At the edge of the bed she bent down and kissed him on the forehead.

"I'm surprised you're able to awaken at all, after the wicked things you compelled me to do." she whispered.

Kobe noted that her small white teeth were exposed as she whispered.

"Perfect teeth," the young Partisan thought, "they match the rest of her."

"Marta, I don't know what to say," he responded once his observation of her beauty was complete.

Kobe tried to project his feelings in German. His hand pulled her head close to his.

"I've never done... I've never felt..." he couldn't finish the thought. The words he wanted to use didn't seem to fit. His eyes took in the smooth hairless skin of her bare back and buttocks and the desire that she had stirred the previous night began to return.

"Don't say anything, Eli. Don't tell me you love me," she responded in a pleading tone.

She turned her eyes from him. Tears welled up within her as she walked away from him to stand naked in front of the window.

"We'll talk about plans. The future. You. Me. But not now, not here. Here we are content, far from the weight of the world, the war. Leave it at that for the moment."

Outside, snow fell steadily on the square. The flakes were white and pure. Marta extinguished her cigarette in a bronze ashtray forged in the shape of a clam. She folded her arms across her breasts in a sudden urge for modesty and tried to control her tears.

"I'm married, Eli. I have no business seducing a young man. But now, you're all I have, you're the only thing that I can trust. I love you but please do not love me. It will only cause you pain. I have a husband; I'm the enemy. No matter what we mean to each other, you'll always know that."

Her face began to tremble. Again, she turned away. Kobe pushed the weight of the quilt off of his naked body. He stood up and walked across the void between them, a void of culture, of war, of circumstance. He reached out. Gently grasping her wrist, he drew her body, its contours soft and warm, close to him. He became determined in that moment to lead their next dance. He lifted her, surprised at the lightness of her body, and carried her to bed.

"We shouldn't," she murmured softly in protest.

But there was no sincerity behind the words.

"Do not love me," she whispered. "Please, do not love me."

He gently placed her in the center of bed. She buried her face against the sheets.

In a soft, tenor voice, he began to sing a Slovene lullaby his mother taught him as a child. He stroked Marta's hair, inadvertently touching the bare skin of her shoulders and collarbone with rough, battle-hardened fingers. She turned on her side so that she could study his eyes and listen more closely to the unfamiliar words of the song. He concentrated his gaze on her eyes and gained a fleeting glance into her soul.

"But I do love you, Marta. You cannot change that. And it will always be so," he whispered in German as he drew the sheets over their naked bodies.

They embraced beneath the dirty light of an English dawn. Beyond the walls of Marta Essen's bedroom, the snow continued to fall and the City of London rose to claim another day. And sometime that morning, the pupil taught the teacher another step in the dance.

The Legacy

Chapter 11

February 25, 1943

The Englishman arrived at Marta Essen's room unannounced after first trying room 224–Kobe's room. He suspected that Ms. Essen and the Partisan were close. He guessed that they were together. Deakin tried her room. He was right.

"How can I help you?" Kobe said in halting, English as he opened the door.

The Partisan managed to enunciate clearly enough so that Deakin understood him. The Englishman surmised, from the young Yugoslav's appearance, that Kobe hadn't left Frau Essen's room in several days. Their eyes met. A hint of guilt seemed to flash across the young man's face, like he'd been caught stealing apples.

"Mr. Kobe? My name is William Deakin, Captain, British Army. Mr. Churchill has sent me. He wants me to make a more in-depth inquiry into the status of the war in Yugoslavia, so we can learn what your lads and the other groups are doing, look beyond the atrocity you and Frau Essen discussed."

Even in the hallway, Deakin could detect the strong musk of passion coming from the room. He smiled and handed Kobe a copy of the *Times*.

"Not that the story you told isn't important. It is. And you'll see by the latest article in the *Times* that your King is still getting quite a bit of mileage out of it."

The newspaper Deakin handed to the Partisan was folded neatly so that the article in question was visible.

"I can't read English," the young man said in slow, deliberate words. "You read it to me."

"Well, certainly. It says here that independent sources and a German National have documented mass executions on the Sava River in Yugoslavia. Also indicates your King, Peter, was quoted as saying that the killings clearly point out the need for Allied support of the Chetniks."

"Chetniks? He asks for help for Chetniks? Not Partisans?"

"Sorry. No mention of your bloaks in the article. Just the Royalists got the press, I'm afraid."

The Slav raised his eyes from the printed page to Deakin, his face flushed in anger.

"This article. It mentions only Milhailovich's Chetniks?"

Deakin nodded in agreement. Kobe continued, "It says nothing about my comrades? Why does the King ignore us? Was he hearing when I spoke? When Marta spoke? Is the blood of my father no loss? Not worthy of his help?"

The younger man's voice cracked with rage. He slapped the newspaper out of the British officer's hands. It fluttered to the floor.

Deakin spoke softly:

"It appears that your king has his reasons to mistrust this man you call Tito. We know nothing of him here in England. Your king apparently views him as a bit of a challenge, an antimonarchist. These comrades of yours, they must be seen by the king as a danger to his throne."

Deakin paused. The Captain was speaking Slovenian. It took great effort for him to convert his native English into the difficult language of the Balkans.

"I ask you, Mr. Kobe. Are you a Marxist? Do you seek to overthrow King Peter?"

A smile crept across Kobe's face. The Partisan, sensing he was being teased, felt his anger abate. His face returned to color.

"I'm a soldier, a fighter, a believer in whichever leader will annihilate the Germans and the Ustashi."

The words rolled off his tongue like venom from a snake. He spit out the word "Ustashi." Deakin had no difficulty seeing the bitterness, hearing it in the man's diction.

"As for whether I'm a Marxist or a Monarchist, I can't say. I fight with the communists because the Chetniks run and hide. They are cowards and will die cowards. But do I want them beaten? Do I want the King off the throne? I don't know. But if wanting to fight makes me a Marxist, then that's what I am."

Kobe realized he was dressed in his robe and little else. He motioned for the Englishman to step inside the room.

Deakin picked up the crumpled copy of the *Times* and followed the Yugoslavian into the apartment. It appeared that the woman was gone. A lingering fragrance of her permeated the room's atmosphere despite her absence.

The Officer cleared his throat and sat down at a drawing table.

The Legacy

"I'll be frank. The Prime Minister is fed up with reports we're getting from our man with Colonel Mihailovich. Chap by the name of Bill Hudson. Good fellow–brave, honest. Mihailovich keeps telling Hudson the Chetniks are in control, will mop up the Germans shortly. Then Mihailovich gets in pitched battles with your people. Makes alliances with the Italians. According to Hudson, the man can't soldier and isn't telling the truth. Spends more time bedding young ladies and combing his beard than he does fighting Germans."

From the look of interest on the young Slav's face, it was obvious that Hudson's assessment of the Chetnik leader was on target.

"We know about the nasty business in October and November of '41 when the old boy refused any more joint raids with you folks. Nazis retaliated for your combined attack at Kraljevo. Executed 6,000 there on October 20. Another 7,000 at Kragujevac. 100 of your people for every Nazi killed. 50 for every Nazi wounded. Hitler's direct orders. Hudson was there. Witnessed the fighting between the Chetniks and the Partisans after the massacres. According to Hudson, Milhailovich's boys started it. Germans killed their families so they attacked you. Great way to win a war, eh?"

Kobe was surprised that the British knew so much about the political strife in his country. Deakin left the table and stepped around the Partisan to admire a painting on the opposite side of the room. His curiosity satisfied, the officer turned towards Kobe and spoke:

"Churchill is tired of the Chetniks. He wants to find out more about this man, Tito. In fact, he wants to send me as his personal envoy. Can you get me there? You know the language, the country. Would you go back with me? It would mean parachuting in. Night jump. Personal risk."

Deakin's plea was not what Eli Kobe had been expecting. It was certainly not what the Partisan wanted to hear. He was eighteen years old, in love, safe in a warm, familiar room in an ivy–covered English manor. He had escaped death and treachery. Despite his earlier vows of revenge, the peace he had found in London had released some of the poison, abated some of his festering passion for retribution. He was not at all sure he wanted to go back to Yugoslavia.

An eerie silence filled the room. A powdery haze of coal dust rose, disturbed by vibrations from the street outside. As the dust ascended it became caught in the spare light filtering in from outside. A fine haze separated the two men, forming something of a wall between them.

Sounds of a key turning in the lock caused them to avoid further unease. Marta opened the door and stepped into the room, carrying a small bundle from the market under one arm. In her other hand, a frayed glove grasped tightly to the narrow neck of a bottle of French wine, a scarce commodity in war–torn London. She nodded to Deakin.

Placing the package and the bottle on a small end table, she advanced towards Eli. She untied her wool scarf, tilted her head and kissed the Partisan. The suppleness of her bare neck, her elegance and grace, reminded the British officer of women he'd seen depicted in Renaissance paintings. Tiny drops of rain fell from her hair onto her lover's forehead.

Kobe grasped her hand and pulled her towards him. He looked at her face and gestured towards the Englishman.

"Marta, Captain Deakin has asked me to help him find Tito. Parachute into the mountains. Fight with the Partisans once more. I don't know what to do."

Kobe's eyes were fixed and vacant. He was obviously overwrought, a characteristic of his personality that she found compelling. But the extreme power of Kobe's mixed emotions confused him, made him unsure of what course to take. Love for Marta bade him to stay. Hatred for the Ustashi and the Germans bade him to go. There was no easy choice to be made.

Marta placed her cold soft hands on his face. She looked away from Eli, trying desperately to gain control of her own internal thoughts. Despite her marriage, despite Franz, she was with the only man she had ever loved. To lose him would be death. But to deny him this chance would be worse. If he did not go back, it would eat at his soul; it would haunt him and consume him as the bile of a diseased liver consumes the drunkard. It would eventually turn him against her. It would make her just another German, an enemy like all the rest.

"Eli, I love you. You know that. And I know that you love me. But you must go with Captain Deakin. You must return to your home. There's no other choice."

Eli Kobe studied the woman's wide brown eyes. He detected no deception, no lies hidden in their beauty. He turned away from their power, afraid they would make him stay, hold him back, and stared at the irregular boards of the floor. After a moment, he looked up at the Englishman.

The Legacy

"Alright, I'll go."

The English Officer touched the brim of his cap and exited the room, leaving the German woman and the Partisan to examine their future under the bitter light of circumstance.

Chapter 12

April 13, 1943

The steady drone of the C-47 Transport's engines filled the belly of the airplane with unrelenting noise.

"Blessed Virgin Mary, protector and mother of Jesus Christ my Lord, grant me safe passage tonight," Kobe prayed.

He mumbled to himself in Latin, the meaning of the words lost to the Anglicans around him. Inwardly, he admitted he was terrified. Outwardly, he showed no fear. He wore armor of nervous bravado, weaving the cloth of bravery from the knowledge his presence was important to mission. He was to accompany Captain Deakin, Captain W.I. Stewart, and several other English officers to Mount Durmitor for a meeting with Tito. It was to be the first parlay between the Western Allies and the Partisans.

"What'd you say?"

Deakin sat next to the guerilla. The Englishman leaned tightly against the interior metal skin of the plane. The Yugoslav looked away from his companion and shook his head:

"Nothing. I said nothing."

Though there was no tremor or emotion audible in his voice, Deakin detected the familiar signs of fear as he sat in close proximity to Kobe.

"There's no reason to be afraid, son. I've done night jumps dozens of times. So has Stewart. It'll pass quickly, much more quickly than you can guess. It's the landing, not the jump, that's crucial. Remember that."

Kobe smiled weakly. The Partisan found that the officer's advice didn't change reality. Responsibility weighed upon Eli's shoulders like provisions piled atop a pack mule. Looking out the ice-covered windows of the airplane, Kobe stared into the bottomless pit of the night sky, into a premonition of his own death. A tremor of regret caused the guerrilla to turn away from the window and close his eyes as the engines of the airplane droned on.

It was a long flight from Egypt to the mountains of Yugoslavia through skies controlled by the German Luftwafte. The transport was unarmed, unescorted and at the mercy of the Axis if detected. The slow-moving plane would be an easy target for German fighters, the Focke Wulfs, the Messerschmidts. Its only protection, its only armor, was chance.

Deakin reached out and touched Kobe on the shoulder.

"Here we go, old chap. Time to fall into the night, to feel the rush of the wind. You'll love it, Kobe—once you've done it."

"I hope you're right, Captain."

After a brief interlude, the Partisan stood up and shuffled forward. Deakin nodded towards an open door. A gale of stiff winter air burst into the hold of the plane. The wind slapped Kobe's face, bringing with it a heightened sense of alertness.

The jumpmaster, a man named Harrington, a short bulldog of a man, wore his sandy hair shaved to the scalp. The British soldier managed the line with intimidation. As each candidate approached, he stared deeply into the man's eyes, and if appropriate, authorized the soldier's progression to the place of demarcation.

Harrington studied the face of the young Yugoslav by the red glow of the jump light. Kobe saw a hint of recognition in the Englishman's eyes. The master did not know Kobe. But he, like Deakin, knew the face of terror, terror he had witnessed across the face of every green recruit in the British Army. Every man that came aboard Harrington's airplane jumped with or without the master's assistance. Power lines, trees, enemy fire; all awaited the paratroopers as they plummeted blindly towards the surface of the earth. There was no end to the ways one could die during a night jump.

"No need to be nervous, son, I ain' t lost no one yet. You pups are all alike, all ready to piss your britches when you try it the first time. No need to fret, lad, just close your eyes, put one foot in front of the other and jump."

Eli didn't understand all of the English words. But the calming tone of the man's voice was sincere, discernible in any language. The Partisan relaxed ever so slightly.

Deakin clutched Kobe's arm as they approached the doorway. The strength of the onrushing air chilled the bare skin of their faces as they braced for their turn, waiting for the red light to turn to green. Deakin's grip reminded Eli of his father's embrace–firm and strong. It conveyed a father's message. It was an embrace of safety, of protection.

Stewart stood immediately in front of them. The cold assault of the April night at ten thousand feet took their breaths away. Stewart smiled, gave the "thumbs up" signal and stepped out into the evening sky. As Kobe inched towards to the door, the soldiers behind him shifted forward in turn.

"May God speed, Eli."

Deakin's voice seemed distant and completely removed from the reality of the place. Kobe did not acknowledge the Englishman. Closing his eyes, he stepped out into the void, embraced the vast emptiness of the Balkan night and dropped noiselessly away from the airplane.

"Hail Mary, full of grace...."

Kobe kept his eyes clamped shut. Before he could finish his prayer, he snapped free of the tether line.

"Our Father, which art in heaven, hallowed be thy name. Thy Kingdom come, thy will be done, on earth as it is in heaven..."

Desperation was replaced by an acknowledgment of freedom, of unrestrained flight.

"Heaven," he thought," I'm in heaven. Please God, let the chute open, let the silk come free."

A tremendous jolt pulled him back towards the distant airplane. His plunge to earth slowed to a delicate decline as his parachute unfurled behind him.

"Praise Jesus, Praise the Blessed Virgin, I'll live."

The words were shouted, no longer reserved for himself, his voice echoing across the evening's quiet. After his outburst of joy, Kobe drifted serenely through the night air. With each passing moment the air above Mount Durmitor became thicker. The increasing texture of the atmosphere rustled the thin silk of Kobe's chute as he floated down. It was too dark to see the others, too dark for Kobe to see his companions striking the uneven surface of the mountain.

He sensed the ground's presence long before his eyes could make out the details of the landscape. He strained to see the terrain falling away before him. It was hopeless. The darkness that protected Kobe from detection made it impossible for him to focus with certainty. Sensing he was about to touch down, he braced himself. The shock did not disappoint. After his legs took the initial jolt, a sharp pain shot through his knees and hips. Then he was down, rolling through the mud of his homeland, trying to stay clear of the rigging of the chute.

The others landed safely in groups of twos and threes. Only Stewart suffered injury. His chute caught a gust of wind as he touched down. The sudden draft twisted the Englishman's body around itself without warning, causing a badly sprained ankle. Free of his parachute, Stewart tried to walk with his comrades. His progress was marked by a noticeable limp and an expression of pain across his brow.

"How goes it, Kobe?" Deakin whispered as he bundled his chute, moving quickly to help the guerrilla do the same.

"It was beautiful." Kobe related in a breathless tone. "I hope I never have to do it again."

The British Officer chuckled softly and slapped the Yugoslav on the back.

"Once you've done it, t'isn't that easy to refuse the second time. Jumping is like drinking fine wine, or making love. The more familiar you are with the experience, the more enjoyable it becomes. You'll jump again."

"I'll need to remember more of my catechism if I do. I think I used up most of the prayers I know on the way down."

The men gathered their parachutes and placed them in a pile for the Yugoslavians to salvage for use as tent and clothing material. A small contingent of Partisans materialized, emerging as individual shadows from underneath the cloak of the forest's rim. One of them approached Deakin.

"Captain Deakin, I presume? Milovan Diljas, Tito's attaché to the outside. Pleased to meet you," the guerilla said in exceedingly clear English.

Diljas extended a large mottled hand to the British officer. Deakin shook it firmly.

"I'm pleased to make your acquaintance, Comrade Diljas. This lad at my side, one of yours. Kobe, a Slovenian. He was at the battle at Ljubljana, fought with Petrich in Dalmatia, escaped to England with the Essen woman. Have you heard of him?"

Deakin tried to gauge whether the Partisan knew the story of Marta Essen's defection, whether the intelligence of the communists was as solid as he'd been lead to believe.

"Ah yes, Comrade Kobe. Good things have been said about this boy. Brave.

A Ustashi hater. With him, like so many, it is personal. We know about the woman. Haven't verified all of it, but it's accurate to a degree. There was indeed a mass murder along the Sava, that much we know."

"She's believable. I met her, spoke to her. Kobe here is in love with her."

"What's this? Kobe, you surprise me, falling in love with a German. How can this be?"

Eli Kobe held his Mauser firmly, trying to appear resolute and mature.

"She's not like the rest. She's different. She saw the bodies, held the babies as their souls flew to God. There's nothing more to say."

Diljas nodded, accepting the explanation.

"War does strange things to men, eh Captain? Let's go, before Germans, ones who are not so understanding, find us."

Surrounded by twenty of Tito's handpicked elite, members of the First Proletarians, the combined force formed a single column.

Though his rudimentary parochial schooling touched upon the geography of Montenegro, Kobe was better schooled in the mountains of his native Slovenia. That night, they might as well have been traversing the Alps in Switzerland as much as he was able to discern in the dark. After a time, he gave up trying to determine their location and contented himself with stumbling along behind Deakin, wondering what use he was to the English in a land he was not familiar with, in dealing with a leader he'd never met.

Unknown to the tiny guerrilla force laboring through the forested hillside, the German 12th and 2nd armies had combined on the plains surrounding Mount Durmitor. The purpose of the German unification of force was to surprise, engage and extinguish the Partisan army camped nearby. With Tito silenced, the German High Command intended to sweep into Serbia and exterminate the Chetniks while Mihailovich sat pondering whether his Serbian troops would fight or wait out the war.

Ignorant of the Nazi strategy, Tito gathered his guerrillas in Montenegro. Nineteen thousand men and women rested in the shadows of Mount Durmitor and awaited his orders. Surrounding the beleaguered Partisan force, oblivious to the steady winds and heavy rains of April, two veteran German armies totaling in excess of fifty thousand soldiers, supported by Panzer armor, heavy artillery and air superiority, took up positions and awaited the signal to attack. Hitler, having conceived the battle plan for the campaign in Montenegro, would personally order their advance.

Unaware of the silent convergence of Nazi might, the British envoys and their escort wound their way to the Partisan encampment. Dawn's epiphany, resplendent in purple and violet, rose from behind the foothills and washed the valley in a subtle blanket of color. Light from the birthing sun caught Kobe's eye and he smiled.

If the young Slovene had been able to see through the thick vegetation of the forest below, he would have realized that the pastoral scene before him was yet another cruel illusion.

Chapter 13

April 15, 1943

Eli Kobe had never met Josip Broz. Kobe was a nominal communist. He joined the Partisans to fight the invaders, not to debate politics and ideology. The Kobes were simple farmers and peasants.They sided with the faction most likely to eradicate the Nazi cancer from their homeland.Their only goal was to liberate Slovenia from the death grip of the Germans without giving any thought to what would come after the war was over.

"And this fierce looking young man, Comrade Tito, is Eli Kobe, survivor of the battle of Ljubljana, but more importantly, lover of German officer's wives. Isn't that right, little brother?"

Djilas' sense of humor did not strike a chord with the young Partisan. Being in the presence of Tito for the first time, in his quarters, Kobe thought better of making it an issue. He smiled.

"Comrade Djilas is misinformed. It is Frau Essen who has converted me into a National Socialist, one of the Master Race." They roared at the joke, Tito laughing loudest of all.

"A remarkable boy, one who can tame German women. Even Djilas with his vast experience with the opposite sex cannot boast of such a conquest," the Partisan leader observed.

Had it not been Tito who called his love of Marta Essen a "conquest", Eli might have angered. Instead, he ignored the slight, accepting it in the light-hearted vein it was offered.

Tito extended his hand to Deakin.

"Welcome to our place of refuge in mountains. I trust your trip here was safe and uneventful, Captain?"

The Partisan leader made it a point to shake hands with all of the British officers. Tito's legendary persona mesmerized the young Slovene. Here, only a meter away, was the most wanted man in all of occupied Yugoslavia. A man who, nearly single handedly, organized a rag-tag assortment of peasants, factory workers and miners into an effective underground force which had handcuffed the Nazis and their allies.

The Legacy

Gregarious, studious and intelligent; well–versed in the moods and beliefs of the squabbling nationalities within Yugoslavia, Tito had little trouble forming an intense personal bond with Kobe in a very short span of time. He embraced the young Partisan during their first meeting as if Kobe were his son. It was a solid, manly embrace, conveying sincerity and trust. The gesture was meant to insure that Kobe would reciprocate philosophically, politically, and embrace Tito's Marxist pragmatism.

By the sparse light of the new day, they arrived at Tito's lair: a natural cave carved from the summit of the mountain by ice and water millennia ago. The guerillas' position was well concealed from Nazi airplanes. The Partisan leader's location was protected from the eyes and ears of traitors. Though damp and cold in appearance, the cavern on Mount Durmitor was well equipped. There was room enough for Tito, his female secretary and paramour Zdenka, for his personal bodyguard Djuro, for Milovan Djilas and for Tito's dog, Lux.

"What is your situation here, Comrade Tito?" Deakin said, accepting a small glass of very bitter wine from Djilas as he spoke. The pungent beverage was the best the camp could offer. It was musty and spoiled, having nearly turned to vinegar. It curled the Captain's tongue. Deakin did not betray his disappointment with the beverage.

"Excellent wine, Comrades. Excellent. I'm surprised that you live so well."

"It's shit. You English must drink rat's piss if you think this is good wine," Diljas observed. "It's the war. A man can't find a good glass of wine or plum brandy anywhere. Maybe in the cities. But the damn Germans drink it all before we get there.

"How are you faring against the Germans?" Stewart asked. "Our reports from the Chetniks indicate you're on the verge of collapse."

The Englishman spoke from a seated position. He occupied the smooth leather of a cavalry saddle tossed absently on the bare dirt floor of the cavern. His injured ankle was wrapped in gauze and elevated. Lux lay next to him, asleep. Stewart's hand gently stroked the dog's belly as he talked. The officer winced painfully when Lux pressed his weight against the man's injured leg. The landing had done serious damage to the muscles supporting the ankle and foot. The British officer was not prepared for Tito's angry response.

"Why do you stupid bastards listen to the Chetniks? They're nothing but profiteers, simply hoping to hold out in strength until a peace is negotiated. The monarchist devils will try to create a feudal Greater Serbia, their warped and time dishonored dream, punishing those who disagree with their plans. I can't understand how the Allies can listen to their reports. Do you listen to the German's version of how the war in Russia goes? Or do you ask Stalin?"

Tito's voice was loud and animated. Kobe grinned. He liked the man's fervor, his outrage.

"Surely there's some truth that you've had, shall we say, close calls? Narrow escapes from the Germans and the Ustashi?"

"Yes, that's true. But the Chetniks use those stories to exaggerate our weakness'. In reality, the "close calls" as you describe them, tell of our strength, right Djuro?"

The big man nodded in agreement. A smile formed slowly, interrupting the stern expression occupying Djuro's face.

"Tell them about the River, Comrade General," Djuro prodded.

"Yes, the River. That's a tale that will bring home the point about the Chetniks. Here, around this cave, nineteen thousand Partisans are gathered. The core of our resistance, a formidable underground fighting force.

These people, these peasants and workers with guns, are survivors of the battle of the Neretva River. Operation Weiss (White), the Germans called it. I'll tell you about Operation Weiss."

Sensing the story would be involved, Kobe sat down. He wedged his British-issue field pack against the wet stone wall of the cave. Tito stood over him, telling the story as if he were a troubadour of old:

"In January of this year, Hitler launched Operation Weiss to push us out of Bihach, away from Zagreb, the capital of Croatia. They came at us with eight divisions, together with Ustashi and over 12,000 Chetniks. Their plan was to surround, overwhelm and annihilate my command. Operation Weiss was the final breaking point between Mihailovich and me. It marked the flaming of the torch of hatred between us and there's not enough water on this earth to extinguish that fire."

Tito bent to pat Lux's head. He stared at the ceiling of the room, collecting his thoughts:

"By luck, I'd been forewarned of the plan by an Austrian woman, one not so different from Kobe's German friend. Leaving most of our heavy guns and mechanized equipment behind, we marched south towards Montenegro an hour ahead of the enemy. Twenty thousand Partisan soldiers, men and women. Thirty five hundred sick and wounded comrades. Followed by countless civilian refugees. It was quite a sight, eh Djilas?"

The emissary yawned, obviously having heard the same story over and over. Diljas winked at Kobe and Kobe winked back, like two schoolboys bored with class.

"Very well, Comrade, we'll see if the history books yawn at Operation Weiss" Tito scolded. "We took everyone we could with us. By the end of February, because of the sick, the wounded and the countless thousands of civilians, the Germans caught us.

We found ourselves trapped against the Neretva River. The watercourse was swollen. Passage across was impossible. It was ironic that we were unable to cross because we were the ones who had demolished all the bridges. Thankfully, we weren't as thorough as we thought. The bridge at Konjic remained intact. We had failed, for whatever reason, to destroy that one. I sent a single Partisan company, one hundred and fifty men and women, to capture and hold the remaining bridge. But in a bloody battle, the Germans, two regiments strong, took it and wiped out our entire defensive force. The defeat at the bridge eliminated any chance of our escape. We were, as Zdenka said at the time, going to be pushed into the river to drown, like a litter of unwanted kittens."

Kobe moved closer to the warmth of the wood stove as Tito continued to relate the story of the Neretva. Kobe was far from bored by the tale. And he wasn't alone. Deakin and Stewart were awe struck as well. The English were beginning to see the genius in the man, beginning to see that Yugoslavian hopes rested upon the shoulders of Tito.

"Pushed by the enemy, we came to the burned ruins of Jablanica where Djuro found the remains of a bridge that we had earlier destroyed. Fortunately, our demolition work on that bridge was less than complete. Our explosives did massive damage to the span but a portion of the superstructure still crossed the Neretva. A single, thin, iron girder was our only way out. To buy time, I ordered a counter-offensive against the Germans. A select unit of my personal body guard, some of the same men who brought you here, crossed the wreckage of the bridge at Jablanica and overran a Chetnik position on the opposite bank. The wounded crossed first, then the civilians. When all the noncombatants and wounded were across, the main contingent retreated over the bridge. By a single stroke of luck, some imagination and the courage of my men and women, twenty five thousand souls escaped the Germans to live and fight again.

Tito's voice was calm and quiet as he concluded the miraculous tale.

"We crossed the Neretva and smashed those Chetnik bastards, didn't we Djilas?" the Yugoslav stated in a retrospective voice. "We proved to Mihailovich that it was stupid to cast his lot with the enemy. His forces across the river were annihilated, pushed far into this country. Some surrendered. Some joined us. We welcome any Chetniks that want to fight with us. But most are too stubborn, too stupid. Most die."

Tito's eyes glared in the flickering, hazy light of a kerosene lamp. A yellow pall clothed his short frame, extending his shadow across the rough stone wall of the cavern. Djilas grunted in approval.

Deakin looked intently at the Partisan commander. He'd already made up his mind about the man, about the clean-shaven guerilla leader with the dark penetrating eyes, the fine cheekbones and the deep black hair. Tito knew exactly who he was. A liberator. A warrior. A leader. There was no doubt about it. The Englishman believed the man could be all those things to a united Yugoslavia.

Deakin pondered what to say, how to indicate his views. He uttered a cursory statement of approval while he thought of something more profound to say.

"A most remarkable tale, Comrade Tito. Most remarkable."

Deakin turned towards Stewart to obtain the Captain's input. Before another word could be spoken, the roof of the cavern collapsed in a cascade of dirt and boulders. They were under attack.

Amidst the falling debris, Deakin caught a glimpse of Lux, Tito's dog. The animal's entrails were fatally exposed. It whimpered once and died. More shells collided with the dirt above and around them; more rocks and soil fell onto the cavern floor. The stale underground air became choked with dust. Incoming artillery fire from German guns pounded the mountainside, raining debris upon them.

"Damn the Germans, they've found us," Zedenka cursed as she was thrown to the ground by another explosion. The bright yellow wool of her sweater was covered with the blood of Captain Stewart. She tried to rise from the cavern floor but her legs were too weak to support her.

"My God, look at the man. His blood is all over me."

The secretary rambled incessantly, disoriented by the weight of the dead man upon her. Stewart's life ebbed away from him with the last glimmer of lamp-light, a single piece of shrapnel having severed his head from his body. The Englishman had become the first casualty of Operation Swartz (Black).

Kobe lay on the floor, bewildered but unharmed, his eyelids tightly clenched against the turmoil, trying to battle the memory of his father's death on the mountain. Nothing had changed. The smells, the sounds, the terror remained the same. He trembled, unable to move, unable to cry.

With an efficiency of movement learned from countless prior retreats, Djilas and Djuro collected maps and documents by the light of a carbide lantern. A second wave of shells shook the dirt ceiling. Rounds from the distant German guns continued to pound the bosom of the mountain.

"Get out, Comrades, get out before the roof disintegrates and you're buried," Djilas screamed. Despite the volume of his voice, his words were difficult to discern over the din of the enemy guns.

Partisan soldiers appeared at the cavern's mouth carrying additional lanterns. They feared Tito had been killed in the onslaught. Deakin tried to rise from the cavern floor and escape to the source of the light.

"I'm hit. I can't move my leg. I'm pinned."

Deakin's leg was trapped beneath a stone. He couldn't pull himself free.

"Come on, English. I don't want the blood of another of Churchill's pups on my hands. You'll not die here, Captain, not while I'm alive," Tito whispered as he pulled Deakin towards freedom.

Djilas remained behind, looking for Kobe. He assumed the young man was dead. To his amazement, the Partisan found the young Slovene cowering near Stewart's corpse. Djuro pushed the dead Englishman's body off of Zdenka and ascertained that she had not been injured in the attack. Djilas screamed at the Slovene:

"This is no time to hesitate, to be afraid. If you're a Partisan, act like one and get the hell out of here!"

Djilas's admonishment forced Kobe to immediately regain his footing. All around him, soldiers were dragging the wounded and the dead out of the cavern. Zedenka sat unescorted along the far wall of the cavern. Kobe went to her. With minimal effort, he pulled the Partisan woman to her feet.

"We must hurry before another shell collapses the roof."

The woman coughed. She staggered through the thickening smoke and haze. Kobe encouraged her to move forward, towards the light of the waiting lanterns. Incoherent and sobbing, she emerged from the tunnel to embrace the April dawn.

Below, Deakin limped behind Tito on a narrow trail leading into the valley. The two men were trying to make their way to the front.

"Stay close, English. Someone might mistake you for a German. We'll get close to the action. You'll see how we fight. This is what you came to see, no? Partisans killing the enemy? Stay by me and you'll see many Germans die."

Dodging projectiles and small arms fire, Tito and Djilas made their way to the heart of the battle. The Englishman marveled at the Partisans' ability to quickly organize effective resistance. As they approached the front, a scout appraised them of the situation in urgent terms:

"We've seen huge numbers of Ustashi, Germans and Italians joining the attack," the soldier explained.

"Take heart, Comrade. They bleed just as we do. Take steady aim, make the bullets count."

Battle-hardened faces smiled as soldiers nearby heard Tito's voice. Again Deakin witnessed the strength and resilience of the man's personality. The English officer saw firsthand Tito's ability to inspire a weary, outnumbered force caught in a seemingly hopeless situation.

"Only a few men I've met," Deakin murmured to himself, "Could lead men and women to the gates of hell and ask them to smash through them. This man is one of them."

Higher up the trail, Kobe supported Zdenka as they moved down the mountain. The path was rough, the footing treacherous. His grip remained tight.

"I've got you. Soon we'll be down. Keep up with me. We'll live, sister, I promise you, we'll live."

Eli found it difficult to maintain his balance as they struggled along the narrow trail. The footpath snaked its way through dense brush and scattered pines. All around him, he detected the muzzle flashes of small arms' fire. He caught glimpses of the Partisan column fighting its way through the pinchers of the enemy, the flanks of the communists' retreat protected by loyal troops. To their rear, up the hillside, Kobe heard muffled explosions, evidence that the Partisans were destroying their abandoned fortifications.

Near the base of the mountain, the path intersected a well-worn cartway worn deep into the soil by centuries of horse-drawn traffic. Drawn into the deep shadows of the woods, Kobe and the young woman became caught in the surge of the retreating army. Disappearing in the mass of soldiers, they were swept ever downward until they reached the cool, still air of the valley floor where dawn's light teased the horizon. As the sun rose, the orange glow of morning allowed the Partisan officers to gauge the success of the retreat.

A small contingent of female Partisans from a village near Sarajevo secured a gap through the Axis lines. Blunting an Axis counter-offensive, the women held the Partisans escape route open against terrible odds. Fighting hand to hand, the women maintained their position. German units rushed to close the breach just as the main Partisan column crossed a small stream. Caught in the rush of the retreating soldiers, Kobe and Zdenka waded through frigid water. Dragging themselves over the ice-covered boulders defining the opposite bank, slipping in the frozen mud of the lowlands, Kobe and the woman reached the far shore and vanished with the others into the rugged wilderness of a lowland marsh.

Their mission complete, the female soldiers withdrew. They sought to make the other side of the stream, to escape through the tangled underbrush of the wetlands when a platoon of the German SS surprised the Partisans in mid-steam.

German bullets tore into the unprotected flesh of the women. The force of the rounds striking the female guerillas caused their bodies to spin uncontrollably, creating a brutally disorganized ballet. The soldiers' cries, the repetitive bark of the gunfire, added a surreal symphony to the hideous choreography orchestrated by the Nazi's. The cruel artistry of the ambush ended when the last Yugoslavian body fell into the frigid water and remained perfectly still. The flowing water caused the wounds to clot quickly, leaving only minute traces of blood to foul the stream.

The Partisans spilled out into the valley below Mount Durmitor. Deakin tried to keep pace with the Yugoslavian commander as the Englishman offered an observation out loud, to no one in particular:

"I've just witnessed one of the great strategic retreats in military history and Stewart isn't here to see it. Damn, that man's luck couldn't hold."

But Stewart or no Stewart, the British envoy was not about to miss Tito's next move. Churchill's hunch had been correct. Josip Broz was a man to be reckoned with.

The Legacy

Chapter 14

September 25, 1943

Deakin sat transfixed. He watched Tito swim in a Montenegrin brook near the Adriatic Sea, the general's thick back shrouded by the mist of early morning. In the distance, the Partisan forces could be seen encamped in a tentative perimeter around the Port of Split. They had come west, to the relative peace and safety of the coast after the failure of Operation Schwartz. Tito was determined once and for all to shake the pursuing Germans.

Escaping the Nazi trap at Durmitor accomplished more than merely securing the Partisans' survival. The miraculous retreat from the mountain prompted the beginning of the end for the Fascist regime in Italy. On September 8, 1943, after repeated defeats in Yugoslavia and North Africa, the Italian government collapsed and surrendered to the British, leaving Tito and his forces to face only the Germans and the Ustashi.

Deakin's assessment of Tito didn't diminish during the intervening months. The Englishman made a point to communicate his opinions directly to Churchill. The Captain's views became the foundation for the commencement of British airdrops to the Partisans. His reports were also the basis for a decline in similar support to the Chetniks.

Tito emerged naked from the tepid waters of the creek. His new dog, Tiger, greeted him.

"Even the man's pets are a source of amazement," Deakin observed to himself.

A German officer once owned Tiger. On the march to Split, Tito had "liberated" the animal and made it his own.

"He takes what he needs," thought Deakin, watching the Partisan dry his ample body with a ragged towel, "something to remember."

"Deakin, you look lost in thought. Tell me, what occupies your mind on this glorious day?" Tito asked, breaking the Englishman's train of thought.

"Nothing, Comrade General, nothing. I was only dreaming of England, of Hill's Church and the orchards of my family's farm there. How different the hills there are, how occupied, how less wild."

Deakin misrepresented his thoughts and sought to keep his admiration of Tito to himself.

"These aren't mere hills, Captain. These are the beginnings of the Dinarics, of true mountains. How can you compare puny English hills with our mountains?"

Before Deakin answered, Tito waved his hand, indicating there was no need to respond.

"But of course, at least your hills, however small they may be, are not soiled by the presence of the Germans, eh English?"

Tito slapped Deakin on the back. A wide smile formed across the Partisan's face.

"It's time for us to get back to camp. I can smell lamb roasting from here."

Walking back to the Partisan camp, Tito and Deakin chatted briefly about the German offensive pouring into Dalmatia.

Determined to drive the communists from the sea, from easy resupply by the British fleet, the enemy had regrouped and pursued the guerrillas. The sound of German Panzers and big guns firing could be heard in the near-distance. Unnerved by the closeness of the enemy, Deakin decided it was time to broach an important topic with the Partisan:

"Fitzroy Maclean, a friend of Churchill's, a former member of Parliament, is convinced that your resistance to the Germans is critical to Allied success," the British Officer offered as they began to walk uphill.

The Yugoslav set a brisk pace. Tito stopped for a moment to look back at the British officer. Deakin caught his breath and continued:

"Maclean's just the man to convince those snooty bastards in London that you're for real, the horse we should back. He's en route to Split as we speak."

If Tito heard the information, he didn't acknowledge it. He simply continued the same, quick tempo of their walk.

Deakin tried to stay close to Tito. His leg, the one injured on Durmitor, remained weak and unsteady. The uncertainty of his gait forced Deakin to pick his route carefully. Impatient at the slowness of their progress, Tito grabbed Deakin's arm and helped the Captain along.

Kobe walked behind the two men, cradling the Mauser. Four grenades hung from his cartridge belt. The grip of an Italian bayonet protruded from the top of one boot. A German pistol, scavenged from a dead Wermacht Major, was holstered to his hip. Kobe tried to eavesdrop on the conversation as they made their way to the Partisan camp. A determined breeze distorted the officers' words so that he heard only bits and pieces of the discussion.

Tito released the Brit's arm and spoke:

"Why shouldn't Churchill be convinced? My Partisans, brave young farmers like Kobe here, sisters from the mills, a mob that fights with hunting rifles and stolen cannon, it ties up fourteen German Divisions–

140,000 men, soldiers that would be in Italy or Africa killing British and Americans."

Tito's smile faded. The man's demeanor became stern. Deakin withdrew slightly from the Partisan, knowing that Tito's temper was unpredictable.

"I'd say its about time the damn British sent someone other than a lowly captain to talk to me."

As he formed the words "lowly captain," Tito's lips returned to a smile, making it clear his message should not be taken as a personal attack on Deakin but as a reflection of Tito's frustration with the slowness of British diplomacy.

"I've convinced four thousand Italians, my Garibaldi Division, to fight for me. I turn German friends into German enemies. German pets into Nazi biters. I work miracles, escape ambushes, march across mountains to defeat traitors. For all that, Churchill sends me crates of flour and useless, antiquated rifles from the Great War. Maybe I should see what the Germans have to offer."

It was a ploy Tito had brought up before, the threat of negotiating a separate peace with the Axis. Deakin had come to realize that it was a bluff. Tito hated the Germans. He wanted them beaten as badly as Churchill did.

Catching bits and pieces of the dialogue between the two men, thinking of his time with Marta, Kobe smiled. Rarely did he get to see Tito in such a mood, so confident, so disarmingly frank. Despite his ego, Tito was reasonably honest in assessing his personal achievements.

In the summer months after Mount Durmitor, Kobe himself became more confident. After Operation Schwartz and the terror he experienced cowering on the floor of the cave, he never again felt fear. In the pitched battles to take Dalmatia and the seaport of Split, he killed the enemy with steady precision and steely–eyed vengeance.

For his valor, Kobe was handpicked by Tito to join an elite bodyguard. He was assigned to follow the Partisan leader wherever he went. Tanned and strong from the months of campaigning in Bosnia and Dalmatia, Kobe became an archetypal Partisan. Resolute. Loyal. Ideologically Marxist. He was no longer a soldier without a creed. His transformation mirrored that of the Yugoslav nation. Change swept through the land eliminating what little power was once claimed by the Chetniks. The changes were destined to sweep away the Germans as well.

"Good Lord, don't be so hard on us. You've got to remember we have no experience outside our monarchy. Even if we've stripped our royalty of power, we still love the crown. With such an infatuation with tradition, is it any wonder London is reluctant to abandon the Chetniks? They're the last salvation, the last hope of King Peter, the heir to your country's throne."

Deakin realized his words might be misconstrued, that Tito might think the Captain was attaching some legitimacy to the young king's claims. The British Captain stumbled. His ankle turned over. Tito deliberately refrained from assisting the Englishman.

The Yugoslavian's eyes flared as he grabbed the British soldier by the lapels of his uniform and voiced his displeasure:

"Christ said, 'My kingdom is not of this world.' So too it will be for King Peter. His kingdom has been swept away by the Nazi tide. It's no longer of this world."

Though said with obvious bite, Deakin detected no personal malice in Tito's words.

It was an expression, an affirmation of what must be, an acknowledgement that things had changed, that power flowed to those, like Tito, who stepped into the void and faced the oppressor.

Their walk brought them to the small farm. Tito motioned for Deakin to remain outside the farmhouse serving as his headquarters. The Partisan leader disappeared into the cottage.

The structure housing Tito's command post was typical of the farm homes of Dalmatia. Small stones, retrieved over the ages by the occupants from the surrounding fields, formed the building's foundation. Crude bricks, bleached nearly white by the sun formed the exterior walls of the building. Cracks in the aging mortar allowed small plants to take root and prosper along the walls, adding to a general air of disrepair. Tito pushed aside the remnants of a wooden door, which hung precariously from a single hinge, and entered the house.

Djilas leaned over a large map of the Dalmatian–Bosnian border placed before him on the dining room table. Field commanders stood to either side of him engaged in conversation. The soldiers stopped their discussions when Tito came into the room. Djilas motioned for the Partisan leader to join him at the map.

"Josip, there's little doubt. The Germans are close to breaking through. If they do, we'll be encircled."

Djilas' voice was insistent but without panic. The information was factual, not emotional.

"A breakthrough will allow German armor to push into Split. If that takes place, without armor, without heavy guns, we'll be forced to collapse into the sea."

"And, Comrade Minister?" Tito queried, knowing full well the outcome of such an assault would be disaster.

"The result would be annihilation. Total annihilation."

Tito nodded. He scanned the details of the German troop positions on the map and looked up from the parchment, into the faces of his commanders.

"What say the rest of you?"

His eyes remained riveted upon his officers. The intensity of his gaze was palpable. No one spoke, no one wished to repeat the obvious, no one wished to acknowledge that the Partisans, despite all their victories, had no alternative but to turn and run for the safety of the wilderness.

The silence between them cast a depressing pall over the room. Stana Tomashevich, a female Partisan commander, stepped forward to speak. Her voice was quiet and slightly tremulous:

"We've assessed our success in Dalmatia. We've taken enough weapons, ammunition and equipment from the Italians to raise another ten divisions. To stay and fight, to challenge the Nazis in a battle we have little hope of winning—and every likelihood of losing, would destroy all we've worked for, all you've accomplished over the past three years. I know I speak for my brothers and sisters when I tell you we must withdraw. We can regroup and begin anew to lash out at the Germans from the protection of the Bosnian hills."

Her eyes flashed with brilliance. Tito took full measure of what she said, took full measure of her beauty as well.

"What a war," Tito thought, "only such a conflict could steal a woman from her home, from her village. She should be carrying a baby across her back, nursing a child upon her breast, not carrying a rifle into battle. Such a war."

He sighed.

"You show courage speaking when your brothers will not. Do you all agree with Sister Tomashevich? Should we leave and take refuge in the mountains?"

Before the others could respond, the remnants of the front door, hanging loose upon its hinge, were pushed aside. Exquisite light from the seacoast flooded the room. Deakin limped across the floor followed by a young man, lean and slight of build. The stranger wore the uniform of a British paratrooper. His dress was absent rank or insignia. A dirty beret covered his blond hair. Djuro raised the muzzle of his submachine gun in the general direction of the unfamiliar soldier.

Deakin walked cautiously in front of the Partisan commanders and placed himself in front of Tito.

"I'd like to introduce Brigadier Fitzroy Maclean. The chap I was telling you about."

Deakin gestured towards the newcomer. All eyes were fixed on the Yugoslav leader. Tito was known to explode if interrupted. Unexpectedly, the Partisan smiled and extended his hand.

"Well, Maclean, you English seem to turn up at the worst times. You drop in uninvited, just as Deakin did on Durmitor, right in the middle of a major German offensive. We were just discussing, with Comrade Tomashevich here, the necessity of evacuating. I've been advised to leave Dalmatia at once, which is what we'll do. I'd suggest that you and Captain Deakin come along—unless you'd rather talk to the Germans."

Maclean smiled and turned in the direction of Stana Tomashevich:

"I've no wish to discuss tactics with the Germans. From the looks of things, I'm sure I'll find Partisan hospitality, even on the run, to be more than satisfactory."

The English General's eyes remained fixed on those of the young woman.

He spoke softly, in perfect Serbo–Croatian. His directness caused Tomashevich to blush. She turned away, obviously embarrassed by the attention. Tito, knowing that Stana was more than a match for the Englishman, laughed.

"Careful, General. Sometimes the most beautiful apple is full of poison."

"I'd dare say, sir, that I'd risk the poison for a taste of that apple."

Tito chuckled and slapped Maclean on the shoulder. Relieved that the exchange was over, Tomashevich retreated from the cottage. Maclean's eyes followed her departure, intrigued that her battle-worn fatigues did little to conceal her feminine form.

As Eli Kobe stood sentry outside, his attention began to wander. He tried to focus his attention on the slow rustling of the pasture grass. His thoughts carried him down the hill, past the limits of the farm's closely cropped fields, beyond the shores of the Adriatic, across Europe, across the English Channel to Marta.

Chapter 15

September 27, 1943

Marta escaped the depressing, thick, Autumnal fog of London. She flew to Cairo aboard a RAF Hudson. Once there, she sought out Sergie Makiedo and Joze Podvje, Partisan operatives, men who were capable of smuggling her back into Axis-occupied Yugoslavia.

Makiedo and Podvje were in North Africa, sent by Tito, to convince the Allies to sponsor a fleet, a fleet that would supply the communists by sea. A Partisan stronghold existed on the Island of Vis, a short distance from Hvar. From Vis, Mikos Pappas continued to operate his trawler as a shuttle between the Greek ELAS resistance fighters and the Yugoslav communists. From Vis to Corfu and back, the Helena constantly defied Nazi patrols. The Partisans believed that larger vessels could successfully run the same gauntlet and shuttle badly needed ammunition and supplies to the guerrillas.

The British High Command remained convinced that airborne resupply to Milhailovich's Chetniks and Tito's Partisans was the best course militarily and politically. Sea-borne efforts required the allocation of sparse warships and transports, resources better used to facilitate the invasion of Normandy.

By the time Marta met with the Partisan agents in Cairo, they had managed to find other, more receptive ears for their plan. Representatives of the American Organization of Strategic Services, the OSS, agreed to find vessels and provide financial assistance to the Yugoslav resistance. The ships purchased by the OSS would become known as the "Splinter Fleet"– a rag tag assortment of outmoded trawlers, leaking ketches and rusting tramp steamers assembled to reprovision the Partisans by sea.

Major Louis Huot of the OSS sat with two Yugoslav Communists in an outdoor cafe in the heart of old Cairo. The force of a fierce autumn sun blanketed their table. It was warm for September, warm even for Cairo. It was also quiet. Rommel and his forces had been pushed out of Egypt. Peace had been restored to the African desert.

Against the powerful glare of the sun, a diminutive figure appeared. A woman, neatly dressed in western-style clothing, approached the men as they talked.

The Legacy

Though her blond hair was cropped unnaturally short, a slight breeze gently stirred the scant wisps of hair remaining about her forehead. Her eyes, deep pools of brown, presented a stark contrast to her fair complexion. Her pale skin was distinctly out of place when compared to the sun-weathered bodies of the native Egyptians moving through the city behind her. It was obvious to the men at the table that she was European.

Huot studied the woman's features. He squinted severely so as to see her better. To his surprise, the woman stopped directly in front of their table and addressed the group in English:

"I'm Marta Kobe, the wife of a Partisan soldier, a member of Tito's bodyguard. I'm desperate to travel to Vis, to be near him."

Her voice was calm and steady, without any hint of anxiety. She told a little lie. It was of no consequence to her that she and Eli were not married in the eyes of the church, that in fact, she remained married to a German SS officer. Her passport, procured through the Yugoslavian government in exile, was in the name of Marta Kobe. It listed her as Yugoslavian. That was enough. In her heart, in Eli's heart, they were husband and wife. No power on earth could dispute that.

"I'm told that you have a vessel, the Marija, bound for Italy and Vis. I ask for passage with you, to find my husband."

Makiedo spoke first. He looked intently at the strangely confident young woman:

"May I see your passport?"

She pulled a document from a well-worn bag hanging from her shoulder and handed him papers enclosed in leather.

"Thank you."

The Yugoslavian operative glanced at it, convinced himself it was genuine and returned it to the stranger. He noted that she looked worn and tired from the dust and heat of Cairo.

"Please sit. You seem tired."

Makiedo motioned for her to join them. She walked hesitantly to an empty chair and sat down heavily. A gasp of hot breath escaped from her lips. It was obvious she was thankful to be off of her feet and out of the sun.

Makiedo looked at her, trying to gauge her essence.

"You speak English well, Mrs. Kobe. But I note a trace of an accent. German perhaps?"

His eyes narrowed as he studied her face, trying to determine if they could risk her presence. She smiled.

"I'm German born. I came to your country with my first husband, a soldier, an SS officer. I left him and married Mr. Kobe. I could no longer stomach the war my country brought to your people. I could no longer watch their killing. I escaped Yugoslavia and came to England, to bear witness to the atrocities I'd witnessed."

No emotion broke through to punctuate her words. She pulled an envelope from her bag. It was her trump card. She handed it to the man. The others at the table leaned in to watch Makiedo open the envelope.

Makiedo held a letter from Brigadier Fitzroy Maclean. The memorandum detailed Marta Essen's service to the allies. Makiedo passed it to the others.

"A celebrity. I should've known the name. I've heard of the matter at Ljubljana. It is but one of the hundreds of such incidents, massacres. I'm sorry I didn't remember."

Podvje looked over his warm ale as he spoke. The tumbler filtered the extreme sunlight, breaking the fragile beam apart until the light formed a small spectrum, a miniature rainbow, over the table. His voice was far deeper, more resonant than Maikedo's:

"You're welcome to come with, Mrs. Kobe. But it won' t be an easy trip. The Marija is old, a schooner built before the turn of the century. She has no accommodations for passengers; she's a transport, not the kind of ship for a woman. But we'll take you. We owe you that much."

Huot, the American, remained silent. He was lost in thought. His eyes were not fixed upon the woman, but focused off in the distance. When he finally looked at her, the color had vanished from her cheeks. She was as white as new snow. She took a few, slow breaths of the acrid air. Her color returned.

"She's a remarkable woman", the American thought. "Remarkable and beautiful."

It was obvious she was deeply in love with her Partisan. Still, Huot could not restrain himself from touching her. His small, effeminate hand reached out and gently found hers.

"You'll be one of the first to see whether the Splinter Fleet can be made to work. If this trip is a success, your husband's Partisans will be able to receive ammunition and arms by water in far greater quantities than the English can deliver by air."

Huot's hand was moist with perspiration. She gently removed it from hers. He continued to look at her with American directness, making her nervous and uneasy.

"Thank you, Major. Thank you for understanding. I promise not to be a burden to you or your men."

"I could never see you as being a burden to anyone."

Huot's comment shocked her. It was too personal, too familiar for the time and place. She wanted to leave, to seek the safety of her hotel room.

"Waiter, bring Mrs. Kobe a bottle of your best white wine," Huot called out to a passing servant. Turning to the woman, he continued in the same casual tone:

"I trust white will do nicely, Mrs. Kobe?"

"Thank you, Major, but I'm really very tired. I don't wish to appear rude, but I should get some rest."

"Nonsense, madam, nonsense. I insist that you allow me the small pleasure of buying the best this poor excuse for a cafe has to offer."

The waiter, resplendently dressed in starched whites, his exotic skin shining in the brilliant heat, returned and presented a bottle of locally produced wine. Huot examined the label, frowned and paid the man. The Egyptian produced a corkscrew and labored to open the bottle.

"Pop."

Marta tried to listen politely as the American talked about the details of some military adventure he'd been involved in. Finally, after what seemed to Marta to be an inordinate length of time, Huot filled her glass with pale, yellow liquid. He handed her the thin stemmed vessel and raised his tumbler of ale in toast.

"To you, Mrs. Kobe. To a safe journey."

She feigned a smile. The others raised their glasses as well.

"We'll be leaving in the morning, at first light. I'll meet you in front of your hotel."

The American's statement was spoken without importance, as if an aside. She couldn't determine from the tone of the words whether Huot truly welcomed her on the journey or not.

"I will be there," she assured.

Her stomach turned over, upset by the unfamiliar air and climate. The nausea reminded her not to drink too deeply of the wine. She lowered her glass and thought of tomorrow. The faces of her new companions blurred. Nothing mattered except Eli. Tomorrow she would be on the sea, racing back to him.

"Thank you for your assistance. I' m afraid that I'm not much company. The wine has gone to my head, Major Huot. I really must retire."

Straightening the folds of her navy blue skirt, adjusting the buttons of her thin, white cotton blouse, she took her leave. She continued to feel the directness of the American's stare as she walked away. She knew that Huot's gaze never left her until she turned and disappeared from view.

"There goes one hell of a woman," Huot murmured.

The others nodded in affirmation, their eyes studying the thick bottoms of their empty glasses. Huot ordered another round. The American felt like indulging himself.

That night, Marta Essen sought to sleep in the stale, unmoving air of the hotel. Each time she drifted off, the night noises of the city disrupted her slumber. In the dark, passionless grip of the night, she wondered what Eli would say when and if she found him. She wondered how he would react to her subterfuge of marriage. Exhausted, she collapsed into sleep.

It didn't take long for the Marija to clear the Port of Cairo. The ship was world-weary but fast, a mistress of the sea; all sails and well-oiled oak, a lioness who would not be tamed or vanquished by the Germans.

From Cairo to Algiers the vessel rode the winds, loaded to the gunwales with medicine, ammunition and small arms. She was bound for Italy, for Bari, to take on light machine guns and four-pound howitzers.

The first day following their passage, Marta welcomed the relative calm of Bari after a wrenching trip across the Mediterranean. Her stomach settled. Her strength returned. She began to accompany the men as they searched the wharves and docks of the ancient city for additional ships to augment the Splinter Fleet.

The Legacy

Marta Essen possessed no particular expertise regarding vessels or the sea. She knew nothing of sailing. Huot relished being with her, being accompanied in public by the beautiful young woman. He had become polite and restrained, unlike his demeanor during their first encounter. Though they became friends, she made it painfully obvious that their connection would never advance beyond friendship. Huot accepted the limitations she placed upon their time together. Even if he had not been so accepting, her need to leave the salt-encrusted Marija overwhelmed any sense of caution she may have retained about being escorted by the American.

"How long has it been since I made love with Eli?" she thought.

Though certain details of her time with the young Partisan had faded, Marta's ability to recall his touch, his embrace as they made love, had not. The autumn sunshine, the fresh breeze, the flocks of birds on the move along the Italian coast triggered her memory. Walking the streets of Bari took her mind off of the final leg of their journey, the voyage across the Adriatic to Vis.

"She sails straight and true, Mrs. Kobe," Huot remarked, invading her private thoughts.

Huot stood at the rail of the ship, watching the Marija crash through the weather-roughened waters.

"Yes, Major, the boat is able, as is the crew. I, unfortunately, am not faring so well."

The German woman's face was drawn and gaunt. But for the faint pink of her lips, her face was off-white, the color of children's paste. The seasickness that plagued her during earlier voyages had returned. Being under sail, at the mercy of the winds, only heightened her nausea.

"Two days, Marta, two days and you will be off this hulk, I promise."

She cringed. Huot had taken to calling her by her first name sometime during the voyage. It made her uncomfortable and caused her to question his true motives. He was so friendly, so engaging, so direct. She decided to confront him.

"Are all Americans that way?"

"What way, Marta?"

"That way. Using the first names of people they barely know, speaking in the familiar with a married woman, a woman they know little about, without a second thought?"

From the expression of bewilderment on his face, she knew that Huot had no idea what she was feeling. She decided to soften her words:

"It's just that, where I come from, it takes many, many hours of friendship and conversation before such barriers are let down, before one feels comfortable enough to call another, especially one of the opposite gender, by their first name."

His face seemed to brighten. He spoke in a quiet, respectful tone:

"Americans are always in a hurry. Always trying to get things moving, to make friends, make money, become important. That's what we value, that's how we are. I guess that's not how you Germans, or the Slavs, for that matter, do things. We're always afraid there will be no tomorrow. We don't have your history of a thousand years of culture to fall back on. We make ours up day by day, as we go along. If I've been too direct, it's only because that's how we're taught to get along, to communicate. If I offended you, Mrs. Kobe, I'm sorry."

The look in his eyes seemed genuine. She smiled, careful not to encourage him by showing false emotion.

To her, Huot was not a handsome man. His face was essentially nondescript, his eyes were unremarkable; absent any definable color. He was short, shorter than she, and appreciably heavier; not fat, but thick; thick wrists, thick neck, thick body but thin feminine hands and delicate fingers.

"Perhaps I spoke too harshly, Major. I understand that you don' t mean to offend me. It's just another difference between our worlds, that's all."

He smiled, showing his less-than-white teeth, and walked away. From his slow, deliberate gait, Marta was certain she had caused him pain.

"I'll have to try to accommodate him as a friend without encouraging his interest in me as a woman," she thought. "A most difficult task."

She turned her eyes to the sea and watched the old ship as it fought to make progress through the water. The decking creaked and the hull groaned with the slap of each whitecap against the ship's sides. Around her, men worked at the ropes, trimming the sails, moving with haste to capture the best of the wind. She watched with interest as the Marija's crew, an international mix of Greeks, Italians and Yugoslavs, coordinated efforts with little spoken communication. She knew Huot was the lone American. Huot was not a sailor. He spent his days, for the most part, inside, out of the wind and elements.

Though the churning froth was by no means a tonic for Marta's weary constitution, the young woman took solace in the fact that each jolting fall of the boat's bow brought her closer to Eli. On October 10, 1943, the Marija finally came to rest at Vis, Yugoslavia.

With the successful completion of the ship's maiden run, Huot was convinced that the Splinter Fleet could turn the tide for the Partisans. The successful replenishment of the Partisans, using OSS contacts and Allied munitions, could be accomplished by water. Huot's orders forbade him to make direct contact with Tito, the Balkans being in the British operational theater. But the American could not restrain his curiosity. He was determined to disobey Eisenhower's direct order and search out the Partisan leader and discuss with Tito his ideas for the Splinter Fleet.

"Do you know Eli Kobe? He comes from near Jesenice?" Marta asked a bearded Partisan working the docks.

"What unit is he with?" the man replied in an irritated tone.

"George Petrich's," she responded in slow, rudimentary Serbo-Croation.

She was exhausted from fighting her own body. Her words, laboriously delivered in a language she had come to learn in a limited fashion since the Sava, slipped out of her mouth, barely audible due to her fatigue.

The man stood on the decaying dock, working the ropes securing the Marija. He appeared patient in his work, impatient in his dealings with strangers. As he responded, he pulled heavily on the ropes, easing the ship closer to the pier:

"Petrich's unit is with Tito, in the mountains, near Jajce, in West Bosnia. If you're looking for someone who's with Petrich, that's where he'd be."

"I was told Petrich was here."

"Was, Miss, was. This is Yugoslavia. If Tito stays put for more than a few days, he's a dead man. The Germans and the Ustashi want him, want his head on a platter. If he stops running, fighting, he's dead."

She knew the man was right, that a guerrilla unit's survival depended upon its ability to travel swiftly, to vanish into the steep canyons and hills of the countryside at the hint of an enemy attack. Marta stepped over the gunwale and walked gingerly down the gangplank to where the man worked. She gently grasped the Serb by the arm and tried to gain his undivided attention.

"How far is it to Jajce?" she asked in a concerned voice.

The dockhand sensed the woman was troubled. His attitude softened.

"Depends on where the Germans are. My best guess is that you could make it there, on a good horse, in three days."

"On a horse? Are there no trains to Jajce?"

"There were. Tito blew them all to hell to make it more difficult for the Germans to move their armor. You'll either go on horseback, or you'll walk. If it were me, I'd take a horse. A good mount can cover a lot of ground in the hills."

He politely removed her hand from his sweat-stained workshirt and returned to tying off the mooring line.

She felt a wave of fear intrude upon her mind. She had taken riding lessons as a little girl. That was years ago. She had never ridden a horse in mountainous terrain. But there seemed to be no alternative, no other way.

"Thank you for the information. Can you tell me where I can find a horse?"

The man smiled a tired smile, an expression of mild annoyance. His patience was wearing thin, unused as he was to answering a woman's questions.

"Major Huot would know. I hear he's planning to find Tito. He's taking a squad of Partisans with him. He should be able to help you."

"Thank you. I'll ask him."

Leaving the man to his work, Marta Essen went aboard the Marija. She needed time to think, to contemplate how she would approach the American.

She had made up her mind long ago, before she left England, that she would find Eli Kobe no matter what it took. As she stood on the deck of the Marija, she weighed the risks of a trip into Nazi-occupied Yugoslavia. It had to be done. It was that simple.

Huot appeared from below deck, greeted by a fierce, ashen sky. Clouds rapidly closed in upon the harbor like a shroud. Huot scanned the horizon and cursed under his breath. Marta heard the words plainly. She pulled the hood of her cloak close around her face and left her belongings near the rail. At the stairway to the hold, she extended a hand to the American.

"You haven't been well. I can do this," the Officer demurred.

"I'm fine, Major, really I am. Being on solid ground has set my sense of balance right. Let me help you. Your arms are full."

He relented and allowed her to lift a small duffel out of the hold. He climbed the stairs and joined her on the wind swept deck.

Sensing the moment was right; she looked intently into the American's face, her eyes brilliantly visible from within the depths of the cloak. Pellets of rain began to fall, distorting her features. She thought the man looked weary. The softness, the curiosity she had seen in his eyes in Cairo, had vanished.

"Major, I understand that you're going to Jajce. I must go there too. My husband is there. You'll take me, won't you?"

They were nearly the same height. She studied his face. The boldness of her gaze was uncharacteristic. It forced him to look away. "I'll be traveling through German lines, on horseback. It's not a journey for a city woman."

"I can ride," she responded. "I'm an excellent rider. All I need, Major, is a mount. And as far as being a woman, the women who fight for the guerrillas face more hardship, more pain, than I'll experience on one short trip into Bosnia."

His focus remained downcast. He appeared to be studying the planking of the deck. He thought of the reasons why he should not take a delicate woman through German lines into the mountains of Yugoslavia. Huot discovered he was too tired to argue. Still, he tried to dissuade her.

"As God is my witness, Mrs. Kobe, I pray that you don't ask this of me."

"I ask you for nothing, Major, other than help in finding a horse. Once I have a mount, I will not bother you further. I'll ride with you but if I delay you, if I imperil you in any way, you're free to leave me."

"That's unlikely. I wouldn't leave you in the mountains to whatever fate might be in store for a German woman who sympathizes with the Partisans."

"Major, I won't accept no for an answer. With or without your help, I will go. Be assured of that."

Huot's colorless eyes met hers. It was obvious she would not accept his reasoning. Yielding to her, he said:

"Alright. Tomorrow morning we'll find you a horse, one that you can ride without breaking your foolish little neck. What happens after that, I guess, is up to God and the Germans."

Though he agreed to help the German woman find her Partisan husband, Major Huot silently prayed that Eli Kobe was dead. To avoid her detecting his true emotions, he turned away. As Huot turned, Marta Essen carelessly dropped the American's duffel. Down it tumbled, down it spilled, until it came to rest at the bottom of the gangway. The bag teetered precariously on the edge of the wharf, threatening to fall into the cold waters of the Adriatic. The dockworker stooped down, picked up the bag and deposited it safely on the pier. The German woman grasped Huot tightly around the neck. Her tears streamed into his face.

"Thank you, Major, thank you. There's no way I can ever repay your kindness."

The OSS officer stood in the bleak air of the harbor, silently ashamed that he had wished her lover dead. The warm water of the woman's tears slid down his face, mixed with the cold rain and spoiled the cigarette clenched tightly in his lips.

Alone on the waterfront of Vis, soaked to the skin by the persistent rain, Major Huot listened to the echoes of Marta Essen's gratitude and the pounding of his less-than-honorable heart.

The Legacy

Chapter 16

May 25, 1944

The British Prime Minister sent aid to the Partisans. He also sent his only son, Randolph, as part of the English military mission to the guerrillas. Brigadier Maclean's reports convinced Winston Churchill that, regardless of the politics, Tito was a man worthy of support. At Churchill's insistence, the British airdrops were re-directed to provide unqualified assistance to the Partisans. As a consequence, Milhailovich's Chetniks watched the supplies they had previously received from the Allies dwindle to nothing.

The munitions the British supplied by air, coupled with the tons of munitions disgorged weekly by the Splinter Fleet at Vis, insured that, by the end of 1943, the communists were well–nourished and well-equipped. The Partisans were no longer a ragged contingent of shadow troops striking only under the cover of darkness. They were rapidly becoming an army, the strategic equal of the German Wermacht in Yugoslavia; they had always been superior to the Axis in terms of bravery and spirit.

"Are you ready for the trip?"

Marta, round of belly and eight months pregnant with her first child, was busily preparing pork over the open hearth of a campfire. It was May, springtime in the mountains. The sun sat high making it hot during the day. The nights still held the chill of the recently departed winter.

"The sooner we escape this place, Eli, the better I'll feel," Marta lamented. "This child does not wish to wait much longer."

The young Partisan reached around his lover's waist and rubbed the faded fabric of her dress where the garment stretched tightly across her belly. He nuzzled her ear, blowing fragments of hair away from her face as he uttered words of love to her in Slovenian.

"Stop it, Eli. That's what got me pregnant in the first place," she complained. "Besides, you have no business starting something you don't have time to finish."

Exhausted from trying to keep up with Tito, Eli welcomed the chance to rest in Vis. His direct commander, Djuro, made it plain there would be no objection to the young bodyguard being absent from the front for two weeks. If the child didn't come on time, there would be no extension of Kobe's leave. Two weeks was all the Partisans could afford to be a man short.

"Marta, stop that for a moment."

Kobe's voice became serious. She knew it was time to give him her attention. She stopped rolling the bread dough before her. He leaned close to her face, feeling the soft down of her neck against his coarse skin.

"I want to marry you."

When Marta was in England, Eli contemplated approaching Father Utyro, the lone Catholic priest traveling with the Partisans but Kobe's nerve failed him. He did not speak to the priest during Marta's absence.

His inability to talk to the Father changed when Marta appeared with Major Huot in early October. Seeing her thin, nubile form dressed in castoff fatigues and a red woolen cloak, sitting astride a white Spanish mare, his emotions soared. His longing for her, his desire to be with her, became unbearable. During their first few moments together, he sensed the agony of the American's disappointment seeking to engulf them in a cesspool of jealousy.

There was the problem of the woman's prior marriage; a nasty problem that ate away at Eli Kobe from the day she arrived in Jajce. He tried to put the idea of marriage out of his mind. He tried to console himself by repeating that she was married, she was a German, the wife of a Nazi butcher.

"Our love," he reasoned silently, "was born out of the strange, brutal haze of war."

He told himself that such love could not last, could not be used to construct a marriage. Even if such a thing was possible, which it was not since she was already married.

Through the winter they lived together, moving with the Partisan camp, making love and talking about their dreams. From time to time, Eli would disappear into the forest with his comrades. When he returned, his clothing soiled, muddy and smelling of battle, Marta would not ask where he'd been, what he'd done; and he didn't offer to tell her.

As the snow melted and spring returned to the mountains, it became obvious that Marta was with child. The time had come for Eli Kobe to claim, for all eternity, what Franz Essen had lost. What, through the turmoil of war, was now Kobe's. The Partisan grew increasingly tired of watching Huot's eyes following Marta whenever she encountered the American.

"But Eli, I'm married."

Her fingers stroked the bare skin of the base of his neck, where his shirt was open. She curled and uncurled the sparse hairs of his chest as they embraced.

"I've spoken with Father Utyro. I thought that might be a problem. He assures me it isn' t."

As Eli stared into her eyes, his tone became deadly serious.

"How did you come to be married to the German?"

"It was a civil ceremony, at the town hall of his home village. Is that important?"

"Was there a priest, a man of God, present to bless the union?"

"Franz is an atheist. He refused to have a minister there. I'm Lutheran. I wanted a church wedding, for my parents' sake. He was vehement, said he wouldn't allow a homosexual follower of fables and old wives' tales to bless his marriage. He was so insistent, so angry, I let it pass."

"You may be married in the eyes of Hitler, but not in the eyes of God. Utyro says that, without the Church's presence, your marriage to Essen is of no consequence to God or to the priest. You're a free woman, Marta Essen," he stated evenly. "Will you marry me?"

Her fingers tensed causing her to pull harshly on his chest hairs. She turned away from his face, seeking to quell her gathering tears. There was a moment of awkward silence as she fought to control her emotions sufficient to respond:

"I'll marry you. After all, our little daughter needs a proper family, doesn't she?" she whispered through a slight smile.

"You mean our son, don't you? From the strength of the kicks, it is definitely a son."

She was unable to look at him directly as she continued:

"When should we get married?"

Her German inflection had all but disappeared as she spoke in the language of the Partisans. It had become rare that she ever needed to think, to grasp in her mind, for the appropriate phrase or word. He laughed. The sound made her look at him.

"You speak Serbo-Croatian very well. I think I'll have to speak more

Slovenian around you. You need to learn the language of my village."

There was a brief pause before he continued.

"Why not tonight?"

"Learn Slovenian tonight?"

"No. Get married."

"But Eli, it's Tito's birthday. There'll be much celebrating, much music. Who'll notice a wedding with the General's party going on?"

"Tito's asked that the wedding take place before the whole camp. We'll be married long before they all drink too much slivovica, long before the music becomes too loud for the baby's delicate little ears."

She returned her eyes to meet his.

"And Marta, then we shall dance."

"I'm afraid you'll be dancing by yourself. I'm a bit out of round for dancing," she said, her eyebrows knitting into an intense frown. "But what am I to wear? I've nothing that will do a wedding justice."

"Don't worry. Madame Bolinka, you know, the fat one who is such a good seamstress? She's prepared a dress for you."

"I'll ask for nothing more, Eli, nothing more. To have a man who loves me, to carry a healthy child close to my heart, these are things I could only dream of before I met you. I'm no longer sad that fate brought me to this land."

"Nor am I," he whispered, pulling her swollen body close to his.

She did not protest. She did not murmur words of discouragement as he led her into their tent, its brown canvas faded by the intense sun of the thin mountain air.

"Close the flaps. Someone might see, might make gossip," she urged in a low, careful voice.

He drew the door panels shut. With one hand, he secured the flaps with twine. With the other, he unbuttoned his shirt and threw it into a dim corner of the tent.

"No one will see, Marta. No one but you and I."

She reclined so that her belly rose above her thighs. With a sense of urgency, Kobe undid his trousers and tossed them in the general direction of his shirt. Kneeling over her, he undid her blouse with deliberate, slow care, releasing her engorged breasts. His mouth enclosed the nipples, erect with excitement, enlarged with milk. He suckled on each breast patiently as his left hand loosened the waistband of her skirt. Shifting her weight, she allowed him to pull the garment down. His hands moved to her exposed buttocks, kneading the flesh, its texture firm and youthful. He felt her breath quicken under his touch. His fingers began to gently probe, circle, and encompass her innermost flesh. Marta let out her breath. A tiny cry of amazement rose from her lips as her thighs began to quiver. As their passion reached the point of explosion, only the canvas walls of the tent disguised their exuberant lovemaking. He rolled her over onto her left side, her breasts and her womb propped by a pillow.

In the privacy of their tent, he placed his stomach and thighs directly behind her, his hands softly stroking her neck, his mouth nibbling along the skin of her shoulders. One hand followed the soft, feathery fibers of her hair, the color bleached nearly white by the intensity of the mountain sun. He slid his hands under her arms, following the graceful curve of her ribcage. He touched her belly, the taunt skin of her chest, until his hands rested under the fullness of her impending motherhood. He lovingly pressed each nipple between his thumb and forefinger. He whispered her name.

"God, Marta. I must have you."

She did not answer. The words she would have said were lost within her, floating near her soul, caught in the building crescendo of orgasm. Sensing she was near the limit of her endurance, he entered her from behind. The muscles of her buttocks pressed tightly against his thighs and he surrendered to the most primitive of human feelings, allowing the evolution of his kind to guide him. Their bodies moved in perfect unison, in harmony, until at last, their souls merged as one in a singular instant of release.

"Mr. Kobe, I think we'd better see the priest. I'm almost certain that we just broke some sort of Catholic law," she said breathlessly into his ear.

Her right arm draped across his naked torso. The sparse light of the fleeting day danced upon his bare skin, upon his hips and legs. A narrow shaft of light intruded, casting shadows across the walls of the tent. An unexpected gust of wind loosened a door flap. The fabric slapped noisily in the passing breeze.

"You're right, Mrs. Kobe. But I think you' re the cause of my demise. Maybe only you need to see the priest," he replied with a sheepish grin, kissing her on the chin.

"Now isn't the time to worry about who has sinned. We have a wedding to get ready for," she teased.

Kobe kissed the woman's bare belly, slightly below the navel, and rose from their bed. Slipping on his fatigues and a clean wool shirt, he vanished through the door of the tent. Marta recoiled contentedly within the thick wool blanket and searched for dreams of their future together in Yugoslavia. The memories of her life in Germany with Franz Essen sought to intrude but were bested by her love for the Partisan. She fell into a deep sleep.

Hours later they stood before Josip Broz and his camp. Eli was dressed in a black formal jacket borrowed from Djuro; Marta concealed her pregnant form in a hand-sown white muslin wedding dress.

"Do you, Eli Kobe, take this woman, Marta Stuva, as your lawfully wedded wife, to have and to hold, in good times and bad, for richer or poorer, in sickness and in health, to love, honor, and cherish, until death?"

The priest avoided using her married name, Essen and referenced her maiden name, "Stuva", as if she'd never been married to Franz Essen.

"I do."

"And do you, Marta Stuva, take this man, Eli Kobe, as your lawfully wedded husband, to have and to hold, making the same promises to him, and in addition, making to him the promise to obey him, until death?"

"I do."

"Then by the power vested in me by the Holy Roman Church, I pronounce you man and wife. You may kiss her."

Eli placed his lips forcefully against Marta's as the flames of a Partisan bonfire framed her face, accenting her high cheekbones and the exquisite curve of her jaw. His kiss was one of admiration and love, not passion, his passion having been quenched earlier that day.

"Comrades, I give you Mr. and Mrs. Eli Kobe."

Their Partisan comrades cheered until strong, persistent hands forced the couple apart.

"Now, little brother and little sister, we dance. For your future and for my birthday," Tito announced in a jubilant tone, "We dance."

Tito motioned for the musicians to begin. Kobe smiled and moved aside as the General offered his hand to Marta.

The Legacy

"Mrs. Kobe, let me be the first to dance with you."

"Only if you promise not to be disappointed by my laziness, Comrade General. You'll have to be satisfied with a few slow, clumsy steps. My balance isn't what it was before this child decided to make its presence known."

"Nonsense, Sister Marta. You'll do just fine."

With a gentle tug, Tito pulled her out into the circle, where others were already dancing to the strains of an impromptu orchestra.

"Guess how old I am," Tito quipped.

The Commander whirled her around, at a pace faster than she thought she could physically handle. But his style seemed so effortless, so under control, she had no difficulty keeping up.

"Forty five, Comrade General."

"Bless you. No, I'm 52 tonight. An old man, fighting an old war. Do you agree?"

"With what, Comrade? That you are old or that this conflict is old? Which premise do you wish me to address?"

"Ah, Mrs. Kobe, you're perceptive. Please address both."

"I think, Comrade General, that at this moment, you're not old, you're not young. You're mature but still able to dance better than most young men because you have experience," she said with a coy, flirtatious smile.

"As for the war," she continued, "what choice do you have? My country attacked. Whether the conflict is old or new matters little when your families are dying at the hands of the Germans."

Tito pondered her response and replied:

"I thank you for your insight, into both my dancing abilities and the just nature of our cause. I think I see a jealous husband coming to claim his bride."

Through the crowd of twirling men and women, Kobe approached. Tito placed Marta's hand upon the young guerrilla's shoulder and left them to the music. Long before the celebration quieted and the celebrants passed into the deep sleep of the grapes, Marta and Eli Kobe said their good-byes and retired to their tent, leaving the party to continue on without them.

For Tito's birthday, elaborate cakes were prepared. Beer, wine and plum brandy were in abundance. The music, music of the mountains, rang long into the night while Tito danced with Zdenka. Twirling, spinning like mad tops out of control, they fell to the earth together, laughing as they sat upon the cool ground.

"Comrade sister, you're too good a dancer to be stuck in the mountains with an old man. You should be in Belgrade, with the ballet, no?"

"General, I recognize your motives. Tonight, your flattery will not get you into Zdenka's bed. Tonight, Zdenka will not go to bed. Instead, I'll dance until the day arrives," the dark-eyed beauty asserted.

"You tease me, you lead me on. We'll see who is in whose bed when morning comes. I'll wager that you and I will be together, no matter whose bed it might be."

"I doubt it, Comrade General. But who is to say? Anything is possible."

"Let's get a drink," Tito proposed.

"Beer. I need beer to quench my thirst," the woman responded.

"Then beer it shall be."

Tito helped his secretary up from the dirt. Zdenka brushed the dust of the country from her blue cotton skirt as they walked away from the dancers.

Above, the silhouette a German reconnaissance plane flew past the camp. Disguised by thick clouds, the sound of its motor could not be heard over the music.

Within an hour of the plane's silent survey, six hundred German SS soldiers landed by parachute and glider in the fields surrounding the Partisan position. The enemy's silent descent onto the neighboring farms of Drvar precluded the possibility of an organized defense.

Using tactics perfected in thousands of villages and towns throughout Europe, the SS rounded up the villagers of Drvar and slaughtered them. There was no reason for the killing. The villagers were purposefully unarmed, left so by the Partisans to prevent the enemy from claiming that the peasants were active in the resistance. The civilians held no arms; this fact meant nothing to the Germans as they butchered helpless old men, women of all ages and children along the streets and roads leading to Drvar. The murders were only a bitter reprise of countless other atrocities orchestrated by the SS in Yugoslavia; murders which made no military sense, which served no military purpose.

They marched on. Each SS soldier carried a photograph of Tito. Each was armed with a submachine gun and hundreds of rounds of ammunition. They were, in essence, six hundred assassins with one goal, one objective; to find and kill Josip Broz. Undetected by the Partisans, the German paratroopers marched over rain–soaked pastures, trampling neat, cultivated rows of freshly germinated grain. They swarmed, by tens and twenties, upward into the hills, the noise of their advance veiled by the din of Tito's birthday party.

Without warning, weapon fire from the SS advance punctuated the evening. Mortar shells sliced through the heavy, warm air, slamming into the wet earth underlying Tito's hidden camp.

A small, isolated cottage stood at the center of the guerrilla encampment. A cave was located behind the cottage. Djuro insisted upon a cave. Tito insisted on a cave. For just such a circumstance. The German mortars sought to strike the cottage in hopes that the Partisan leader was already in bed.

"Germans! Take up your arms and follow me," Djuro shouted to those men and women gathering around him near the remnants of the party. The soldiers scurried away into the darkness to retrieve their weapons.

"They've broken through!" someone exclaimed.

"Hurry now, to the front," Djuro commanded.

The enemy completely surprised the Partisans. Outnumbered one hundred to one, the SS retained the element of confusion on their side. Their advance was reckless, without quarter. They knew that their objective was to sacrifice themselves to silence Tito. If they accomplished their goal, they would be Teutonic heroes, their names worshipped through the next one thousand years of the Reich.

Eli grabbed his Mauser and bandoleer and pulled on his trousers as he quickly exited the tent. Confused by the brutal suddenness of battle, Marta slipped on a cloak, covering her naked, pregnant form and followed her husband outside. There was no time to talk. No time to say goodbye. He grasped her arm.

Leading her away from the sounds of the firefight, they encountered Zdenka hiding beneath the shadows of the trees.

"Protect her, sister," Kobe requested.

"I will," the tall woman responded hesitantly, her eyes desperate with anxiety.

The woman restrained Marta as they spoke. Before the German woman could protest, Zdenka pulled the pregnant woman away from the soldier.

"Eli, don't leave me," Marta Kobe screamed hysterically, struggling against the strength of the Yugoslavian woman.

"I'll be back, Marta. I swear I'll be back," Kobe yelled as he moved through the thick underbrush towards the fighting.

As her husband's form disappeared into the trees, Marta strained against Zdenka's strength. She could not break the woman's grip.

"Let me go. If he's dying tonight, I want to die with him," she pleaded.

"He's not going to die. But even if he does, you must protect his son, his daughter, growing inside of you."

Zdenka continued to compel Marta Essen towards the safety of the cave as she spoke:

"Think, woman. The baby is more important than either of you."

"I can think of nothing but him. Let me go."

Despite the German woman's opposition, Zdenka pushed her towards the confines of the cavern. Marta Kobe did not see her husband scramble over the thick brush of the mountain's slope, down into the inferno raging against the helter–skelter line of the Partisan defense as she cried. But she knew that was where he would be. It was his duty. It was their destiny.

Another hand reached for her and forced her deep into the cave. The hand was coarse and masculine. A male voice addressed her:

"Don't worry about your husband. No Nazi dog can kill him. No bullet will harm him. He's a magician. I've seen it, seen him dodge death many times. He'll be back in your arms soon enough".

It was Tito. The tone of his voice contained such utter calm that she believed him.

"We must escape. The Germans mean to kill me. They want no one else, only me."

The group followed the wall of the tunnel until they emerged in a narrow ravine. Despite the poor light, Marta discerned that the rocky ground had been excavated to accommodate a railroad grade. An unbelievable sight awaited them.

In middle of the forest, a locomotive and two cars waited for Tito's party on the narrow gauge tracks. The Partisan leader directed Marta and his secretary to the first car. Deakin, Maclean, and Churchill followed. Djuro, Tito's bodyguard, was not with them. The train began to roll. Tiger ran behind, barking nervously at the locomotive until Deakin leaned out over the tracks and grabbed the dog's collar, effortlessly hoisting the animal onto the train.

In the unequal light, Marta saw armed, faceless members of the resistance operating the train. Scores of Partisan soldiers grasped tightly to the rusted wrought iron railings and ladders of the locomotive and cars, their weapons raised and poised for a fight.

Units of the select guards, the OZNA, held the tree line along the tracks. Bullets from German light machine guns struck the engine's boiler, throwing sparks, as the locomotive gathered steam. Zdenka forced Marta's head down, below the windowsill, out of danger. Repetitive "pings" echoed across the night, as enemy bullets struck metal. Marta could not see Djuro or her husband in the darkness of the overhanging forest. She could hear the cries of the bodyguard, the OZNA, as they rallied to beat back the SS, allowing the engine to gather speed. She knew Eli was with them.

For five kilometers the train plummeted down grade, down towards the main Partisan force, breaking through the tightly drawn Nazi line, outrunning the chatter of the German guns. Intermittently, cries of anguish greeted them from the forest's edge. Here and there a SS paratrooper broke through only to be gunned down by the withering fire of the OZNA. The tenacity of the enemy's onslaught made it clear that the Partisan force could not hold the tracks. The Nazis had isolated the train's defenders from the main Yugoslav force.

Ignoring Zdenka's repeated admonitions to remain low, Marta looked out the shattered window. She scrutinized the forest as the train quickened its pace down the slope. She could, from time to time, make out the vague forms of retreating Partisans running alongside the cars, clutching at the ladders, clambering onto the platforms, onto the roofs. Some made the safety of the apparatus. Others crumpled in pain, torn free from the splintered wood or the rusted metal of the train by the ferocity of the Nazi gunfire. It was too dark for her to see their faces.

"Eli," she prayed," May God speed you back to me."

She turned away from the battle. She could not bear to dwell upon her husband's fate.

The OZNA was beaten back. The SS stormed the tracks. But the accelerating grade of the spur and a surge of steam quickly advanced Tito's train out of danger. Wind whistled around them. All of the windows were shattered. The wooden sides of the cars were pockmarked by thousands of bullet holes. It became more and more difficult to hear gunfire.

"Comrade Djilas, give the order to withdraw."

"It's already been done, General."

"Huot, come with me." Tito said to the American Major as the train coasted to a stop at the base of the mountain.

"But your position seems secure. Why withdraw? Why not stand and annihilate them here in the forest?" Huot inquired.

Tito didn't smile.

Tito grimaced at the American's question. It was obvious from the pained expression on the Partisan's face that he'd run out of patience for Huot. Tito's reply was curt:

"Because, Major, after the drones comes the Queen."

"What?"

"Tomorrow this mountain will be surrounded by fresh divisions of the German Wermacht. If we don't retreat now and flee these drones, the queen will come to sting us."

The Partisan leader astutely surmised that the raid on Drvar was merely a prelude to another Axis offensive. Indeed, as Tito and his advisors stepped off the train, thousands of German troops were advancing towards Drvar. The Axis forces hoped to search out and destroy the beleaguered communists, seeking to trap them as they streamed away from the assault in disarray. Tito anticipated the trap and responded quickly to place the men and women under his command out of harm's way.

Safely within the ranks of the evacuating Partisans, Marta Kobe was placed in a horse-drawn wagon for the retreat; she would not be going to Vis to give birth in the comfort of a Yugoslavian military hospital; her child would be born, as its father had, in the harsh countryside of Yugoslavia.

Marta Essen knew none of this. She collapsed as she was taken from the train. She remained unconscious, protected by the rigid straw bedding of the cart, oblivious to her destination as the wagon carried her away from danger.

Bleeding profusely from a thigh wound, Eli Kobe hid beneath the dense branches of an evergreen. His left leg hung uselessly beside him. Spasms of pain cut through him like lightning. The anguish made it difficult for him to concentrate on the fury of the skirmish. He grasped the tail of his shirt with both hands and ripped a piece of fabric off. Biting his lip, he bound his thigh as best he could. The flow of blood soaked the rag until beads of blood worked through the cloth and dripped slowly to the ground. He looked up.

Two uprooted pines formed a natural wall in front of his position. Seeking their shelter, he pulled himself along the wet ground with his bare hands. The Mauser slid down his left shoulder and scraped the dirt. With determined effort, he found temporary respite in the cover of the fallen timber. His labor left him breathing heavily; pain blocked out his ability to concentrate. He heard the voices of his retreating comrades.

"Soon," he thought, "I'll be alone once again. If I call out, if I ask for them to carry me, I'll slow them down, I'll cause more to die."

He remained silent.

From the black depths of the woods, they came. Twenty or more. He heard their muffled footsteps, heard commands barked in German as they advanced. With his remaining strength, he pulled himself up so that he could rest his rifle on the smooth bark of one of the dead pines.

Movement on his right drew his attention. A man ran towards him. Eli Kobe shifted his weight and felt the hip fracture announce its presence. He trained the muzzle of his rifle on the running man. His right index finger began to squeeze. An instant before he reached the point of no return, he recognized his target. It was Djuro. Behind Djuro, coming out of the thick brush, Kobe saw other men. Germans.

Selecting one of the enemy as a target Kobe slid the rifle across the tree trunk and placed his sights on the advancing soldier.

"Djuro. Look out."

Kobe fired at the shadow, saw it collapse and merge with the darkness of the forest floor. Another soldier took the dead man's place. The line of the enemy continued to advance, training deadly, concentrated fire down upon Kobe's position. He had succeeded in buying his friend time; time to escape.

Djuro vaulted the logs and slid down beside the injured Partisan.

"Thanks. They were gaining on me. Too much cake at Tito's party."

Djuro was breathing hard. His attempt to joke about their circumstances was distorted by an edge of concern to his words. He concentrated his gaze on Kobe's face and recognized that his companion was severely wounded and in pain. Djuro contemplated their predicament. The wounded Partisan squeezed off another round. Another German soldier fell. The remaining attackers sought refuge in the trees at the sight of their comrade's demise. After a prolonged silence, the Germans began to move forward, using the trees as cover.

"We can't stay here. The forest is crawling with Germans. We must leave, try to make the base of the mountain. I heard we're retreating. Can you walk?"

Even in the close light, it was obvious, from the disrupted alignment of the man's hip, from the mottled blood on the crude bandage, that Kobe could not move. Djuro knew it. Kobe knew it.

"My hip is shattered."

A German, not more than twenty paces from the barricade aimed his rifle at them. A blast from Djuro's submachine gun sliced through the man. The dying soldier's screams filled the night air. Djuro ducked down behind the debris as Kobe fired again.

"I'll cover you. You must run, try to make camp. Tell Marta I love her. Will you do that?"

Djuro shook his head, "no". He had no intention of leaving one of his soldiers, not much more than a boy, to die alone. Concentrated fire from the enemy forced them down behind the timber again. This time, the assault did not let up.

"You must leave. I'm of no use to you. I don't wish to end up a cripple, a one–legged fool begging for food on the streets of Belgrade. Even if I could leave this place, I'll lose the leg. Go while you still can."

The chatter of German small arms continued. There was little time. Recognizing the truth of Kobe's words, Djuro relented. Grasping the stock of Kobe's Mauser, Djuro exchanged weapons. Sliding a grenade from his belt, Djuro pulled the pin and held the detonator tightly in his fist. Djuro's voice, spoken in a mere whisper, was choked with sadness:

"I'll tell them of your bravery."

"Don't forget my wife. Promise me you'll tell her that I love her."

"I will."

The withering fire of the enemy sliced through the underbrush. Bullets slammed into the trunks of the trees protecting them. Each incoming projectile landed with a dull "thud." Drawing a deliberate breath, Djuro released the detonator on the grenade and threw it towards the dark rim of the trees. In an instant, a loud thunder erupted. The enemy guns fell silent.

In a single motion, Djuro pushed himself up from the dirt and dodged off into the darkness. Kobe remained within the protection of the fallen trees. As the smoke cleared, he studied the forms of the advancing soldiers. When the Germans were within a few yards, he raised himself high over the timber and squeezed the trigger of the submachine gun. The thick forest canopy distorted the "rat-a-tat-tat" sound of the automatic weapon. Three more SS fell. But there were too many.

Chapter 17

September 1944

Within minutes of leaving Drvar, Zdenka knew that Eli Kobe had fallen. The Partisan did not share this information with the German woman, for, at that moment, Marta Kobe was deep in the discomfort of childbirth.

Fate dictated that Marta would bring her first born into the world amidst the unyielding straw of a horse cart, beneath the steady blue blanket of an autumn sky. She did not complain. She uttered no cries of pain as her new son's sturdy head burst through her flesh, releasing him to the world. When it was over, when she'd rested enough to regain her strength, with the infant suckling at her swollen breasts, Zdenka finally told her that Eli was not with the Partisans. She did not have the heart to tell Marta what his true fate had been.

For several days, Marta did not speak. She rode in the wagon, her features drawn and devoid of life while she stared blankly and clutched the baby.

John. That was the name Zdenka gave the infant. At first, Marta ignored the child, forgetting to nurse him until Zdenka or one of the other women placed him on her nipples. She demonstrated no mothering instincts, barely tolerating the baby's intrusion into her personal space as the guerilla column wound its way towards the safety of yet another mountain sanctuary. Marta stared back towards Drvar, where the love of her life, the only love she had ever known, remained.

In time, the sunshine and fresh air of the mountains commenced working their magic on the young mother. A faint smile began to appear on her face whenever she watched John sleep. It was then that the others knew she would survive.

Tito himself did not follow the column as it was continually assaulted and harassed by the enemy. At the suggestion of Maclean and Deakin, the Partisan leader was airlifted to Italy and then to Vis. His disappearance prevented the Nazi's from succeeding in their attempts to eradicate him. Without Tito, the main Partisan column continued to retreat further into the mountains of Bosnia, prodded and pursued by the enemy, protected at length by British fighter cover and bomber attacks.

The Legacy

There was no way of delicately telling the young German woman her husband was dead. Like most Yugoslavians, and certainly like most Partisans, Zdenka was adept at speaking her mind, at telling it straight. She'd been taught at an early age to state the truth without delicacy or subtlety. She knew she couldn't ease Marta's pain. After weeks of rough travel, the Partisan woman realized there was no escaping the agony her revelation would cause. It had to be done. She waited until the mother and child were left alone.

Marta was in her tent with the baby, ignorant of Eli's passing, unaware that his body remained uncovered, his corpse sheltered only by the overhanging trees of the hillside. Zdenka entered the tent unannounced. The woman's presence was a surprise. They were not close friends. The women tolerated each other. That was all. The taller woman's entrance into her tent, while John lay asleep at her side, seemed to Marta to be an unwelcome trespass.

"Marta, I've news to tell you."

Zdenka's face was blank. Her hand touched Marta's. The Partisan woman's skin was cool, nearly cold. Marta felt her heart jump with joy.

"Eli has been found," she thought. "With the main force. Perhaps wounded. But alive."

She was elated. She smiled. The baby gurgled, squirming against the soft fabric of the blanket.

"There was no reason for it, Marta. No reason for it to be Eli instead of me. Or someone else. But it happened. Eli died. Near the tracks, protecting the train. Comrade Djuro was with him and saw him fall. There is no doubt".

A tightening of the Yugoslav woman's hand conveyed an expression of pity. Marta didn't feel the gesture. She became numb, expressionless. It was as if her soul had been cut out. Her head went spinning until she fell forward on the blanket. Then nothingness, only the black void of the nether world. Marta Kobe didn't hear Zdenka's words as the Partisan woman attempted to relay Eli Kobe's last expression of love to his young wife.

Two days later, the German woman regained consciousness. For forty-eight hours she swooned in and out of deep sleep. Conscious, unconscious. Writhing in pain. Zdenka stayed with her through it all, washing the perspiration from the smaller woman's forehead, combing her blond hair; its silky sheen of gold having faded to the color of burnt corn, the color having been altered by the rigors of the road and by childbirth. It was necessary for Zdenka to find surrogate mothers to nurse the infant. Marta's breasts refused to supply nourishment for the child.

When she awoke, Marta Kobe broke down in a flood of sobs and uncontrolled convulsions. For the entirety of the third day she was utterly silent; she chose to simply remember her husband, their love and the brief interludes of peace they had shared amidst the war-torn lunacy and terror surrounding them.

On the evening of the fourth day she asked:

"Did they find Eli's body?"

Marta was nursing the baby. Holding him tightly to her, protecting the last remaining physical connection to Eli. She inquired of Zdenka in a yearning voice.

"The body was never found. Our retreat from Drvar left many of our people, dead and wounded, behind."

The young mother cast her eyes downward. She thought of her husband's corpse, exposed and rotting. The image made her shiver.

She strained to see Eli as he had looked on their last night together, their wedding night, dancing before the light of the fire. A smile, a floating kiss, his rifle upraised as he left to defend Drvar against the enemy. His last kiss still sought to reach her on the wind, suspended in time, just out of reach.

Zdenka broke the silence.

"What will you do now?"

"I suppose I'll continue on with your people. I have no place else to go."

Marta brushed a lock of dirty hair away from her eyes. It was hard to tell the true color of her hair in the dim candle light of the tent. She continued, looking thoughtfully at her child as she spoke:

"My son is Yugoslavian. His father, his grandfather, his aunts, his uncles, they all died so he could grow to be a man in this land. I see no other place, no other future for Eli Kobe's child."

"I suppose that's so. But don't say 'your people.' Your testimony, your witness makes you one of us. You are the mother of a Slovenian child. There is no longer a Marta Essen from Germany. There is only Marta Kobe."

Touched by the woman's compassion, Marta reached out to her. The German woman's grip was strong. Zdenka reciprocated. They clung to each other, weeping long into the night, locked in the embrace of sisterhood.

After Drvar, the fortunes of the guerrillas soared due to the intervention of the allies and the persistence of Partisan attacks in Serbia. Recognizing the success of the communists in the Balkans, Churchill sought to prod Tito and King Peter II into an uneasy truce. As a step towards attempting to unify the Yugoslavs, Churchill convinced the King to disavow the Chetniks, ending their claims that they were the legitimate defenders of Yugoslavia. But the dream of unity among the factions was fleeting.

For his part, Tito listened to Churchill, continuing to accept the military advice and hardware the British and Americans provided. But he made no commitments towards unity with the other Yugoslav political groups. The only commitment he made was that his Partisans would fight the Germans.

Throughout the summer of 1944, Tito's forces did exactly that. By August of that year, it was clear that Mihailovich and the Chetniks were through as Partisan forces routed both the Germans and the Chetniks from most of Serbia.

On the 12th of September 1944, in a radio broadcast from England, King Peter finally urged all Yugoslavians to unite and join in an uprising of the people. He also urged the formation of the National Liberation Army under the leadership of Tito. Once the announcement was made, Mihailovich lost the support of the monarch and the Chetniks disbanded. Some fled with their leader. A few joined the Partisans. Many simply went home to their farms and villages to await the outcome of the war.

Through the summer and early fall, Marta Kobe and her son followed the swarm of peasants and workers that formed the National Liberation Army. No longer confined to a horse cart, Marta and John rode in the relative comfort of a captured Nazi motor transport. The infant and his mother traveled beneath the taunt canvas canopy of the truck with other refugee women and their children. A contingent of the OZNA, Tito's handpicked men, guarded the convoy.

Once Tito's personal bodyguard, the OZNA had been reorganized as a secret police force, a police force with one mission: To find and exterminate members of the Ustashi and unrepentant Chetniks foolish enough to continue to fight. The OZNA was commissioned to perform its function in the same deliberate, ruthless manner the SS and Ustashi had.

To the young widow and her son, the members of OZNA were not killers or assassins. They were liberators, providers of justice and revenge in an unjust world. Revenge for Anna, Maria, Stefen and Josip. For Frederick. And for Eli. The OZNA were his friends, his brothers. No amount of bloodletting could extinguish that bond.

In early October 1944, the Partisans came into direct contact with Soviet armored divisions, divisions which swept across the Hungarian border to assist the Yugoslavians in the siege of Belgrade. Though wary of the Soviet Union's ultimate political intentions, Tito recognized that he could not storm the Yugoslavian capital without much loss of life and delay. His guerilla forces possessed little heavy artillery or armor. Both were needed to assault the fortified positions of the Germans in the city. To acquire Stalin's assistance, Tito struck an uneasy bargain with the Soviet Union. The two forces would attack Belgrade as one.

Marta Kobe had never been to Belgrade, the capital of Serbia, and the largest and most symbolic city in Yugoslavia. On October 19th, 1944, the National Liberation Army stopped short of the capital in preparation for a final assault.

The young mother climbed a low hill south of the city to watch the Partisan attack. Yellow, red and orange flashed across the cheerless night sky in a constant, unyielding barrage. The concussion of each shell resonated across the distance; the explosions of Partisan and Soviet munitions blanketed Belgrade in a brilliant cascade of artificial color. The big guns' recoil shook the ridge, moving the soil beneath Marta's Kobe's feet as if a terrible ogre was waking from sleep.

The infant pressed himself tightly to his mother as he sought refuge from the noise. He was used to the sounds and disruptions of combat. This bombardment was different. Even the child sensed the intensity of the onslaught; massive, concentrated, deadly.

"Isn't it beautiful, Zdenka?"

Marta stood dangerously close to the edge of the ridge holding her son as she studied the bombardment consuming the city. The fighting was removed and distant. She was oblivious to the fact that thousands of soldiers, the enemy and her friends, were dying in the spectacle.

"It's something to behold. Tito says that by tomorrow Belgrade will fall. And with the city, the Germans. It's their last stand here, the last cancer to be cut out."

"Will we enter the city tomorrow?"

"That's hard to say. Keep in mind that that the beauty you find in tonight's sky is a terrible beauty. Men and women of courage are dying as we speak. The Germans may not be ready to leave."

"I know they die, Zdenka. I don't forget. I'll never forget."

"What's more important is that children like John never forget," Zdenka said in a conciliatory tone.

The Partisan woman reached out to the infant and instinctively stroked the baby's warm, pudgy hand. John looked up at her, his face framed by the light of the artillery assault and cooed. She tried to concentrate on the battle but her mind was elsewhere.

She had grown fond of the German woman and the child. They were a foreshadowing of what would be right with the world once Belgrade fell. They were symbols of life, especially the boy, a child born of a father he'd never see. Life conceived, delivered, from the death of war.

Sensing this was the right moment; Zdenka opened her shirt pocket and pulled out two small silver medals on thin silver chains. The medals bore the profile of Marshall Tito and were inscribed "1944." The word "OZNA" was etched in the reverse. She opened Marta's hand and placed the medals in it, closing the widow's fingers over the cold, smooth surface of the silver disks.

"From Tito," Zdenka said, "With love. For you and the baby. In memory of your husband."

There was nothing more she could say. Illuminated by the light of the distant city on fire, Zdenka turned and walked away, seeking the quiet of the Partisan camp.

Holding the medals to her cheek, Marta Kobe pulled John close to her and turned to follow Zdenka.

The next morning, Belgrade fell to the Partisans. Marta Kobe, former wife of a German SS officer, widow of a Yugoslav Partisan, rode into the capital of her adopted homeland. Strapped across her right shoulder, she wore Eli's well–worn Mauser. Djuro made sure the weapon found its way back into her hands. Holding onto her shoulder tightly, in apprehension of the crowds, her infant son clutched her left arm. To all the cheering citizens lining the streets, the tired looking young woman carrying a child and a battered rifle epitomized the spirit of a nation's resistance.

For her part, looking out into the crowd of celebrating Yugoslavians, Marta Kobe knew that she and her son were destined to remain in the land of her husband's death.

Chapter 18

May 25, 1944

Franz Essen's fortunes took a turn for the better after the atrocity on the Sava. For his brilliant concealment of the murders, for his organizational skill in prompting the Ustashi to run wild throughout Slovenia and Croatia, he was given an elite command: a platoon of SS paratroops. Damos Tomich, his Ustashi collaborator, served him as his interpreter and guide. Their descent by parachute into the woods surrounding Drvar on May 25, 1944 had been routine and uneventful. Not a man was lost in the jump; no injuries were sustained.

Essen's unit was assigned the task of securing Drvar itself, of lining up hundreds of women, children and old men in the town, of slaughtering them in the town square, in the streets, in their beds, against the stone walls lining the edges of the town. It was easy work, safe work, the kind of work the Lieutenant excelled at. It was over in a matter of minutes.

From the town, Essen's unit clambered up the mountainside, through the underbrush and rocky debris left from innumerable landslides. Each soldier carried a photo of Tito. Believing they could not fail to find him, to execute him, Damos Tomich wanted to be there when it happened, when the scourge of the Ustashi was eliminated.

Tomich carried the same rifle he hunted with in the mountains and valleys of Croatia before the war. It was an old Italian weapon of World War I vintage given to Tomich by his father. The rifle boasted a solid walnut stock, once beautiful, now stained by the rain and scarred by the rigors of battle. Though the bolt action of the weapon was cumbersome, the rifle itself was deadly in the hands of the man who carried it.

Through the trees and wet leaves, Tomich moved with Essen and the Germans. The Ustashi carried his rifle at the ready, with the safety off. The Germans sought the most direct path into the heart of the Partisan camp. In the distance, Tomich detected the sounds of a party, a celebration.

"Ah yes. Tito's birthday. What better day for the pig to die."

Tomich smiled and tapped Essen on the shoulder.

"It's Tito's birthday. Let's throw him a party."

Essen's thin lips parted in a silent laugh. The officer tilted his steel pot so that he could look into Tomich's face. In the reflection of the Partisan fires, the German determined that the big Croat was excited by the thought of battle.

Essen turned his attention to his men. Using hand signals, he directed them to surround the Partisan inner circle. Passing within feet of sleeping sentries, the German soldiers took their positions.

From the left, machine gun fire erupted. The noise was not the report of the small caliber weapons carried by the SS, but the deep resonance of a Partisan machine gun. German mortar rounds began to "whoosh" through the thin air towards the Partisan camp. The intruders had been discovered.

At the center of their line, Essen's men forced the battle towards the sounds of the party. Crashing through the dense brush, the Germans ran headlong into the Partisan sanctuary. Bursts of submachine gun fire snorted from the platoon. Here, a scream, there, a confused cry of alarm. Essen gauged the return fire from the startled enemy, noting it to be panicked, uneven. From the response, he knew the assault was a complete surprise. There was no coordinated resistance.

A bullet whizzed by Essen's head. The round struck a tree trunk. Bark exploded and showered Tomich with debris, reminding the Croat that war was serious business.

"Best to keep my wits about me," Tomich thought.

Through the smoke and haze, Tomich made out the shadowy forms of Partisans in retreat. He crouched to one knee, steadied his heavy rifle, careful to exhale before the trigger struck the limit of its guard, and fired.

"Crack."

Black smoke, a muffled cry from a stricken Partisan, then death, another Partisan shot through the head. Tomich pulled the cumbersome bolt back and ejected the spent casing. Another cartridge slid from the clip into the chamber. A second enemy soldier bent to check the corpse.

"Crack".

Another dead communist. The Croat smiled.

"Like shooting pigs in a pen."

In contrast to the big man's slow and deliberate sniping, Essen fell prone, protecting himself with a line of boulders, and poured steady fire into the retreating Partisans. The thin defensive line of the guerillas collapsed into chaos. No more than two to three hundred armed Partisans were left defending the lair. German intelligence had been perfect.

Reloading a fresh clip, Essen watched a young Partisan woman toss aside her British-made rifle, its chamber jammed by a misfired cartridge. She raised her hands in the air. The SS officer looked directly at her. He studied her face for one, hesitant moment. In the glare of the explosions around them, he could make out her rounded chin and smooth cheeks. He noted that she possessed dark, fearless eyes. In another place, another time, he would have considered her to be a pretty girl. Now he knew her as simply another communist. Another dead Partisan. Essen's clip clicked into place. The muzzle erupted. Bullets tore through her woolen shirt and chest like a buzz saw. Blood spurted from her neck. The woman's body tumbled downhill, rolling until it came to a stop at Tomich's feet. Her eyes remained open as she labored to breathe. The Ustashi towered over her and raised his rifle. In an uninterrupted motion, he lowered his heavy weapon, crushing the woman's skull with the butt of his rifle. The German officer turned away, confident that he could not have done it, could not have been so brutal. But the deed was done. He regained his composure and pushed ahead. There was no time for remorse in battle.

"Soldiers that contemplate ethics on a battlefield," Essen thought, "are known as casualties."

The Partisan retreat became more organized, more stubborn. The Yugoslavians fought from position to position, allowing Tito time to escape. Though surprised, the enemy made Essen's work difficult. Twelve of his platoon died before they reached the camp. Eight more were unable to fight, wounded and in need of medical attention. He pressed on.

Entering the compound, it was clear that the Partisans had left most of their provisions and ammunition behind. Within the small frame house that served as Tito's command post, Essen found food, liquor and Tito's birthday cake sitting undisturbed on a table. A quick search behind the house revealed the entrance to a cave. SS intelligence hadn't factored a cave into the equation.

Sensing they'd been out-smarted, the surviving SS poured into the cold confines of the cavern. Once inside, they encountered an unexpected sound. Essen recognized the repetitive discharge of a steam boiler as he entered the damp chamber behind his men.

"Damn him," the German murmured. "Damn the magician. He's getting away on a train!"

Shouting madly at his troops to clear the cavern of the Partisan rearguard, Essen's men collided headlong with five Partisans left behind to slow the Germans.

The defenders were dead within seconds. Having run out of ammunition, they were reduced to swinging their rifles like clubs until each slumped to the ground, torn apart by the withering Axis fire.

Racing into the fresh air at the end of the tunnel, Essen and Tomich saw the outline of the departing Partisan train. A platoon of Partisan rifles discharged in sequence, concentrating fire wherever there was movement. A heavy machine gun mounted on the last car chattered. Screams of stricken SS paratroopers echoed beneath the trees as the gun sprayed death into the darkness of the night. Essen saw that there was no hope of catching the train from the rear. The communists cut down his soldiers in turn as they emerged from the cavern. Sensing the futility of the situation, the Lieutenant ordered his men back into cave.

"You can't give up. We have him. We finally have him in our grasp and you're letting him go."

The big Croat loomed over the slight form of the German officer. Tomich's eyes were filled with desperation. Essen shook his head:

"No, Major, we don't have him. We've merely flushed the wolf from its den. But his fangs are too dangerous for us to pursue. It's up to others to catch him now that the trap is sprung."

"Essen, I beg of you, don't do this. You'll never have another chance like this. Send them out after the train, before it's too late."

The German could not be moved. He would not, despite Tomich's protestations, pursue the train. Eyes wild with rage, the big man left the officer and stomped off through the heavy air of the tunnel. At the cave's exit, sheltered by a stone arch, Tomich surveyed his chances of breaking out into the open, into the night. In his mind he saw himself dodging Partisan fire, throwing a grenade in front of the rolling stock, killing Tito. But it was an illusion. The train's downhill momentum had taken over, its speed increased with each turn of the locomotive's great wheels. Tito would not die by the Croatian's hand tonight.

The Legacy

Disgusted, Tomich began to walk back through the cave. His attention was drawn to a large wooden crate. The container was tucked away in a far corner of the tunnel, out of view unless one happened to glance directly at it. Unable to read English, Tomich could not decipher the words on the container's label.

Curious, he pulled out a knife, a bone-handled blade he used to gut sheep and goats on his parents' farm, and walked over to the crate. Each board was nailed separately, forcing him to use the blade of the knife as a lever. The wood groaned as the Ustashi strained to free the planks.

Inside, the box there were scores of thin blankets and fatigue jackets. He recognized the emblems on the lapels and shoulders of the clothing. The material was cheap cotton duck.

"American," he muttered, "worthless shit."

Striking a match, he lit a small candle he carried in his cartridge belt. By the flickering light, Tomich stooped to examine the contents of the crate.

"Too thin for the mountains."

The candle's glare reflected back at him from deep within the container. What Tomich discovered beneath the field jackets and blankets astonished him.

Damos Tomich had never been rich a man, had never held much money or wealth in his hands. When he picked up the first gold ingot from the crate, its weight and form beyond what he'd ever imagined, he could not believe his luck. Casting a glance over his shoulder, he forced his hand deeper into the crate. More bars. Hundreds of them. A fortune. His fortune. A birthday gift from Tito. But how to carry it, how to conceal it from the others? His new found wealth created as many problems as it did opportunities.

A noise. A disturbance behind him called his attention back to reality. Footsteps; he heard the sound of steady footsteps coming towards him. Someone was coming back into the cave. Tomich raised his rifle. For the first time in his life, Tomich found it difficult to hold the weapon steady.

"I'll have to kill anyone who sees this," the Ustashi thought.

A stale breeze blew through the tunnel as a figure walked into the meager light cast by the candle. A sparse wind caused the man's shadow to gyrate on the rock wall. Tomich's finger touched the trigger of his weapon.

"What have we here, Major Tomich?"

A high, thick German voice caused Tomich to relax. It was Essen.

"At least it's someone who, given the right incentive, might be trusted. Half a loaf is better than none," Tomich reasoned to himself.

Essen bent over and retrieved a bar of gold from the crate. Like a dog with a meaty bone, he turned it over and over in his hand. He examined its every attribute, its flawless beauty. He smiled, stood up and faced the Ustashi.

"We must pack the crate back up, Major, and have some of my men commandeer a truck to carry it. No need to tell them what's in it, right? After all, we are partners in this war."

The German's gap–toothed smirk loomed sinister. Essen's cheeks appeared hollow. One eye seemed raised, as if the German was scrutinizing his newly proclaimed business associate.

Essen continued to fondle a bar as he studied the Croatian. When he felt confident that Tomich's discovery was real and not a dream, the German gently deposited the bullion in the crate, turned and walked out of the cave, leaving the Ustashi officer to conceal their secret.

The Legacy

Chapter 19

October 19, 1944

It had been a difficult escape for Franz Essen and Damos Tomich. Belgrade was completely surrounded by Tito's Partisans and the Russians. The only means of departure; a single, unscathed Junker 88 which survived the bombardment, hidden in a concrete hanger at the last remaining Axis airfield in occupied Yugoslavia. Repeated shelling failed to dent the hanger's four-foot thick concrete exterior. Though the rest of the squadron was caught in the open and destroyed the lone surviving JU 88 was spared because it was in the hanger for servicing.

Essen and Tomich, desperate to protect their treasure in the final hours of the Nazi occupation, deserted. Their commanders did not note their departure from the front until hours later, until long after the Junker roared out of its hanger, down the pockmarked surface of the dirt runway, into the air of the Yugoslavian night.

Northwest. They headed Northwest to avoid the Russian guns and the squadrons of British fighters flying in from captured Italian airfields. Their fuel supply low, Essen landed in Gorizia, the last remaining enclave of German occupation in Italy; a city located just over the Slovenian border, in the direct path of the American Army's assault up the Italian peninsula. If they had to surrender, they determined it would be to the Americans.

If they surrendered to the British, they would be handed over to

Tito and summarily tried as war criminals. Their participation in the Sava affair was widely known due to King Peter's pronouncements of the same from London. Partisan bullets would not be wasted on them. It was far likelier that they would be paraded back to Slovenia, to be beaten by a mob of peasants, decapitated and dismembered, all of the blood and death to be captured by some amateur photographer for posterity. No, they could not afford to turn themselves over to the British.

And of what use would it be to surrender to the Russians? Brothers in Marxism to the Partisans? Their fate would be the same. Tito and his army would salivate and whine until Stalin forced the Red Army to disgorge them to the Partisans. There would be no chance of salvation in the Bolsheviks' camp.

That left the Americans, whose advance up the Italian Peninsula was stalled within miles of the Austrian border, nearly in sight of Gorizia. It would be in Gorizia, they decided, that they would surrender.

Franz Essen worked long and hard on the plan. He spent hours photographing documents from the staff headquarters of the German 12th and 2nd Armies. As an SS officer, he had unrestricted access to both offices throughout the course of the occupation. His private collection of reports, charts, memoranda and other writings regarding the Balkan campaign, including detailed summaries of the activities of the Gestapo and the SS, filled two attaché cases. These were to be chips in the game of poker he would play with the Americans.

Damos Tomich had already made his contribution to their escape. He'd found three hundred and fifty pounds of pure gold. Half for Essen, half for Tomich. That would buy a lot of forgiveness from the right American officer. Tomich had also gathered countless reams of documents captured from the Partisans regarding Soviet troop strengths in Eastern Europe. The papers contained accurate designations of the reserves being placed by Stalin in the occupied areas of the East to solidify his hold on the region once the Nazis retreated.

In addition, Tomich managed to acquire detailed knowledge and documentation highlighting the activities of the Yugoslav, Greek and Albanian Communist Parties. If, as Essen impressed upon the Croat, the East and the West were destined to meet in an ultimate showdown in Europe after the collapse of Germany, the materials Tomich secreted from the Ustashi regarding the communists would be invaluable to either side. Economics of life being what they were, Tomich and Essen resolved to share the information with the side most likely to allow them to live.

For fourteen days and nights after they crash-landed, Essen and Tomich contented themselves with hiding in the cellar of the Hotel Gorizia. They existed on a single square of rotting mare's cheese and a liter of stale bottled water. In their self-made prison, they endured stifling claustrophobia and a deep-rooted unease brought about by the constant fear of discovery. In the darkness of the cellar, Essen began to experience the pangs of anguish similar to what he'd inflicted on the Jews and other undesirables he'd hunted in Austria, in Yugoslavia. The two men remained hidden, cramped like rats in a hole, awaiting the inevitable, ultimate termination of their lives. They were murderers and deserters, hunted by both the Allies and the Nazis.

On the fifteenth day, the Americans took Gorizia. There was little the Wermacht could do to halt the Allies. The German farm boys and old men forced to fight in the waning days of the Italian campaign expressed no will to die in battle, no pride in National Socialism, no belief in the Supreme Race. They faced combat–hardened American veterans to no real purpose. The reality of the folly of the Third Reich brought their quick retreat, a mad, disorganized scramble out of Italy by a mob intent on running back to their homes in Mother Germany.

"What've we got here boys?"

Essen felt the sharp point of an American bayonet firmly placed against the thin, unshaven skin of his jaw. His eyes tried to focus on the soldier's face. The words were English. The SS officer understood them clearly.

"It's a Kraut and his pal, I think."

Another voice, higher pitched, younger. The second soldier pressed a submachine gun to Tomich's temple. They'd been discovered.

The cellar door to the outside remained open, allowing a stream of brilliant, white light to penetrate the damp basement. More shouts in English disturbed the unnatural silence of their tomb. Tomich and Essen were pulled from the cellar and unceremoniously shoved out into the streets of Gorizia. Their eyes burned from the brightness of the sun. Their captors showed them little courtesy. The two men were marched at bayonet point to Allied headquarters. Speaking heavily accented English as he was rushed along the dirt street, Essen demanded to see someone in authority, someone of rank.

"Shut up and get moving. You'll see someone soon enough. Maybe too soon for your own good."

"I'm an officer in the German SS. I demand to see someone of rank as required by the Geneva Convention."

"Shut your yap, Kraut. Geneva Besheba. You guys don't play by the rules, why should we?"

"Ya, clam it, Adolph. You'll get your chance. An officer, eh? Well then, we'll take you to see the General. Right boys?"

"That's right, Sarge. If it's an audience the man wants, then it's an audience he'll get. With the top man himself."

Major General Shane Austin's attitude towards the captured German officer and his Ustashi partner was less than charitable. It took Franz Essen only a minute in a room with the American, the air heavily choked with cigarette smoke, to assess that Austin was not their man.

Nearly sixty, balding and a chain smoker, Austin plowed his way through Italy with his armored division like he plowed his way through life. He didn't like many people. He didn't have much compassion, especially for the enemy, whatever enemy his country asked him to fight.

"Lieutenant, I just don't see why I shouldn't turn you over to the British.

That's standard operating procedure. This is their theater, I'm just along for the ride. The Croatian with you complicates things further. I'd rather not get involved in politics. I think its best that we turn you over to the British."

Austin spat a wad of flem near a German shorthair curled at his feet. The spit stained the floor. The dog slept on.

"Herr General. I would do exactly as you say if I were in your shoes."

Essen decided to play to the man's obvious weakness, his ego.

"That is, I'd turn over those captured to another command. That would free my troops for further duty. Fighting. I would do that too unless I knew that the prisoners were privy to valuable information."

The German smiled a bit. Let the words rest on the older man's brow.

"Information?"

Essen had Austin wrong. This American wasn't interested in stroking his own ego.

"You've got something to say you think is important? Too important for the Brits, eh? What is it? What's so goddamn important that I should be wasting my time here talking to a mere pup?"

The general's eyes narrowed, looking not at Essen but at Tomich. His stare was one of obvious disgust.

"The material Major Tomich and I possess concerns two topics. Number one, I have detailed data regarding the German occupation of Yugoslavia. Dates, names, details of the unfortunate civilian 'incidents' you may have heard about."

His use of the word 'incidents' clearly piqued the man's interest. The American's eyes shifted back to Essen.

"And Major Tomich possesses equally vital information regarding the Soviets, the Partisans, the ELAS in Greece, and a number of other communist organizations. Again, very useful to your intelligence unit. What is it called? The OSS?"

At the mention of the OSS, Austin sat down. He leaned heavily to scratch behind the dog's ears. The American continued to stare at the German as he stroked the animal.

"Alright. I'll contact the OSS. Get someone up here to talk to the two of you. In the meantime, you'll be treated exactly like any other prisoners of war."

Austin stood up and looked out the window devoid of any glass. Bullets had splintered most of the trim. He turned to address Essen. Though the American General's voice was quiet, the words were clear.

"What about this information? Is it with you?"

He guessed not. But maybe the Kraut wasn't as smart as he seemed.

"Why General, if I were so foolish as to allow us to be captured with such vital data, I wouldn't have much leverage with the OSS, now would I?"

Austin nodded and called the MP's back into the room to escort the two POWs to the holding area. It was hours before he contacted the OSS by field telephone and explained what had happened.

Captain Marvin Field was the OSS man who arrived two days later to interrogate the prisoners. Top of his class at West Point, Field started in armor, but was selected for OSS duty on the strength of his language skills. He spoke fluent German, Russian, French and Italian. A splendid dresser, his uniforms were always pressed and sharp. His boots were polished to a mirror finish despite the slime and mud of the combat zone. A fanatic about his Clark Gable looks, his pencil thin mustache matched the jet-black color of his hair. He was of slim physique, though his face was distinguished by a square, powerful jaw. Once Franz Essen saw him walk into the interrogation tent, he knew it was possible. This man could be bought. The question was; would it take more than an exchange of information? More than the interests of country?

"Yes," Essen calculated, "this one will require more. A personal stake. Something for himself."

"So, Lt. Essen. General Austin tells me you have information which may be of interest to the OSS. Why haven't you turned it over to us? Might help you in the long run. Better treatment, fancier food, all that."

Field was smoking a pipe. Looking like a German baron. Essen knew him well, had grown up with such men, hating them. Soulless, selfish. Perfect for this deal.

"Captain, let me speak frankly. You will not repeat this, yes?"

Field nodded, indicating the discussion would remain confidential.

"My friend and I, we must not fall into the hands of the Partisans. And if I had not taken the precaution of protecting these documents, we'd likely be in British hands, ready for transport back to Belgrade."

His words were spoken softly, with calm. Field sensed these two were due to hang or be shot if the Yugoslavs got hold of them.

"Since we're being frank, Herr Essen. I need to know exactly what it is you fear in Yugoslavia. What did you do?"

Essen could see that the American had already decided the payoff would have to be huge to allow the two of them to escape death.

"Unfortunately Captain, there are those in Yugoslavia that mistakenly believe Major Tomich and I were involved in an incident along the Sava River. Something about noncombatants being killed. We could plead our innocence but do you really think the Partisans would listen to a German and an officer of the loyal fascist army of Croatia?"

"You mean the Ustashi, don't you. Tomich is a member of the Ustashi. They killed almost a million fellow Yugoslavians by our count, Serbs, Jews, Gypsies, Moslems, other minorities. And you of course, you were indeed at the Sava. Your wife was the one who brought that story out of the occupied territory. She brought out the evidence. The Brits made us aware of her."

Field knew that the news of the wife's defection had not previously been conveyed to the German. The SS Officer's young face, though trained to avoid any display of upset or weakness, was pained. He was obviously ignorant of the fact that Frau Essen was the one who had broken the silence, who had given testimony against her own husband.

"Let's get to the point, gentlemen. You want to live, I want information. I can, if the materials you possess are significant, guarantee that you will not be handed over to any other command. Beyond that, there is little I can do. Do we have a deal?"

"Captain, we want more than a mere chance to avoid death. If either of us remain in Europe in American hands, especially if what you tell me about my miserable wife is true, we will surely face the firing squad. Death will only be postponed. We want not only life, but also new identities and transport, preferably to Brazil.

I have many friends there, friends who saw the light before me and got out. No, for the valuable material we have to offer, we will require new passports, identification and transportation to Brazil."

Essen hesitated to say more. Field stood up and walked towards him. With one hand, he grabbed the lapel of the German and said:

"What makes you think my country wants you to live? Or that I want you to live? What makes you believe that the information you have is worth the lives of those peasants you shot in the back? Tell me that."

Field dropped Essen roughly back into his chair. Tomich's shoulders bulged, ready to strike, ready to beat the American officer to death with his bare hands. Field sensed the danger. He turned to rebuke the man.

"Tomich, I'd suggest you relax. There are four MPs outside of this tent. You touch me, you so much as snarl at me, and I'll have them come in and execute you two on the spot."

The intensity of Field's eyes backed up his words. Tomich grunted in defiance but slumped back into his chair.

"I understand your anger Captain. But I'm not here to debate what may or may not have happened in the past. There is more at stake here than mere information..."

Essen left his words dangling in the air, left his thought unfinished.

"What do you mean?"

"I mean gold, Captain. Gold. 350 pounds of it, liberated from the Partisans. It's hidden where only Tomich and I can find it. But we'll gladly share one–third of it with your government, if we can come to some arrangement along the lines we've discussed. We'd leave it up to you personally, of course, as to how your portion of the gold is transferred to your government."

Essen regained his composure. From the interest shown on the man's face it was obvious that this new approach made sense to Captain Field.

"Are you asking me to take a bribe? To accept over fifty thousand dollars in gold to allow you to escape the firing squad? When by all rights of law, that's where the two of you should go? To Belgrade. To the Partisans. This offer of yours shocks me. It shocks me."

He continued to stare at the German, ignoring the Ustashi as if Tomich wasn't in the room.

"Don' t label it as such. Call it payment for services rendered. How you dispense or account for the gold, as the receiving agent for your government, is up to you. Consider the gold to be a gift from us. You give us the gift of life, we give you the gift of gold. Repayment, of sorts, for kindness and hospitality. Not a bribe."

Essen was grinning now. He knew he'd completed the deal and cemented the preservation of their lives.

"Gifts are acceptable. The American government could accept a gift. Might be a problem if the Yugoslavs assert the gold is theirs, but since the Partisans are not officially the regular Army of Yugoslavia, the gold doesn't belong to the empowered government of the land. Probably stolen by the Partisans from the Croatians in any event."

It was well known to Field and others in the OSS that the Ustashi had taken as much as 720 million dollars in gold and silver from the Jews, Gypsies and Serbians of Yugoslavia during the Nazi occupation. The pro-Catholic Croatians sent much of the money to the College of San Girolamo, a Vatican-associated institute in Rome. The Vatican in turn utilized portions of the endowment to assist in the relocation of Ustashi leaders, most notably to South America. In some instances, the Catholic Church provided transportation, money; clothing, false identification, Vatican passports and new careers for the exiles. Field took this information into account as he mulled over the German officer's proposition.

"I still have to convince my superiors that the documents you have are worth your freedom. There's a hell of a political risk to my country for saving your necks if this ever leaks out. Hundreds of Germans and Ustashi will doubtlessly hang for war crimes. It'll take a hell of a lot of reliable intelligence data, raw and virgin to our operatives, to cement this deal. I'll need a representative selection of what it is you've got to convince the higher ups. A sample. Then I'll see what I can do."

Essen reached into his boot and pulled out several compacted sheets of paper containing the master list of all Gestapo contacts in Southern Austria.

"A good start," Essen thought.

The German handed the documents to the OSS officer. Field unfolded the writings and scrutinized them. The words were German but he understood them. He clearly understood the document's importance. It was enough.

The American placed the papers on his desk and walked confidently towards the prisoners. His voice was low, as if he wanted to insure the MPs outside couldn' t hear him. He spoke in German.

"One more thing, partners."

His use of the word "partners" was coated with venom, mistrust.

"Our agreement is half, not a third. After all, the joy of giving is directly proportionate to the size of the gift."

Essen could hear the American chuckle to himself as he walked out of the tent, appreciably richer than he had entered.

BOOK TWO: THE HUNTER

The Legacy

Chapter 1

November 1 (All Saints Day) 1991

"This is Agnes Budaslavich. I live up on the Whiteface Reservoir. My husband Adam, he's 72. He went out deer hunting this morning and he's not back yet."

The dispatcher, a twenty-year veteran of the St. Louis County Sheriff's Department, had taken thirty calls like this in his career. Most times the wayward husband either showed up the next morning after spending a night in the woods or was found by the volunteer rescue squad. Either way, few if any of the calls turned to tragedy.

"Ma'am, I'll notify both the deputies on patrol and the rescue squad. Could you tell me the area your husband was hunting in, the type of clothes he was wearing and give me a description of him?"

The dispatcher tried to maintain a soothing calm as he asked for information; routine to him, frightening to the person on the other end of the line.

"Oh yeah, one more thing. Was he with anyone else?"

Mrs. Budaslavich proceeded to tell the dispatcher that her husband was hunting alone, was hunting in the Wasoose Lake area, stood six foot two and weighed about 230 pounds, was wearing blaze orange hunting pants, jacket and cap (the kind with ear flaps and a brim) and was supposed to be home by 5:30 p.m., an hour after legal hunting ended. The dispatcher patiently took down the specifics and tried to reassure the obviously distraught woman.

"Squad 18. Squad 18. This is dispatch. We've got a lost hunter up on the Wasoose Lakes, off the Long Lake Road near Palo. Rescue Squad's on its way and will meet you at the guy's home."

The dispatcher then related details regarding the hunter's description, clothing and address to the deputies and the rescue squad. It was 8:00 p.m.

Deputy Dave Swanson was one of two deputies in Squad 18 when the call on Mr. Budaslavich came in. His partner was Deputy Debra Slater. They'd been partners for six years. Both were married – but not to each other. They were on afternoons, patrolling the sparsely populated reaches of the County from 3:00 p.m. until 11:00 p.m.

Mark Munger

Emerald green eyes, auburn hair hanging to her shoulders when she wasn't at work, when she didn't tie the soft, reddish mane up and off her neck, Debra Slater was attractive. Not dazzling, not perfectly featured. More like the girl next door, the kind of face that attracted men, made them feel comfortable. Her eyes were set wide apart. Her square, Nordic jaw and distinctive cheekbones hinted at her Icelandic heritage. Slater was her married name. She had been an Iversen before that. She wasn't thin—her job placed too many demands upon her physical strength for her to stay model thin. But it was obvious from her well defined figure that Debra Slater took great pains to stay in shape.

Her partner, Dave Swanson, also fit his Nordic surname. Blond hair cropped into a short crewcut, steel blue eyes. Narrow nose and angular jaw. He seemed taller, bigger than he really was because of a narrow waist and broad shoulders. Shoulders built over time working out at Stan's Spa in the West End of Duluth, Minnesota, a blue-collar neighborhood defined by its many taverns and the ore docks, docks where the lakers loaded their holds with iron ore. He'd been born there, gone to school there. He'd likely die there.

The St. Louis County Sheriff's Department covered the entire length and breadth of St. Louis County, largest county east of the Mississippi. Two squads handled all the calls after 5:00 p.m. Hundreds of square miles of rugged country, spanned only by logging roads and long–abandoned railroad beds. Partly woods. Partly thicket. Mostly swamp.

Swanson and Slater took dirt forest roads from their location in Brimson near the Lake County line. They were at Budaslavich's home in forty minutes. The rescue squad had not arrived yet.

Adam Budaslavich's home appeared modest. A light blue or gray ranch with a two or three stall garage. A large metal pole barn in the rear yard, filled to overflowing with antique automobiles and parts. Dead or dying vehicles of various makes and vintages piled high in the yard; protected by two mean looking dogs of indiscernible breed but discernibly vicious dispositions. It was cold, no more than ten degrees above zero. Not a night to spend alone in the woods in Northeastern Minnesota.

An inch of snow lay on the ground–none was in the air. There was a full moon and no clouds; there was no need for a yard light, though one illuminated the front porch.

Mrs. Budaslavich, a short portly woman looking to be about sixty to sixty five, answered the door and let them in.

"Thank God you're here, officers. I can't understand where Adam is. Do you think he's all right? This is so unlike him. I'm worried sick. What can you do at night? What if he had a heart attack? Not that he has any problems of that sort, you know. He's strong as an ox, still cuts pulpwood. Still works fulltime at the mine in Hoyt Lakes. Still acts like a big kid. What could be wrong?"

Mrs. Budaslavich's voice convulsed as she ran out of breath, sobbing into the handkerchief Deputy Slater supplied.

Deb Slater put her arm around the old woman, trying to calm her. Swanson glanced around the interior of the house in idle curiosity. He was nervous; uneasy at the woman's upset. Swanson sensed that the modesty of the home's exterior was not duplicated in the home's interior. Antique furniture cluttered every available nook and cranny of the main floor. Paintings and prints covered virtually all the surfaces of the walls. A state of the art audio–video system took up a large portion of the north end of the room.

"This a picture of your husband, Ma'am?"

Swanson gingerly removed a photo from a marble-topped chest of drawers. He stood slightly stooped, his upper body leaning over the distraught woman, the photo positioned in his hands so she could see it.

"Yes, officer. That's pretty much current. It was taken last summer at our family reunion in Virginia. You can take that if you like – if it'll help."

She turned away from the two deputies.

"Don't worry, Mrs. Budaslavich. I'm sure your husband will be O.K."

Slater looked at the older woman, wondering what she'd feel if she were the one with the missing husband.

"I'd feel even worse," Slater thought, "Rick is only twenty eight."

Revolving amber light flashed across the front room's picture window. The St. Louis County Rescue squad had arrived, volunteers whose job it was to find the lost, the injured, at any hour, in any weather, simply for the hope of a "thank you" when their work was done. Slater walked to the glass.

"Good. It's Jimmy Nelson and his crew. Best bunch of guys we've got, Mrs. Budaslavich. They'll find Adam and bring him home to you, sure as anything."

Swanson stepped closer to the grieving wife. He asked whether she knew where her husband would have parked, what make of the vehicle he drove. Details, more details. She told them. Ford F150 4x4. Black. Camper Special with a Holiday Camper in the bed. He'd be parked right on the forest road leading to the Wasoose. Probably by the second of the three Wasoose Lakes. The truck would likely be there.

Slater and Swanson thanked the lady, left their cards and their home phone numbers. They told her they would call her immediately if they found anything. Did she have someone to stay with her? Yes, her daughter Joan from Aurora was coming down. They left, followed by the rescue squad.

"Christ, I bet the guy had a fucking heart attack three miles back in some swamp."

Dave Swanson was driving; Slater was listening, as the tan Chevrolet Suburban bounced along Highway 4, a two-lane spit of blacktop that would take them to Long Lake Road. Ten miles from the Budaslavich's, they turned onto the gravel path that led to Long Lake. Another two miles, a left and they were fighting their way through overgrown ruts and aspen saplings towards the Wasoose Lakes.

Actually lakes is a misnomer. Maybe four thousand years ago they were lakes. Now the Wasoose were merely three potholes surrounded by hundreds of miles of swamp, with the only high ground for ten miles to the North, between the primitive road and the waterline. The rest of the landscape was a bleak, desolate, massive bog filled with sawgrass, spruce and balsam. Swanson knew the area; he'd hunted ducks on the first two potholes in the chain.

The third Wasoose wasn't even big enough to put a canoe in. Ducks didn't much like it either. It was too brackish, too dark, the water like motor oil in thickness. Thousands of years of decaying leaves and weeds and the slowness of the black water seeping from the first two Wasoose into the third left it stagnant, nearly dead. One wouldn't want to fall into the third Wasoose. Swanson had. He stunk like a sewer for days.

They hadn't said anything about the old man since Swanson's comment back on the blacktop. Slater finally responded to her partner as they neared the first Wasoose:

"We'll probably find old Adam sleeping in his camper. Probably changed his mind. Stayed overnight."

The thought of deer hunting gave her the creeps. Untrained dopes walking around in the woods with high–powered rifles, blasting away at the first sound or motion in the brush. She hated deer season. Hated hunting. She carried a .357 because she had to, not because she wanted to. She was a hell of a shot at the range, best in her class. But she still hated hunting.

"Hey, maybe the old buck's got himself a young doe out here.Ya Know? He's rocking and rolling some hot number from Eveleth or McKinley in the back of his camper while the old lady thinks he's lost."

Swanson chuckled at his own imagination. Most of his imagination seemed to center on such topics.

"There you go again, Dave, talking through your zipper. Is that all you guys ever think about? God, you're all the same."

"Is Rick as bad?"

Swanson loved getting Slater to admit that Rick, her beloved, was as screwed up as her partner, or all men for that matter.

"You know Rick's a saint.You know all teachers are.They only think about what's best for the kids. Never have time to dream up warped scenarios like you Swanny.You've got too much time to think, that's your problem".

Slater glanced at her partner, his face illuminated by the pale green light of the dashboard. He was grinning from ear to ear as he drove, obviously enjoying the banter.

The Suburban finally bounced to a stop, nearly rear–ending Adam Budaslavich's pickup.The headlights of the County vehicle cast eerie shadows across the forest. Behind them, the rescue squad came to a similarly abrupt halt.

Swanson pulled out his flashlight and exited the Suburban. The cab of Budaslavich's Ford was empty. Swanson felt the grip of the night's cold. It chilled him to the bone. Above, the moon stood full in the sky. At first, there was near silence. Only the purr of the vehicles could be heard. No wind, no birds. Nothing. Then, out of the North, a flock of wayward Canadian Geese could be seen in silhouette against the moon's yellow globe. Their voices, their honks, echoed along the Wasoose. Swanson watched them as the birds continued south. There was no open water here. Only the black ice of a new winter.

"Let's wake him up, Deb."

Swanson walked to the rear of the pickup and knocked loudly. There was no answer. The deputy grasped the door to the camper. It was locked.

"We gotta find out if the old man's inside or not."

Slater and three members of the rescue squad crowded around the camper door.

"Hey Nelson, got anything to break open this door?"

"Sure Swine. There's a fire ax in the truck. I'll get it."

Jimmy Nelson began to walk back to his vehicle when Swanson grabbed his arm. Not roughly, but with a smile. A Cheshire grin that Nelson was able to see in the bright light of the headlights.

"Shit no Jim, we just want to open the damn door–not break it up for fire wood. Deb, we got that pry bar with?"

Swanson's partner nodded yes.

"Good, let's try that before Paul Bunyan here splinters the door with his ax."

The door to the camper opened with modest effort. There was no one inside. From the look of things, Budaslavich hadn't used the camper since fishing season. Waders, fishing reels, rods, lures and assorted junk lay strewn about. There was no sign of any food, sleeping bags or anything else to suggest that Adam Budaslavich had intended to stay the night.

"Jimmy, I guess we better search the immediate area for the old guy. You guys bring flashlights?"

Swanson looked at the clear sky above the treetops again as he spoke. Almost too cold to search. Surely too cold to spend the night in the woods without shelter. Nelson reached into the rear of the rescue squad vehicle and pulled out three Halogen lanterns.

"Here."

Slater and the rescue squad members each took a lantern.

"I don't think they'll throw much more light than the full moon. Use 'em if you need to, otherwise, the moon will probably be enough. I'll keep Morrison here at the van, me; Johnson and you two should spread out and comb the high stuff between the road and the lakes. Morrison can use the loud speaker to call the old man. What's his name?"

"Adam," Slater answered softly.

The quiet in her voice came from her realization that Mr. Budaslavich was lost somewhere out in the desolation of the Wasoose.

"Adam. That's easy enough. Morrison, you use the speaker. Call him every minute or so. Hopefully if he's just disoriented, he'll follow the sound. Or at least fire a couple rounds. Tough to see how he could be really lost. Not much room before you run into swamp. And if he went off in that stuff, we'll never find him tonight."

"Look's to me like he's in trouble, Jim, not lost."

It was Slater again speaking in the same quiet tone. She pulled her gloves on as protection against the cold's embrace and buttoned her parka to the chin. Winter had come early, in force.

"Welcome to Northeastern Minnesota," she mused softly to herself. "They're probably still golfing in Minneapolis."

The searchers fanned out between the road and the first Wasoose. The moon cast shadows over the birch, popple and spruce. The shadows bowed and curtsied in a slow, elegant waltz as the wind freshened. All was silent save for the muffled calls of Morrison on the P.A. There was no response from the forest.

It took twenty minutes to walk the area bordering the first Wasoose. Nothing. No sign of Adam Budaslavich, other than a few sets of boot prints leading directly from the pickup onto a well–worn snowmobile trail. But the trail was so worn that the light of the lanterns or the moon could not illuminate the old man's prints. A deer stand set in a triangle of birch trees overlooked the first lake. It appeared to Slater that the stand hadn't been used; there were no piss marks in the snow, no candy bar wrappers, no empty soda or beer cans surrounding the platform.

There were boot tracks in the area of the stand, all right. But none leading directly to it.

"Whoever came by this stand," thought Slater, "either didn't want to climb into it, or had some other destination in mind."

The stand's integrity was suspect. It looked rotten. A good place to break an ankle. The floor, rails and ladder rungs were all made of slender popple, nailed to three birch trees with spikes, spikes long since rusted by the harsh, wet weather of the boreal forest. Most of the rungs were cracked.

Slater stood quietly near the stand, listening. The others were slowing making their way back to the vehicles. Slater focused the beam of her flashlight on the packed snow of the trail and began to walk back towards the road. The surface of the uneven ground revealed few deer tracks. Every few hundred yards she'd hit a set. Mostly small. Probably doe. No good if you didn't have a doe permit. Without one, you could only shoot the males, the bucks. Slater hoped Budaslavich didn't have a permit. Spare a doe, spare next year's fawn.

After half an hour, the four returned to the road. They found nothing, no sign of the old man. Every so often, a lone white cloud, sitting high in the night sky, would drift across the moon's face and restore a somber interval to their task. A surge in the wind from the Northwest made the frozen tree branches sing.

"Let's try the second Wasoose, eh Jim?"

Swanson was looking at the squad leader over a thermos cup of hot chocolate. The Deputy held the silver receptacle tightly in his gloved hands. Steam from the liquid curled slowly upward until it disappeared.

"Sure Swanny. But I'm starting to agree with Slater that the old man is in trouble. Probably Alzheimer's; walked off into the swamp, never to be found. Hell, he's likely half way to Meadowlands by now, if he's alive."

Nelson shook his hair. His efforts loosened a spruce cone the wind had deposited in the hollow where his bare neck met his shoulders. He reached for Swanson's cup and took a long gulp. Steam escaped from the corner of his lip.

Swanson grabbed the cup back in mock upset.

"Jimmy you don't suddenly get Alzheimer's like a cold or the measles. This guy was in good shape. Probably in better shape than any of us. Except Deb."

He winked at his partner, knowing she didn't appreciate locker room humor.

"God, you are something, Swanson. I don't know how I ever got you for a partner. Or why I stay with you. I guess I'm trying to straighten you out, salvage your soul. If I can't do it, no one can."

Slater gave her partner a kick in the shins and motioned the men to get back to work. Swanson rubbed his leg. The kick was supposed to hurt. It did. He looked at Slater.

"Shit Deb, even Linda has given up. You'll spend your career harping on me. I'll never change."

They kept walking. Again, the snow revealed few tracks. None human. The terrain became more difficult; the ground sometimes firm and treed, other times full of rushes and swampy. A faint "crunch" could be heard each time they stepped off solid ground, their feet breaking through the thin ice that formed over the marsh grass which grew in the peat bog surrounding the lake. A snowy owl hooted from beyond the shore of the second Wasoose, its call muffled by the woods. The owl's lament was a haunting, spooky sound. It made Slater's neck hair stand upright against the slick nylon of her parka's collar.

She walked the furthest east, heading towards a tall stand of cedar trees, which framed the Lake's edge. A ruffed grouse burst out from beneath the snow, exploding through the cedar boughs. It flew off into the night, its wings sounding like a draft horse crashing through a window. The tempo of Slater's excited heart beat in time to the rhythm of the partridge's wings.

Back on the forest road, Morrison kept calling. There was no answer.

Then she found them.

Footprints. Two sets. One large. One small. They came from the West. Men's Sorels. The larger prints were in front. Both sets appeared to be evenly spaced, indicating a steady walk. She bent down to look at them more closely by the artificial light of her lantern. The lantern's batteries were failing. She began to follow the footprints, pausing when clouds hid the moon's light.

All around her, the cedar boughs hung low. She moved slowly, bent close to the ground so as not to lose the prints. As her shoulders brushed past the frozen tree limbs, wet snow fell into her hair, down the neck of her sweater. The snow was cold, stinging like the prick of a needle. Its touch numbed her bare skin. She halted. The smaller tracks vanished before her. She brushed the snow away from her neck. The larger tracks kept going.

Ahead in a grove of black alder, a thicket really, she saw the triangular form of another deer stand. It looked like the large footprints stopped at the base of the stand. The snow on the ladder leading to the stand's shooting platform had been brushed away by someone or something. The stand was empty. She looked back at the smaller prints and retraced the larger prints to where the smaller ones stopped. She knelt, balancing herself with one hand. She could no longer hear Morrison or the others. She heard only the deliberate pattern of her own heart.

Slater removed a glove and reached into the snow which was only an inch or so deep. The snow's grip was intense and crisp. It stung her bare hand; like snow-cone ice at the State Fair stings your tongue. She groped for an object she thought she'd seen. She was certain it had glimmered briefly at her, reflected by the moon's light, when she'd walked by. She feared she'd lost it. She hadn't. She found it. The metal was so cold it stuck to the flesh of her palm as she closed her hand around it. She'd found a rifle cartridge. The bullet was missing.

She found nothing more, nothing except the footprints. Slater followed them to the stand in the alders. She climbed into the stand. Looking out from its height, hating the thought of the sport that the platform represented, she tried to scan the forest floor by the faltering glow of her flashlight.

It was from the height of the stand that she found Adam Budaslavich. He was lying on the ground, face down in the snow, ten feet to the south of the deer stand. Even from a distance, Deputy Debra Slater knew that the old man was dead.

Chapter 2

November 2, 1991

It took an hour for the Sheriff's Department investigator to drive from Duluth to the Wasoose. Al Pagotti was the man. Eighteen years with the Department. Twelve as a homicide detective. Five foot nine, two hundred and forty pounds, Pagotti was a living testimonial to the levels of starch found in Italian home cooking. He came alone.

Slater and Swanson were there. They hadn't moved the body, hadn't touched it. It wasn't their business, now that the old man had turned up dead. Real dead. Many hours dead by the stiffness in his limbs, by the color of his face.

A large red blotch in the back disrupted Budaslavich's orange jacket. A large hole interrupted the fabric and was covered with frozen blood. His blood. One hole, one bullet. That's what Slater thought when she approached the body from the deer stand. He'd dropped right in his tracks. There were no other footprints near the body.

A Browning 30–06 rifle lay underneath the man. Semi–automatic. Belgian made. Expensive. Swanson found it as he came to Slater's side after she'd cried out. Only the stock and the trigger mechanism were visible. Swanson used his flashlight to read the make, model and caliber off the receiver.

Pagotti trudged slowly through the snow with Jimmy Nelson. Slater and Swanson had stayed with the body. Other than the sound of frozen branches cracking, the Wasoose forest was silent. It wasn't difficult to hear the progress of the detective as he stumbled through the brush.

When he appeared from behind the trees, a shadow in the light of Nelson's lantern, Slater understood why Pagotti's approach through the undergrowth had been telegraphed long before he arrived. He wasn't dressed for the woods and it was obvious the fat man was annoyed.

He wore a suit, a black London Fog overcoat and highly polished black wingtips, which were badly stained by the wet snow and debris of the woods. Pagotti wore no gloves or hat. It was easy to see he was cold and unhappy.

"Whatawegot here, Slater?"

The words rolled off his tongue. He bent down to look at the body.

"Looks like the poor sucker tripped on a branch and did himself in, eh Swanny?"

Pagotti studied the dead man as he talked to Swanson.

"I dunno Sarge, this guy lived his whole life in the woods. I could understand it if he'd busted through a stand and shot himself. Just doesn't add up that he'd walk around with the safety off and shoot himself falling over a branch or a stump," Swanson replied.

Pagotti took out his Minolta and flash. He shot the body as it lay. The camera's light erupted in the darkness of the alders. He took photos of the body from every angle, took photos of the dead man's footprints. When he seemed satisfied he'd preserved the death scene, he rolled the body over.

"Well, sure looks like he shot himself. Look here, there's a spent cartridge, a 30–06, lying right under the body. Must have ejected automatically. Seems to be one entry wound here, right over the heart. Poor bastard."

Pagotti continued to photograph the scene, making sure he preserved the cartridge, the rifle, the entry wound, just as they'd been found.

Slater looked at the face of the old man. His skin looked frigid. Having been denied the warmth of life; the exposed flesh was the color of fireplace ash. She'd seen dead men and women in her job. Not too many. But some. Some more pathetic, sadder than others. A baby beaten to death by an alcoholic father. A husband shot to death in his home, in front of his family, by a nutcase angry at a call the victim made while officiating a youth hockey game. Having experienced other deaths didn't make Adam Budaslavich's death mask any less disturbing, didn't make the old man's demise any easier to accept.

"Deb says there are other footprints a few hundred feet North of here."

Swanson tried to bring his partner back from the depths, back from the unrest he saw sweeping over her face.

"Maybe you want to get those on film too, eh Sarge?"

"Ya. Sure. We better," Pagotti mumbled.

Pagotti stood up from the body and brushed the dirt and snow off his coat.

"Too damn late at night to be out here rolling around in the snow with some dead Bohunk," the detective mumbled.

"Jimmy, cover the damn fool thing. Ambulance will be here in a few minutes. You help 'em get the body into their rig."

Nelson nodded. He had Morrison fetch a blanket from the Rescue Squad van to cover the body while they waited for the ambulance.

"Here Sarge, here's where the smaller set of prints follow the larger ones. From the size of the large ones and the direction, I'd guess they were the old guy's."

Deb Slater was kneeling again. Her right knee rested on the ground. The joint turned numb in the snow.

Pagotti fumbled with the camera.

"Too cold to be out taking pictures of footprints in a swamp," he thought. "Especially when it's clear that the old man stumbled and shot himself."

At least that's what the detective opined to himself as he shivered uncontrollably.

"It fits," Pagotti told himself. "One shot, one shell."

The direction of the wound; snow disturbed on a low branch where he probably tripped, then stumbled, not appreciating that the stumble would cost him his life, all added up to an accidental death.

"Careless," Pagotti murmured through his chattering teeth. That's what the man was; simply careless."

Even so, Pagotti snapped photographs of the footprints. In doing so, he saw that who ever had walked on the same trail as Adam Budaslavich had returned by the same route. Looked to be a man by the size and depth of the smaller prints. But one could see that whoever had made the smaller prints did not follow the old man to the stand in the alders, did not walk the several hundred feet to the place of the man's dying.

Beyond the shores of the first Wasoose, a train whistle blew the mournful wail of a Duluth, Winnipeg and Pacific engine crossing the forest twenty miles to the south. A wolf howled in response. Not the yip of a coyote but the long, throaty call of a timber wolf. Slater glanced upward, into the night sky. Thousands of brilliant stars, their distant light illuminating the earth in varying levels of intensity, competed with the thin canopy of clouds. For a brief instant she forgot why she was on the Wasoose.

Pagotti lumbered to his feet and signaled he was done. His awkward gestures brought Slater back to the job at hand. The ambulance boys emerged from the forest. Nelson brought them to the body. A stretcher covered by another wool blanket was placed next to the body. Hands reached beneath the corpse and rolled it onto the platform. No one spoke.

Deb Slater removed her wet gloves and hung them on her belt. Thrusting her hands into the pockets of her jacket for warmth, she started back towards the squad. Swanson and Pagotti remained behind, making small talk about a boxing match at the Duluth Arena that the fat detective was missing. As she began to walk, Slater's left hand brushed against cold metal. The rifle cartridge.

Snow that had once adhered to the brass casing began to melt in the warmth of her hand. She stopped in the light of Swanson's flashlight and looked at the shell. For the first time, she examined its base. It was not a 30–06 shell. It was a freshly fired cartridge but it was not from the old man's rifle. She walked back and handed the piece of metal to Pagotti.

Chapter 3

November 2, 1991

Deputy Slater sat back in her chair on the second floor of the St. Louis Courthouse in Duluth. Yesterday's snow had melted; it was completely gone, exposing dormant, brown grass and frozen soil. She looked out her window, a window that was not really hers by rights. She shared her cubicle with Swanson. She was alone as she studied the skyline of the City, its buildings cloaked in the faint, cheerless light of winter in Northeastern Minnesota.

Slater sighed and brought her attention back to the desk. She hated working in the office, felt she was more effective, more useful to the department away from her desk, interacting with people, real people, not just other cops.

At twenty-eight she was secure in her job with the department. She loved her work as a patrol deputy. She liked her partner. Even those days or nights she had to be the bearer of bad news did not deter her love of police work out in the field, out of the office.

She'd delivered that kind of news last night. It wasn't until 2:30 a.m. that she and Swanson made it back down Highway 4 to the Budaslavich home. Six years of telling widows and widowers their spouses were gone. Six years of watching the slow terror of loss build as reality spread over the faces of those left behind. She always tried to remain controlled, calm, sympathetic. But, after six years, it hadn't gotten any easier. It never became routine. It was always painful.

Mrs. Budaslavich's reaction was severe. She wailed. She screamed. She denied her husband's death. Though her daughter Joan was outwardly less emotional, Slater's instincts told her the daughter was no less shaken by the old man's death. Her "thank you's," as the officers left, rang hollow. It was obvious that the mere closing of the Budaslavich's front door would not contain the anguish the family was experiencing over the old man's death. Slater felt the sorrow as they drove back down the dark path of the highway to Duluth. She still felt it the next day, forty-five miles away.

Anyway, there she was, staring down at the paperwork or out the window. Thinking about Adam Budaslavich. Wanting to know more about the man.

How he died. Someone knew. Someone who walked in the man's footprints at the Wasoose knew how and when Adam Budaslavich died. She did not. At least, not for certain.

Once Pagotti finished, Swanson and Slater marked the death scene with yellow police ribbon, encircling the fatal grounds in a perimeter of poly tape. The tape enclosed the stand in the black alders, the footprints of the victim, the area where the small footprints stopped and where the second rifle cartridge was found. That was all the deputies had been able to accomplish in the night's chill.

"Maybe," thought Slater, "the forensic lab at the Bureau of Criminal Apprehension in St. Paul can do more."

Pagotti read Slater the riot act for handling the cartridge. Her inadvertence destroyed any possibility of checking the casing for prints.

"Dumb," Slater thought. "Just plain dumb."

She found herself using an adjective to describe her in a way she'd spent six years trying to avoid. Some male cops thought dumb and female were synonymous. Now here she was using the hated term on herself.

She'd been a good student in high school. Nothing spectacular, but steady. She won no scholarships based upon her grades or for her athletic achievements, though she'd lettered in volleyball and track for three years. She was not a brain, not a jock. Simply dependable and hardworking, always achieving a bit more than expected but never a star.

Deb Slater brought these traits and far more to the Sheriff's Department after two years of law enforcement training in Alexandria, Minnesota. At Alex, she was tops in her class. There she was a star. Her pistol accuracy, her physical training scores, her skills course ratings and her classroom grades were beyond reproach. She excelled in a training system dominated by males, by the "good ol boys."

Moving to Duluth from the small farm community of New London, Minnesota where she grew up had been tough. Duluth, while hardly Chicago or the Twin Cities, seemed ready to swallow her and Rick alive when they arrived as wide–eyed kids from the prairie six years ago. But Rick's presence, his love, made the transition easier. And the advantages of living in the northern part of the state soon proved worth their initial anxiety.

Duluth was close to the lakes, close to the woods, close to camping, canoeing. It sat right on the shores of the big lake, Lake Superior. She learned from living there that the great body of frigid, fresh water always overshadowed the lives of those near it, and in some mysterious way, controlled the ebbs and flows of the City and its inhabitants.

Its sheer size often made the weather change in an instant, made the seasons wholly unpredictable.

She could see the Bay of the St. Louis River from her window. Its copper–red water flowed through the Western end of the City and was held back from rushing into the Lake itself by a tiny spit of sand, Park Point. The Point was a neighborhood located in the very center of the City, isolated by geography and spirit from the rest of Duluth. The Point's only link to the mainland; a century-old lift bridge, a short span of steel and asphalt, which is raised to allow vessels to enter the harbor.

To actually see the lake, to see the blue waters of the big lake, she had to go outside, which she did at every opportunity. Lake Superior was a sight Deb Slater never got enough of. Even now, after years of living near the water's edge, she never grew tired of watching whitecaps roll in upon the Point, the frenzied mountains of blue-green water dredged up from the shallows, pushed up by the winds out of Ontario, out of the Northeast. Their terrible beauty continuously challenged the survival of the fragile landform that separated river and lake. In those storms, the dangerous gales of autumn and early winter, over the hundreds of years of navigation on the lake, countless men and ships had perished, crushed by the fury of the swells, drowned in the unforgiving cold of the water. Some were lost but a stone's throw from the innocence of the sandy shore, their bodies taxed and exhausted by attempting to survive the water's intense cold only moments after they entered its grasp.

Still they sailed. Rust colored ore boats, outbound from Duluth to the steel mills of Michigan, Indiana, Ohio and Pennsylvania, heavily laden with taconite, the dirty gray low–grade iron mined on Minnesota's Iron Range, compressed by technology into quarter–sized pellets. The high quality ore, bright and red because of its high iron content, had been played out years before, leaving the gaping emptiness of hundreds of abandoned open pit and underground mines to pockmark the landscape.

There were also the black–hulled salties, ocean going freighters, their painted steel hulls peeling from the saltwater of the oceans, their exposed steel plates further stained by the corrosive toxins lurking in the harbors of the Great Lakes ports. Their cargo holds were loaded in Duluth and Superior, Wisconsin with grain raised and harvested in the Midwest, stored along the wharves and eddies of the Bay. The ships wallowed under the weight of their cargo, carrying precious grain to Europe, Africa and the Far East.

All of the boats and ships passed, inbound and outbound, under the delicate span of the Lift Bridge. To Debra Slater, a farm girl from the prairie, the scene was surreal. It was as if God had lifted a scene from Europe and set it down in the middle of North America.

The lake was the reason she and Rick moved away from New London, a sleepy little dot on the map in Western Minnesota with no big lake, no crazy weather. Nothing unexpected ever happened in New London. Constant sameness, that was New London. Not a bad place, really, simply a good place to be from, to leave upon growing up.

Swanny sat his butt down on Slater's desk, disrupting her daydream. It was supposed to have been their day off. Adam Budaslavich's death changed that.

"What do you think, Deb? What do you make of this Budaslavich thing? I mean, Pagotti still wants to call it an accidental shooting. Accidental on the part of the dead guy, I'll buy that. But what about the cartridge you found? Al says its likely another hunter, from who knows when, simply shot at a deer in the same area. No connection at all to the old guy winding up face down in the snow, right?"

Swanny was looking directly into Slater's eyes. He was reaching for affirmation of Pagotti's theory, the theory that Adam Budaslavich had stumbled, his gun had gone off, and he had died. Slater's cartridge wasn't evidence, had nothing to do with the old man's death. He'd killed himself, that was all there was to it. At least, that was the theory.

"You know what Swanny? I can't get over something you said out at the scene. Remember, you said the old guy wouldn't walk around with the safety off. He was born in the woods. Remember that? That's what's eating at me. Here's a guy who lives in the boonies, walks the woods year 'round. Hunts grouse, ducks, bear, deer. Traps, fishes, cuts pulp and firewood. Not a Joe Tourist deer slayer from the Cities up for an opening weekend of beer and deer. And he shoots himself with a 30–06 rifle on level ground? I don't buy it."

"Deb, you gotta stop listening to me, you really do. I was talking from my heart out there on the Wasoose."

Her partner clearly wanted to get the matter over with, to bury the old man and then bury the file. Case closed. Slater looked up at her partner, his frame leaning over her, shadowing the desktop and the uncompleted paperwork. Adam Budaslavich's paperwork.

"No Dave, you were talking from experience. A hunch. Your guts. No, I think there's something more to this than an old man simply shooting himself."

Slater turned back to the file folder containing her rough notes on the investigation. Nothing really leaped out at her or grabbed her attention. Despite the cursory findings of the medical examiner's autopsy, she didn't buy the old man's death as mere accident. It just didn't feel right. The dead man was not a victim of his own carelessness, that much Deb Slater believed. He just wasn't. She said nothing more to Swanny. Her hands moved over the keyboard as she began to type.

Slater worked until she finished the report and then dragged herself home. It was nearly 11:00pm. Rick was fast asleep and snoring, an act he always denied he was guilty of. She sat down in their living room with a cup of hot tea, trying to watch David Letterman. The host was insulting some poor woman and her counting cocker spaniel.

She'd brought the file home. She stared at its pages in the dim light of the television. What had Pagotti missed? What had she and Swanson left out? The entry wound was clear. Only one shot killed the man. The exit wound matched. Again, one shot. Where could she look further, what was there left to review? The bullet. If the bullet itself had exited, it was still somewhere out on the Wasoose. In the trees, maybe in the swamp. A bullet in the swamp. A needle in a haystack. But if it could be found, ballistics at the BCA could determine the origin of the fatal shot, or at the very least, tell if it was from the old man's rifle. Then they'd be certain, no guesses.

Tomorrow before her shift, she'd call Inspector Phil Chen of the BCA. He was in town. In town to look at a nasty double homicide–arson case in West Duluth. Chen was an old friend; he'd be willing to visit the Wasoose. And he was a crackerjack forensic investigator. Together the two of them might be able to recreate the final minutes of Adam Budaslavich's last deer hunt.

Chapter 4

November 3, 1991

Slater met Inspector Phil Chen for breakfast at a greasy spoon in Duluth's Central Hillside. Pat's Flapjacks, Pat MacGregor proprietor. Five foot four. Three hundred pounds. Or more. Pat obviously ate too many of his own flapjacks. Far too many. But his place was the local cops' home away from home when they were on duty and hungry. Lot's of food, cheap and strong coffee. A brew served with or without whiskey, depending on the officer and the season.

Slater ordered an omelet. She was hungry. She hadn't slept. Chen lowered himself into the booth ten minutes after her food arrived. Sliding across the cracked red vinyl seat, silver duct tape holding the stuffing in, Chen folded his arms and placed them on the linoleum top of the table. Bev, the waitress, snapped her gum and smiled. The BCA Agent ordered toast and coffee. He'd driven up from BCA headquarters in St. Paul for the murder–arson case that morning. Two and a half-hours on the freeway. He needed the java. To wake up. To get warm.

"So tell me Deb, what's so peculiar about this hunting accident that a BCA bigshot like me needs to take a look–see?"

He was grinning. All the local cops, the city police, the county deputies, held the BCA in awe at times, in disdain at others. The beat cops by and large praised the forensic abilities of the Bureau but damned the lack of "street smarts" some of the lab coats exhibited in analyzing the facts behind the evidence.

Chen was one of the rare ones who had worked the real world. He'd been a beat cop, he knew people, knew cops. And he knew Deb Slater well enough to sense she had good reasons to bring him in on the case. Maybe it was only based upon her instinct, upon a hunch about a dead old man in the woods. But he trusted her hunches, her instincts.

"Phil, I gotta tell you, Sheriff Prescott would raise hell if he knew I was going behind Pagotti's back on this one. I mean, Pagotti's so damned sure that the old guy was walking through the woods with his safety off, tripped and fell, "boom," kills himself. Pagotti's got Swanson convinced of it. He wasn't convinced before, but now, for the record, he is. I just can't buy it. I mean, no one can explain the cartridge I found. No one. And the other boot prints. There was another hunter out there. Someone. Whether he accidentally shot Budaslavich or simply saw the body after he died, I don't know. But something tells me he saw the old man, dead or alive."

She looked at Chen. She could tell he was interested.

They'd met in Alexandria, Minnesota, in the Western part of the state, in cop school. They'd dated a few times. Nothing serious. At least not in Slater's mind. It wasn't that Chen was Chinese or from California. That didn't enter into it at all. He was handsome, dark skinned. Good build, athletic. A hell of a shortstop in high school. At least that's what he told her, and she believed it. Dark eyes; brown disappearing into black. They had held a certain attraction for a brief time. But she'd always thought of him as a confidant, a friend. And even then she'd known that Rick was the one she loved. No room in the hotel of her heart for two lovers. But plenty of rooms for friends. Phil Chen had a floor of rooms there all to himself.

The BCA agent took a long swig of the coffee from a chipped porcelain cup. Hot. Damn hot. It woke him up.

"Well, if you're so sure this thing doesn't add up, let's go out and take a look. Off duty of course. At least for your sake. So Pagotti and Prescott don't get all hot and bothered. How about tomorrow afternoon?"

He knew the arson scene would take all day. An elderly couple had died in the fire. Messy. Disheartening.

Slater nodded.

"Let's meet here tomorrow at noon. Not for lunch. Once a week at Pat's is more than enough for me," she said.

He smiled. Nodding in agreement.

"Yeah we both could stand to watch our cholesterol, what with the onset of advanced age and all."

She left Chen with the bill. He made her; he always paid. She'd given up arguing. He told her it made him feel like he was still dating her. It was a little crazy but sweet.

Chen watched Debra Slater walk out of the café. For a long while, the BCA investigator sipped contentedly on his second cup of coffee. He watched the sun rise over the harbor through an oily film of grease coating the glass. He noted that there were no clouds floating above the lake as a brilliant pink glow climbed the horizon above the Wisconsin shore. The officer took in the shimmering blue–black water, its calm disturbed by crashing waves. He seemed at ease, at home, studying the lake. He was born and raised in another hilly city, on another body of water. San Francisco. Duluth was a lot like his hometown except for the cold. Damn cold.

Chen took a final sip of the bitter brew and forced himself away from the table. Pulling the collar of his woolen peacoat as high as the fabric would go, he paid the bill, securing the buttons of his coat as he strolled out onto First Street, out into the morning cold.

Not far down the hill from Pat's, Sheriff Dan Prescott sat at his desk in the St. Louis County Courthouse pondering the next departmental budget.

"Shit," the Sheriff thought, "damn Republicans have cut so much federal revenue spending that the county is either going to have to raise taxes two hundred percent or make cuts across the board," he murmured to himself.

Personnel, equipment, benefits would all suffer. Prescott figured his department would be hit hard, despite all the political mantra regarding law and order. The math was simple. There were, according to the County Commissioners, the politicians who ran the county, too many deputies for a county with a declining population. Decades of falling steel prices, of cheap foreign imports, left diminished demand for the region's iron ore. The decline in the demand for Minnesota ore caused the Iron Range to waste away like a huge ghost town.

And the Russian grain embargo in '74 hadn't exactly been a boon for the port of Duluth, its dockworkers, or the truckers that transport the grain. All of the people hit by those hard times held on as long as they could, surviving by selling off bits and pieces of their lives to stay long after common sense dictated it was time to leave. Then, desperate to save their families, they eventually surrendered to the finality of it all and moved to Texas, Florida, Arizona, or the Twin Cities of Minneapolis and St. Paul to find work. To many who left Northeastern Minnesota in the 1980's, the South was the promised land, where there was no winter, where all the money and jobs had gone.

St. Louis County sustained a loss of thirty thousand people in ten years; thirty thousand out of a total population of somewhat over 200,000. Prescott sat thinking about all those Minnesotans lost to the tropics. Were they yearning to come home? Did they miss the snow, the wind, the rain? The Sheriff tapped the desktop with his pencil and thumbed the pocket of his dress shirt. An Arrow. Not too expensive, not too cheap. Sharp looking. White. Always a white shirt with a tailored gray or blue suit. Every day he alternated between the two colors. He had three of each in his closet at home. Lucy, his wife, bought them and always bought gray or blue. To go with his eyes, she said.

All the powers in the courthouse, the judges, the court administrators, fought for the corner offices in the building. The corner offices boasted views of the lake. If you couldn't get one of those, you settled for an office on an outside wall facing east or north where the windows offered at least a partial view of the lake or St. Louis Bay.

But Prescott's office faced the hillside. By choice. He liked looking at the small houses stacked atop one another up the steeply treed slope, especially when the seasons changed. Every three months, four times a year, he felt privileged to watch the magic of that change. He'd been born in Duluth. He, like Dave Swanson, would die in Duluth.

This time of year, the hillside was lifeless. The orange, yellow and red pastels of autumn had been blown away by early November winds. Winter was not quite present, at least in town. The scant snowfall that remained in the forests and swamps had vanished from the city. The lake did that. It acted as a natural air conditioner in the summer, cooling the City. But in winter, the vast expanse of fresh water retained the sun's warmth, raising the temperature five or ten degrees above what was found only a few miles inland. Because of its size and the action of the waves, Lake Superior's surface rarely froze solid beyond a stone's throw from shore. The open water helped warm the cities of Duluth and Superior, though warm in January and February was always a relative term.

Prescott watched a school bus climb the hillside between the black cliffs of gabro, craggy remnants of ancient volcanoes that formed the Sawtooth Mountains. He thought of his kids. Both boys were in high school, pleading, begging for a car. Their days of riding a big yellow bus were over. The Sheriff smiled, remembering the three of them playing all-star wrestling on the living room floor, Lucy screaming at the top of lungs as the lamps and vases teetered near destruction.

Someone opened his door. The distraction pulled him back to reality. Al Pagotti let himself in. Prescott took his feet off the window ledge and turned to face the detective.

"What's up, Al?"

Prescott disliked Pagotti. Thought he'd become lazy, complacent. The detective had lost the bulldog tenacity that'd made him the top investigator in the department. Pagotti shuffled forward.

"Nice suit, Dan."

The insincerity in his subordinate's voice made the sheriff wince. Pagotti was always awkward with his boss. Most likely because he had stood twice for election as Sheriff and lost miserably both times. Pagotti was, in his boss' opinion; too apolitical to deal with the County Board, too thin skinned to accept criticism. In addition, the man was unable to instill confidence in the men and women that served in the Department.

Pagotti himself knew the Sheriff's perceptions were accurate. It made him resent Dan Prescott. Prescott could accomplish all that Pagotti could not and do so without breaking a sweat.

"I've got some interesting news on the Budaslavich thing. You know Channel 10 had a reporter up there? Got the whole story about accidental shooting, the works. Even broadcast the details about the scene. That was all the day after. This morning before their early morning show someone leaked 'em the contents of Slater's report. About the stray shell. You know, the one Slater found at the scene? And another set of tracks. Not the old man's."

Pagotti wasn't telling these things to Prescott, he was asking the Sheriff to confirm them.

Prescott nodded. Old news. Except for the part about the leak. But there were always leaks. And they were always an embarrassment, though there wasn't much that he could do to stop them. He was irritated that the fat man was wasting his time.

"So what's the point Al? I'm sure the department's highest ranking detective isn't telling me this for my health."

He was going to say 'best' detective but thought better of inflating Pagotti's ego.

"Well chief, right after the 7:00 a.m. broadcast, I got a call from Mr. Tuomi from Cotton High School. You know, the football coach? Seems the Coach and his son Jason were hunting the Wasoose at about the time Budaslavich was. Same day. The kid apparently had a doe permit, kicked up a small doe between the First Wasoose and the Second. Got buck fever. Doe fever, whatever. He got excited."

Pagotti was looking at Dan Prescott with a grin from cheek to ruddy cheek. He was obviously relishing the fact that the sheriff did not know where the story was going.

"What's the punchline Al? Did the kid see Budaslavich's body? Get scared? Or did he talk to the old guy out there on the Wasoose?"

Prescott wanted Pagotti to get to the point. The budget was still on his desk, still begging to be redlined. Deductions. Corrections. Pagotti's grin turned into a smile. He'd caught the boss preoccupied. He hadn't been following the story. The detective was pleased he could break it to the Sheriff. Pagotti's jowls quivered. He was happy, real happy.

"Coach Tuomi thinks the kid shot the old man. Wants to come in with the boy and give a statement."

Prescott stared down at the budget papers cluttering his desk. He was annoyed at not guessing the ending to the fat man's story. He should have.

"Well Al, see to it that you don't scare the hell out of the kid. His dad's a good guy and I'm sure the kid's from the same stock."

Pagotti nodded and left the room, closing the door as he walked out, gloating to himself as he shuffled down the hall. Prescott looked back out onto the hillside. He couldn't help but smile.

"Maybe old Al will get back to being himself if I let him catch me a few more times. Nothing important or crucial," the Sheriff mused. "Just let him win a few of the little points where he can't hurt me."

With that, the sheriff resumed staring down at the ledger sheets in front of him. He returned to thumping the eraser of his pencil against the desktop. Now if he could only get Pagotti to solve his budget problems.

Chapter 5

November 5, 1991

Slater didn't meet Phil Chen the next day. Pagotti cornered her to tell her about Jason Tuomi. The kid was coming in at 9:00 a.m. the next morning. She had to be there. Pagotti insisted. She knew the interview process and the paperwork would keep her past noon. She called Chen and told him they'd have to meet another day.

True to his word, at 9:00 a.m. the next morning, Coach Tuomi and his son were in Pagotti's office, sitting between piles of old McDonald's wrappers and styrene cups half full of cold coffee. Remnants of stale donuts and sweet rolls lay scattered atop the detective's desk. His office was crammed with an old Air Force surplus metal desk and stacks of manila folders. Stacks on the window ledge. Stacks on the floor. Most were not open cases but dead files, brought back to life to help Sheriff Prescott build a case for his budget. Pagotti had yet to review any of them.

The older Tuomi sat sternly erect. Back straight. True to football coach form, he was tall, lean and looked 45 at 55. The boy was a younger, thinner version of the father, more arms and legs than muscle at this point. Slater leaned against a stack of files looking at the boy. She could tell it was all he could do to hold back the tears.

"Coach, I just want you to tell Deputy Slater here what you told me. No need for Jason to go over it just right now. Understand he's upset about it. Especially two weeks before state playoffs."

Pagotti looked up from the Budaslavich file open on the top of his desk. He was thumbing through the photographs of the scene that he'd taken.

"Uh, Deputy, it's like this. Me and Jason were hunting the Wasoose. November one."

He said "one" not "first."

"Probably an old military habit," Slater noted to herself.

"I left Jason by the first Wasoose. Plan was for me to stay on the forest road. Walk north. Back towards Long Lake then turn into the woods. Walk South towards Jason pushing deer."

The coach stopped, eyes moist. He wasn't doing much better than the kid.

"About an hour and a half after I hit the woods, I hear a shot–can't recall how loud or how close. One shot, that's all I heard. So I keep walking south, kicked out two small doe. To myself, I'm thinking it could have been Jason who shot, but it could have been the owner of the pickup that was parked there. Couldn't tell."

Slater studied the Coach's face. The emotion faded. His face became cold, empty, without passion. The Coach was back in control, merely relating facts. In the corner, Jason Tuomi hung his head and sobbed quietly.

"Jason and I meet. I ask him, 'Did you shoot?' he says 'No.' So we pack it on out to the road. The other pickup's still there. I remember because I was thinking to myself as we drove by it that the owner must be a real meat hunter, a real venison lover. We drove back to Cotton on the Three Lakes Road and had a burger at Edna's on Highway 53."

Pagotti shifted his buttocks in the chair, obviously impatient for the Coach to get on with it. His throat strained from too many years of cheap scotch, he asked the elder Tuomi to continue.

"Then Jason saw that newscast."

Jason shuddered and wept more audibly. His father reached over and grasped his shoulder. A gesture that seemed to say, "That's OK kid, the fumble wasn't your fault."

"So we're watching TV yesterday morning. Channel 10, the early report before "Good Morning America." On comes Wendy what's–her–name. She starts talking about a shooting over the weekend up by the Long Lake Road. An empty shell found at the scene. And Jason's watching, he gets agitated. Starts crying, worse than now. I ask him what's wrong. He tells me he thinks he's the one that shot the old man. So I call Pagotti here. Saw his name on the television as the guy in charge. Came here to make a clean slate of it. Right Jason?"

The father's eyes betrayed emotion. He looked with deep sadness at his boy. Jason Tuomi could not lift his head to respond.

Slater pulled herself up and faced Coach Tuomi.

"Mr. Tuomi, is it all right if I ask Jason about some of the details of the incident? You know he's entitled to a lawyer and he doesn't have to talk to me or say a thing. It's really his decision to make."

Mark Munger

Slater looked down at the boy. He managed to stop crying though his letter jacket showed the stain of his tears.

"I'll talk to you Ma'am," he whispered in a careful, delicate voice.

Slater noted that it was not the type of voice you'd associate with someone reckless enough to shoot another hunter. Jason Tuomi began to relate all he knew about November first on the Wasoose.

"I left dad, just like he said. Walked east until I hit the shore of the first Wasoose. I stopped frequently to listen and watch. Saw no deer. Worked my way south along the shoreline. I was wet, it was tough going. I carried Grandpa Tuomi's 30–30 Winchester."

In her mind, Slater pictured the weapon. An old, silver-plated saddle gun with black electrician's tape muffling the noise of the saddle ring so as not to scare the deer when the boy walked. She'd seen hundreds of them over the course of her lifetime living in Minnesota.

"Go on."

"Got any water? I'm really thirsty," the boy asked, his throat raspy.

Slater poured tepid water from a plastic pitcher into a waxed paper cup and handed it to the boy. He drank slowly, as if he wanted to avoid rushing into telling the rest of the story. He placed the empty paper cup on the desk top and continued:

"Sometime around ten thirty I heard a tree branch snap. Nothing much, just one of those noises that's different. Not the usual sound of the forest.

I stopped. Ahead through the cedars I thought I saw four tan-colored legs. A deer. Never did see the head. Didn't matter. I had a doe permit. I pulled up the Winchester, placed it against my cheek. My heart thumped, not a simple rush like before a big game but a pounding in my chest like I've never experienced. The force was so overwhelming it shook my arms when I tried to aim. The legs moved. Or I thought they did. I couldn't tell for sure. I squeezed the trigger. One shot. Loud. Very Loud. No other sound.

Can't remember if the legs moved after that or not. I lowered the rifle, walked ahead a few steps. There was no deer. No blood in the snow, where the deer should've been. Ahead in a small clearing in the alders, I seen someone's deer stand. No one in it.

But to the right, a man's body. A dead man. The dead man on Channel 10."

"Did you check the body, Jason?" Slater asked, edging closer to the boy, protective but still professional.

She wanted to pull every detail out, to learn the full story.

"Yes, Ma'am. I walked over to him. There was blood all over his back. One hole. He was dead, not breathing. I knew it. I couldn't touch him. I couldn't."

The boy turned away from the officers, towards his father. Tears fell again, landing on the soft leather sleeves of his letter jacket.

"Jason, you're sure you walked over to the body and checked it? Checked to see whether Mr. Budaslavich was alive?"

Her voice hinted of disbelief. Something in the back of her mind told her there was something odd; something missing.

"Come on Deputy, I believe the boy. Let's not pry further. At least right now."

Pagotti's voice cut through the tension of the moment. He was using his Catholic Priest routine, the saintly protector. He was ending the interview.

"Coach, why don't you and Jason go on home now. We know where to reach you if we need anything more."

With Pagotti's dismissal, Coach Tuomi pulled the limp form of his son out of the office and walked the boy down the hall. It was obvious the kid had been through hell in telling what had happened.

The glass door shook as it slammed into place. Pagotti's face was scarlet. His head looked like a tomato ready to burst.

"What the hell was that Slater? Why were you pushing the kid so hard? He told you he walked over to the body. What else did you want him to say?"

Pagotti was obviously beyond mere upset. Always dangerous to get your boss angry. But not so dangerous when he's being stupid.

"Al, either Jason Tuomi was lying or he flew the last hundred feet to the body. He's a size nine boot. Same as the small tracks we found in the snow. Budaslavich is a twelve. Minimum. There weren't any size nine footprints within 100 feet of Adam Budaslavich's corpse."

Chapter 6

November 6, 1991

Phil Chen's eyebrows knit together. Pencil thin, they matched the angular gaze of his eyes. He was looking at the contents of Adam Budaslavich's pockets. Swanson and Slater had gathered the old man's possessions from the body at the St. Luke's Hospital Morgue the day after the Wasoose.

There wasn't much of interest. A wallet. Standard pictures of wife and kids. Driver's license. Visa. Sears. Social Security card. LTV Mining Employee's Credit Union number. Three or four deposit slips for the credit union. Some cash, a twenty, five ones. A deer license and a tag. A Citizen watch, standard K–Mart issue, steel band. Three sticks of Juicy Fruit, two wrappers. Nail clippers. Nine intact cartridges for a 30.06 rifle. One spent matching cartridge was found beneath the dead man's body. The used cartridge had been removed by Pagotti and placed in a clear plastic receptacle separate from the man's worldly possessions.

There were also items of clothing and personal property. A 5" Buck knife with black sheath. Brown leather belt. Pin–on compass. Two pairs of socks. Orange hunting pants. A bloodstained red woolen shirt, a bullet hole in the front and back. White T-shirt and boxer shorts. A blaze orange hunting jacket from Sears. The holes perforating the jacket matched those in the shirt. The jacket was blood stained. Dirt and leaves were mixed with the dead man's blood, staining the edges of the torn fabric. The inventory also included a small, dime-sized medal dangling from a silver chain.

"Perhaps," thought Chen, "one of the saints? Thomas? Christopher?"

Being Methodist, he didn't know. On the back of the medal, one word had been engraved. The word meant nothing to him. He placed the medal to one side.

"Sure can't find anything of significance here, Deb. Looks like the pockets and wallet of two–thirds of the working guys in Minnesota. Especially during deer season."

He tucked away the contents of each plastic ziplock bag in turn. Marked with black marker, preserved for posterity. Slater stood next to Chen, watching his thorough review of each item. Always amazed at the painstaking forensic investigation her friend conducted. Like an anteater combing an anthill. Sucking out each ant, one by one. Spitting out those that didn't taste right.

After the baggies were secured, Chen turned his attention to the photographs of the scene. Looking at each under a magnifying glass. Combing the preserved evidence of Adam Budaslavich's final resting-place. He found nothing in the grainy photos which meshed with Jason Tuomi's version of what had happened. Nothing he saw explained the lack of the boy's footprints around the body. A computerized enhancement might show the details better but it was only available in St. Paul.

"Yes," thought Phil Chen, "enhancement is what the photos need."

He'd do it as soon as he got back to the lab.

"Anything in the pictures that shows Tuomi's story makes sense, Phil?"

Slater was in plain clothes. Off–duty. Looking directly over Chen's shoulder as he scanned the photos. To Chen, she looked as she always looked. Beautiful. Radiant. The same Deb Slater he'd fallen in love with in school. She didn't seem to notice how intoxicated he was by her presence. Too bad. He hoped she would have noticed.

"Gonna have to run a computer enhancement on these. I want to get a better look at the snow. The footprints. Pagotti's no master with the camera, eh? I think he's a stop or two off on these. Or shooting through a pair of nylons. They're fuzzy. Can't tell if I'm missing something obvious. Just can't tell. Computer should help."

He loved working with technology. Being part of a new breed of cop. A new generation. Science assisting justice. A perfect match in the case of Phil Chen.

"I still think we should go out and take a look at the scene. Give it the once over in the daylight. Even though the snow's melted and the footprints are likely gone, it might help me to get an idea of the place. And we can run a metal detector over the area. Maybe the bullet that killed Budaslavich will turn up."

Out at the Wasoose, it had drizzled off and on following Adam Budaslavich's death. The crime scene retained no footprints of discernible shape. All that remained were slight depressions in black soil softened by the rain. Much of the snow had washed away, leaving the top layer of dirt exposed to the sun. Slater and Chen worked within the yellow ribbons that marked the scene. Chen fixed his attention upon the dial of a metal detector. The growling wind defused the audible "beep, beep, beep" of the device as the detective worked the area. The current came from the South, a relatively warm, mild breeze, for November.

Chen passed the instrument over the area where Budaslavich's body had been discovered. Traces of blood still stained the leaves and other debris covering the soil. The BCA agent concentrated his efforts based upon the boy's story. A theory. He searched an area consistent with the reported path of the boy's bullet. One shot. If indeed it struck the old man, it would have hit him in the chest, spun him around. Budaslavich would have landed on his stomach, the bullet exiting out his back. Shot north to south, the bullet would have exited to the south. Towards the cedars.

Chen and Slater worked an arc twenty feet wide from the spot the body was found. A steady "beep." Nothing, no old pop cans, no old nails, no metal at all. Chen poked the detector up into the trees, looking for evidence that a bullet had lodged in the bark. Nothing. After an hour of fruitless search, they sat down under a spruce, the tree's needles dripping with melt. They sat very near where Adam Budaslavich had met his Maker.

"Just doesn't seem right, Phil. I mean, the kid tells us he walked over to the body. Photos show us only one set of tracks, the old man's. The autopsy makes it clear there's only one bullet. One shot. That's clear. That's consistent. The kid shot once, dad heard only one shot. No bullet lying to the south in a path from where Jason stood and shot. That's not consistent. We should have found the slug based on what he told us and what the autopsy showed regarding the entrance and exit wounds. I just don't get it."

She looked at Phil Chen with puzzlement. Waiting for him to clear up the mystery. She'd come to expect that.

"I know. It's the kid's story that I can't follow. If he walked up to the body, where are the prints? If he shot the old man, where is the 30–30 bullet? The cartridge you found clearly isn't his. It's a 9mm of some sort."

He paused, to make sure Slater was following him. She was.

"And the kid's bullet, after hitting the ribs, it should be relatively close. In a line to the south. It isn't."

Chen pondered a minute. He pulled a manila folder from under his jacket. Reread the autopsy report. Organ by organ described. Hematoma, pneumothorax. Blood, blood and more blood. Entry wound to the front.

They agreed to spend another hour on the search. Another hour of attempting to find the needle. At 3:00 p.m. on November 6, 1991, they found the needle twenty-eight feet from the final resting place of the old man. Four feet up from the ground, imbedded in the trunk of a birch tree. Hidden from view except for a tiny spark of silver which caught the investigator's eye.

From its location in the birch, Chen pieced together a solution to the inconsistencies in Jason Tuomi's story. He surmised that the slug had traveled from a location to the south of the body, not north. The fatal shot had come from a direction directly opposite from where the boy had been. As he stood looking at the scene, putting it together in his mind, Slater photographed the bullet's resting place and Chen held a tape against the trunk of the tree to show the height of the slug from the ground. Preserved as evidençe in the photos, Chen carefully pried the projectile from the tree's embrace. Looking at it closely, he could tell it had passed through something. Maybe a body.

"This is an odd looking slug, Deb. It's definitely not a 30–30. Not a 30–06 either. I don't know what caliber or type, never run into one quite like it before."

He held the bullet gingerly in the steel tines of a tweezers, gazing at the piece of lead as if it could speak, as if it could solve the riddles. But the bullet's presence didn't answer the riddles, or the questions of the two officers. It only brought to mind a hundred more.

Chapter 7

November 7, 1991

BCA Headquarters occupied a nondescript building along University Avenue, isolated from other law enforcement facilities in a neighborhood of pimps, whores and users who live in the gut of the City. Despite the allusions to New York or LA, the neighborhood was by and large safe. Safe in the daytime, safe at night. As long as you did your business and got out; kept your thoughts and eyes to yourself.

It was November 7th. Phil Chen planned to be back in California to visit his family. Those plans were made long before he dug the bullet out of a tree trunk on the Wasoose. The mystery of the slug intrigued him, made him stay over a few extra days in the cold of the Minnesota winter.

During the course of his career, he'd examined many deadly projectiles; bullets pulled from bodies, pried from the concrete of basement walls or out of the thin, punctured metal of car doors. He'd seen the remnants of bullets from heavy artillery (high–powered rifles), stop 'em in their tracks handguns (.357's, .44's, .45's), and the less lethal stuff (.38 service revolver's, .25 and .22 Saturday Night Specials). But he'd never seen a slug like the one he pulled out of the tree. He was forced to admit he couldn't identify it; that he needed help.

Ballistics expert Marv Hankinson sat looking at the slug perched on his lab bench down the hall from Chen's office. Hankinson stared at the bullet through a stereo microscope, gently turning the object, stopping every so often to look carefully through his ballistics manuals, trying to find a match. Chen crowded in close behind the man. He didn't allow Hankinson space to breathe.

"Phil, for Chrissake, can't you give me some room? I can't work with you trying to crawl down my shorts!" the technician said half in jest.

Pudgy, beet-red in complexion, with the sandy yellow hair of his Norse forefathers, Hankinson didn't need Chen standing at his elbow to make him perspire. Simply trying to breathe did that; the sweat formed effortlessly on his hairless forehead, rolling slowly down the arch of his nose. Once there, the moisture hung from the tip of his nose, in midair, poised to drop onto whatever work Hankinson had before him. Seeing the perspiration begin to form,

Chen moved back a step and gave the big man room.

Hankinson continued to study the markings on the slug, markings left by the rifling of the weapon that fired it.

"It's clear this slug is a 9mm. I've never run across one quite like it. The process that molded this bullet is not something I recognize. The striations on it caused by the rifling of the weapon's bore are an oddity. They're archaic, outdated."

Hankinson wasn't talking to Chen, or anyone else in particular. He was thinking aloud.

Flipping through another ballistics catalog, the technician turned to a section on foreign–made weaponry. Pages of stuff on Warsaw Pact small arms. NATO. Japanese. Scandinavian. Israeli. Nothing seemed close. Many examples of 9mm bullets but nothing matching what lay before him on the table. He picked up a volume on 20th century weapons and ballistics no longer in production. He searched for the section on discontinued foreign arms. At page 205, he stopped. There it was, big as life. The cartridge was a Zulsdorf. Made for a 9mm German Mauser. Dates of production: 1935–1945. Country of origin–Nazi Germany. Bingo.

"Here it is Chen. Here's the cartridge. And next to it, there's your murder weapon. Zulsdorf made the bullet and cartridge. Produced during World War II for the war in Europe and North Africa. Look at the rifling on the sample in the book. Then take a gander at the slug you brought in."

Chen glanced at the glossy photo in the catalog and then into the microscope.

"See the rings worn near the impact point on the slug's end? A tell–tale marking that confirms this is the culprit."

Hankinson pulled his chair away from the bench to allow Chen a better look. He stood up and stretched his back, hands on his hips. It had taken six hours of diligent search. They now knew the origins of the bullet.

"I guess the next question, Marv, is whether or not this slug could have made the entry and exit wounds we found on the old man's chest and back. We've got a bullet, we've got a gun—we can put those two together. But we still have the Tuomi boy at the scene. No other footprints. It's getting more confused, crazier, not simpler. An antique bullet found in Northeastern Minnesota forty-five years after the war is over. Christ, this is a mess."

Chen looked up. He wasn't smiling. He wasn't happy. He'd hoped he'd been wrong, hoped the slug from the tree was a match with Jason Tuomi's 30–30. Or the old man's 30–06. Proving he was wrong simply meant more work, meant there was more than one needle in the haystack.

"Well, wouldn't be that unusual for someone who fought over in Europe during the war to have bought back a German weapon as a trophy."

"No, you're right Marv. Probably a few thousand guns like that in the state. But the bullet doesn't make sense. Why would someone use a fifty-year-old cartridge? Take a chance of a misfire? Or even have one laying around, for that matter?"

"Good question, Chen. I'm just a technician, not a mind reader. Afraid I can't answer that one."

"Let's go down and see if Nancy came up with anything of use."

On the first floor, BCA Agent Nancy Claus took the out–of–focus images Pagotti had captured at the death scene and fed them into the agency's Mac computer through a high-detail scanner. Using a custom graphics program, she enlarged the detail in each photo and sharpened the imagery. Laid out on her finishing table were twenty-four laser printed, enhanced enlargements of the snow, the footprints, the body.

Chen and Hankinson entered Claus' laboratory. Leaning over the edge of her lab bench, the men stared at the finished product. Claus stood up, moving in behind them. She was a very tall, very pale woman. Her hair was dyed jet black. Large-framed eyeglasses concealed most of her face. The spectacles made her look older than her forty years. She seldom smiled; she never laughed. A loner or alone, Chen couldn't decide which it was. In any case, he'd given up kidding or joking with her. She possessed no sense of humor. She was all business. He suspected she was lesbian, but didn't really know. He was certain of one thing. The lady was a computer genius.

"Inspector Chen, if you look at the photos of the large footprints in sequence, from where we presume Jason Tuomi's smaller prints stop, to the body, you'll see that there are brush marks, from the detail. It appears as if the marks were made with a pine or spruce bough. Like someone wiped the surface clean."

Claus was pointing with a yellow–tipped highlighter to a series of very regular brush marks on the snow's crust. The markings were disturbed by a single set of large Sorel prints. The bootprints looked to be about size twelve. Adam Budaslavich's size. His prints. Chen nodded in understanding.

"Whoever attempted to wipe the area clean missed a few footprints of interest. Take a look at this enhancement of the large footprints, the ones that appear to be the dead man's, leading to the place his body was found. What do you see?"

Chen bent down closer. Claus handed him a magnifying glass. He peered at the enlarged detail of the prints.

"Geez, Nancy, I can't really see anything unusual. What am I supposed to see?"

Chen cracked a smile and turned to see Hankinson grinning. He winked at Claus. She wasn't smiling.

"What you're supposed to see, Inspector, is the obvious. Within the large footprints is a second, smaller set of footprints. The second set match the tread style and size of the Tuomi boy's boots."

Chen grew more puzzled. He was thoroughly lost.

"So what are you saying, Claus?"

He called her Claus rather than Nancy to reinforce his rank over her. To convey his impatience with the game. She seemed too sure of herself for his liking. Women weren't, in Phil Chen's book, supposed to be so self-confident. She didn't yield to his subtle claim to power.

"What is clear, Inspector Chen, is that Jason Tuomi did indeed walk to the body of Adam Budaslavich. The smaller prints are his. What is not clear is why someone would walk on top of the Tuomi boy's prints with a larger sized boot, a size twelve boot, in the exact footprints Jason Tuomi left. What's more, whoever walked in the Tuomi boy's tracks, walked backwards–facing the dead man's body. It's also clear that the larger tracks you see in the photograph are not from the dead man's Sorels. I've looked at the old man's boots. They've got a clearly visible crack in the right sole, which leaves a distinct impression in snow. You can see that in the large tracks right next to the body. Right here."

She pointed to a set of boot prints next to the body of Adam Budaslavich, the corpse's face white and lifeless in the flash of Pagotti's camera.

"Those are the dead man's. These other tracks that leave the body and head towards where the Tuomi boy was standing when he shot, they're the same size as Budaslavich's boot would make. Same pattern. Except they're new or almost new. The tread isn't worn and there's no crack in the right sole."

Chen glanced at Hankinson. Both turned to Claus with questioning looks on their faces. Her expression bore no grin, no smirk of triumph, and no recognition that she'd uncovered major secrets regarding Adam Budaslavich's death. She'd established that someone else had been out on the Wasoose on November 1, 1991. Someone, who, in all probability, insisted upon using fifty-year-old Zulsdorf 9 mm rifle cartridges. Someone who quite probably murdered Adam Budaslavich.

The Legacy

Chapter 8

November 10, 1989

Philip Chen was going to miss Thanksgiving in San Francisco. After the revelations of the 7th, he called Slater and filled her in on the BCA's findings. She was interested, damn interested in looking deeper into the death of Adam Budaslavich. Chen drove north on I–35 again the next day and spent the afternoon in Slater's office by himself, reviewing the file. Digging. Searching.

They met with the St. Louis County Medical Examiner, Dr. Bruce Johnson. Johnson was a pathologist, a forensic medical specialist, at St. Luke's Hospital. His conclusions were as Chen had suspected. The 9mm slug was consistent with the entry and exit wounds found on the old man's body. By size, by the rib damage and the impact to the bullet's tip, Johnson was fairly certain the slug was the one that killed the man. Not a sure thing, but consistent. Probable. And from the angle of entry and exit, Johnson confirmed Chen's suspicion that Budaslavich had been shot as he turned around to face the direction of his assailant. He turned to the South. The theory was consistent with the physical evidence. It was time to pay Mrs. Budaslavich another visit.

Other than the follow–up by Slater and Swanson in the early morning hours of November 2nd, and a contact by Sheriff Prescott relating the Tuomi boy's story, no one had spoken to the old woman about her husband's death. There had been no reason to bother her in her grief. Now there was. Now it looked like someone other than the Tuomi boy was involved. Now it looked suspiciously like murder. Chen and Slater wanted to find out why; why anyone would want the old man dead.

It took Slater half an hour to bring Mrs. Budaslavich up to speed. Going through the Tuomi boy's version, pointing out the conflicts in the story by reference to the evidence the BCA had found. Missing footprints, differing rifle cartridges and slugs. Presenting the notion that her husband had been killed deliberately. Not an accident. The widow listened. She remained silent, emotionless.

She did not cry because she'd shed her tears at the funeral. Now her husband rested beneath the cold, cruel dirt of the Catholic Cemetery of St. Catherine's in Aurora. After the Mass for the dead, after some nice words from Father Joki, Adam Budaslavich was lowered into a grave and covered with dirt. That's when the tears ended for her. Despite the absence of tears, Slater guessed the woman's pain was still there, behind a mask and private, not for public display.

The widow Budaslavich looked up from her pale, venous hands and spoke in a nervous, uncertain voice:

"But why, Deputy Slater? Why would anyone want to kill Adam? He didn't fight with nobody. Didn't have any enemies. Why?"

It was obvious from her expression that Mrs. Budaslavich was truly puzzled.

Chen cleared his throat.

"Ma'am, that's why we're here. To try and find out anything about your husband that might be helpful, anything that signifies a possibility. We need to detail everything you knew about him, anything you can tell us about where Adam was on the day he died, who he spoke to and saw. Anything you know might help."

"Well, like I told the deputies when they were here, isn't much to really say. He's worked at Erie Mining, now LTV, up in Hoyt Lakes since 1955. That's the year he came here from Yugoslavia. Left because of threats from the communists. Never spoke much about his life there beyond that. I could tell it was too painful. Never spoke about the war or his family."

Mrs. Budaslavich looked across the coffee table at Slater. The Deputy thought the widow was seeking the comfort of another woman's support, perhaps searching for a soul mate as she struggled to deal with the reality of her husband's death once more.

"We met in 1956, went together three months. Knew we were right for each other. Built this house in 1958, children after that. He never got laid off, even when the mines were shut down. He could fix anything, any machinery. His boss didn't want him to retire because he could take parts others would throw away and make them work," she reported with a slight tremor to her words.

Her eyes drifted away from the police officers and focused absently on something beyond the glass of the living room's big picture window, the edges of the glass framed in white hoarfrost. She hesitated, then began anew:

"Cut pulp every winter. Used Frank Hauptman's skidder and flatbed. Frank was his best friend. He's got a little 3.2 beer tavern over on Comstock Lake.

Good German food. Anyway, Adam still cut pulp into his 70's, never tired, never slowed down. Outside of Frank and a few fellows at work or at the Moose in Aurora, he didn't have too many friends. Can't tell you much more than that."

She turned her attention back into the room and stared intently at Inspector Chen. A single tear ran down the right side of her nose, poised in space to fall to the floor.

"How 'bout the day he died, Ma'am? Do you know where was that day?" Slater's voice was respectful. She didn't want to offend the widow by appearing demanding. She asked the question as gently as possible. The old woman stood and smoothed her dress. Picking up the empty coffee cups from the table, she walked into the kitchen, and looked out a window. Her eyes swept past the metal storage building, past the yard-a small rectangle of grass cut out of the spruce jungle, past her private, orderly world and into the vastness of the forest. After a time, Mrs. Budaslavich turned to face the officers. She seemed composed, her voice once again calm:

"I think Adam left the house about 4:30 in the morning. Went to his hunting spot over there by the Wasoose. He didn't make lunch. I would have found a mess left for me to clean if he had."

A small smile came across her lips.

"I don't know for sure, but I'd guess he went to Frank's for lunch. Maybe a glass of tap beer. Hamburger, you know. That sort of thing.

He wasn't with anyone. He hunted alone. Said he could think better. The woods were like being in church for him," the widow said, clearly finished in her revelations.

Slater nodded and offered:

"Thanks your patience. I can't imagine what this has been like for you, Ma'am."

The officers rose from their chairs to leave. As she passed the old woman, Slater gently placed her hand on Mrs. Budaslavich's shoulder. Her gesture was fleeting, just enough to let the woman know she cared. Chen shuffled out in silence, obviously uncomfortable in the situation. Not knowing the right words to say, he said nothing. He simply closed the door.

Slater spoke first as they drove the twenty minutes to Comstock Lake:

"Phil, did you notice anything unusual about the place. I mean, the way it was furnished, the details?"

She was betting to herself he hadn't, that he'd been so uncomfortable talking to the old lady he hadn't taken in his surroundings. She was wrong.

"I know what you're getting at. Those dishes she was serving us out of, my mom's got a set just like'em. Some kind of fancy china, isn't it?"

"Bone china, Phil. English bone china."

"Yeah, that's it. Same stuff mom has, though this lady has a lot more of it. Did you see the furniture, God I've never seen a real leather recliner like that outside a catalog. How in the world could a working stiff like Budaslavich afford all that stuff?"

Slater thought as she drove. She was pleased that Phil Chen had come to the same realization that she had, a realization that there was more to Adam Budaslavich than one could learn from a glance.

"Did you check out the photos? I missed them when Dave and I were there. Too busy gawking at the prints and paintings. I can't imagine how those two saved up enough to visit Russia, Australia and most of Europe on his salary, no matter how good the guy was with his hands. Hell, I've never been out of the country except to Canada."

Chen was about to say something when a rut caused the squad to toss wildly about. Slater shook her head, abruptly cutting the conversation short.

"Gotta keep my focus on this damn road," she indicated.

It was true. She had to concentrate on negotiating the vehicle around potholes, big potholes, pits in the road that made the squad bounce and swerve nearly out of control, while trying to anticipate the innumerable sharp angles which narrowed the road to one lane at the corners. Cognizant that they would have a long walk to the nearest farmhouse if they went in the ditch, she slowed down.

They pulled into the parking lot of the Comstock Lake Inn. Slater noticed it was quiet. There were no cars in the lot except a Cadillac Seville. The car was near new and rich burgundy in color. She guessed the car belonged to the owner, the German. She had expected to see other vehicles, belonging to a hunter or two, who'd come in from the wind and the November chill for a sandwich, a tap beer. Curiously, the Caddie was the only car in the lot.

Though it was noon, a mercury vapor lamp burned dimly over the gravel parking area. A dusting of last night's snow remained undisturbed along the cement walk up to the tavern. The snow bore no footprints. The sign hanging on the wooden screen door read:

Open Daily
6:30 a.m.–1:00 p.m.
Monday through Saturday
Closed Sundays

The place should have been open. It looked closed. There were no lights on. Slater opened the screen door and tried the tarnished brass knob of the interior door with her gloved hand. The door was constructed of crudely hewn planks of white pine held together by blackened hardware. The wood itself was varnished and shiny.

She found the main door unlocked. She pushed. The hinges creaked eerily as the door swung in. Walking through the portal, Slater expected to be met by warmth. Instead, it was cold, colder than outside. It didn't feel like the heat was on, or had been on for quite some time. Chen slipped in behind her and flicked on the lights.

Across the room, the bar stood, covering one wall. Because it was a 3.2 beer joint, there were no liquor bottles lined up behind the bar, only a mirror and several dozen beer glasses. A couple of tappers for 3.2 beer kegs were hidden under the counter. Trophies and plaques crowded the available wall space surrounding the oval mirror. Multi-colored fishing lures hung from the ceiling on thick wooden pegs. The pegs were coated with the same thick, dark varnish that protected the log walls. The lures were for sale, just like the pork rinds, the beef jerky, the pigs' feet, the spicy sausage, the chips and the candy bars. The later items were lined up, neatly displayed, in their cardboard cartons or jars along the bar.

The planked pine floor was clean, spotless; it was well polished and newly swept. Behind the bar, Slater heard a tiny scratching sound, followed by a muffled scurry. A deer mouse popped its head out from atop the back bar, its oversized ears twitching. The mouse darted behind a dust-covered fishing trophy and disappeared.

Five tables with four chairs each defined a small eating area. The tables were set with napkins, utensils, catsup, mustard, salt and pepper. The tavern was clearly ready for business. And yet, there was no business to be had. A great stone fireplace occupied one wall. Wood for a fire was stacked neatly on the fire irons but had not been lit.

Chen walked over to the bar. The counter had been wiped clean, the ashtrays emptied. Nothing seemed out of place. Slater left the main room and checked the solitary, unisex restroom. Entering the darkened lavatory, she called out:

"Hello? Anyone here?"

There was no answer. The faint echo of her voice replied off the log walls and rafters. The moose head over the fireplace didn't respond.

Searching the small kitchen, Chen noted that all the plates, pots, pans and cooking equipment were clean and put away. Nothing appeared out of order. The kitchen appeared ready for a new day's activities. The BCA Agent noticed a small door, off the kitchen, labeled "Pantry". He tried to push the door open but it stopped short, blocked by something. Spreading his legs, Chen braced his trailing foot and put all of his back, buttocks and weight into the door. It opened generously. Slater approached. Straining her eyes in the dim light of the pantry, she sought to make out the contents of the room's interior. The shelves were stocked with staples: crackers, cereal, noodles and canned goods.

She discerned the outline of a man's shoe. Chen fumbled along the interior of the pantry looking for a light switch. He couldn't find one. Slater's eyes became more accustomed to the darkness. It wasn't long before she was able to determine that the shoe she was staring at was still attached to its owner.

The two officers crouched alongside the corpse. Slater guessed they'd found what was once Frank Hauptman. He was lying face down, spread eagle on the cold concrete floor, arms outstretched to either side of his torso. His back was torn open. A single bullet appeared to have ripped through his blue flannel shirt, saturating his apron with blood. The scene looked curiously familiar.

Chapter 9

November 11, 1991

Sheriff Dan Prescott and Detective Al Pagotti waited patiently for Slater and Chen to explain what they were doing investigating a death that was officially assigned to Deb Slater's superior. From her brief conversation with the Sheriff on the phone, Slater could sense that her boss was unappreciative that Frank Hauptman had been discovered murdered in his own bar. What had begun as a routine hunting accident now appeared to be substantially more than that. Pagotti was a simple man. Complexities annoyed him. The death of Hauptman made everything far more difficult.

The similarities between the two deaths made it so. One shot, through the heart. Slater could tell by Dan Prescott's voice on the other end of the phone when he called her that the Sheriff was substantially pissed off. He berated her for not running the investigation by Pagotti. She also sensed the Sheriff was curious, curious to hear more about the two dead men who'd been friends.

Slater was uneasy as she rode the elevator up to Prescott's office. She'd been off duty, investigating a suspected homicide that wasn't assigned to her, accompanied by a BCA agent who had no real authority to do anything at all. And then there was the fact that she hadn't bothered to tell her own partner, Swanson, what she was up to.

"I'm in deep shit," she thought. The elevator bell chimed. The door opened. "Deep shit," she muttered to herself walking out into the hallway.

Phil Chen looked at her quizzically, trying to hear what she said. She didn't repeat it. Chen shrugged his shoulders and followed her down the hall to Prescott's office.

Pagotti and the Sheriff were situated behind the Sheriff's big oak desk. Prescott sat in his chair, swinging the quarter-sawn oak antique back and forth in nervous anticipation. Pagotti leaned against a window ledge. The desktop was clear of all the paperwork that routinely cluttered it. The desk was clear of budget estimates, of arrest reports; clear of anything distracting or intrusive. Slater saw the telltale condition of Prescott's desk as she walked through the open door. She didn't like it. The desk being clean meant Sheriff Dan was ready for a limited agenda. And She and Chen were it. The BCA officer closed the glass door behind them. Slater picked the chair closest to Prescott, trying to insulate Chen by interjecting her body between the Sheriff and the Agent. Her friend sat down next to her and began to speak, carefully measuring his words:

"Dan, I know you and Al want an explanation as to what the hell I'm doing up here, out of my laboratory, wasting my time on some dead deer hunter, stirring up trouble."

It was obvious he hoped his speaking first would defuse the two superiors. Slater was sure it was having the opposite effect. She watched Pagotti's face turn from merely pink to scarlet as Chen spoke. It didn't seem to faze Chen. He kept going:

"I'm sure Deb told you, turns out the old guy, Budaslavich, he was bumped off. Deliberately shot. The Tuomi kid had nothin' to do with it. Nothin' to do with the guy dying at all. 9mm got him, foreign job. World War II vintage. Footprints were wiped clean by the killer, backtracked to make it look like Budaslavich was the only one around."

Pagotti's face lost some of its color as he listened. He was interested. Prescott was another matter. Slater couldn't tell whether the Sheriff was still intrigued by the tale or was merely being polite.

"Killer slipped a 30.06 casing under the body to complete the illusion. Nearly perfect. Nearly."

Chen paused again to gauge his audience's reaction. The two superiors remained silent. Chen plunged ahead:

"So Deb and I decided, rightly or wrongly, after going over this stuff, decided to see the widow. She fills us in on a relationship with Hauptman, tells us it's likely her husband was there for lunch the day he died. So we show up there. And Hauptman greets us face down in the pantry with a 9mm hole through his chest. Laid out stiff as a board, no evidence he even knew what hit him. Near as I can tell, the slug we pulled out of the pantry wall and the cartridge we found there match those from the Wasoose. But no fingerprints. No footprints. Everything spick and span, wiped clean. Not nearly perfect. This time the killer got it perfect."

He'd rambled on without a breath until he was forced to stop for air. The men across the desk studied the BCA Agent with less than friendly eyes.

The Legacy

"That's it in a nutshell. Maybe we should've cleared seeing the old lady with Pagotti, to avoid stepping on toes. But going it alone was my idea. Thought we should hit it quick, while the old mind was ticking. That was my idea, plowing ahead. Not Deb's."

He lied a little, looked at Slater, hoping she'd appreciate him taking the heat.

"That's not true, Dan. Phil's taking too much on himself. I was just as gung-ho on this as he was. I wanted to get out there and take a second look, see Mrs. Budaslavich, follow up with Hauptman," the deputy reported.

She was looking directly into Prescott's eyes and she knew her approach, taking the blame, was working. Her honesty unnerved her boss. He looked away.

"It's my fault Al and Swanny weren't in on it. I just thought it'd be a lot easier and cleaner if Phil and I just poked around."

Deb Slater knew she was perspiring because beads of sweat were rolling down her upper arms. She knew Pagotti would never buy an explanation of any sort from her. She also knew she couldn't tell Prescott the real reason she'd stepped out on her own; it would be unprofessional to point out Pagotti's lack of work ethic, lack of interest in doing a thorough job and his incompetence in this setting. She braced for a response.

Prescott wasn't about to reprimand Slater. She didn't know it, but he'd already grown tired of Al Pagotti's slow decline into mediocrity. He wasn't angry, at least not with Slater for bypassing Pagotti. He was angry that she'd excluded her partner. Swanson was a good cop, a hard worker, the kind of guy who'd appreciate being shown his first inclination was wrong, that there was more to what happened out on the Wasoose than was obvious. But his partner had ignored him. That kind of disregard for a partner could cause a rift, could split up a good team.

"O.K. Slater, I accept that you and Chen are equally to blame. But you did some good police work here. You two put together physical facts that make sense out of a pile of crap that made none. But you left Swanson out in the cold. Your own partner, for Chrissake. That can cause problems, real problems. And you didn't keep your direct supervisor informed. Sergeant Pagotti's got the right to know what's going on in his unit, on his own file. You two used poor judgment. I'll let it slide on this one because no one got hurt. But from now on, you'd better walk the straight and narrow, by the book."

His voice was cold, hard-edged. But both Chen and Slater could tell from his posture, his body language, that the display was more for show, more for Pagotti, than anything.

Prescott leaned away from the desk and looked at the ceiling.

"One last thing. You keep Al here informed about anything you find, any hunch you have, any hard evidence you dig up. Got it?"

The Sheriff suppressed a smile as he caught a glimpse of the Italian's profile: lips pursed, cheeks bulging, like Pagotti was trying to control an explosion. The Detective wanted satisfaction, wanted Slater and Chen called on the carpet, whipped like dogs. Prescott made it clear that wasn't going to happen.

"Now, take a hike," Prescott commanded.

Chen and Slater left quickly. Behind the glass of the closed door, they could see Pagotti gesturing wildly. They could hear his voice rumble off the drywall. Dan Prescott sat looking at the officer, slowly shaking his head from side to side. It was clear from a distance that the Sheriff was not supporting Pagotti's pleas for justice, for obedience.

Slater and Chen walked rapidly down the hall to avoid riding the elevator with Pagotti.

"Al's really burned up. I can't believe Prescott let us off like this. I mean, sure I'm not one of his. But I know better. You know better. We should be working all this through the fat man. Did you see his eyes bulge? Man, he looked like a frog with a firecracker in him."

Chen chuckled out loud. Slater gave him a stern look.

"Very funny Phil. But from now on, we keep Pagotti advised. And Swanny. Prescott's right. He's my partner, I've gotta keep harmony in the family."

On the second floor, they found Swanson looking over another deputy's shoulder in the lunchroom.

The two men were studying Miss March, Ms. Elizabeth Violet Hollander, who hailed from Sweetwater, Texas. Slater glanced at the fetching Miss Hollander in the altogether and grunted in disgust. Swanson saw she was behind him and flushed red. Miss Hollander disappeared in a flurry of paper.

"Weren't you paying attention at the sexual harassment seminar, Swanson?" Deputy Slater queried.

Her partner, embarrassed, his face slowly returning to flesh tones, remained silent. The three officers entered Slater and Swanson's cubicle.

"Mind if I have a look at Hauptman's personal effects?" Chen inquired.

"Sure but there's not much of interest," Swanson replied, dumping the contents of a small manila envelope onto his desk.

Hauptman's personal property made a very small pile. A plain brown leather wallet. Fifty dollars in cash. Small change. MasterCard. Driver's license. Assorted other cards. A small religious medal. Silver chain. Silver medallion. St. Thomas. St. Christopher. Something like that. Chen couldn't really tell as he held it to the light. It was inscribed on the reverse, in a language he could not read.

Chen and Slater hadn't inventoried Hauptman's possessions at the tavern. They left that for the detectives. They checked the scene, determined that the cash register was still locked and found the key still attached to a ring hanging from Hauptman's belt. Three hundred odd dollars in cash and checks were found in the till. They had ruled out robbery as a motive. But they had not done a detailed inventory of the man's pockets or his wallet. They hadn't seen his personal effects until Swanson dumped them on his desk.

Chen quietly examined the medal while the two deputies checked the other items against an inventory sheet. He lifted the object, gazed at it. The necklace was finely crafted, delicate, light to the touch, a mere wafer of silver, no larger in size and weight than a communion host. He looked at Slater. She caught his eyes and recognized that the BCA Agent was onto something. She slid her chair next to him. Without a word, he handed the medal to her. She looked at it closely for the first time. Her eyes focused on the inscription. Turning the medallion over, she concentrated on the likeness etched on the obverse.

She had seen this medal before in the personal effects of Adam Budaslavich. The emblem hung, suspended in midair, spinning in Deb Slater's hand on a thin mesh chain. Like a mysterious top on a string, it twirled in the light, over and over and over.

A medal. A face of someone they did not recognize and could not place. And one word. A one word puzzle connecting the bodies of two old men. As the medallion slowed to a stop in her hand, Debra Slater handed the artifact to Dave Swanson. It was late. The significance of the pendants would have to wait for another day.

Slater was tired. It was after five and she was due for a back rub.

"I think I'll call it a day and head for home. I need to get some sleep. See you tomorrow."

Her partner smiled.

"See Ya Deb. Phil and I are gonna go get a beer or two." .

Phil Chen smiled, nodding in agreement.

"Night Deb," he said.

"Night Phil. Keep Dave out of trouble."

She pulled the sleeves of her winter coat over her arms and left, walking down the hall to the elevator. Slater rode an elevator car to the top floor of the concrete parking ramp and stepped out into the dank cold.

Behind her, in the dim fluorescent glow of the cubicle, Chen and Swanson stared at the medal in silence, as if hoping divine intervention would tell them its secrets. After a minute or two, Swanson carefully tucked all of Frank Hauptman's possessions, including the medal, back into their manila resting-place.

Tired, thirsty, and in need of relaxation, the two officers headed for Eddie's Place to have a beer and talk about Miss March's vision for world peace.

Though unplanned, somewhere during the night, after two or three beers brightened their intellects, they talked further about Adam Budaslavich and Frank Hauptman. About why anyone would want to murder two old men in the middle of nowhere. But even the beer didn't help answer their questions.

The Legacy

Chapter 10

November 12, 1991

Deputy Dave Swanson sat at a table at the Comstock Lake Inn surrounded by piles of paper; Frank Hauptman's life as represented by financial records, tax returns and bank receipts. A mountain of paper cascaded from the table onto the varnished floor.

After obtaining a search warrant, the Deputies spent hours combing through the dead man's living quarters, looking through his desk and file cabinets; probing for something, anything, that would tell them about the life of Frank Hauptman.

Another visit to the widow Budaslavich provided no further leads. There seemed to be no link between the two men's deaths other than their friendship.

From conversations with neighbors on the lake, mostly seasonal cabin users, those in and out of their lakehomes on weekends to ice fish or hunt, the deputies were unable to find another soul who claimed Frank Hauptman as a friend, or claimed to know any details about the man's life.

One neighbor described him as moody, grumpy. Another called him a hermit; plainly satisfied to open the tavern every morning, wait on patrons with a gruff, "Vat do you Vant?" and do little more. Few of the locals bothered to talk to the man outside of ordering beer or food while in his place. Even talk about the weather or fishing seemed to irritate Hauptman.

Swanson's indepth conversations with Mrs. Budaslavich on these points puzzled him. The widow maintained that her visits with Hauptman were always pleasant. She thought that his thick German accent made people uneasy, wary. His naturally gruff manner and speech, she believed, came from his upbringing in Germany. It wasn't his personality but his heritage that forged a distance between the man and his patrons.

To the widow and her husband, Hauptman had always appeared to be a charming host and a good friend. Single, Hauptman was never interested in Mrs. B's eligible woman friends. Adam always insisted it was because Hauptman lost his wife to an allied air strike during the war, only a few months after their marriage. It was her husband's contention that Hauptman simply lost his ability to love after that. Even still, Mrs. Budaslavich admitted that Hauptman was a recluse. He kept to himself the majority of the time. He was not one to volunteer anything about himself or to step out of the shadows.

Hauptman's books and records were standard fare. The tavern eked out money year after year but it wasn't much. A net of fifteen or twenty thousand a year. No mortgage. No frills. No financial indicators sufficient to cause Swanson to suspect excessive debt or money problems were involved in the man's death.

The one oddity was the dead man's ability to take frequent, extensive trips abroad. Trips to South America. Europe. Hawaii. Australia. All apparently paid for in cash. No large credit balances of any type. It didn't fit the image Hauptman portrayed to his customers.

Deb Slater concentrated on Hauptman's personal effects. A few photographs. No letters to speak of. Citizenship papers showing that Hauptman became an U.S. citizen in 1955. 1955. The year caught her eye. The same year Adam Budaslavich came to the United States from Yugoslavia. She looked more carefully at the documents. She needed to follow up regarding the German's American citizenship. The dates were too coincidental. Another link where there had appeared to be none. Another piece of evidence defining the relationship between the two dead men. Or perhaps, nothing.

"Deb, these bank and tax records aren't too interesting. Guy made a few bucks, spent hardly anything other than for travel. Can't seem to find his savings and checking ledgers though. Other than that, simple cash in, cash out existence. No bad loans, no red ink."

As he spoke, Swanson was looking at a safety deposit key envelope. The envelope sat on the table, partially covered by last year's tax returns.

"Funny," he thought, "I didn't see that before."

Small and inconspicuous the key had been lost in the avalanche of paper. "First National Bank of Minneapolis" was printed across the face of the envelope, a brass clasp fastening the flap down. Swanson picked the envelope up. He knew there should be two keys inside. Two keys to a box owned by Mr. Hauptman. Opening it, he found a single brass key.

He closed the clasp and placed the envelope in a plastic evidence bag.

Something to check out. Maybe a long shot. You could easily misplace a small key like that. But then again, maybe it was significant. He'd tell Slater about it later.

His partner continued to plod through the personal effects. Most of the photos Hauptman possessed were relatively new and showed the tavern; stringers of crappies caught from Comstock, the fish held up in front of smiling vacationers, customers of the resort next door that had once been part of the bar, once owned by Hauptman. Pictures of deer shot in the recent past, their bellies slit, their bodies hanging from the big oak tree in front of the inn. Smiling hunters surrounding the dead animals as they swung, stiff and cold suspended in the air by rope.

"Brutal," she thought. "Wanton killing for killing's sake."

Disgusted, she tossed the photos aside.

Thumbing through the remaining papers, she pieced together bits and pieces of the man's life. She guessed it to be a lonely, solitary existence of little joy. A calendar notepad. Doodles of cartoon characters. Odd geometric shapes drawn in the margins. Shopping lists, the items scratched off as the orders were apparently filled. A few telephone numbers. Budaslavich's name and number. Neatly printed on November 1. A small portion of the calendar was missing, torn away near its edge. And next to it, beneath the date, a notation under Budaslavich's name:

"J. Johnson to meet Adam. Call Adam."

J.Johnson? She'd seen the name somewhere before in connection with the case.

Slater walked over to the evidence envelopes arranged in front of Swanson. Some of the clear plastic bags contained the personal effects of Adam Budaslavich that had been previously inventoried and tagged.

She couldn't contain herself. Fumbling with the zip–lock of one of the bags, she was desperate to confirm what she'd seen before in Swanson's hands back at the Courthouse, in the cubicle. Slowing herself down, she dug deep into the personal property for a well–worn leather wallet that she knew must be in the bag. As her fingers felt it's soft, cool texture, she exhaled.

The dead man's billfold bore the monogram "A.B." stamped into the black cover. In one of the hidden compartments, she found what she was looking for:

a small crumpled slip of paper, made of the same fiber as Hauptman's calendar. She held the scrap of paper up in front of her. The piece fit the missing portion of the calendar exactly and bore information in the same pen:

J. Johnson. (219) 777–3333.

The same name, linked to both dead men, linked by the calendar to the day Adam Budaslavich died. She slid the torn piece of paper into the corresponding space on the calendar. She called Swanson over.

There was no doubt in Deb Slater's mind that J. Johnson, whoever he might be, had something to do with at least one, and possibly two, murders. But though she believed she now knew the who and the how, she still did not know the why.

The Legacy

Chapter 11

November 13, 1991

"I'm sorry, that number is no longer in service. No further information is available for number 777–3333."

Click. The recording ended. Dave Swanson placed the receiver down and looked across the conference table at his partner.

"I told you the number would be disconnected."

Swanson's attitude wasn't helped by the hangover he was nursing from last night's bowling outing with the boys. The fact that the number was inoperative only made his head pound worse. He looked at Slater through the heavy fog surrounding his brain, the alcohol rolling off of him like steam off of a pond. His voice carried an edge of impatience:

"Why don't you see if you can follow–up on Hauptman's citizenship. Maybe take a look at Budaslavich's papers as well."

Having been around her partner when he'd over done a good time, Deb Slater knew better than to say anything, knew better than to kid him. She simply nodded and left the room. His solitude affirmed, Swanson clumsily picked up the phone and called his contact at the Phone Company. He asked if they would run down the address of the last person using the disconnected phone number. He hoped he could uncover the address without having to obtain a warrant. He could get a search warrant if necessary. He wanted to skate through the day if possible, hit the road home early and get some sleep.

Deb Slater went right to work on the details of Hauptman's immigration into the United States in 1955. She dialed the local INS office in Minneapolis. A nasal toned female voice told her that the records that far back would have to come through Washington.

"That," intoned the emotionless voice, "could take months. Years. Data privacy, etc... Best to contact INS in Washington. Blah, blah, blah."

Slater tried to be polite as the voice rambled on, disgorging irrelevant information. She'd heard the same voice, the same drone from hundreds of city, county and state bureaucrats over the years.

"Thanks for all your help."

She hung up on the woman, cursing under her breath.

Instead of spending useless hours, maybe days, trying to find the right person in Washington at INS, she called Herb Whitefeather. Herb was the sole FBI agent assigned to the Bureau's Duluth office. A big man, six foot six, two hundred and thirty pounds, he'd played pro basketball in the ABA when there'd been a franchise in the state, briefly playing forward for the Minnesota Muskies, long after the Lakers had left; long before the Timberwolves were conceived.

Herb was receptive to Slater's call. He'd been kept informed of the murder investigation as a matter of professional courtesy. Not every detail but enough to make sure the FBI could crank up its machinery if need be. Herb said he'd contact a pal in the DC offices of the Bureau to see if the INS couldn't fax key documents from Hauptman's file to Herb's Duluth office. As they talked, Slater also asked Herb to check on Adam Budaslavich's file as well.

"Might as well call in as many favors as you can, Herb," she quipped.

"I'll give it my best, Deb," the agent promised.

Through the rapidly dissipating remnants of his hangover, Swanson managed to track down the address behind the disconnected phone number. 501 5th Avenue West. Room 102B. Swanson recognized it as the Happy Holidays Inn. A ten-dollar-a-night, fifty-bucks-a-week apartment building located in the City's Central Hillside neighborhood. Seedy and derelict, the building had been condemned for human habitation countless times. It often served as transitional housing for impoverished families; families cramped together in one room efficiency units. The Happy Holidays boasted substandard electrical and plumbing, and was a haven for the vagrants, drunks and the less desirable elements of the City. Swanson had been there many times to back up the City police in response to domestic violence, rape and assault calls. He'd seen bodies punctured with bullet and knife wounds, sometimes those of small children, dragged from its rooms.

Swanson craned his neck into the cubicle, told Slater where he was headed.

"Not without me, you aren't," she responded.

Swanson, too tired to complain, waited for her.

It was a short walk to the old, rambling four-story brick building. The Inn had once been a stately vacation haven for tourists. At the turn of the century, visitors from the Cities and Iowa flocked to Duluth in the summer. The tourists basked in cool Lake Superior breezes, attempting to escape the sizzling heat and high humidity of summer in the Corn Belt.

In its prime, each room had been elegantly furnished, equipped with an ornate fireplace and expensive crystal light fixtures. Carefully pruned rose and lilac bushes once bloomed along the blue stone foundation, accenting delicate cedar lattice beneath a covered porch. Now the place was run down and dirty. Bricks hung loose from the mortar. Broken stairs punctuated the once stately front entry. Stains discolored the ornate carvings and woodwork underneath the eaves. Moss grew full and green beneath the shingles. Where roses once flourished, beer cans and wine bottles occupied the scant snow around long-dead bushes.

A poorly painted sign tacked to the front door indicated the office was inside. Slater and Swanson stepped into the building, escaping the light drizzle that was falling. Sitting behind an antique counter, the manager stared at a tiny black and white TV. Her hair was in curlers. The woman appeared matronly and unkempt. A steady diet of pastries and fried foods had lead to the lady's decline, a decline that matched that of the building she was in charge of.

Swanson showed the manager his badge and a search warrant for the room. Mrs. Tinsley, Agnes she said her name was, grunted in annoyance at the intrusion:

"Yeah, I can show you his room. Ain't gonna do you much good though. He's long gone. Left a day or so ago. No notice."

"Did he say where he was headed?" Swanson asked hopefully.

"Hell no, I never even talked to him about his leaving. Like I said, he just up and left."

"We'd appreciate seeing his room, all the same," the Deputy continued.

"No problem, I can walk you down there."

The woman stood up, pushing the hem of her dress down to cover her milky white thighs. Slater smiled as she watched Agnes struggle out of the easy chair. The worn casters of the chair creaked as the woman's great weight was released.

Mrs. Tinsley turned the lock to room 102B and opened it:

"Empty, just like I told you," she asserted with an air of self-importance in a voice sounding very much like the croak of a toad.

"This guy, Johnson, paid cash for the days he stayed. In advance. Got to do it that way with these creeps," she offered in a less prideful tone.

She stepped inside and motioned the officers in.

"Funny, though. He wasn't like the others we get here. He was well mannered, handsome, well dressed. He didn't fit the decor, if you know what I mean."

Slater stood next to the portly landlady, listening to the woman's description of the man they were looking for. Swanson drifted into the room, looking it over.

The old woman went on to describe Johnson as Slater took notes: Forty to forty-five. Medium build. Dark eyes, maybe black or deep brown. Brown hair with a touch of gray at the sideburns. Nondescript except for his penetrating eyes, the old woman said.

"He rented the place for a week. Paid for a private phone. I found that odd. But here, you get used to odd. Anyway, a day ago, I'm walking by and I decided to talk to him about something that had bothered me. I find the door unlocked. I pokes my nose in. He's gone. No notice, no nothing. Just vanished."

Mrs. Tinsley was obviously fatigued from the ordeal of recalling events. She shuffled over to an overstuffed chair, plopped her buttocks down and let out a groan. Slater walked by the woman, watching her partner inventory the place.

A bare 75-watt light bulb hung dangerously from its wiring, illuminating the room. Other than the chair occupied by the puffing form of Mrs. Tinsley, the place was virtually empty. A couple of old Rockwell reproductions were tacked to the cracked plaster walls. A beat up pullout couch that doubled as a bed took up the greater portion of the living room. Mouse droppings surrounded the feet of the upholstered furniture. Black and white linoleum tile defined the eating area. Two folding chairs and a card table sat atop the tile, along with combination sink, stove and refrigerator, all 1940's vintage. Remarkably, the appliances were clean. There were no dirty dishes. All the utensils and plates were stacked neatly in open shelves. The walls of the kitchenette were painted a bright canary yellow, here and there streaked brown by cooking grease.

An interior wall separated the unit from its bath. The lavatory walls were decorated with cheap ceramic tile, each square a bright bluebird blue. The tiny bathroom contained a toilet, a sink, and a tub. There was no shower. Rust marks from the antique pipes stained the porcelain of the tub, sink and toilet near the drains. Again, the room was empty and clean.

The officers looked around the tiny rooms. They checked the single closet, the sparse drawers in the kitchen. They opened the couch. Nothing—they found nothing. No scrap of paper. No cigarette butts. No trace of anything left behind to show who or what J. Johnson was. They were at another dead end.

Slater noted that Mrs. Tinsley was no longer in the room. She'd apparently left; presumably having grown tired of their search. Slater flicked off the light as they left Room 102B.

They followed the decaying sidewalk back to the front of the building to say their good-byes, to leave their cards with the manager. As Slater handed her a card, the old woman pulled out a large cardboard box from beneath her desk. Looking at Slater with one eye, her other crazily focused on the television, the manager began to talk to Slater, her voice muffled by a ham and rye sandwich occupying most of her mouth:

"I found this here empty box in Johnson's room after he left. Seemed too good a box to simply toss out. You want it for somethin'?"

Slater reached out and accepted the container, a box that had not so long ago held a new pair of size 12 Sorel Northlanders. Johnson had purchased new boots. The same size as Adam Budaslavich.

"Thank you Ma'am." This is important. Thanks for remembering it."

Slater tucked the box under her arm and was about to leave when she recalled her earlier discussion with Ms. Tinsley.

"Ma'am, you said you were coming to talk to Johnson about something that bothered you. That's when you noticed he was gone. Do you remember why you were going to see him?"

Slater was leaning up against the counter, studying the manager. Hoping she'd never look that way, never allow herself to fall apart like that. Varicose veins. Mismatched nylons. Crumpled, dirty dress. Swanson stood behind his partner still within hearing distance though not intruding upon the conversation.

"Like I was telling you, I didn't like him leaving his windows open. Especially when he had that hunting rifle in plain view. Any kid could just climb right in and steal it. Then you cops would be in a hell of a mess. Can't trust these kids 'round here a lick. I was coming down to tell him to keep his windows locked."

Mrs. Tinsley was standing with her hands on her hips looking vastly more confident, more important then she'd been only a minute before.

Slater tried to suppress the urgent interest in her voice.

"Rifle, what sort of a rifle?"

Slater and Swanson looked at each other, trying not to telegraph the importance of what the old woman had to say, hoping she'd relay the facts and not exaggerate.

"I don't know. It was long. Black. Wooden underneath. Telescope on top. And a round–thing–a–ma–job on the end. Like a car muffler or something. With little holes in it. Never seen one like it before. Saw it a couple of times. Kept it right out in the open. By the couch. Figured he was going deer hunting."

It was clear that the lady's powers of observation had been honed to a fine edge, enhanced by years of living in the toughest part of the City.

"Thanks again, Ma'am. You've got our cards. If you think of anything else, give us a call. O.K.?" Swanson requested.

"Sure thing, officer, sure thing."

They walked back out into the November day. The drizzle had turned to sleet. An off–lake wind blew ice pellets into their faces as they struggled back to the Courthouse. They fought to keep their faces covered, proceeding gingerly down the dilapidated stairs of the porch. Mrs. Tinsley's form lumbered out into the cold behind them. Her booming voice called out to the officers over the noise of the gale:

"One last thing. This Johnson. His last name was sort of peculiar. Didn't match him. I mean, I heard him talking on the phone when I was cleaning the room next to his. Walls are paper-thin, separate what used to be one big apartment into two small ones. Anyway, he was talking Russian or something like that. Thought you'd want to know."

Before Swanson could launch a followup question, Mrs. Tinsley was gone, having retreated to the relative warmth of the Inn.

Swanson looked over the edge of his collar at his partner. Standing on the hillside, the ice stung their faces as it fell. Their visit with Ms. Tinsley had been fruitful. They now knew that "J. Johnson" was a man. Medium build. Good–looking. That was all relatively clear.

What wasn't so clear was the rest of what they'd learned. Upon the best information they had, Johnson was also Russian–speaking, had taken up temporary residence in Duluth, Minnesota, all the while carrying a sniper's rifle, equipped with a silencer, for the sole apparent purpose of stalking and killing two very old and ostensibly harmless men.

It made Deb Slater wonder if Ms. Tinsley might not have watched a bit too much TV.

Chapter 12

November 14, 1991

Slater's phone call to Phillip Chen regarding the safety deposit box caught the BCA investigator off–guard. He thought he'd seen the last of his active participation in the case. Sheriff Prescott seemed to suggest as much during their last little "chat" in Duluth. But Chen wasn't about to ignore Deb Slater.

The envelope with the remaining safety deposit key and the warrant arrived two days after the call. It was easier, quicker, for someone in Minneapolis to inventory the box than to send a St. Louis County Deputy to do the job. It was also budget time. Chen was happy to oblige.

Minneapolis had survived the first major storm of winter with little ill effect. A few inches of snow remained on the ground as Chen drove I–94 from St. Paul to Minneapolis. Traffic was light, at least by Chen's standards. He'd been raised in the bumper to bumper chaos of California's expressways. As he drove, Chen thought about the Twins opener coming next spring, wondered if they'd ever get back to the Series. Knew their chances were poor. They'd be lucky to break .500. He'd play more golf.

He pulled up the off-ramp near First National of Minneapolis, the warrant and the safety deposit key secure in his briefcase. The attaché was a nice brown imitation snakeskin piece. A Christmas present from his mom two years ago, the case looked ten years old. He parked the unmarked squad car and walked down the four flights of stairs of the ramp, emerging into bright sunlight. It was warm, thirty-five degrees. The snow was melting, running downgrade, pooling into little lakes and streams along the curbs. Gathering force, the water rushed along until it disappeared in massive storm drains, eventually emptying into the Mississippi River somewhere near St. Anthony Falls.

The melting snow painted a false portrait, gave one a false sense of security. He knew spring wasn't in the picture. Spring was four and a half months away. He dodged the puddles on the sidewalk as he approached the bank lobby. He wasn't quick enough. His wingtips got wet.

At First National, he took the elevator to the subbasement, to the safety deposit level. A mature woman greeted him from behind a plate glass window.

The Legacy

Her voice crackled over a tinny speaker:

"May I help you sir?"

She looked to be about fifty. Five feet tall. Black-rimmed glasses. Graying hair. She wore an inexpensive woman's suit.

"Morning, Ma'am." I'm inspector Phillip Chen. BCA. I've got a search warrant to look at the safety deposit box corresponding to this key."

Through a slot in the window, he handed her a copy of the warrant, displaying the judge's signature on the original warrant to her through the pane of glass. Because the boxes were coded, he passed her the key through the small slit in the bottom of the window. The coding meant that you couldn't tell by looking at a key which box number the key would fit unless you had the master list. She possessed the list. She frowned as she read through the legal papers and explained:

"I'll have to call Mr. Epson in legal. He'll want to O.K. this."

Chen nodded. He watched her call Epson. He daydreamed about what Epson looked like, where he officed in the monolith owned by First National. Chen envisioned Epson to be a 60 year old, balding guy with a potbelly, lounging up on the 25th floor behind a cluttered desk. Epson, Chen surmised, would have a great view of the city and the River. Plaques and diplomas likely covered Epson's office walls. The tinny voice interrupted his dream.

"Mr. Epson says it's all right. I'll buzz you in."

Chen walked towards a thick door of polished metal. He heard the latch click open. He turned the knob. Once inside, he followed the woman past row upon row of safety deposit boxes. At box A1256, she stopped and inserted Chen's key and another looped around her wrist into two keyholes. Turning the keys simultaneously she opened the drawer.

"You can either look at the contents here or over there, in one of the cubicles."

She pointed in the direction of three enclosures which offered privacy for those viewing treasures held by the boxes. Her expression was stern, like that of a schoolteacher as she continued:

"Oh yes, Mr. Epson says he wants to see you before you take anything with you pursuant to the search warrant. He also wants me to make sure you don't go without leaving your card."

The BCA agent dug deep into his pocket and pulled out his wallet. He opened the sleeve of soft leather and handed her a business card. She looked at it, reading it carefully. Without a word, she nodded and walked back to her perch behind the glass wall.

Chen pulled out the metal drawer and walked over to the first cubicle and sat down. His hands were wet with nervous anticipation. The stool was cold and uncomfortable. He grabbed a ring on the cover of the gray box and pulled it open.

There was not much inside.

A United States visa in the name of Frank Hauptman dated April 4, 1955. The document was stamped with a point of departure for the United States; Rio De Janeiro, Brazil, and a point of entry; Miami, Florida.

Under the visa, Chen retrieved a single photograph. The snapshot was black and white and old. The edges of the picture were yellowed and contained writing in German along the white margins. Chen knew the language well enough to make out a date: December 12, 1942. The photograph depicted a young man in a finely tailored military uniform, Chen guessed German, with his arms around another young man. The second man in the picture was much larger, six three or so, and wore a uniform as well. But the larger man's garments were of poor quality and were ill tailored. Both uniforms looked to be gray in color, though he couldn't be sure since the snapshot was only black and white. The bigger man wore an odd cap, with an emblem Chen couldn't make out in the center of the cap. There were stripes on the seams of the big man's trousers and a large clump of impressive looking braiding over the left breast of his jacket. The smaller man, the one Chen guessed to be German, wore similar trousers but a more traditional cap. His uniform was sharply tailored in marked contrast to the big man's loose-fitting clothing. The smaller man's cap bore a German Eagle squarely in the garment's center, above the brim.

On the reverse of the photo, Chen found more writing in English. It read:

Adam Budaslavich
Minnesota

He flipped the photograph over to concentrate on the faces of its subjects.

The men appeared to be posed in front of an ornate building of some kind. It was a church, some sort of Orthodox Church, as best Chen could make out, from its onion dome and Greek or Orthodox cross. He placed the photograph and the visa to one side.

The final item in the box caught Chen's eye. At the bottom of the metal drawer, he found another small red envelope with a brass hasp securing a flap. He knew, without opening it, that it was another set of keys for another safety deposit box. The writing on the envelope read:

"Northland Savings Bank, Duluth, Minnesota."

Opening the hasp, Chen dug inside the packet. Both keys were gone.

Phillip Chen pushed his chair away from the cubicle and the few items of little or no value that sat on the desk in front of him, items that begged more questions than they answered. Chen flipped through the visa. He looked at the photo of Hauptman. Several things struck him as he held the document up to look at its detail. One, it was odd that Mrs. Budaslavich advised Slater and Swanson that Frank Hauptman had immigrated to the United States from Germany. He hadn't; he'd come from Brazil, ten years after the war ended.

And then there was the black and white photograph. By comparing the visa photo of Hauptman and the two faces in the snapshot, Chen identified the smaller man as Frank Hauptman. It was obvious from the uniform that Hauptman had been in the German Army, most likely during World War II. From the name on the reverse of the photograph, Chen assumed that the larger man was Adam Budaslavich, which made no sense whatsoever. Budaslavich was Yugoslavian. He immigrated to the U.S. to escape the communist regime. He wasn't German.

Chen settled on trying to inventory what he did know. There was only one key to safety deposit box A1256 at the First National Bank of Minneapolis. One key to Frank Hauptman's box in Minneapolis was missing. There were also the two missing keys to Hauptman's box at Northland Savings Bank in Duluth. Whoever had taken the one key from the Comstock Lake Inn had likely taken the two keys from box A1256. That much, Chen felt sure of.

Putting the contents of the box into an evidence bag, Chen took care not to obliterate any fingerprints. On his way out, he remembered to stop and leave a copy of the box's inventory for Mr. Epson. True to form, Epson never descended from his office to actually talk to the inspector.

Outside, Chen braced himself against a northwest wind sweeping across the plains. The steady surge of cold air, straight from Canada, cut through his thin overcoat. Walking back to his car, his body bent against the weather, Phil Chen mulled over what he knew at that point. He'd investigated many deaths. Murders for money; killings over jealousy, rage, sex or drugs. These murders didn't seem to fit any of the patterns. They didn't seem to follow any of the rules. Each time Slater dragged him back into the case, each time another bit of evidence turned up, it didn't get easier. It grew more complex.

By the time he walked up the four flights of stairs to his car, Phil Chen decided there was something far more sinister, far more unusual going on than either he or Deb Slater could conceive of. And he was determined to help find out what it was.

Chapter 13

November 15,1991

Sheriff Dan Prescott was livid. His face looked like it was on fire. He sat at his desk with his legs tightly crossed.

"His calve muscles are so tight," Slater thought, "he's cutting off the circulation to his feet."

The tenor of his voice conveyed the same tight, unhappy frame of mind.

"Goddamn it Herb, what do you mean Washington says the INS files of Hauptman and Budaslavich are sealed and marked 'confidential'? I got two stiffs, two murders, and the FBI can't get me a peek at the immigration files of the victims? Especially when it's clear this isn't your typical murder? Somebody whacked two locals with a silencer for no apparent reason and your boys in DC say we can't look at the files? Christ, what the hell is going on?"

Before Herb Whitefeather could respond, Prescott uncoiled his legs, reached over and slammed the phone receiver down. The force of the Sheriff's efforts sent the phone sliding across his desk and crashing to the floor.

"If you'd like to make a call...."

Slater picked up the telephone and placed it out of her boss' reach. She knew better than to say anything. She'd leave it to Swanson or Pagotti to calm him down.

Prescott's voice was shaking. His upset was accented by the uneven texture of his words.

"Can you believe it? First double homicide in five years and the Feds tell us our biggest lead can't be followed because some asshole bureaucrat in Washington wrote 'confidential' on the files."

He wasn't calming down as the words rolled off his tongue. In fact, there was a very real danger that Sheriff Prescott was just warming up.

Pagotti stepped into the breach to keep the Sheriff from emotionally imploding:

"Dan, calm down. We've still got the stuff Chen pulled out of the safety deposit box in Minneapolis. Still got the description of this Johnson character from the landlady. With Chen's people dusting the box for prints, who knows what'll turn up. Deb and Swanny are on to something. It's gonna take time. Time to separate the wheat from the chafe. But it's coming together, at least some of it is. Some of what we've got is beginning to make sense."

Pagotti wasn't sure anything about the case made sense. But his words seemed to calm Prescott down.

Swanson listened to his supervisors from his perch on top of a file credenza. His revolver and holster hung over the edge of the cabinet as he carefully studied the Sheriff's face. He made no attempt to enter into the discussion.

He and Slater had followed up with Phil Chen regarding the safety deposit box. The print results weren't ready yet. Attempts to pin down an expert to review the old photograph had bogged down. No one with the armed forces stationed in Duluth was of any help. No one could identify the location of the photograph or the military units represented by the uniforms worn in it. But all in all, outside of some guesses and suppositions, they didn't really know very much. Pagotti was really gilding the lily on this one. That was reason enough to stay clear of the Sheriff's rage.

"What about the safety deposit box in Duluth, Dave?"

Prescott appeared calm. He looked at Swanson with penetrating eyes.

"What do we know about Hauptman's Duluth box?"

Swanson took a sip of coffee and noted the beverage was brutally bitter.

"Dan must have made this shit," the Deputy thought, before relating what he knew:

"Deb and I went over to Duluth First Trust yesterday. They took over Northern Savings back in the late '70's. We served the warrant on them but without the box number, they couldn't be positive which one was Hauptman's. Their records don't list Hauptman ever being an account holder. They're putting together a list of box holders going back to 1954. It'll take a few days. The old stuff is on microfiche and has to be retrieved."

"Likely another blind alley anyway," Swanson thought to himself. By the downward twitch of Prescott's lower lip, he could tell the Sheriff agreed.

"What the hell, Al. You tell me we're making progress. Seems like if GM and Ford made this kind of progress, we'd all be pitching hay and cleaning up horse shit. I got two dead guys, both shot at close range. Same weapon. A possible killer with no known address and a phony name. No witnesses. No motive. No arrests. The media is screaming for details. They want the killer and have been pounding at me since the Tuomi kid's confession turned out to be more fiction than fact," the Sheriff observed.

Prescott stood up and faced Pagotti. He leaned over the fat detective. Pagotti was dressed in obvious poor taste: a crumpled faux-leather sports coat, time-worn polyester slacks, pink short-sleeved dress shirt and a Pepsi-stained tie.

"I got three TV channels, the local paper and the Minneapolis Tribune barking at me. Calling me on a daily basis for updates," Prescott insisted. "What should I tell them today, folks? That we've made progress but we don't really know what progress it is that we've made."

The Sheriff's face was red again, rapidly turning purple. Outside the office, a phone jangled. A secretary buzzed Prescott. It was Phil Chen calling for Slater. She excused herself, thankful to escape the Sheriff's wrath.

"Deb, we got a good set of prints on the box. Other than mine, of course. Stupid of me not to wear gloves in opening it. Anyway, a clean set. Sent'em to the FBI Crime Lab. Also to the INS on the hunch this Johnson fellow might be an immigrant."

Chen's voice was upbeat. So was his news.

"Finally," she mused, "finally something's going our way."

"Great news Phil. I can't tell you how wound up Prescott is. He just slammed down the phone on Herb Whitefeather. You know, the FBI man up here. INS says we can't look at the victim's files. Marked confidential. But if these prints do match someone named Johnson, or someone other than Hauptman, maybe the thing will start to make some sense."

She paused. She could tell Chen was impatient, had more to relate.

"I went back to talk to the lady at the safety deposit window after I pulled the prints. She remembered taking someone matching Johnson's description to look at Hauptman's box. He didn't sign the sheet when he came in. That's why she didn't tell me about him until she'd thought on it for a time. Assumed it was Hauptman. But thinking about it, she began to recall more. The guy spoke with an accent. And get this; she thought it might be Russian at first. But he said something as he opened the box that she recognized. It was a word in Serb or Croat. You know, Yugoslavian. Turns out she's Serb herself, still goes to the Orthodox services in St. Paul, the one's done in Serbian. She's convinced the man she let examine the box is Yugoslavian. What do you make of that?"

Deb Slater listened to the BCA agent. Hearing the words, she tried to recall what she'd seen before. As Chen continued to speak, later searched through the personal effects of the two dead men contained in the evidence folders placed on her desk. She was looking for items that seemed to form a connection between the two victims.

She located the objects. Both items contained identical inscriptions. She wrote the word down on a notepad. Her fingers carefully measured the reverse of Hauptman's silver medal.

"Thanks for the help, Phil. You're a life saver. Gotta go. Somethin' just clicked."

"Hope it helps, Deb. Hope it helps you nail the sonofabitch, whoever it he is."

"It's one step in that direction, Mr. Chen. One step. See ya."

She didn't wait for a response as she hurriedly placed the receiver down.

Across the hall, she stopped at a door marked "Detective Michael Stoyavoff." Stoyavoff was the Department's resident Bohunk, a member of the Serbian Orthodox Church, a Macedonian. She knocked.

"Come in."

She opened the door and walked into Stoyavoff's office. The brightness of the lights caused her to blink. Stoyavoff always had too many lights on. He was sitting behind a mound of files and old newspapers, surrounded on all sides by photographs of his four kids. All smiling, dark skinned, brown–eyed, just like their father, their ages newborn to eighteen. A picture of Lisa, his wife, was hanging by itself behind his chair.

"How are the kids?"

Slater didn't inquire to make small talk. She was genuinely interested in his children.

"Same as always. They spend most of their time trying to tie Lisa and I in knots. One day Jay's got a basketball game, Jill is at tumbling. The next day Emily is at swimming practice then volleyball. It never stops. Hell, Marcus, the baby, you'd think the infant would be the toughest. He's a piece of cake compared to three teenagers. Sports. Who the hell decided to get kids involved in organized sports?"

The Legacy

He looked tired. Slater smiled, thinking to herself the chaos that must reign at the Stoyavoff house on a Friday night.

"Mike, I hate to bother you, but you know that double homicide Swanny and I are working on?"

She stopped. He looked up from the mess he was plowing through. The maze of detail created by the paper web trapped him, made him oblivious to her. A wry grin spread over his face. He looked up at her with dark brown eyes.

Deb Slater wondered if the officer would ever start to show his age. Stoyavoff was nearly forty-five. He looked thirty and was extremely handsome:

"Damn handsome for any age," the female deputy thought.

"Especially so for a man over forty."

"Yeah Deb, I've kicked it around with Al a bit. Russian killer, eh? Sounds like a James Bond movie, not sleepy old Duluth."

He paused to gauge her response.

"So what gives?"

"Phil Chen down at BCA told me he's got a witness, a Serbian woman who works at a bank down there who'll swear this Johnson guy is Yugoslavian. Serb, Croat, anything but Russian. Heard him speak in Serbian. So I figure, if you got a Bohunk as a number one suspect, I should check it out with our number one Bohunk cop. Right?"

She used the term "Bohunk" without fear that Stoyavoff would find it offensive. He'd grown up hearing it on the Iron Range as a common way to refer to anyone of Yugoslav decent. To his father and grandfather, the term had been an insult hurled by those afraid of the immigrant Slavs' Orthodox religion and their faith's adherence to the Gregorian Calendar. With time, the term's poison had been diluted.

"Can you tell me what the hell these are and what this inscription on the back means?"

Slater pulled the two silver medallions that had once adorned the necks of Adam Budaslavich and Frank Hauptman out of a manila evidence envelope and handed them to the detective.

Stoyavoff turned them over and over in his hands, slowly reviewing their detail. He noted that they were identical but he could not identify the face on the medals. The figure depicted was not a traditional saint, not Thomas or

Christopher, and seemed more contemporary looking than that. Clean—, definitely a man's face, approximately middle-aged. Underneath the profile, a Roman numeral."XXXXIV". Forty-Four. On the reverse, the word "OZNA" written in Cyrillic script.

Michael Stoyavoff, resident Bohunk of the St. Louis County Sheriff's Department stared at the two medals in his hand. He stared at the word. He had absolutely no idea what it meant.

The Legacy

Chapter 14

November 17,1991

Michael Stoyavoff made certain that Deb Slater was with him when he visited Father Sanjina. If anyone could tell them the significance of the medals, or explain the meaning of the Cyrillic word written on the reverse, it would be Sanjina.

In his early eighties, Marko Sanjina had been a young Orthodox priest during World War II. A native of the province of Bosnia, he had joined the Serbian Chetniks in 1941 and traveled with them throughout the country. He spoke most of the languages and dialects of the diverse Yugoslav peoples. He could read them as well. He was valued in the Minnesota Slavic community as a historian, as a scholar, as well as a religious leader.

St. Elizabeth of the Nativity was not a large church. Its tiny chapel was home to less than two hundred parishioners. But its onion skinned dome in the Gary–New Duluth neighborhood on the southern edge of town served as the focal point of Duluth's Serbian Orthodox community for nearly a century.

Dense forested slopes rose above the City's skyline. St. Elizabeth's resided in the shadows of the hills, the setting mirroring that of many Orthodox churches found in the mountains of the old country.

It was this similarity of place which originally drew the churches' immigrant parishioners to the valley. Most came for the jobs, for the work; work in the blast furnaces of the steel plant, the coke plant, and the wire bailing plant. There had been plenty of jobs until the factories and mills rusted into obsolescence and shut down. By the early 1970's, less than one hundred years after iron ore had been discovered in Northeastern Minnesota, the mines were played out. The good paying jobs disappeared. But the descendants of the immigrant Slavs, and a few of the octogenarian first-generation immigrants themselves, clung to their homes in the valley, clung to their neighborhood, their piece of the American Dream.

Father Sanjina proved to be a tiny man. Bearded, he dressed in the black cassock traditional to his church, and boasted luxuriant silver hair. Great tufts of gray and white sprouted out over each eye like the tufts of a Great Horned

Owl, the hair thick and curly despite the priest's age. He had light brown, almost yellow eyes, punctuated by an obvious twinkle that never retreated. He opened the door to let the two deputies into the rectory:

"Michael, what a pleasant surprise."

The old man spoke English in a heavy accent which tended to cut the words off before they actually ended.

"What brings you to church in the middle of the week? And with such a lovely young lady, a fellow officer, no?"

"How've you been, Father?" Stoyavoff asked in Serbian. Before the old man responded, the officer continued in English:

"This is Deputy Slater, one of the officers I work with. Deputy Slater, Father Sanjina."

"Come in, Come in. You'll catch a death of cold out in that wind," the priest exclaimed, obviously excited to have company.

The two officers made their way through a fresh blanket of powdery snow. Light flakes drifted gently to the ground, covering the sidewalk and front stoop of the rectory as they entered the house.

The men embraced. Sanjina extended his hand to Slater. It was pale and deeply veined but the old man's grip was surprisingly strong for his age. The officers removed their overshoes and followed their host into the parlor.

"I'm very pleased to meet such a beautiful young lady, Officer Slater. Michael always did have fine taste in partners."

"I'm pleased to meet you, Father. But, unfortunately, Michael and I aren't partners. Just working together on one case."

She tried to be professional yet congenial. The priest's manners, his style, were Old World. She would be careful to honor those traditions while she was in his home.

Books lined the walls of the rectory. Wherever one looked, wherever one walked, there were books. The priest's reputation as a student, as a scholar was clearly reflected in the volumes lining every available inch of space in the house. Books in Serbian. Italian. English. German. Paperbacks yellowing prematurely. Decaying manuscripts hundreds of years old. Recent editions in glossy jackets, each author's face displayed on the back cover for posterity. There seemed to be no end to the shelves and the knowledge stacked upon them.

"Please, have a seat. Would you like some tea? It will help chase away the season's grip," the priest offered.

"Sure, Father. Whatever you're having, if its no trouble."

"No trouble at all, Michael. And you Ms. Slater?"

Deb Slater nodded her head. Sanjina motioned for them to sit on an overstuffed couch in the center of the parlor. He disappeared behind a rack of books. When he returned, he was carrying an elegant silver serving tray and tea set. Steam rose from the freshly brewed tea and filled the air. The tea's strong aroma blended curiously with the musty odor of the books. Thickly glazed windows interrupted one wall of the library and displayed the patterns of fresh snowflakes. Newly captured snow pressed against the cold exterior of the glass. To Slater, the room seemed to be the most purposeful, peaceful place she'd ever been in. Her attention was brought back into to the room when the priest coughed. The cleric poured her a cup of tea.

"Father, Deputy Slater is investigating a couple of murders that took place up on Highway 4. You've probably read about them in the paper. Looks premeditated. More like assassinations actually. Have you followed it in the news?"

Stoyavoff was holding a fragile teacup between in his hands as he studied the priest. The Father nodded but did not direct his gaze at Stoyavoff. Instead, he stared at Slater measuring her face, her soul. At least, that's how Slater felt about the intensity of the man's look.

"Anyway, one of the links between the two men, Budaslavich and Hauptman, seems to be the medals they both wore."

The detective produced the familiar envelopes from his briefcase. He pulled the medallions and chains from their resting places and passed them to Sanjina:

"I don't recognize the likeness on these. Doesn't seem to be any saint that I was taught about here at Saint Liz."

Stoyavoff winced a bit. He knew he shouldn't have used the slang "St. Liz" in front of the Father. If the breach in etiquette concerned Sanjina, the priest didn't show it. His small frame remained doubled over. It was evident he was straining to look at the objects in question. After a brief inspection, the little man chuckled to himself. The chuckle turned into a laugh; a deep belly laugh. Obviously enjoying some private joke, the holy man shook uncontrollably with spasms of amusement.

Slater looked quizzically at Stoyavoff. Her hair was wet from the snow. The melting flakes dripped from her eyebrows onto her cheeks, sliding down from her chin into her tea.

Sanjina noticed that he was the only one laughing, the only one who apparently got the joke. His spine straightened. He looked at Slater:

"Miss Slater. Or is it Mrs.?" the old man asked.

"Mrs."

She would have rather had him call her "Deputy" but decided not to push it. "Well, Mrs. Slater, you see the reason I laugh is because I thought I trained Michael well in religion class. I thought I'd worked some measure of magic, created some small margin of success in conferring upon him the history and majesty of our faith. It seems I overestimated my abilities as a teacher, or Michael's ability as a student. One or the other."

Sanjina stopped and chuckled to himself again as he looked intently across the room at a row of books. He appeared to be reading the titles of the volumes through his square bifocals. His head was tilted towards the floor as he tried to focus. The little man rose from his chair and shuffled towards the shelves, his eyes riveted upon a particular volume. The officers watched patiently as they tried to figure out what was so damn funny. Reaching up as far as his short stature would allow, Sanjina pulled out a thick, dust covered text, walked slowly back to his chair, and placed it on the coffee table in front of his guests. Sanjina's arthritic thumb began to turn the pages of the book in studied appreciation. The priest's search ended in a section of the volume containing photographs. Each picture was captioned in English. Sanjina fixed his tired eyes on a black and white portrait of a man. Holding the page open with his index finger, the cleric placed the medals over the photograph:

"Come closer and take a look," the priest invited.

Slater and Stoyavoff moved closer. The profile in the book was identical to the face etched into the medallions. Sanjina pushed the volume across the table, but said nothing. It was obvious he enjoyed prolonging the mystery:

"Here is your long–suffering saint, your religious martyr."

A bony digit pointed to the book's title at the top of the open page. It read "Tito" by Vladimir Dedijer. The photograph which occupied the majority of the page was entitled "Tito at Drvar, May 25, 1944." Even to Slater's untrained eye, it was obvious that the medals found on the necks of the two dead men bore the profile of Josef Broz—Tito.

"Why would a German and a Yugoslavian immigrant who supposedly left his home to escape the communists, wear medals with a communist dictator's likeness on them?" Stoyavoff queried, his mind raced ahead.

Innumerable questions began to formulate in his mind. From the expression on her face, Slater was similarly perplexed by the priest's revelation.

"And what about this word printed on the back. What does 'OZNA' mean?"

Stoyavoff's voice betrayed a pleading quality underlying a request that the priest stop the game and solve the riddle. Father Sanjina's grin broadened. It was obvious to Slater that this was the most fun he'd had in years:

"You see the marking under Tito's head on the medal? '44'? That's 1944. In 1944 at Drvar, I believe it was May or June, a force of Nazi paratroopers attacked Tito's hidden lair. Each was armed with a submachine gun and a photograph of Josef Broz; Tito as he was called by the Partisans. The paratroopers had but one purpose.

To find and kill Tito. To destroy the mind behind the communist resistance. They failed, Tito escaped, saved by the personal bravery of his bodyguards, an elite, hand selected unit of Partisans fanatically loyal to Tito. These men and women later became the foundation of the Yugoslav Provisional Government's Secret Police-the OZNA. These medals seem to commemorate that event."

Sanjina held the silver medals close to his eyes as he spoke:

"They both bear the date of May 25th under the 44. The same date as the photograph. Tito's fifty-second birthday. The day the Nazis attacked," he explained, his words trailing off.

He stopped speaking, seemingly lost in a past that he'd almost forgotten. But he was watching; watching to see if the officers followed the story. Slater's eyes remained riveted on the Priest's face. He continued:

"After the communists defeated the Nazis, the OZNA became an arm of the communist government, an agency who's fundamental mission was to locate and destroy Croatians who'd become Ustashi; allies of the Nazis. Ante Pavelich was the Ustashi leader. Me, I was a Royalist. I marched with the Chetniks until it was obvious we could not prevail."

Father Sanjina's gaze focused on the gaily-frosted windows. Ignoring the natural beauty of the snowfall, his attention became fixed on the silent, crumbling smokestacks of the abandoned US Steel mill looming in the near distance:

"This Pavelich. He persecuted and killed over one million Moslems, Jews, gypsies and Orthodox Christians. But once the Ustashi were hunted down, the OZNA went after my old comrades, the Royalists, the Chetniks—those that supported a return to the monarchy. Tito caught up with Mihailovich, our Chetnik commander, had him shot and put in an unmarked grave. I was destined for a similar fate because I opposed the communists. But in the end, even Tito grew tired of the slaughter, the shedding of blood. Most of us were spared. We avoided the firing squads of the secret police. Once I escaped OZNA's noose, I came to this country. I didn't give them a second chance."

The old man's voice developed a slight tremor as he came to the end of his thought. Whether it was due to anger or age, the deputy couldn't tell.

"So OZNA is the name of the Yugoslav secret police?" Slater asked, not certain that she had grasped the entirety of the story.

It made little sense to her that two old men, one a German and one an avowed anticommunist, would be found wearing medals commemorating Tito's escape from death forty-some years ago. It made no sense, no sense at all.

"Was. In 1946, through internal reorganization, OZNA was renamed UDBA and its attention turned outward–to include those enemies who'd escaped from Yugoslavia during the war. Some selected agents became much like the Jewish Nazi hunters we're all familiar with, searching out Ustashi and Germans who'd committed war crimes but escaped."

Sanjina bent close to Slater as he completed the sentence. The deputy looked up into the old man's face. She perceived he was anticipating her next question.

"So why would these two dead old men in Duluth, Minnesota be wearing medals honoring a communist war hero of Yugoslavia?"

Stoyavoff thought that one over as the words rolled across Deb Slater's tongue. He had a headache. All this history about a heritage he did not know. It gave him a splitting headache. He moved his head from side to side, cracking his neck.

He gave the priest a sidelong glance. Sanjina would know. Yes, the old man would know. Especially if he saw the photo Chen retrieved from the safety deposit box in Minneapolis. It was in the briefcase, secure in Hauptman's evidence envelope. He pulled it out and placed it before the priest.

Slater kneeled on the carpeting in front of the table, looking intently at the photo. Though there were years between the photograph and the murders, she was certain. The German officer in the picture was Frank Hauptman. There was no mistaking the narrow beak of a nose, the aristocratic chin, and the high, blade-like cheekbones. And the big man, no doubt, had to be Adam Budaslavich. Fifty pounds lighter. Many years younger. But it was he. She turned to Sanjina:

"If Hauptman is the German officer in this photograph and the other man is Budaslavich, what does that all mean in relation to the story you just told us?"

Slater's words came out slowly, deliberately. She was beginning to sense something of what the old man was trying to tell them. The wood fire burning in the cavernous stone fireplace was pulling the chill out of her wet uniform and hair. The tea was warming her, insulating her against the dampness and the cold.

The priest stared intently into the weathered skin of his own hands as he spoke:

"I would say that your Mr. Hauptman was an SS officer in the German Wermacht stationed in Yugoslavia. The uniform, the church in the background; they are all familiar to me. They are of the mountains, the war. And Budaslavich. As for him, there's no doubt. The uniform he's wearing is that of the Yugoslav Army. Again an officer. A major. This picture is obviously one of two friends. Taken sometime after the Nazis defeated our Army in April of 1941. By the uniform and the timing, Mr. Budaslavich can be only one thing.

A Ustashi, a traitor, a fascist follower of Ante Pavelich. Definitely Croatian, most likely Catholic."

Pleased with his deductive powers, Father Sanjina sat back in his threadbare recliner and sipped strong black tea.

Stoyavoff remained deep in contemplative thought. He stood up and walked towards the windows overlooking the garden, its greenery dormant and covered with a thin veil of freshly fallen snow. The snowflakes waxed and waned with the wind. Some fell upon the wrought iron fence where summer's warmth would sprout grapevines. He sighed and walked back to the couch.

He grasped the back of the sofa and leaned forward, extending his torso over Slater as she sat on the carpeting. She looked at the priest as she spoke:

"So what we've got, Father, are two dead enemies of Tito wearing Tito medals, stamped with the name of the Yugoslav secret police. Booty from the war, from a battle both fought in and became friends?"

It was a question. Not a statement. Slater wasn't sure of anything at this point.

Sanjina grinned. His teacup was empty. He placed it in its saucer. His voice returned to its full volume and throaty vitality:

"More likely calling cards left by the killer. Or killers. My guess is that whoever killed the two men in this photograph left the medals on them. This Mr. Johnson you spoke of. If he is the killer, then I'd say he brought these fellows two gifts. One was the gift of these medals. The other was the gift of death. And you can bet, officers, that the second gift has something to do with whatever brought Hauptman and Budaslavich together in Yugoslavia some fifty years ago."

From the tone of the priest's voice, it was clear he had no more to say on the subject. The conversation had obviously taken a toll, had rekindled long-forgotten memories. Stoyavoff nodded to Slater. The two officers stood up, intent upon leaving.

"Thank you, Father, it was good to see you again."

"Yes, Father Sanjina, thank you. You were most helpful. And thank you for the tea."

"You're quite welcome, Mrs. Slater. Come again, anytime. Old men relish the company of beauty. You, Michael, have become a stranger. Don't limit your visits to worship. Come and see me whenever you can."

"I will, Father," Stoyavoff replied sheepishly.

The officers retrieved their boots and coats. With their garments closed tight against the wind, they let themselves out of the front door. Behind them, the old man pulled on his heavy woolen overcoat. Wrestling himself into the garment's protective warmth, he pulled on his gloves and grabbed a snow shovel leaning against the wainscoted wall of the foyer.

Sanjina opened the front door, walked onto the porch, down the stairs, and began to clear the sidewalk of snow.

In the fading light of another November day, a flock of wayward mallards on the wing drew the deputies' attention up into the swirling clouds. They could not see the speeding ducks breaking a path through the sky. They could only hear their distant calls, sounding like the spirits of long dead warriors from another time calling out to them, taunting them.

On the steps of the rectory, Father Sanjina brushed away the last of his tears and pushed aside the drifting snow. The priest found solace in working. The steady labor of lifting the light, crystalline snow lessened his pain, ended his tears. With the onset of dusk, the only sound heard beneath the shadow of the silent hills was that of the little priest scraping the bare cement of the walk with his shovel.

Chapter 15

November 20, 1991

There were no entries on the computer printout listing a Frank Hauptman, F. Hauptman. None. Adam Budaslavich, A. Budaslavich. None. According to the records of the bank, neither man had held a safety deposit box. Not dating back to 1954, at least. Slater had read and reread the listing but could not find any names remotely similar to those of the two dead men. Whatever Mr. Johnson had done with the keys he took from the Minneapolis safety deposit box, she was convinced he'd found a similar box in the Duluth bank. But how?

Deb Slater put her legs up on the coffee table. The tabletop was smoked glass framed by oak veneer. A candy dish, a copy of *Life Magazine*, and a display of dried wildflowers in a small vase rested randomly on the glass. She sat in her pajamas, two piece silk, powder blue, and a terry robe of deeper blue belted tightly around her waist. Rick sat next to her on the davenport, reading yesterday's history tests, correcting them, lost in his own world as she was in hers. A fire burned brightly in the brick fireplace a short distance across their family room.

She gingerly massaged the glass in her hand as her eyes followed the discrete tongues of the fire's flame. A single lamp stood above Rick's shoulder illuminating his half of the couch and not much more. The wine warmed her, made her content. The liquor didn't stop her mind from wandering back to the two dead men, to their story, their mystery. The brutal deaths gnawed at her through the momentary distraction of the wine. The liquor was merely a buffer. The alcohol was not strong enough to stop her mind from probing into the murders as she sat before the fire.

She rose from the couch seeking to get closer to the fire's warmth. Reflexively she picked up a wrought iron fireplace tool and poked at a birch log being consumed by the flames. Embers shot upward, caught in the chimney draft like lazy fireflies on a hot summer's night. Holding loosely to the tool, she leaned towards the hearth, prodding logs, encouraging the flames.

Sometime ago, she had convinced herself that Johnson had been at the Duluth bank, had been in the safety deposit box and taken whatever he wanted, whatever he killed for. He had also taken whatever secrets one could hide in a small metal box.

Intrigued by the fire's dance, she promised herself that she would interview all of the safety deposit clerks and officers on her next shift. Tonight she was going to climb in bed with her husband after another glass of wine and give him a lesson in history. Their history.

"So you believe a man fitting this description, with a slightly foreign accent, was in here a few days ago?" Deputy Slater asked.

Debra Slater sat behind a desk in the safety deposit department interviewing Edna Simmons, the officer in charge of the department. Though Simmons appeared to be well over sixty years old and ready for retirement, the woman seemed diligent, eagle–eyed, like most bank employees who've worked their way up from teller windows to positions of authority.

Ms. Simmons was convinced that a man fitting the description of Mr. Johnson had been in to look at a box only days before. She was certain of it. So certain, she pulled the registration sheets containing all of the signatures of the customers who'd entered the department over the past two weeks.

There it was March 23. An entry signed "Frank H. Essen." The address listed next to it: "Comstock Lake, Minnesota." Nothing more. The signature was delicate, neat. Not the work of a man in a hurry. Slater puzzled over the name. Essen. That was a new one. Slater asked for a photocopy of the page. Ms. Simmons obliged.

When the older woman brought the photocopy back, she stopped short of handing it to Slater. She looked to be deep in thought.

"You know, he didn't fill out the box number he looked at, this Mr. Essen, or whatever his name is. My fault, supposed to make sure they do. But I remember bringing him to it. He was so polite, so good looking. And that accent. Reminded me of some foreign movie star. That's why I remember the box he looked at."

Ms. Simmons motioned for Slater to follow her. Down two rows, one to the left. They stopped. The banker pointed to a small box in the bottom row. Box T4356.

"That's it, all right. That's the one Mr. Essen was interested in."

Slater thanked the woman and told her she'd be back with a search warrant to have the lock drilled. The Deputy promised to be back before her shift ended, provided she could find a judge to sign the warrant.

Just before closing time, Slater and Swanson returned to First Trust, a search warrant for box T4356 in hand. Slater called ahead and made arrangements for a locksmith to be present. When they arrived at the safety deposit counter, Ms. Simmons was still at her post. She was all smiles, obviously thrilled to be part of a police investigation. In a matter of minutes, the locksmith completed his work and box T4356 was open. Slater fully expected that it would be empty. It wasn't.

Inside the shallow metal walls of the box lay two dog–eared deposit slips. Each was inscribed "Deutchesbank Rio de Janeiro." The writing on the slips appeared to be in German. Both slips bore the names "Frank Hauptman und/oder Franz Essen." There was one transaction listed on each scrap of paper. On March 13, 1946, it appeared Mr. Hauptman or Mr. Essen, or both, deposited $100,000.00 in gold with the Brazilian bank. And on December 10, 1955, he/they withdrew the gold. There was nothing else contained in the box.

Swanson gingerly picked up the slips and deposited them in a plastic bag as evidence. The BCA would have another chance to come up with fingerprints that meant something. Thanking Ms. Simmons for her help, the two deputies walked out onto Michigan Street. They remained silent; there was nothing either could think of to say.

Two forty-six-year-old bank slips from a bank in Brazil had been left for them to find by Mr. Johnson. That they were sure of. But what else had been in the box that Johnson had taken with him? Or destroyed? Wordlessly, like dogs wandering home on instinct, they shuffled up the hill.

"Deb, I don't know about you, but this case doesn't seem to be getting any easier, does it?" Swanson remarked.

The two officers sat in a booth at Pat's. Sweat rolled down Swanson's forehead. A touch of the flu, or as Slater called it, "the Duluth Blues," was beginning to take its toll. Slater's partner looked haggard, tired and ornery. She sensed he was about ready to call it quits on the murders. Nothing made any sense. Slater looked at him over her hot chocolate, spiced with a little mint, Pat's winter specialty. The cup was cracked, the saucer stained by years of use. She winked.

"But I've got the whole thing solved, Dave. We're obviously dealing with a love triangle. That's right, Mrs. Budaslavich is Mr. Johnson. Just a clever disguise. When Adam found out she was sleeping with the Kraut, she did 'em both in and took the insurance money. Got the house. Got whatever was in the two safety deposit boxes. Let's bring the old lady in."

She grinned, showing shiny white enamel except where small spots of chocolate remained stuck in the spaces between the two eyeteeth in the front. Swanson groaned.

"Be serious, Deb. I mean, what do we got? Two dead men killed by antique 9mm slugs. Both friends, both immigrants. Both served together in Yugoslavia during the war. Against the communists, so the priest said. They both end up here in Minnesota. A few miles from each other. Out in the middle of nowhere. And they live happily ever after for nearly forty some years until a nut calling himself 'Mr. Johnson' checks into the Central Hillside. Comes up for a little people hunting during deer season. Does 'em both, takes some safety deposit box keys, leaves clues that make the priest believe there's more to the story."

The big deputy sighed. The fever was beginning to take its toll. Dispassionately, he continued his observation:

"Now we find out that Hauptman has a buddy named Essen, or is Essen. Was or were in Brazil before coming here. Had loads of gold. From somewhere. That's what we've got and it makes no damn sense whatsoever".

Swanson's right hand stroked his tender, sore throat. The sweat didn't let up. The deputy's underarms were damp, wet like a swamp. He needed sleep.

"So you don't like my theory, Dave?"

Slater finished her chocolate. She pulled her down gloves over her hands as she sat across the booth.

"It sucks."

Swanson stood up, hovering over her for a brief instant as he responded in a weak voice.

"You're forgetting the best part, Slater. The INS, the FBI, whoever, they won't let us look at the files. That tells me that the two stiffs are definitely important, too important to let two badges from Duluth snoop into the past. That's what Herb said. That's where the story may well end."

Slater smiled at Swanson's frustration, left a tip and pulled her partner towards the door.

It was after 6:00 p.m. Outside, the night was moonless and thickly dark. A few courageous stars managed to peak through the clouds. The tiny, distant specks cast dim light against the depth of the sky. The glass of the courthouse windows was trimmed with frost. Slater sat down in her cubicle and looked at her message spindle and sorted through the pink memo sheets. One in particular leaped out at her. It was from Herb, marked "urgent." Whitefeather's office and home numbers were on the slip. 6:00. Herb would be at home. She dialed the number.

A female voice answered. Herb's live–in. Susan Salminen. Deb recognized her voice. They exchanged greetings, nothing of substance. The two women didn't really know each other well enough to engage in an indepth conversation. Herb came on the line.

"What's up Herb?"

There was a short pause. Giggles and ruffling noises in the background.

"Ah–ah," thought the deputy, "I caught those two in the middle of the 'naughty thing.'"

Whitefeather quickly regained his composure and began to talk. Slater had all she could to keep from laughing, visualizing how flushed and embarrassed the big man would be.

"Deb, you're never gonna believe this. I kept harping on my contact at INS, a little old redheaded Cherokee lady I dated in school at Quantico. She was at George Washington Law. Anyway, I've been on her ass to get me something, anything on your homicides. For days, nothing. Not a crumb. I'm out there last week, in DC, for a meeting of the Regional supervisors. Anyway, I meet up with her at a cocktail party. A sort of 'be kind to Indians bash', AIM, Fonda, all that shit."

Slater could hear the door slam in the background. Susan obviously wasn't happy that Herb had visited an old flame. Whitefeather paused, momentarily lost in thought.

"Anyways, where was I? Yeah, after a few drinks, we start talking about the old days. Then she asks, real coyly, if I'm still interested in taking a peek at your dead guys' files. 'Am I?' I says? 'Damn right. When?' I ask. She says 'Right now.'

Just about blew my mind.

So we leave the party. Boring shit anyway. Jane standing next to Ted talking about my rights. Someone reading a letter from Brando in Tahiti, a letter from God I suppose. So we leave. Walk right into the INS offices. She's got top clearance, gets us to her office. No problem."

His voice became a whisper.

"I gotta say this part quiet. Don't want Sue to come unglued.

She pulls out two file folders from the top drawer of her desk. Manila folders marked 'Confidential.' She hands me the files and then pulls me towards her and starts unzipping my barndoor. Right in her fucking office."

Slater started to giggle again, picturing the huge Indian dressed in his best suit, always in the best of taste, being seduced by a red-haired coquette with top security clearance.

She suppressed the urge to laugh and said, as straight as she could, "Well, I suppose she just wanted you to return the favor, Herb."

She could tell the big man wasn't amused.

"Damn it, Deb. It wasn't funny. I'm thinking to myself that this might even be a setup. Who knows? So I back off, calm the situation down. I tell her maybe after we take a peek at the files, we'll go have some coffee, dinner. Anything to get her off of me. She looked pissed but agreed."

Over the receiver, Slater could hear the stereo being turned on in the other room. Loud. Obnoxious heavy metal rock and roll. Sue was obviously not in a happy mood. Whitefeather sighed on the other end.

"We sit down at her desk, look at the two files. One marked Frank Hauptman. One marked Adam Budaslavich. You'll never believe what was inside."

He paused. Making her wait for the secret to be revealed. Making her uneasy. A little revenge for the joke she'd cracked.

Deb Slater grew anxious. Tired of the case, the dead ends. She wanted answers, not more games.

"Herb, get to the point, would you?"

"The point is, Ms. Slater, that Frank Hauptman, according to his sealed INS file, is really a man known as Franz Essen. A native of Germany. Born October 12, 1916. Immigrated to Brazil, August 8, 1945. From, and get this, Belgrade, Yugoslavia. Then from Brazil to the U.S., December 19, 1955. Visa in the name of Frank Hauptman. Citizenship sponsored by General William Porter, United States Army, OSS. And Budaslavich, he came along for the ride. Real name, Damos Tomich. Born July 8, 1916. Zagreb, Yugoslavia. Immigrated to Brazil, August 8, 1945. And then... you guessed it, Brazil to the U.S. on September 19, 1955. Citizenship courtesy of? Yep. General William Porter."

He paused for effect. Certain he'd confused the deputy by the whispered revelations.

"What the hell are you telling me, Herb? That some army officer in Washington helped these two come to the States. A Nazi and a Croatian traitor? Under assumed names? Why the hell would the United States Army get involved with something like that?"

She was thoroughly confused. And upset that, with every new discovery, the murders became less and less understandable.

"Deb, you don't even know what the OSS is, do you?"

She could tell from his voice that he was grinning from ear to ear on the other end. She had to admit she didn't. She'd never heard of it.

"Well, the Army probably wasn't interested in bringing a Nazi and a Yugoslav traitor to this country. But for some reason, the OSS was. General Porter was the chief officer of the OSS in Northern Italy. Seeing he was the top brass, those men were mighty important to someone in the OSS."

He paused to let the information sink in.

"You see, Deb, the OSS is now known as the Central Intelligence Agency of the United States of America. The CIA, Deb. The goddamned CIA brought your two dead men to Minnesota."

Deputy Debra Slater of the St. Louis County Sheriff's Department sat on the other end of the phone, gazing across her desk at a photo of her and Rick taken years ago, at some long forgotten wedding or party. She held the phone far away from her ear, all the while staring blindly at the photo, for no particular reason other than her eyes were fixed upon it.

Instinctively, without removing her gaze from the photo, she replaced the receiver. She hadn't recovered from the shock of Herb's revelations to say goodbye or to ask what happened in the INS office after the little red head delivered her part of the bargain. None of those things seemed important. Deb Slater's head felt like it was ready to explode. It was time to go out into the chill of the night air and get home.

Chapter 16

November 21, 1991

"You were right Deb. Here's the name you got from Herb."

Dave Swanson was sitting inside the safety deposit vault at Duluth First Trust reviewing several hundred pages of computer printout, alphabetical listings of all box holders going back to 1950. Slater sat next to him at the brown metal table looking at another hundred or so sheets of names, most of the people long since dead. Swanson pointed to the name: Franz Essen-Box T4356, the same box they'd looked at and found the deposit slips in. Slater scanned further up the page. Nothing for Adam Budaslavich. But further, under the "Ts." Bingo. There it was. Damos Tomich. Another box. Date opened: November 21, 1954. Box B7345. They summoned Mrs. Simmons again.

Box B7345 was heavy. It was difficult for Mrs. Simmons to pull out once the locksmith drilled the lock out. They thought about asking Mrs. Budaslavich for the keys. They decided it was better to go with a warrant. The widow Budaslavich had been through enough. It would serve no purpose for her to know that her husband wasn't who he claimed to be.

The box was so heavy it took both Slater and Swanson to lift it onto the table. Slater guessed it went a good seventy-five pounds or more. She opened the lid. The contents caught her off guard.

Stacked neatly within the metal confines of the safety deposit box were ten or so small yellow ingots bearing an imbedded seal, the words foreign and unfamiliar. Slater carefully picked one of the bars up by the edges, feeling its heft, its weight. From the density and color, there was no doubt. The deputy knew it to be pure gold.

Swanson reached in and lifted two ingots, one in each hand. Amazed and in awe of the brilliant sheen each cast when exposed to the light, he whistled.

"At least we've finally come up with something of substance," Slater whispered. "Something tangible. Gold at least gives us a motive."

Her partner nodded in agreement and continued to hold the bars, envying their weight. Debra Slater carefully placed the bar she was holding to one side of the table. She looked into the box, to discern the value of the treasure. The female officer turned her gaze from the treasure towards her partner, and spoke in hushed tones:

"This stuff is beautiful, all right. And heavy. Say, maybe you and I could use a couple of these for paperweights. Think Mrs. Simmons would miss one or two of these?"

Dave Swanson smiled at his partner's joke. He looked sheepishly over his shoulder at the bank clerk as she watched them. She was carefully scrutinizing their every move.

"Yes," thought the deputy, "Mrs. Simmons would miss them."

"I don't think we could pull it off," he said quietly.

At more than four hundred dollars an ounce, the ten bars weighed seven to eight pounds apiece, which meant they were worth $50,000.00 per bar. Deputy Dave Swanson made the calculations in his head as he admired the weight in his hands.

"Well, at least we know what has Mr. Johnson so interested in Northeastern Minnesota. I mean, if you're gonna kill two old men, this would just about make it all worthwhile."

Swanson spoke to no one in particular as he placed the bars down next to the safety deposit box. Slater looked up at her partner.

She was inventorying what she knew about the dead men in her mind. The men were intertwined in a relationship forged during a different time, a different age; intertwined in life, intertwined in death. They now had the motive: money, one of the most common, most elementary of all motives for murder.

She reasoned that, whoever Johnson was, he'd known about the gold, had come to get it. But it was puzzling. The description of Johnson made him too young to be a disgruntled partner of the victims. Fortyish, the landlady had said. A Yugoslav, that seemed definite. How did he know? How had he come to know about the fortune that lay in the safety deposit box? She shook her head and got back to the matter at hand:

"Dave, I think it's clear we know why Johnson came here. I mean, just suppose that Johnson knew Hauptman or Budaslavich, or both, had this kind of wealth. He comes for it. First he tries to get it through Budaslavich. The guy's married. Doesn't keep evidence of the box or the account at home. Suppose that's true. Trying to keep it all from a wife who has no idea about the OSS, his past. The secret identity. So Johnson kills Budaslavich in frustration. Then he goes to Hauptman. Finds there what he needs. But can't leave any witnesses, so he kills Hauptman as well. Goes to Minneapolis. Uses Hauptman's keys to get into the box there. Follows the trail back just like we did. Gets whatever Hauptman had of value in his box. Probably gold. But Johnson can't find Budaslavich's box, the old Yugoslav's gold. Doesn't know where it is, or even if it is."

She paused, out of breath. Hoping she was making sense.

"O.K., I'll buy that. But answer me two questions. Number one, why does he kill Hauptman after he knows where the keys are? I mean, he could have broken in at any time and grabbed the keys without doing the old guy. And two, how in the world did he track the two of them up here to the boonies? Forty years after the war. Thirty years after they immigrate with assumed names," Swanson said, shaking his head in disbelief.

"I'm beginning to believe the guy we're chasing has someone or something powerful behind him. No one could do that kind of tracking on his own. No one."

Mrs. Simmons watched the deputies put the three bars they'd examined back into the box. They agreed that the locksmith would need to replace the lock cylinder and provide them with a key. They would leave the gold in the trusted hands of the bank for the time being. That amount of wealth, Swanson argued, would be too tempting to leave in the confines of the Sheriff Department's property room.

A new lock was installed. The locksmith provided them with a key. Slater and Swanson gathered up the computer sheets, notebooks and papers. It was time to get back to the office and try to make some sense of the twists and turns their investigation had uncovered.

"Thank you for all your help, Mrs. Simmons."

"You're welcome, officer. Just keep me updated on what happens. I'd like to know what you find out."

"We'll do what we can, Mrs. Simmons. We'll do what we can."

Slater's voice trailed off as she followed her partner out into the teeth of a November blizzard. The two deputies trudged through ankle deep snow up the hill to the courthouse. Neither spoke. Both contemplated the silent, natural beauty of the storm.

Twenty minutes after the Deputies departed; Ms. Linda Olson relieved Mrs. Simmons in the dungeon of the bank. Tall and thin, a firm believer in aerobics and nautilus training, Ms. Olson looked eighteen. She was thirty-two. Her usual watch over the safety deposit vault desk fell from 4:30 until 5:00 p.m., from the time Mrs. Simmons caught her bus until closing. After closing, Ms. Olson went to work for the remainder of the evening as an auditor in the bookkeeping department. There were seldom any customers in the safety deposit vault on her brief watch.

This day was different. At 4:55 p.m., a well-dressed man of medium build exited the middle elevator. His coat draped over one arm; he pulled a briefcase behind him on a caddie, the kind commonly seen in airports. He wore an expensive winter-weight suit. Ms. Olson glanced up from her desk as he approached. The man had intensely brown eyes and thick, wavy black hair. Hints of gray flecked the temples. The visitor was handsome.

"Good evening, Ma'am," the stranger said through a wide, careful smile.

"How may I help you sir?"

He handed her a business card. It read:

Douglas P. Jones.
Assistant St. Louis County Attorney.

"County Attorney sent me to inventory the box owned by Mr. Budaslavich. I believe two deputies were by earlier and secured it."

His manner was polite, sincere and believable. His speech bore a trace of a slight accent, an accent Ms. Olson did not recognize.

"Sure. Come in."

"Thank you. Quite a nasty storm outside, eh?"

"I'd say. At least I'm on the night shift. Should let up by the time I'm off tomorrow morning."

Ms. Olson buzzed him through.

"The box you want is right down here," she explained.

As she walked in front of Mr. Jones, she felt a strong arm curl around her neck from behind. She tried to scream but could not.

The Legacy

A handkerchief with a pungent smell passed over her nose and mouth. She fought the odor as she kicked at the handsome man in the expensive suit, striking downward on his instep as she'd been taught. But her foot merely pounded into the granite of the floor, her movement having been perceived long before she could execute it. In a brief instant she was overcome by the fumes and fell unconscious towards the floor. Mr. Jones caught her body as it collapsed, gently lowering it onto the cool stone.

Working quickly, the man located Budaslavich's box, an orange St. Louis County Sheriff's Department property tag still affixed to it. Opening his briefcase, Jones removed a round cylinder holding a series of key blanks. Within seconds, he opened the tumblers of the new lock. No damage, no alarm. He went to work.

Not more than five minutes later, Attorney Jones exited from one of the bank's lobby elevators, bound for the skywalk system of downtown Duluth. Entering the maze of elevated walkways connecting the major buildings of Duluth's downtown; Jones became another blue suit in the evening crush of blue suits. No one paid any attention to the strain upon Jones' face as he shuffled along, burdened by the weight of the black briefcase being pulled behind him.

None of the weary dregs of the corporate world walking past Mr. Jones realized that, beneath their feet, a half million dollars in gold had just been liberated from the Duluth First Trust Bank. It would be several minutes before anyone in the bookkeeping department thought to look for Ms. Olson.

Chapter 17

November 22, 1991

Minneapolis and St. Paul were not Deb Slater's favorite places to visit. She hated the traffic. Too fast, too many cars, too many drivers with no manners. Every time she drove to the Cities, everything was changed. Where once the concrete and brick Foshay Tower was the tallest building, the Foshay was now dwarfed by tens of other skyscrapers. New granite and glass monuments to industry, to technology, sprouted like weeds. Straining to touch heaven, the structures blocked out the very sun they sought to worship, making the downtowns of the Twin Cities feel claustrophobic.

Dave Swanson drove a county car, the Beast, a tan 1980 Nova. The automobile, Motor Pool No. 124, was ready to die. It wasn't a squad car, just a plain old brown Nova with a number and "St. Louis County Motorpool" stenciled across the door. Pagotti was in the back seat, snoring, his raspy voice exhaling and inhaling in rhythm, hands securely locked around his fat belly. His rumpled overcoat was unbuttoned, revealing a holster holding a .38 beneath his sports jacket. The jacket was plaid, loud and obnoxious, like its owner. Slater sat up front with her partner, as far removed from the fat man as possible.

At 11:00 a.m., the officers parked in front of the Yugoslavian Consulate in Minneapolis, a turn of the century sandstone mansion converted into offices. The subtle color of the sandstone blended naturally with the brown and yellow backdrop of the early winter day.

When a Democrat of Croatian decent occupied the governor's seat, the consulate was busy, extremely busy. Even now, a year after the seat was stolen by a Republican of Scandinavian extraction in one of the most scandal–ridden elections in Minnesota history, the consulate still thrived.

The deputies were expected. They had official business. A parking space was reserved for them. Otherwise, there would have been no room for their Nova.

"Officers, I'm so pleased to meet you. I'm Gregor Mendevich, Consul for the Yugoslavian Government, such as it is. With the upheaval going on in my homeland, who can say whether I'm still Consul or not? Ah, but I forget my manners. Won't you come in?"

The Legacy

The diplomat was very tall. Thin. Late fifties near sixty. Shortly cropped white hair. Gray eyes.

"Really hazel," Slater thought.

Smiling and polite. Very polite. They stepped into the foyer of the mansion.

"Mr. Mendevich, I'm detective Pagotti, St. Louis County Sheriff's Department. These folks are Deputies Swanson and Slater. It's good of you to see us on such short notice."

Pagotti's sport coat and slacks were disheveled. His eyes were somewhat glazed, looking like he'd just woke up—which he had. The Yugoslav motioned for the officers to follow him into his office.

"Some office," Pagotti muttered to himself as he sat in an antique cherry-wood armchair.

The theme of the place was wood. Cherry, maple, oak. Every piece of furniture or trim finely polished. Original oriental rugs protected oak flooring. Elaborate oil paintings adorned the walls, encased in ornately turned walnut frames.

"Portraits of dignitaries," Slater guessed to herself. She recognized one of Tito hanging over the marble fireplace.

A fire burning in the huge marble fireplace captivated Swanson's eyes. Much of his view of the fire's low flames was blocked by the Consul's desk. Delicate legs of ornate cherry supported a massive slab of marble. The stone of the desk matched the stone surrounding the fireplace and served as a writing surface. The furniture's impressive size seemed intended to place distance between the Consul and his visitors.

"When you called, Deputy Slater, I must say your description of the events in your part of the State were intriguing. The makings of a movie, really. Murder. Gold. Medals of Marshall Tito. It certainly caught my attention."

The Consul talked easily, without the pretense and cool reserve Slater expected from a diplomat.

"Well, sir, the reason I called and the reason we're here is we believe the killer is Yugoslavian. It seems to fit. Both dead men were in the war together in Yugoslavia. Both came to this country under the protection of the OSS. Why, we can't tell you. We don't know. But they did."

Leaning forward, the tall man picked up his cup and sipped hot tea. He made no attempt to offer any of the liquid to his guests.

"That is indeed of interest. From what you tell me, one was an SS officer. The other, Ustashi. I'm Croatian," the Consul offered, "like those who joined the Ustashi. But my father actually fought with one of the Chetnik Brigades, you know, the Royalists."

Fought the Germans. He quit before the war was over, went back to his farm. Through all the purges and bloodletting, he was never harmed. I tell you this so you know that not all Croats were Ustashi."

He paused to take another sip of tea. A faint vapor rose from the cup, encouraged by the pull of the fireplace's draft.

"I make no excuses for Ante Pavelich and his killers. None. One must wonder why the OSS would protect such men," he observed dryly.

His gaze turned to Pagotti as the supervisor, his equal, seeking an explanation.

"Consul, we don't know why the OSS was involved," Pagotti indicated.

"Slater's contact with the FBI is checking that angle out through Washington sources. We do know that the bullets used to kill the immigrants match the time frame for their escape from Europe. 1940's vintage 9 MM. Somehow, this Johnson character who keeps turning up is connected to the war and what went on in your country. That's where we thought you could help."

The fat detective pulled the tail of his overcoat from underneath his buttocks. The heat of the fire was making him perspire.

"I don't know how I could possibly help, Detective," the old man stated. I'll certainly do what I can."

"What we'd like to do, sir, if you can, is track all Yugoslavian passports, all Yugoslav citizens entering the States, going back to late August or so," Swanson interjected.

Dave Swanson decided to spell his boss before the guy had a heart attack. The Deputy stood up and placed his hands on the edge of the marble writing surface for balance as he continued:

"Do you have access to such a list? I know we could go through our State department in Washington but that will take too much time. We can't let this guy keep running around the Northwoods killing off our elderly while we wait for some bureaucrat to shuffle the right forms. Can you get us a list like that, maybe narrow it to those who've visited Minnesota?"

"I can get those names from our Embassy in Washington," Mendevich advised. "Rest assured, it will take but a day. If any of those individuals visited Minnesota, their names would also be recorded. That data will take a little bit more to obtain since its not computerized. But it can be done. Of course, I doubt that you will find any 'Johnson's' on the list. That's simply not a surname you'll find used in my country. It must be an alias."

"I'd have to agree," Slater interrupted.

She spoke quietly, the tone of her voice showing obvious respect. She was entranced by the simple eloquence of the man's demeanor, by the solidarity of his performance. No shred of his personal opinion escaped. There was no way to know what the man was thinking. Slater began anew:

"My thought is, and Deputy Swanson agrees, that whoever Mr. Johnson is or was, he has a connection to the military or the police in your country. He's obtained information on Hauptman, or Essen, or whatever his name really is, as well as on Budaslavich. Damos Tomich, information that even the old man's wife didn't know. And then there are these."

Deputy Slater reached inside the well–worn lid of her briefcase, pulled out a wrinkled evidence bag containing the two silver medals found on the dead men and delivered them to Mendevich.

The Yugoslavian pushed his chair away from his desk as he held the medals in his soft pink hands.

"He has politician's hands," observed Slater to herself, "unlike the rugged hands of his dead countryman, Adam Budaslavich."

A look of utter fascination occupied the diplomat's long face as he cautiously examined the little bits of silver suspended before his eyes. The fire reflected off the polished wood floor and threw subtle light across the medallions, illuminating them like diamonds.

After a moment of contemplation, the diplomat turned his attention towards the officers:

"These are indeed curious, Ms. Slater. Where in God's name did you get them?"

Though Medevich's performance continued to appear flawless, Deb Slater observed a hint of concern invade the Consul's voice.

"He's nervous," she thought.

For the first time since they walked through the door, Mr. Mendevich was unsure of himself. Slater sensed the medals were a key, a key to finding out who the hell the man known as Mr. Johnson was.

"We found one around the neck of each dead man. They're identical. Mrs. Budaslavich swears she'd never seen the medal or the chain before. And Hauptman's customers never saw him wear any jewelry. Not a ring or a watch, not a necklace of any kind."

She paused, allowing the Consul to grasp the significance of what she said. In a hurried breath, Slater got to the point:

"We think the killer put them around the victims' necks."

The tall old man in the expensive Italian suit rose deliberately from behind his desk. He turned his back to the officers and held the twisting medals in one hand. The officers could see that the Consul was looking intently into the fireplace, staring at the flames. After a short while, he spoke, in a voice low and tentative:

"I will see what I can do, officers. I cannot promise anything. These medals and what you tell me change everything; they make it more delicate, more sensitive. I will see. That's all I can promise."

Without moving from behind the sanctuary of his desk, he raised the medallions to Slater. She carefully took the objects from the Yugoslavian as the Consul turned his attention back to the warm glow of the fire.

Pagotti motioned Swanson and Slater to join him out in the foyer. The officers exited the mansion to confront the November angst encompassing the city, Mendevich having made it clear that their interview was over.

Chapter 18

December 1, 1991

Beyond providing a list of Yugoslav nationals who'd entered the country in the early fall of the year, Mendevich was not helpful. The deputies received no list of Yugoslav visitors to Minnesota from the consulate, no further hints or details regarding the origin of the medals; simply a master list from the Washington Embassy with thirteen hundred names on it. Slater knew she'd need Phil Chen's expertise to make the list manageable.

"Deb, if we limit our search for now to males, that should cut down the list by a third. And if we stick to the premise that whoever this guy is, he must have come into the country in early fall, arriving just before deer season, that gets us down to probably no more than a hundred names."

Chen was seated at Slater's desk. He was working on a laptop PC connected to a portable scanner, entering the list provided by the Consulate into the CPU. After he scanned in the list, Chen looked at Slater, smiling a devilish, infectious smile he always used on her.

"Phil, what good does putting this stuff into the computer do? I mean, we could go through the list and sort it by hand, couldn't we?" Debra asked.

The Deputy wasn't comfortable with computers. She didn't use them much and really didn't like them.

"No", she thought, "I don't understand them. That's why I avoid them."

"This list isn't in date order. It's not alphabetical either," Chen observed. "If we put it into the PC, the program will allow us to call up things in a specific order. By date, by first letter. Whatever. We can sort it the same way. Say we want only those names corresponding to October. The program will limit its search to those names and spit them back out at us. Or if you want all the first names beginning with 'T,' it will do that too. It'll take a job that could last a day and do it in seconds. That's the beauty of the beast, Deb."

"O.K. hotshot," Slater groaned. "Let's start with the obvious. Any 'Johnsons' in there?"

She knew there wouldn't be. But it was a logical place to start. Chen typed in the commands, selected the correct search mode and waited.

"No, no 'Johnsons.' Why not try any names, first or last, beginning with 'J'. Let's see if there are any."

Again he typed in the commands and waited as the hardware churned silently. There were numerous names, first and last, beginning with "J," listed. Jochivich, Jodick. No "Johnsons." Slater leaned over Chen's shoulder and observed the blue and yellow screen.

"Try 'John' separately. Johnson is derived from John, you know, John's son."

Chen nodded. His fingers tapped quickly across the white plastic key typing in the name "John." A brief whirl of the harddrive. A list of "Johns" appeared. Twenty or so.

"Now let's see how many of our 'Johns' arrived in the fall. Say between August 1 through October 15."

Again the information request was entered. Again, a brief wait. Five names were left.

"Sure looks easy when you let Chen's fingers do the walking," a voice offered.

Dave Swanson spoke the words as he arrived back from lunch, a smudge of catsup still occupying a corner of his lips. Slater grinned and pointed to the stain. Swanson sheepishly licked it off.

"So we've got five Johns that might be our Mr. Johnson. I'll give Herb a call and see if he can track down where those five are now. If they haven't left the country, maybe Herb can put a hold on their departure until we interview them. He'll need to pull some weight with the big boys to delay 'em but he can handle it. After all, he's a big boy himself," Slater said to no one in particular as she dialed the FBI agent's number.

Whitefeather took down the five names and promised to do what he could through the Washington office of the Bureau. He also had other news for Slater:

"Deb, you remember my little red head in DC? With INS? Well, she called me back about those two names you were interested in. Remember the 'Confidential' boys? She did some more digging with a buddy over at the CIA. While it's all pretty hush–hush on these kinds of things, he told her it was likely your two stiffs had cooperated with the OSS during the war, likely provided intelligence of some sort. That's the most probable reason for the OSS giving them help. Apparently, in some situations, the OSS wasn't above giving aid to known war criminals; minor ones mind you, in return for information. That really pissed off the Europeans, not to mention the Jews and the Soviets. I'm gonna see if I can't get an inkling as to the kind of help your two dead geezers might have given. Must have been pretty special to get free passage to the good old U.S. of A."

Slater thanked the FBI Agent and hung up the receiver. Her eyes glanced towards Chen but she was looking through him, staring out into the whiteness of early winter. After a moment, her mind came back into the room, back from wherever Herb's conversation had taken her.

"Whitefeather says he thinks the two dead men got OSS help because of information they gave our government. Says even some Nazi war criminals got protection. Kind of makes you wonder who's side we're on sometimes, don't it?"

Chen nodded. His smile had disappeared.

"Yeah, I think back to the war. I mean, I'm Chinese. My family was still on the mainland at the beginning. They weren't political. Not Nationalists. Not Communists. But the U.S. sticks its nose in, gives aid to the Nationalists. Screws up the whole damn country. For what? The Communists won anyway, my family barely escaped and came here. It took another thirty years for the Communists to trust the U.S. again."

They kicked around the case a bit more. Chen reminded Slater and Swanson that the fingerprints from the Minneapolis Safety Deposit box hadn't come back yet from Washington. It had been several weeks. Chen promised to get on it. He packed up his PC and left, back to the Cities, his lab. Swanson headed out to check on a fatal traffic accident out in the country, by Fish Lake, the heart of Fredenberg Township, where beer, driving and sharp curves continually proved they couldn't coexist.

Slater turned her attention to the other work on her desk. Other files. A rape out near Floodwood. A couple of burglaries on the Midway River. But it was tough to concentrate with an unsolved double homicide hanging in the background, lurking in the shadows. Her other work was definitely suffering because of it. She closed the rape file folder and dialed Rick's number at school. His voice always got her back into focus and allowed her to come to terms with her job. Rick always had a good story to tell. Today was no exception. He made her laugh.

In the middle of saying goodbye to her husband, near the end of her shift, the great bulk of Herb Whitefeather lumbered into her cubicle. The man paused over Slater like a falcon hovering over a mouse. She hung up the phone.

"What's up Herb? Why the surprise visit?"

The big man sat down heavily next to her. He had a yellow legal pad full of scribbling and doodles. His throat cleared.

"Goddamn it Deb, what in the hell did you get me into? After we talked, I called Red back at INS and asked her to see if she couldn't get some more info on why the OSS gave Budaslavich and Hauptman help. She said sure. Next thing I know, I'm on the line with my area supervisor, Max Reinberg in Chicago. He's screaming at me. No shit. Tells me I'm not gonna see retirement with the Bureau if I don't stop doing the work of the Sheriff's department. He starts reading me the riot act about my job, my caseload, reassignment to Miami. Christ, anywhere but fucking Miami."

Herb looked out the cubical towards Prescott's office.

"So, I ask him, I ask, 'What's wrong with assisting local law enforcement on a case which may well be ours in the end?' I mean, a double homicide involving interstate flight. I might end up with the file on my lap. He screams again, I can tell he's not listening. Tells me that's all well and good on other cases, but on this case and he says it like he means it, he says, 'Lay Off!' Then he hangs up. So I call Red up right away. And she's crying. Her supervisor did the same thing to her, told her there'd be no more helping Agent Whitefeather on the Minnesota matter. Period. End of discussion. All I get from her is a bunch of sobs. Except I did get her buddy's number at the CIA."

The big man stopped talking, trying to calm down, to regain his composure. Taking a deep breath, Whitefeather continued:

"This guy, Agent Fuqua, he's O.K. I mean, I tell him about Red. He's concerned. But tells me he's under the gun too. Already said too much. His boss is ready to can his ass over this thing. So I say, well if they're gonna can your ass anyway, why not give me some help? He thinks about it. Hangs up, then calls me back from a pay phone."

Slater was nestled deep into her chair, fully reclined, her feet resting on the edge of her desk. She found herself amazed. Herb had done more than anyone could expect. He had done the work for her, for their friendship.

"An hour or so later, he calls me back from another pay phone. I'd given him the names you passed along. You know, the 'Johns' Chen and you dug up. He tells me two of the guys are out of the country. Three are still here. One is in Phoenix. A physics professor doing research. One is in Boston going to medical school. The last one is in Chicago, coaching soccer at the University of Chicago on a one-year exchange. He arrived on October 10th from Belgrade."

Agent Whitefeather paused to relax.

"Oh yeah," the big man offered. "Fuqua couldn't find out anymore about the dead men. No one seems to know anything about how they got here. It happened too long ago, or at least, that's what Washington says. I'm afraid that's it."

Whitefeather looked up from the floor, his sad brown eyes seeking approval. Slater got up, took his hand and shook it vigorously.

"Thanks Herb. You're a hell of a friend to stick your neck out for me. What do you think? Think the guy in Chicago is worth talking to first?"

Whitefeather nodded his head. Slater continued with her train of thought:

"I agree. He's the closest one. His date of entry is consistent. He's obviously athletic, in shape. You'd expect that from a trigger man, right?"

Again, the Agent nodded.

Sheriff Prescott poked his head around the corner and smiled.

"Hello Herb. How's the FBI treatin' you?"

Prescott received no response. Shifting uneasily to Slater, the Sheriff asked the deputy if she wanted to go have a beer. It was quitting time.

"Sure," she replied.

"What about you, Herb?" the Sheriff asked.

The big man shook his head no and rose to leave the room.

"Gonna head home to a hot bath and sleep," Whitefeather quietly added.

The FBI agent exited into the hallway and disappeared.

"What's eating Herb?" Prescott inquired as he helped Slater on with her coat.

"He's in deep shit for helping me on the Wasoose investigation. Someone up top doesn't like us poking into whatever went on back in 1955 with our two dead immigrants. He's in danger of being reassigned," Slater responded.

"Too bad. Herb's a good man."

The Sheriff said the words with sincerity. It was true; Whitefeather was a good man. Slater turned off the light over her desk. As she buttoned up the coat, she thought about calling the Yugoslav Consul regarding the soccer coach in Chicago. But it was late. She could do it tomorrow.

As the two officers walked down the darkened hall, they passed a janitor slopping the tile floor in front of the elevators. Slater stopped the Sheriff by pulling gently on his sleeve.

"Is there any problem with Swanny and I going to Chicago?" Slater asked. "Some guy by the name of John Kobe. Yugoslavian soccer coach. His name came up on the list we got from the Consulate. I think we'd better talk to him."

Slater glanced at the Sheriff, uncertain if he was receptive to another unplanned expense forcing the Department's budget further into the red.

Prescott looked back, back into the dark of the hall, before meeting the Deputy's gaze.

"Shit," he thought, "she's serious. All my work on the budget and now this damn case had to come along."

But he knew that if Slater thought it was a good idea, he had to trust her instincts.

"Sure," he responded tentatively.

Nothing more was said as they walked towards the elevators. Entering one of the cars, the conveyance groaned annoyingly as they were lowered slowly to the ground, to where their companions waited a block away at the Outpost Bar. Prescott chuckled to himself, causing Slater to glance discretely at her boss. She was afraid to ask what was so funny.

With a firm bounce, the elevator stopped on the first floor. Prescott held the door while the deputy stepped out.

"You know, Ms. Slater," Prescott said between a grin, "if I'm going to foot the bill for you and Swanson to gallivant up and down the Midwest chasing some Yugoslavian hitman, drinks are definitely on you."

And they were.

Chapter 19

December 2, 1991

The harsh electronic ring of the phone disrupted Deputy Slater's concentration. She was sitting at a table in the Department's conference room, the contents of two murder files and packets full of evidence carefully organized in front of her. She reached across an unopened envelope from the BCA and picked up the telephone. It was Whitefeather:

"Deb, Herb. I just got off the phone with Fuqua again. Seems we've got everyone in Washington hopping mad on this one, stirred up a hornets nest, something like that. He's all through, can't do any more."

The big man stopped and took a breath. He was clearly excited about something. Something important.

"But before he pulled himself off this thing, he did us one small favor. He came up with a name. Not just any name. The guy who had the INS files of your two dead men sealed. Don't want to tell you more on the phone. Can you come over?"

Whitefeather paused, knowing that the answer would assuredly be "yes." Especially since the Federal Building lay only a few hundred feet to the South of the Courthouse. The huge granite blocks of the Federal Building formed a portion of the Duluth Civic Center. City Hall stood to the North, the County Courthouse dominated the center with the East side of the square defined by ornate flower gardens, a war memorial and Priley fountain.

"I'll be right over," the Deputy responded.

Whitefeather's office was a clutter of Native American portraits and symbols. First edition prints of Sitting Bull and Crazy Horse, Whitefeather's Sioux ancestors, adorned the walls. The only non–Sioux portrait was that of Chief Joseph of the Nez Perce. Underneath, his words of surrender to General Crook were inscribed: "I will fight no more forever."

Slater knew Herb raised Appaloosa ponies on his eighty-acre hobby farm in the valley of the St. Louis River. She also knew the reason he selected such a stubborn horse to breed: they were a constant reminder of the Nez Perce, a reminder of the fragile existence that the Native American people clung to in the White world. He told her that once when she asked about the horses, about the photos of his prize brood mare and stallion on the wall. Fifty or so wild Apps ran loose on his pastures. He trained only two or three at a time for sale. The rest never knew the bit. Herb said that kept their spirits wild, like the spirits of his ancestors.

Slater sat down on a long leather-covered couch in front of his desk. Whitefeather leaned back in his chair, holding a pink phone message pad as he spoke:

"Seems that Fuqua was able to get into the backup files on the Agency's network, search by date, INS index, different parameters. Took him a long time, dodged a few nosy data clerks while doing it. Anyway, he eventually pinned down a name. The guy who sealed this thing up, shoved it into the desk drawer where it wasn't supposed to found."

Slater grew anxious, wanting the name. Her friend sensed her anticipation, her desire to know the information.

"So stop with the suspense, Herb. Who the hell is he?"

Slater rose to her feet, tossed her hair to one side and sat on the corner of the desk. He smiled.

"You ever heard of a guy by the name of Marvin Field?"

Whitefeather knew there were probably very few people in the State of Minnesota who didn't know the name. World War II hero. Millionaire. Pioneer of the computer software boom that blossomed in the Twin Cities in the late 1970's.

"Hell, Herb, who hasn't. Field's one of the richest men in the State. You can't be serious. Marvin Field was the man who put the lid on Budaslavich and Hauptman's files? How in the hell could he do that?"

"Can't tell you, Deb. Fuqua couldn't dig any deeper. He suggested you folks tramp on down to St. Paul and drop by for a cup of coffee and conversation with good 'ol Marvin. You know, shake the tree a little and see what falls out."

The agent put down the pad and studied the woman over a warm can of Tab. He sipped the brown syrup slowing, waiting for the deputy to reply.

Slater pulled herself away from the edge of the desk and looked into the tired eyes of Chief Joseph. Her voice grew very quiet. Whitefeather had to strain to hear all the words:

"Swanny and I are going to Chicago. Remember Mendevich, the Yugoslav Consul?"

"Sure do. Wasn't much help as I recall."

"Well, when I called him back to check on a guy by the name of John Kobe, a Yugoslavian working at the University of Chicago on a coaching exchange, I couldn't get the time of day from the Consul. He referred me to the Yugoslavian Military Attaché at their Embassy in Washington."

"What'd the Attaché have to say?"

"Couldn't get a line in, with the civil war going on and all, I've been told it will be virtually impossible to get a call into the Embassy."

"So why are you going to Chicago?"

"That's where Kobe is supposed to be. The way Mendevich reacted to my call, there's no question in my mind that this guy bears a look-see. Swanny and I gotta get to him fast. I don't have time to chat with Marvin Field," Slater stated with emphasis.

"What the hell did you tell me all that for? Now you got my curiosity level up again. Probably more dangerous to my health to elevate my curiosity than my cholesterol. Now I'm gonna have to do some poking around on my own, maybe shoot down to the Cities and stick my nose into your pile o' shit. And if my boss finds out, he's gonna step on the pile. With my nose still in it. But what the hell, this thing needs a guy with some native tracking skills to flush out the truth. Yeah, I'll go see Field for you. Can't see any other way to do it."

Whitefeather kicked up his feet, putting them atop the mass of open files and papers on his desk. His big arms moved in a circle, stretching taunt muscles, releasing tension.

"Tell you what Deb. This is so confusing, so wrapped up in politics, I'm gonna sit down with the boss and ask him to let me work on it. Officially. He'll whine and cry, but once he hears Field is involved, he won't be able to say no. I'll act as official liaison for the Feds. You guys need someone to do some running and quite frankly, there's not shit going on in Duluth for the Federal Bureau of Investigation. There's ample jurisdiction for us to assist. Maybe I can stir this all up so the pot comes to a boil."

Debra Slater stood up from the couch.

"Thanks Herb. Keep me posted on what Mr. Field has to say about all of this."

"Sure thing, Deb. Good luck in Chicago."

The Deputy walked back to the Courthouse feeling like a tremendous load had been lifted from her.

Herb Whitefeather was as good as there was. He'd get something from Field that explained what the hell was going on or turn over every possible lead in the attempt.

Back at her desk, she fingered the unopened envelope she'd received from the BCA. Most likely from Chen. Opening it, she found she'd been right. It was a brief letter from the forensic expert:

Deb:

The fingerprints found on the safety deposit box cannot be identified using sources available in this country. Because of the likelihood that a foreign national is involved, I have sent complete sets of prints to Interpol and Scotland Yard on the off chance that our Mr. Johnson has prints on record overseas. The prints do not match any of the bank personnel or the victims.

I'll keep you posted.

Best Regards,
Phil.

Another dead-end, another blind alley. Slater neatly folded the letter along its original creases and returned it to its envelope. Time to call it a night.

The next morning, December 3, the two deputies had no trouble finding O'Hare Field in Chicago. The Northwest flight landed there as it was supposed to. But the drive to the University of Chicago was another matter.

Neither Deputy had any concept of direction in the Windy City. The map they obtained from the rental car agency showed only the main streets and freeways, not the byways and side streets they needed to follow to locate the University's gymnasium. The trip took three and a half-hours. It should have taken forty minutes.

Athletic Director Ernie Branch wasn't pleased that he had to accommodate two very late, out–of–town cops. It was bad enough much of his time was spent mollifying professors who rebelled when asked to give athletes the same exam twice. In his own mind, he should have been spending his time either finding scholarship funding for next year or supervising his coaches, not holding the hands of two deputies from Duluth, Minnesota. His displeasure at their intrusion was obvious.

The A.D.'s office in the Frank Bartlett Gymnasium was about the size of Slater's cubicle, but it held the A.D., his secretary and all of the department's records. Every square inch of the floor was devoted to piles of computer printouts, file cabinets and boxes of athletic supplies. There was only one cushioned side chair in the office for use by visitors. Slater sat. Swanson stood. The secretary was dismissed.

Swanson and Slater were in plain clothes. Their uniforms and badges meant very little in Cook County, Illinois. They knew it. The A.D. knew it. So why offend him with the pretense?

Branch had been a wide receiver for the Browns back in the late 1970's. Never a star, always a possession receiver. Six or seven hundred yards a year. Average speed. But never a dropped ball. He had been five ten, one eighty-five in the pros. He tipped the scales at two ten these days. Even at that weight, Branch remained muscular, the result of competitive weight lifting after his playing days were over. Branch's eyes shone with the black brilliance of coal. The intensity of his gaze burrowed into the inner sanctum of anyone who dared return his stare. He had big hands, hands that could palm a basketball, or a beachball for that matter. His head was as bald as an egg, shaved that way on purpose. The glossy dark skin of his scalp made him look even more ornery, mean. He liked it that way.

"Mr. Branch, as I told you on the phone, we'd like to talk to Coach Kobe, if we could. We've got some questions we'd like to ask him about his whereabouts a few weeks ago. Do you mind if we see him?"

Swanson took the lead in talking to the A.D. He sensed Slater was taken back by the guy's demeanor. She wasn't used to the athletic bravado, hadn't grown up with it like he had.

"Listen, let's get one thing straight," Branch muttered. "I don't care who you are or what you want. You're not gonna disrupt my soccer team. We're getting ready to play in the Superdome Holiday Classic over Christmas break. I'll be damned if I'll let you two distract the team. No way are you going to walk around here and cause a scene. Or talk to Kobe in front of the boys. You can wait here, I'll go get him myself."

"Certainly, Mr. Branch, anything you say. That sounds fine," Swanson replied.

The Deputy found himself intimidated by the man's presence. Swanson continued to talk out of nervousness:

"Can you tell us whether Kobe was on the campus the last week of October, first week of November? That's kind of crucial to us."

Dave Swanson followed the A.D.'s finger as it thumbed through a big desk calendar. The man's narrow index finger came to the appropriate time frame on the calendar and stopped.

"Looks like Kobe was in St. Paul running a coaches clinic at Hamline College," Branch said. "October 25th through November 7th. Why you need to know?"

"Has to do with some problems in Duluth around that time, Mr. Branch," Slater interrupted, noting that she was no longer intimidated by the man's gruff exterior. "Can't tell you much more than that at this point. Just part of the investigation, covering all the bases. You understand, part of the job," Slater related, smiling falsely.

Whatever the real impact her smile might have had on the man, it never showed. Branch's forearms bulged as he pulled himself away from his chair and slipped on a nylon jacket and baseball cap in one smooth, fluid motion. Without a word, the Athletic Director opened the glass door and walked out of the room leaving only the residual memory of his cool stare.

Swanson and Slater sat silently in the cramped office. An old radiator continually hissed, releasing excessive, wet heat. A plastic Chicago Bears clock on a bare concrete block wall verified Branch had been gone twenty minutes. It seemed like an hour.

In the midst of the silence, the A.D.'s secretary, Ms. Beatrice, a woman of nearly sixty with white, lifeless hair, weighing scarcely an ounce over ninety pounds, opened the door to the office without warning and rushed into the room.

Branch had every intention of bringing Kobe back to his office to meet the two cops. He didn't want to. But, being from Chicago, he knew it didn't pay to argue with the police. He learned his lesson on the South Side, in the projects. Don't mess with the cops, they'll shoot you, plant a gun. No questions asked. They had the power, the courts. He had to keep them happy. Let the Slav talk to them. Then they'd leave.

The Legacy

As he walked from his office to the Fieldhouse entrance, Branch wondered why the cops wanted to talk to Kobe. The guy was a perfect gentlemen. Kobe had learned how to play the University political game early on. Branch hadn't been happy to see his own coach, Bruce Burns, go to Belgrade in the middle of the turmoil in Yugoslavia. But Burns went and Branch tried hard not to like the foreigner, Burns being Branch's only real friend on the faculty. Black and from the Ivy League, Burns was the All–time goal scorer on the Yale soccer team, a man, like Branch, of color. Still, Burns went and Kobe came. The Yugoslav's professionalism, his work ethic, won Branch over. The A.D. had to admit the Slav had probably forgotten more things about the sport of soccer than Burns ever knew.

Walking into the Fieldhouse, the Athletic Director spotted Kobe standing in the middle of the team. Twenty-six young men were vying for eighteen spots on the bus to New Orleans. Branch stopped short of the group and watched Kobe demonstrate a header into the net. Branch waited patiently for the coach to notice him. Kobe glanced up, kicked the ball over to an assistant and trotted over.

"What's up Ernie?" the foreigner asked.

Kobe's black nylon warm-ups were stained from sweat. He didn't teach with a blackboard but by demonstration. The A.D. admired that. The Yugoslav was about the same height as Branch but not nearly as thickly built. Still, the soccer coach's form held definite sinew and strength, especially in the thighs and calves. Branch had always wished he'd been blessed with thighs like Kobe's when he played in the Pros. Kobe was more slender of waist, of shoulder, built for soccer, not American football.

"John, I've got two cops from Duluth, Minnesota who say they want to talk to you. Dunno what they want. Can you take a break, see them now? Then we can get them the hell outta here," Branch advised.

The A.D. looked back at the team as he spoke. Curt Young, last year's captain, now an assistant coach, was taking over, leading a passing drill. Branch didn't really understand soccer skills or strategy. He wanted to keep it that way. He looked back at Kobe.

"I can give you some time now," Kobe responded. "Young can take the practice for the next half hour or so. But I got to be back for the last half-hour,

OK? Putting in some special plays for the tournament. You know, a Christmas present."

Kobe's lips parted in a grin. Branch smiled but not before noting that there was something amiss in Kobe's eyes. As a wide receiver, Branch had always watched the defensive back's eyes; Kobe's eyes flashed a look of concern. About the team? About the police? Branch couldn't tell.

Kobe turned and yelled at Young to take the practice. The tall blond graduate student nodded. He was also a foreigner, an Aussie. "Soon," thought the A.D., "they'll rename this place United Nations University." The two men began to walk towards Branch's office.

They left the bright lights of the Fieldhouse. Branch and the coach entered a long, narrow hallway. As the A.D. turned a corner in the dim corridor, he felt a slight rush of air behind his head as a tremendous blow crashed onto the base of his skull, snapping his neck.

"Sorry, Ernie," Kobe whispered.

Ms. Beatrice's sudden entrance into Branch's office woke Swanson from a brief nap. The old woman staggered across the metal threshold, nearly falling into Slater's lap and looked up into the female Deputy's eyes.

"Mr. Branch has been attacked. Maybe a broken skull," the woman reported.

Ms. Beatrice's body started to shiver as she spoke. Swanson pulled his coat off of the back of Branch's chair and covered the distraught secretary.

"When did it happen?" Swanson asked in a concerned tone.

The secretary's voice cracked, betraying her anxiety, as she answered:

"I don't know. All I know is that Curt Young, the assistant coach, told the campus police that Ernie left with Coach Kobe. He never made it back here. One of the soccer players going out to bring in some pylons from the bleachers found the athletic director. Mr. Branch is still out of it. The ambulance is taking him to County General now."

"What about Kobe? Where's Mr. Kobe?" Slater inquired.

"I don't know. No one's seen him. Not since he left the Fieldhouse."

Miss Beatrice was beginning to calm down. Her breathing slowed. She seemed more focused.

"How are you doing," Swanson asked.

"I'll be fine, officers," she insisted.

The Legacy

The detectives slipped on their jackets and headed for the door. As they walked down the narrow concrete hallway, Slater had no idea what was on her partner's mind. But there was no doubt at all remaining for Deb Slater. John Kobe was their man, fingerprints or no fingerprints. It really didn't matter what Scotland Yard or Interpol had to say. The man known as Mr. Johnson, or John Kobe, or whatever he called himself, was the killer. But where the hell was he?

Chapter 20

October 10, 1991

Before civil war broke out in his homeland, he had been given orders to find Franz Essen and Damos Tomich and bring them in. The war hadn't impacted those orders; those in command of UDBA had not changed; only the enemy had. Once again, the enemy wore Croatian colors. But the reasons behind the war, behind the strife tearing Yugoslavia apart at the seams, were far less clear in 1991 than they had been in 1941. No, the war had not changed his job. He was empowered to bring enemies, old enemies, to the consulate in Minneapolis by whatever means necessary. Petrich would see to it that they were transported to the Embassy in Washington, then on to Belgrade. And then to the grave.

He was also supposed to find the gold, if any of it still existed. That was secondary. It was doubtful, very doubtful that any gold remained after forty-five years.

It had been easy enough finding the two conspirators. UDBA had long ago gained access to the CIA archives regarding the fugitives. Jack Kobe knew he could bring the war criminals in; he always had, he always did. He snared his prey with little fanfare or noise. He descended upon his victims like an Osprey picking up a trout from a pond; a mere flutter of wings, and then, nothing.

When he traveled from Belgrade to Chicago to take the coaching job, ostensibly as an exchange, in reality, as a cover, he wanted to believe he could do it, could meet the killers of his family, capture them and return them to the gallows, without hate, without malice or a need for revenge. It was an illusion.

Essen had been nothing to locate. Despite changing his name to Frank Hauptman, it had been nothing for Kobe to find the man, to sit down in his orange Eddie Bauer jacket and field pants in the bar that Hauptman owned in Northeastern Minnesota. It had been nothing to look like a typical Twin Cities hunter, make small talk with Hauptman about the weather, about the imaginary life Kobe created for himself. From his first glance at the man over the bar, he knew that Hauptman had to die. From the moment their eyes met, he knew that to be the case. Whether Hauptman sensed any danger, Kobe did not know. October 28 was the day. The Yugoslavian determined that Hauptman would die that very day. But Damos Tomich walking into the bar changed all that.

They remained aloof of each other when Tomich, calling himself Budaslavich, first sat at the bar. Two or three stools apart. Each sipping a tap beer. Flat, no fizz. An old keg. Tomich had a Pabst. Kobe, playing a part, ordered the same. The icy silence between them melted when Hauptman said something to Tomich in Serbo-Croation. Kobe smiled and looked up from the cartoons on the bar napkin. He responded in Tomich's native tongue. It made the big man's mouth turn into a wide grin.

For the next half an hour, Kobe lied; blatantly making up a detailed history of the man called Jack Johnson. A man who did not exist. Emigrated from Yugoslavia in 1969. Croatian. Math teacher at Lincoln Middle School in Apple Valley. Up to do some scouting for the deer opener, November 1. Tomich bought the story—all of it. Kobe knew he could wait to deal with Hauptman. The German would be there, behind the bar. Bigger game would be bagged first:

"So friend Budaslavich, where do you suggest a wandering Croat like myself can find a good piece of woods to hunt?" Kobe asked. "I'm new to this area. What do you call it, Comstock? I've always hunted down south, by St. Cloud. Corn fed deer. I wanted to try some real hunting, in the deep woods, like the old country."

Kobe laid it on thick; thick accent, thick lies.

"Well, little teacher, I hunt over by Long Lake, near the Wasoose," the old Ustashi observed. "Always room for one more. Especially a countryman. Frank, you got a map? I'll show you where I mean."

Hauptman produced a USGS square of the Wasoose. The map was well creased, stained by cooking oil and kitchen grease. Tomich stood up and pointed at the document:

"Right here. That's the forest road off Long Lake access. You see these three ponds? They were all good fishing lakes. Now, swamp and muck. Anyway, that's the three Wasoose. Best hunting I've found. You're welcome to try it."

Tomich pointed to a full head mount of a ten-point whitetail buck hanging over the bar.

"See that fella? I got him ten years ago on the Wasoose. Two hundred fifty six pounds dressed. One shot with my 30-06. Big bastard. Right Frank?"

Hauptman grunted, a thoroughly noncommittal response.

Kobe could tell Hauptman was beginning to feel uneasy around him. The UDBA operative caught the flash of a steady stare, actually more of a fleeting scowl, cross Hauptman's face. The German was starting to watch Kobe with particular care. Jack Kobe knew it was time to go.

"When's the best time to hunt there? I've gotta see some friends in Duluth the next few days but I'll back out here for the opener. I'd like to try it."

Another lie. He had no friends in Duluth, just a shabby room in a rundown hotel on the hillside. Keeping to himself kept him alive, had to be that way whenever he was getting ready to kill. He needed total concentration to prepare. A funeral for such a large man, even one getting on in years, took time, took planning.

"I'm gonna be out there on the First, all day. Take a ride up. There are a few stands I can put you in. See my pickup?" the Croatian asked as he motioned to a vehicle parked outside the window. Kobe glanced out the freshly cleaned glass and nodded.

"You'll see the Ford parked where I walk in. Follow the trail. You'll find me. Plenty of room for another hunter. Here's my phone number in case you can't make it. How 'bout yours?"

Tomich seemed genuinely happy writing his telephone number on a napkin. The old man seemed pleased to have a younger companion to hunt with. Kobe thanked him and folded the napkin before placing it in the pocket of his jacket. The bar owner ripped off a corner of the November calendar and gave it to Jack Johnson.

"Hey Frank, put a note on the First so I remember my new hunting partner's gonna be up, will ya?" Tomich added as he watched Kobe write a number on the scrap of paper.

Hauptman obliged the big man and wrote a brief message on the calendar. Kobe folded his number up and passed it to Budaslavich.

The Yugoslav agent wondered how the Ustashi would react when he found out there was nothing but death waiting for him on the Wasoose? He guessed the big man would try to beat him, try to fire first. Age made it improbable that Tomich could take him out, impossible really. Kobe was only forty-six and in top physical shape; a world class athlete in his youth, a world class assassin by profession. Tomich was in his seventies. Still powerful across the buttocks and shoulders, but the quickness, the eyes, the motor skills were obviously diminished by age. The old man had no chance at all, Kobe decided. None.

"I'll be there, friend Budaslavich. Maybe with a little plum brandy to warm us. Yes, I'll be there on the opener. The First," Kobe offered through a feigned smile.

"Perfect day," Kobe thought. "The First, the anniversary of the Sava. All Saints Day."

Hauptman could wait. The German, while mildly suspicious, would never understand the true reason for Jack Kobe's visit to the Comstock Lake Inn. At least, not until he too felt a 9 mm slug tear into his heart.

Kobe's business was completed. He paid his tab and left the dim smoke-filled atmosphere of the bar to confront the crisp snap of the Northwest wind.

November One. Kobe waited in a rental car for the sun to rise from behind a ridge of black spruce blocking the horizon. The Agent was ready. His muscles ached with anticipation. There was no way Tomich could escape.

Kobe waited on the Long Lake Road in the darkness, concealed from view, still able to see the main road, able to see Tomich and tail the man when he drove by. Kobe had memorized the license plate, make and model of Tomich's pickup. When the vehicle pulled by in the darkness, headlights on, it wasn't hard to follow. Kobe kept his distance. He didn't want to arouse the old man's curiosity. Tomich had been a soldier, had played the game, even if it had been forty-odd years ago. One had to be careful; one could not afford to be too cocky. Surprise meant life, success. It meant the old man would fall.

The pickup turned onto a forest road leading to the Wasoose. Kobe continued down the main road, eventually parking his rental car in an abandoned farmyard. The UDBA Agent walked a quarter mile back to the forest road towards the Wasoose where he found Tomich's truck, the engine still gurgling in the cold, the hood still warm. He followed the dull outline of Tomich's footprints in the snow, carefully placing his boots in the tracks of the larger man, concealing his presence from all but the most observant.

Crouching beneath a stand of cedar trees lining the trail, Kobe watched the distant form of his prey amble slowly down the middle of the path. Lazy daylight crept into the forest, making it more difficult to remain hidden. Kobe concentrated on the old man for a minute, debating whether to simply put his sights on him and kill the Ustashi where he stood. But Kobe knew he couldn't risk such an open shot. Not on the trail. He wanted it to be in the quiet of the woods, where he could surprise the man, give him the story, tell Tomich why the man had to die. Then do it. Afterwards, make it look like an accident. Get out, leaving no trace of his presence. That was the plan he'd thought out. That was the plan that would keep Jack Kobe alive.

The sun broke free of the trees but was quickly replaced by ugly, overcast sky. Thick clouds suppressed the day. Kobe stalked Tomich from a safe distance. The Agent stopped when the Ustashi slowed to reach into a buttpack pulled tight across the big man's ample waist. Removing a thermos bottle, Tomich drank coffee directly from the container. The Ustashi screwed the cap back on the bottle. Reaching into his jacket pocket, Tomich removed a tin of Red Man and placed a thick black wad of snuff firmly in the corner of his cheek. Kobe watched Tomich reach into his jacket, pull out a clip, jam it into his rifle and chamber a round. The click of the weapon's metal receiver disturbed the silence of the woodlands. The old man resumed his walk through the forest.

Kobe remained far behind his intended victim, waiting for the man to get settled, to find a deer stand and fall asleep. The younger man wanted to surprise his prey.

A little after 11:00am, Jack Kobe left his hiding place. He began to track the butcher anew. Though Kobe's arms were no longer tense, his fingers were stiff from the cold. It didn't matter. When it came time to pull the trigger, he knew they would be fine.

When Kobe joined the UDBA, he converted his father's antique Mauser into a lighter, more accurate weapon: competition weight and specifications, reduced stock, scope, modified receiver and most importantly, a silencer. It was easy to bring the rifle along, to fill out the appropriate forms, to have the right connections. The rifle was simply a sporting weapon for competitive shooting. The silencer would have been tough to explain. But it was manufactured of non–metallic synthetic fibers making it indiscernible by x–ray. Hidden inside the guts of a laptop computer, the silencer was innocuous, the artful handiwork of the talented craftsmen of UDBA. The silencer never failed him; it kept the deaths he caused secret and unheard.

The Legacy

Shortly after noon, Kobe pulled the bolt of the Mauser and chambered a shell; an original 9mm cartridge left over from the war. His mother had given him the rifle and a box of bullets on his thirteenth birthday. She told him how the weapon was found next to the father he never knew, after Eli Kobe fell at Drvar, fighting the Germans.

The operative slid the bolt forward in a deliberate manner to avoid causing any sound as the bolt seated itself. It was time to send the bastard to hell.

Kobe circled the deer stand. He saw that he had guessed right. The old man was resting high above the ground in a platform supported by birch logs nailed to a clump of black alders. Tomich was slumped over, sleeping carelessly, his rifle leaning against him. The barrel of the Croatian's weapon rested against a crude birch railing enclosing the stand. Kobe stopped short of the platform and called out:

"Friend Budaslavich."

Tomich stirred. The old man raised the brim of his cap and tried to focus his eyes. A look of delayed recognition swept across the Ustashi's face.

"Ah, my young Twin Cities' friend. You managed to find me, eh? And how is it you were able to follow me out here, into the woods?" Tomich asked.

The old man stood up and stretched his arms. His brilliant orange hunting jacket was unbuttoned, exposing his belly. The Ustashi's stomach hung heavily over a distressed brown leather belt.

"I'm a Croat, Adam, just like you. I can't get lost in a little forest like this. Besides, those big feet of yours are hard to miss."

Tomich looked down at his Sorels before observing:

"I guess you're right, friend. Even Hauptman could follow these through the snow."

Kobe opened his coat and pulled out a tin flask of plum brandy- 150 proof. He raised the flask to the old man.

"I brought brandy. Come down and share a snap with me," Kobe offered with an apparently genuine smile.

"You bet," Tomich responded. "I'm fond of that Yugoslav petrol."

The Ustashi used the English term for gasoline even though they spoke in their tongue. Kobe watched as the big man labored to exit the deer stand.

"Arthritis has crept into his knees," Kobe thought. "Another edge."

Tomich's rifle dangled carelessly by a sling from one shoulder.

"Likely on safe. Another advantage," the UDBA Agent thought to himself.

They stood a few feet from each other as Kobe passed the flask to his victim. The old man took a deep swig of the brandy. A drop of liquor escaped the Ustashi's mouth and spilled down Tomich's coarse, white whiskers. Tomich sought to return the flask. Kobe gestured for the man to keep the bottle as the UDBA agent began to speak in a soft, careful voice:

"No, you hold onto it, Damos Tomich. I have other business to attend to."

The Ustashi's attention was momentarily averted as he watched a bluejay flit through the dense undergrowth of the swamp. The old Ustashi's eyes continued to follow the bird as it dodged between evergreen boughs. Kobe noted that the muscles in the old man's neck tensed at the mention of the Ustashi's given name.

"What did you call me?" the former Ustashi officer exclaimed, his words quick and excited.

Tomich's head began to rotate towards the smaller man as he finished speaking. Kobe discerned that the Ustashi's eyes were wild, like the hopeless eyes of a wolf cornered by a pack of dogs.

"It's as it should be," Kobe thought, "The bastard should know fear before he dies."

The muzzle of the Mauser was pointed at the old man's spine. Kobe took a step back. The silencer had been snapped on while the bluejay captivated Tomich's attention. How long had it been? A second? Two? The old man's facial complexion lost its ruddy color. Blood drained from Tomich's cheeks leaving his skin the color of snow.

"I called you by your true name. Your baptismal name. Your Ustashi name," the UDBA Agent whispered.

"Ustashi" slid over Kobe's tongue with a hard-edged, insulting inflection.

"You remember the Sava, don't you? You remember the women and children you murdered there? Four of them were my uncles and aunts. They were killed by you and the Nazis in cold blood, as I will shortly kill you."

Kobe sought to restrain his hatred, strained hard to keep it under control. He found it impossible to contain four decades of anger:

"Turn around, pig. It's time for you to die."

The Legacy

His words crossed the stillness of the cold November morning with an assurance of finality.

Tomich complied and turned around. As he opened his mouth to speak, Kobe observed that the old man was trembling. Tomich was less polished, less calm, facing the barrel of the Mauser, than Kobe had expected. The man was not a soldier. He was a coward.

Begging for his life, Tomich's plea for leniency was uttered in obvious desperation, The Ustashi's words spilled out almost too quickly for Kobe to make sense of them:

"How do you know who I am? Where I was? How do you know of the Sava? That was an innocent mistake. Orders from the Gestapo, the SS, the Nazis."

Tomich took a breath and tried to compose himself. When he spoke again, his voice was lower, his words much more defined:

"I didn't want to. I tried to talk them out of it. I couldn't. Don't you see it was either them or me? The SS would have shot me if I didn't follow through with it."

The old man began to cry, not merely a tear or two, but a flood of tears cascaded onto the bright fleece of his jacket. Kobe steadied the Mauser and began to apply pressure against the trigger:

"Save it, Ustashi whore. My father's brothers and sisters were butchered as little babies. You were there. You and Essen placed your pistols against the babies' heads and sent their souls to God. Your appeal is denied. I am the judge. The jury. The executioner."

Kobe's finger sought the point of no return.

"But I can make you a rich man. I have gold. Tito's gold. Pounds of it. Bars of it. Hidden. And I know another with as much. You can have it all. It's easy to find. I'll give it to you. I have a wife, children. It was a long time ago. Can't you see that?"

Though Kobe's finger relaxed, the Yugoslavian maintained his vigil. One move by the Croatian and the rifle would explode, sending a bullet tearing through the old man's chest.

"Who, Ustashi? Who is this other man with the gold? Is it friend Essen who now calls himself Hauptman? Why do I need you to make that deal? I've got a bullet saved for his black heart as well. I don't need gold. It won't turn me from my task."

Kobe's lips parted briefly in a small smile.

Tomich felt it was the only opening he would have. The old man knew any movement he made would be risky. His own weapon hung useless from his shoulder. But Tomich gauged there would be no second lapse by the little man, no affording of another opportunity.

The big man's quickness surprised Jack Kobe. Before the UDBA Agent could pull the trigger on his Mauser, Tomich pulled the Browning automatic off of his shoulder. The Ustashi was far more agile than his descent from the deer stand had shown. But the bullet's course through Tomich's orange jacket, through the brightly colored felt, through the old man's Pendleton shirt, dropped Tomich before his brain could coax his index finger to squeeze the trigger of the Browning. Death closed the Ustashi's only avenue of escape. The traitor's heart ceased to beat before his body fell heavily onto the sparse snow of the Wasoose.

It had all been perfect. Until the boy came.

Kobe crouched over the cooling corpse of the Ustashi. In the distance, he heard the sound of footsteps against snow. They were obviously human footsteps from the telltale pattern of the gait. Sensing he was about to be discovered, Kobe grabbed a low-hanging spruce branch, broke it off, and swept away the imprints of his boot prints as he retreated into the cover of the alders.

Behind the dark safety of thick brush, Kobe measured the approach of the stranger. Against the peace of the forest, in the stillness of the place, the UDBA agent heard the sound of yet another shell being introduced into a rifle chamber.

"Crack."

The retort of a hunting rifle's discharge disturbed the woods.

"Have I been found?" Kobe muttered to himself.

A bullet sailed by him, missing his hiding place by a few feet. Kobe raised his weapon, intent upon defending himself. The sound of human footsteps resumed. The intruder moved closer at a quickening pace. Just as the Agent was able to focus on the form of the approaching intruder, Jack Kobe's attention was distracted.

The Legacy

"Crash."

A frightened deer bounded through the thicket concealing the Yugoslavian. Kobe heard the hooves pound excitedly over the crust of the snow. A few meters behind his hiding place, Kobe caught a fleeting glimpse of the animal. The doe's slender body, charged with the adrenaline of fear, slashed deftly through the underbrush. Kobe watched the deer's tail, urgent and upright, plunge unharmed into the grasp of intractable swamp.

The UDBA agent's attention returned to the hunter. A boy appeared next to Tomich's body. Kobe watched as the young hunter bent at the knees and haltingly reached out towards the corpse's face. The boy's gloved hand never touched the dead man's skin.

"Oh my God, I've killed him," the youth exclaimed. "I thought he was a deer. Shit! I've got to get the hell away from him. Got to think. Oh Christ, what the hell have I done?" the boy cried out.

Quickly, without further reflection, the boy abandoned the corpse and retreated down the same trail by which he had arrived, leaving Jack Kobe alone in the woods with the body of Damos Tomich.

It took little effort to make Tomich's death seem like an accident. After he was certain the boy was gone, Kobe pocketed a single bullet from Budaslavich's rifle. He removed a 30-06 cartridge, the bullet having been fired by Kobe at a local indoor rifle range, and placed the spent round under the dead man's body. He gambled that the police investigators, if the death was investigated at all, would simply acknowledge the shell and the single wound and conclude it came from Tomich's own weapon without running ballistic testing on the shell.

"An accident, Mr. Tomich. A tragic hunting accident," Kobe whispered as he deposited the shell in the snow beneath the dead man.

Placing the dead man's rifle under the torso of the corpse, Kobe rolled the body over, covering the weapon. All evidence of Kobe and the boy's bootprints were wiped clean with a spruce bough as the Yugoslav retraced his steps, walking backwards in the footprints of the dead man. He would have left the boy's prints at the scene, implicating the young man in the death, but Kobe was unable to do so without leaving his own prints behind as evidence.

His footprints obliterated, Kobe placed the casing of the fatal Mauser round into the pocket of his jacket.

The UDBA Agent failed to realize that the seam of his pocket had been torn open as he struggled through the thick growth along the Wasoose. The Agent was unaware when the spent Mauser round fell from his pocket into the snow, leaving behind a trace that someone other than the old man had been there.

His tracks concealed, Kobe left the Wasoose and returned to his room in Duluth. It was in his room at the Happy Holidays Inn that the UDBA agent realized his mistake:

"Damn. The cartridge must have fallen through this hole. Carelessness, that's all there is to it," Kobe cursed to himself.

For all of his well-thought-out preparations, something had gone awry. The change in circumstances concerned him. But upon further consideration, Kobe doubted that it mattered:

"The police won't likely find one lost shell in the depths of the woods and it's of little consequence even if they do. It was an accident. That's what they'll find. That's what they'll say."

His argument with himself took some serious effort:

"They'll see the old man's cartridge. See no one else has been around. The kid's so scared, he'll never talk. They'll conclude it was an accident—simply an accident."

He gave the lost cartridge no further thought.

Franz Essen's demise was far simpler. Essen had been caught in the middle of cleaning his bar. Kobe knocked on the door. Feigning injury, he dragged his right leg as if he'd sprained an ankle. Essen appeared suspicious of the schoolteacher but apparently saw no harm in letting him into the tavern.

"Hello, Hauptman. I banged up my leg out hunting, need a ride to Duluth. Can I use your phone to call a friend to pick me up?" Kobe requested.

"Seems like an imposition to me, asking someone to drive all the way out here for a minor leg injury," the German observed, "But suit yourself. It will cost you extra. It's long distance to town."

"Thanks. I'll use my calling card," Kobe related. "I see you're busy. I'll call and then wait out in the car."

"I'd appreciate that. I've got work to do."

Jack Johnson, as Kobe was known to the German, placed a phone call to a number in Duluth. It was actually Kobe's own number. After a few brief comments to no one on the other end. Kobe hung up the phone.

"Thanks again, friend. Someone should be here within the half hour," Kobe said, exiting the bar.

The UDBA Agent had determined that Essen was alone. As Kobe walked towards his car, he heard the "click" of a deadbolt: Essen had locked the door.

The Yugoslavian waited several minutes, allowing the old man's nerves to settle, before removing a set of locksmith's tools from his jacket. At the exterior door, Kobe gingerly slid the appropriate tool into the lock, opening it without resistance.

Safely inside, Kobe heard Essen singing. The tune was German, one Kobe did not know. The lyrics were delivered in a plaintive style, without emotion.

Essen worked on, oblivious to the intruder. His aging hands gathered the food needed for his breakfast regulars, five to ten locals who stopped by every morning. The place boasted just enough breakfast customers to make the effort pay for itself.

Kobe's entrance into the kitchen interrupted Essen's preparation of scrambled eggs. The UDBA agent appeared behind the German without a sound. The apparition startled the cook:

"How the hell did you get back in here?" Essen asked, looking very confused. Thick yellow egg coated the German's hands and wrists. Essen had not heard the man come back in or seen him standing in the closed shadows of the unlit bar, watching him work, until the passage of considerable time.

Florescent lighting cloaked them both in a pale golden aura. Essen's eyes betrayed his fear. The muzzle of the Mauser touched the German's chest. Beads of sweat formed on the tavern keeper's brow.

The Yugoslav held his finger against the trigger. The safety was off. He pressed the silencer into the fabric of the old man's apron. The barrel of the weapon moved to every beat of the victim's heart. Kobe didn't waste time. He related the whole story, at least the parts that he knew. He did not know, nor did Franz Essen know, that Jack Kobe's mother had once been the German's wife. Only Marta and those who'd been with her in the war knew that part. It was another secret, like Essen and Tomich's true identities, that had been born of a distant age.

Kobe told those parts of the story that he had learned from his mother just like he'd told it to the dead Ustashi: Why Kobe was there, in Northeastern Minnesota, pointing a 9mm rifle at an old man. Essen's eyes watered. He began to tremble as he heard the tale. His torso shook. Kobe had seen the same involuntary convulsions countless times before. They were of no consequence to him.

Essen shook uncontrollably as he produced a safety deposit box key from his pant pocket. The key became coated with the yellow of the egg yolk that covered the German's trembling hands:

"This is for a safety deposit box in a Minneapolis bank. Take it. You'll find the box filled with gold bullion. It's yours. Let me live. It was a long time ago, another world, a world that was crazy. I was crazy. It made me so."

Kobe reached out with one hand and snatched the dangling key. The old man sensed his life was at an end:

"I beg of you, do not make this mistake. I can make you a rich man."

Essen desperately tried to organize his thoughts to compel the man into leniency:

"It's Tito's gold. More than enough to satisfy any man's lust. It can be yours if you only let me live."

But the German knew that Jack Kobe's intrusion into his life had nothing to do with lust or greed. The Yugoslavian was there for revenge, plain and simple. Four lives wiped out on the Sava had to be accounted for. Kobe made it painfully clear to the German that talk of gold would not sway him:

"I don't need you to tell me about the gold. We know-the UDBA has always known that you and Tomich took it. You haven't told me anything I don't know, Lt. Essen."

There was no time for further dialogue. Someone might see Kobe's rental car parked in the lot and stop by to check whether the bar was open. Or a neighbor might get curious, stop in to visit with Mr. Hauptman. That would complicate things.

"Get in the pantry," the Yugoslav commanded.

"Why? What are you going to do with me in there? Tie me up? Shoot me? I insist on an answer," Essen demanded weakly.

Kobe roughly shoved the man forward.

"You won't regret sparing me, friend. I know of another, with as much gold as mine. I can help you get it. But I can't help you become rich if I'm dead!" Essen pleaded.

Kobe's rage, his wrath, escalated, as he tried to visualize the face of his father, a father he'd never met, and the kind smiles of his uncles, his aunts. He pictured them on the banks of the Sava. The girls holding the babies. Weeping, wailing, begging for mercy.

He replayed the horror in his mind. The cough of the Ustashi guns. The muzzle flashes, the screams. The ultimate silence of murder.

Essen tried to speak again; he tried to talk to Kobe as the agent stood there, eyes staring blankly at the trembling German.

"Join your partner. Damos Tomich is waiting for you."

"Pop."

Kobe relished the man's disbelief. An egg-stained hand groped at the wound in the center of his chest. Essen's palm became stained by surging blood as the German's life emptied out onto the front of his apron. The old man held up his hand, examining the extremity through traumatized eyes. The white skin of Essen's fingers became coated with a mixture of yellow and crimson as the confusion of impending death formed in Essen's eyes. Kobe watched intently, convinced the German's attention was transfixed upon the horror of descending into Hell.

Kobe closed the door and walked out of the pantry. Standing at the kitchen counter, the Yugoslav dumped the eggs down the garbage disposal and rinsed the pan, leaving the kitchen as if no one had been there.

His business completed, Kobe shut the main door and stepped out into the night underneath a vibrant display of the Northern Lights. Above the newly frozen waters of Comstock Lake, the Aurora was joined by thousands upon thousands of stars punctuating the sable night; stars undistorted by the lights of man; unrelenting energy from billions of years past.

As Kobe opened the door to the rental car, he wondered how he would approach retired Assistant CIA Director Marvin Field. That would take some doing. Petrich warned him not to try to talk to the millionaire. But the game had changed. The hourglass was losing sand. It was only a matter of time before the authorities found Essen's body and started to unravel the two deaths. There was no risk in confronting Field now.

Kobe had already killed two men in America. One more wouldn't matter.

Chapter 21

December 3, 1991

Chen called Slater at the Chicago Police Department. His message only confirmed what they already knew: Jack Johnson was Jack Kobe. The Yugoslav's fingerprints were well documented in the files of Interpol and Scotland Yard, as was his handiwork. The Jack Kobe file was thick: dozens of kidnappings throughout Europe; deaths directly linked to an antique 9mm Mauser; all tied to atrocities or murders committed by those Kobe tracked down; atrocities and murders committed when Yugoslavia had been torn apart by war. Kobe's actions were unofficially sanctioned by his government, plotted and carried out by the UDBA.

Slater thanked Chen and hung up the phone.

"Phil Chen, one of our BCA contacts in St. Paul confirmed that Johnson is Jack Kobe, an operative in UDBA, the Yugoslav secret police," Slater related. "My guess, given the backgrounds of the two dead men, is that they had something to do with war crimes in Yugoslavia. I'll have our boss, Al Pagotti, check with Father Sanjina in Duluth to see what he can dig up on those two."

Slater tried to examine the faces of the Chicago cops. She hoped the men were following her rapid-fire discourse. She drew another breath and continued:

"Maybe Pagotti can come up with something on the gold Budaslavich had in his deposit box. Where the hell it came from, does it tie into this mess or is it just a coincidence, a convenience that Kobe got his men and also got rich? He took it but we don't know why, whether it's personal or UDBA business."

She dialed Pagotti in Duluth and filled him in on the events in Chicago. He said he'd get out and see the priest. Today. Swanson took the receiver, added a few details, and hung up.

They were sitting in Detective Adrian McCray's office. McCray's partner, Fred Warner leaned against a cracked concrete wall. Both men were Chicago born, black, and in their early thirties. That's where the resemblance ended.

McCray was fat, over three hundred pounds. He maintained the weight by constantly eating Jolly Rancher hard candy. The candy took the place of the cigarettes he'd given up three years earlier. Giving up smoking may have saved his lungs but added fifty pounds. Bald, with bulging brown eyes, McCray still looked like he was on the verge of cardiac arrest.

"A cigarette couldn't possibly hurt this guy," Swanson thought. "He's already gone."

In contrast, Detective Warner was tall. Six four or five, but maybe one seventy soaking wet. A string bean. His hair was coarse and thick, closely cropped to his scalp. Traces of a thin mustache accented his upper lip. Beneath his lower lip, a small, triangular tuft of facial hair interrupted his lower jaw. He remained quiet. McCray did all of the talking:

"Here's the stuff we pulled out of Kobe's desk at the University."

McCray handed Slater an evidence folder. There was little of interest inside. Some soccer rule books. Several sets of keys with University logo tags attached. Unimportant pieces of paper relating to scheduling. A white memo pad caught Slater's eye.

Picking up the pad, the Deputy discovered notations in English; inventories of safety deposit boxes in Minneapolis and Duluth; an accounting of the gold bars held by each dead man. Adding the two sections together, Slater roughly calculated that there had been seventy pounds of gold in each man's possession. The total of the stolen gold was worth slightly more than one million dollars. Now it was all gone, swept away in the whirlwind of the Yugoslav's departure.

The second page of the notebook contained names and addresses. One name on the list caught the Deputy's eye immediately: Marvin Field. 4300 Field Tower, St. Paul, Minnesota. Phone number- (612) 838–8888. Other names and addresses on the sheet seemed to be those of high school soccer players in the Twin Cities area; players Kobe was presumably trying to recruit for the University of Chicago.

Slater's perusal of the second page of notes stopped at a phone number bearing an area code she did not recognized. She pointed the number out to Swanson. Looking over his partner's shoulder to read the phone number, the big Deputy dialed on McCray's phone:

"Yugoslavian Embassy, Ottawa. Mrs. Zoliak speaking. How may I direct your call?"

Swanson mumbled, "Sorry, wrong number," and hung up the phone.

"That was the Yugoslav Embassy in Canada. Someone within the Yugoslavian Government must be involved, must know what Kobe is up to."

Slater sighed.

"Can I get copies of these?"

She handed Kobe's notes to Warner.

"Sure. No problem," Warner murmured.

Those were the only words the tall man spoke. The detective took the originals and stepped outside the room. McCray's eyes followed the other black man out the doorway:

"Quite a talker, my partner."

McCray stood up and spoke in a low, gravely voice:

"I think we should take a ride over to Kobe's apartment in Oak Park and see what the black and whites have turned up over there. He's definitely gone south on us. Didn't go back to the apartment. Car never left the faculty lot after the assault. We've got the airports and bus terminals covered. Two guys at the main Amtrak. That's about all we can do. Maybe we'll turn up something at his place we can use to narrow it down. Whatdoya say?"

"Sounds good to me, Adrian. Deb and I would like to take a peak at the guy's place. It's the closest we've come to catching up with him on this whole damn wild goose chase," Swanson answered.

Slater listened intently and nodded in agreement.

Warner walked in with the copies.

"What'll we do with our rental car?" Slater asked.

"Just dump it here. I'll have Warner bring it back later. Better that you folks ride along with me. You might get lost, miss out on all the fun if we catch this guy."

Leaving the office, they negotiated the dimly lit halls of the station house until confronted by a narrow stairwell. Descending a dark staircase, the air close and musty, and the officers eventually arrived in a basement garage housing the Chicago Police Motorpool where an unmarked squad car idled noisily at their disposal. Blue exhaust from the decaying automobile surrounded the car. Meager illumination penetrated the confines of the place where single light bulbs hung precariously from the concrete ceiling. The feeble lights presented dubious protection against head-on collisions in the garage.

As their police cruiser burst free of the squalid confines of the place, the car climbed a cement ramp and encountered a brutal wind off Lake Michigan, a current brisk and full of snow.

"It's colder than Duluth," Slater observed as frigid air whistled through uncountable leaks in the vehicle's weather stripping.

"Dunno about that, Slater. Never been to Duluth myself. Never had much reason to. Kind of small for my way of thinking," McCray responded.

"Small, but safe, Detective. At least, until recently," she said, obliquely referencing the deaths of two old, harmless men.

McCray turned up the Plymouth's puny heater. A squealing belt, not more heat, was the cruiser's only response.

The bald detective piloted the car through a maze of streets and alleys. Slater and Swanson rode quietly in awe of the horn-blaring, four–letter word methodology underlying the Chicago cop's driving. They were both thankful that the squad was unmarked.

Kobe's apartment was one of twenty units located in a plain brick building, bordering a nondescript suburban street, a street lined with other identical, generic apartment complexes. No balconies, no swimming pools, no garages. The units were simple boxes bearing no appearance of individuality. Kobe's apartment was No. 319. It was located on the third floor. Two uniformed units were parked outside. The entrance to the place was sealed off. An Oak Park officer stood on the sidewalk directing traffic, keeping onlookers back. The red lights of parked squad cars turning provocatively invited more onlookers to crowd the area.

McCray lead the four officers up the sidewalk to the front door. He depressed the button for the intercom to Unit 319. A voice answered:

"May I help you?"

"McCray from downtown. We're coming up."

"Sure Detective. I'll buzz the door."

An electronic "click." McCray's hand opened the door into the hallway. The officers began a laborious climb. The fat detective stopped at each landing. Perspiration stained his shirt. McCray tried to dab the moisture away from his temple with a handkerchief but his efforts to control the sweat were unsuccessful.

At the top of the stairs, the police officers turned left and stopped in front of an uniformed patrolman posted outside Kobe's apartment. McCray presented his badge. Two more uniforms and a plain clothes forensic detective were inside the room, inventorying the furnishings, dusting for prints.

"Hello, Julie."

McCray offered his meaty, slick palm to a small blond woman wearing a casual pantsuit. The woman had plain, nondescript features. That's how Slater saw her. Slater wondered how the men in the room saw the other woman, how they saw Deb Slater, for that matter.

The woman smiled. She wore no makeup. Her face boasted a round chin and no cheekbones to speak of. Despite the lack of accent to it, her face was gregarious and punctuated by huge, pale green eyes. Her pupils appeared to be nearly white with small flecks of jade thrown in. The female detective stood up from the end table where she was working and accepted McCray's hand, carefully wiping the excess moisture on her pant leg.

"This here's Julie Bradshaw, one of our best forensic detectives. If there's hair, fingerprints or that kind of thing you need, she'll find 'em."

McCray patted her on the back.

"Like another guy," Slater thought.

Warner left the group to talk to one of the uniforms. Slater and Swanson introduced themselves and filled Ms. Bradshaw in on the case, on John Johnson, Jack Kobe, the condensed version.

"What've you got so far, Julie? We're in need of something to point us in the direction of Kobe. He's on the loose and we're not sure where he's headed. He's already killed two old guys in Duluth. Can't afford a third. Say, that's right, there is a third name. In St. Paul. Slater's got a notion that he might be headed there," McCray related in a thickly urban voice.

The rotund detective plopped himself down on a thinly cushioned pullout couch. The cushions sagged under his weight.

Bradford pointed to a collection of papers, receipts and envelopes spread out on the table in front of them. Slater moved forward to get closer to the documents.

Dave Swanson's attention was riveted on a rifle leaning in a distant corner of the room. The weapon was propped against a wall where Warner and two other

Chicago officers sipped cans of Diet Coke. The deputy joined the parlay. He cast an eye towards the rifle: it was old; German, a Mauser. Without a doubt, it was the murder weapon; it had been modified into a sniper's tool. Equipped with a silencer and a shortened stock, it was obviously an assassin's weapon. The silencer was custom made to deaden the discharge of a weapon not ordinarily susceptible to being quieted. Swanson knelt next to the rifle and carefully studied its dark, devious simplicity.

"Deputy Slater, I think your guess about Kobe being headed to St. Paul is a good one. Look at this Amtrak schedule," Bradshaw said, offering Slater a glossy pamphlet she found in the pile of papers.

"He's circled the days and times for departure from downtown Chicago and from St. Charles. If he knows we're on to him and he wants to avoid the likely places we have cops posted, the bus depots, the airports, the downtown train station, he may have cabbed it to the St. Charles station." the Chicago Detective theorized.

Slater nodded and scanned the schedule. The train for St. Paul had just left downtown and would take a while to wind its way west, through urban congestion.

"How long from the University to St. Charles station?"

"About an hour."

"How about from here?"

"Probably the same."

Slater nodded.

"We'll have to hurry."

She found Swanson:

"We think Kobe's taking the train from St. Charles. We need to hurry if we're going to make the station before the next train leaves."

Dave Swanson stopped scrutinizing the murder weapon and rejoined his partner.

"If you and Detective Bradshaw say so, Deb. I'm game. How about you, McCray?" Swanson asked.

"Wouldn't miss this one for the world, folks. No sireee."

The fat man tried to lift his body out of the couch's grip as he spoke. It took two uniformed officers and Warner to dislodge him. The couch released an audible sigh of relief as the big man regained his feet.

Before the four officers left apartment, Bradshaw handed Slater a nondescript vinyl packet.

"You might want to take this with you," Bradshaw advised.

Slater turned and accepted the item.

"It's Kobe's passport. If you've never seen the guy, the photo might come in handy," the Chicago detective added.

Slater stopped next to the woman. Removing the passport, Deb Slater studied the photograph, coming face to face with the killer they had been pursuing. She observed the likeness of the phantom that had committed the cold-blooded murders in her jurisdiction and felt an unusual aspect of surprise well over her:

"Strange", she thought. "His face isn't at all what I expected. It isn't cold, calculating."

The expression preserved by the picture seemed innocent, serene, framed by kind eyes and a puzzling, quixotic smile. His likeness convinced the Deputy that John Kobe was a man of complexities, a man to be cautious of.

Slater handed the passport to McCray.

"We need copies of this to pass out at the station," she directed.

"Not enough time," the fat man responded, tucking the passport under his arm as they walked out into the Chicago snow. Down the street, a small crowd gathered. Spectators appeared to be drawn to the slowly revolving lights of the police squads like moths to a flame.

McCray pushed his way through the bystanders. Warner remained behind. The officers from St. Louis County followed the big Detective through the crowd.

As the big sedan pulled away from the curb, McCray placed removable lights on top of the unmarked cruiser. All eight cylinders roared to life as Slater prayed that the detective's driving skills had improved. She soon learned they hadn't.

They raced down the quiet residential streets of Oak Park, siren blaring, lights flashing. Slater sat in the back seat and tapped Swanson's shoulder through the wire mesh separating them. Swanson turned, a big grin covering his face, obviously enjoying the ride.

Slater wasn't in the mood for smiles. She was puzzled by the name they found in Kobe's notes. Marvin Field. She wanted to know Swanson's views on how Field fit into the picture:

"Dave, what do you think about this Field guy? You know, in St. Paul? What's his connection to Kobe?"

Swanson didn't look at her as she spoke. His right hand clutched desperately to an armrest attached precariously to the passenger-side door with duct tape. Swanson tried to remain seated as the car sped towards St. Charles. Slater tried to listen to McCray's jabbering over the excited blaring of the siren and the industrial roar of the big v-eight.

"Dunno, Deb. Dunno," Dave Swanson responded. "Could be target number three. Why don't we have Whitefeather get the skinny on the guy? Adrian can get Herb working on it. You and I can spend some time poking around the club car on the Amtrak. Maybe even have a drink or two on that tight wad Prescott."

Slater ignored the attempt at humor and focused her attention on a yellow legal pad resting in her lap. Her concentration broken, she shouted above the noise of freeway to make herself heard:

"Adrian, if I give you the number of Herb Whitefeather, FBI man on this thing, can you get him on the horn?" she inquired.

"Sure thing, Deputy. No problem. Once we get to the station, I'll give 'em a call. You two concentrate on finding our man. We've got some local units there now to give us assistance. They'll need to see what the guy looks like," the obese detective shouted.

Slater didn't hear any of what McCray said after that point. Her attention was fixed on where the squad was headed. Traffic passed by in a blur. The sedan dodged in and out of crawling cars like a halfback weaving through the offensive line. It took forty-five minutes to make the run. McCray made most of the corners on two wheels.

Their luck finally turned at the St. Charles Amtrak station: the train had not left. Passengers were still standing in line waiting to buy tickets for the trip to St. Paul. Several dozen ticketed passengers relaxed in the lobby, lounging on uncomfortable hard plastic seats. Some slept, some watched re–runs of "I Love Lucy" on coin–operated TVs. Several diehard smokers, mostly young twenty-somethings, braved the incoming storm and huddled together on a broken piece of asphalt outside the station. The nicotine addicts drew in a venomous combination of smoke and cold air in equal measure.

McCray spotted several St. Charles police officers and introduced the Deputies. Kobe's passport photo was passed between them. The four uniformed policemen split up, systematically scanning the faces of the patrons waiting in line.

McCray shoved his way through the crowd with his customary rudeness until he arrived in front of the ticket window where he brandished his badge.

"Welcome to Chicago," Swanson thought. "City of cold wind and colder manners."

They had discussed a plan of attack on the way to the station. The deputies decided to take the train back to the Twin Cities if the killer eluded them at the station. Marvin Field was in St. Paul. It seemed clear Kobe was going after him. The train was as good a choice of transportation as any.

"Have you seen this man?" McCray asked, showing his badge and Kobe's photo to the ticket agent. "Ruth S." That's what her nametag said. She was a scarlet-haired woman in her fifties. The color of her hair was surreal and unquestionably artificial. She wore an Amtrak blazer bearing her nametag. She studied the passport photo. It was obvious from her reaction that she recognized the photograph:

"He came through not more than ten minutes ago. I remember him because he was so polite. Not like the usual business customers. They're rude. Want everything done now. Not a minute from now. Anyway, he went through. One–way to St. Paul. Seemed like such a nice man. Sweet smile, great accent. Is he in trouble or somethen?"

Ruth S. clearly wanted to know the reasons behind McCray's inquiry. The big man wasn't offering information. She continued:

"I haven't seen him since he bought his ticket. Has he done something wrong?"

"Just routine, Ma'am. You give us a holler if you see him. We'll be looking around here for a bit."

"He was so nice. Paid cash too. I can't see why you'd want to bother him, what with so many other obvious folks to go after."

"I understand Ma'am. Just be sure to let one of the officers know if you see him. Keep this under your hat, will you? Just between us. O.K.?"

McCray stepped back from the window to allow the deputies to buy their tickets.

Slater wrote out a traveler's check for their fares.

"Can we get receipts? Our boss is in the middle of next year's budget. He's pretty sensitive to expenses."

Ruth S. handed Slater a yellow carbon receipt.

"Thanks allot, Ruth," the female deputy remarked.

Detective McCray began to sense a feeling of discomfort as he combed the confines of the railroad depot. Jack Kobe's face was nowhere to be found. The Chicago detective sensed Dave Swanson and Deb Slater could handle Kobe, no matter how clever the Yugoslav might be. McCray's distress was purely physical, unrelated to the search. His internal clock told him that he had missed lunch. His body craved, it demanded a stop at Dunk N' Donuts on the way back to police headquarters.

"A dozen chocolate cake donuts will hold me 'til supper", McCray thought, smiling at the vision of a dozen dark beauties in a white paper sack as he strolled absently through the commuters on the platform. He found the illusion of sweets almost made the gnawing pit in his stomach disappear.

Almost.

Chapter 22

December 3, 1991

Jack Kobe sat by a window inside the Amtrak station. He felt lucky to get to St. Charles station ahead of his pursuers. Now he saw them, out in the hubbub of the place, stalking the lines of those waiting to board, searching for him. Kobe pulled his Chicago Bulls stocking cap over his eyes and lifted the collar of his jean jacket high off of his neck in an attempt to make his facial features less visible. He glanced at a clock on the station wall. The train was late.

Two officers, one male, one female, both in plain clothes, worked the customers about a hundred feet from him. He caught a glimpse of an uniformed officer here and there in the distance. Kobe watched intently as the female deputy pulled out a small vinyl booklet and opened it. The woman stared at it to refresh her recollection of his features.

"Damn," he said under his breath. Always carried the passport with me. Except for today."

He cursed silently, in his head, in Serbo-Croation. His hand gripped a .38 revolver in his coat pocket. His fingers coiled tightly around the gun's smooth plastic grip. It had been pure luck that he had left the handgun in his locker at the University. Pure luck that he had time to grab his jacket and jeans before he left the locker room. Pure bad luck that he couldn't retrieve his passport.

"If I'm going to rely on luck," he thought, "I'll soon be in prison. Or dead. Luck can't hold, never does. Time to start thinking."

Two great diesel engines pulling nine passenger cars, a club car and a baggage car clattered in from Chicago. There was no caboose. "Chicago Northern Line" was stenciled in brilliant yellow across the dull green bodies of the cars. Kobe glanced at the clock again. The train was seven minutes late.

Looking out into the crowd, he saw the two plain-clothed officers take up posts adjacent to the turnstiles. Uniformed police spread out as the passengers shuffled forward, a herd of human cattle bound for St. Paul. The passengers' carry-on luggage slammed through the rotating arms of the turnstiles. Kobe knew there was no way he would make it on the train undetected. He rose from his seat. Using the bulk of an obese, middle-aged woman to shield him from prying eyes, the UDBA Agent walked urgently towards the restrooms. He needed time to think.

Kobe contemplated leaving the station and returning to the city. He could hide in the urban crowds for weeks, months, years, maybe even a lifetime. He could easily find work and fit in. He had his wallet, his fake identification. He could change his name again and hide if he needed to, at least until he could contact Petrich to get him out of the country.

Petrich was protected, protected by diplomatic immunity. The Americans could expel Petrich if they ever linked the murders to the UDBA. But the diplomat couldn't be prosecuted. Not while he carried the papers of deputy ambassador. Kobe had no such protection. He was simply an operator, a collector, as Petrich liked to call him; a collector of garbage left over from the war.

This time, instead of collecting the garbage, he'd burned it. Petrich definitely wouldn't like it. In fact, the diplomat might ignore Kobe's request for safe harbor. Petrich might just let the Americans take him. Kobe wasn't ready to let that happen, not with one more piece of trash floating in the wind, one more piece of work to be done.

The immediate question was: How to board the train and avoid the police? The UDBA Agent glanced out the bathroom window over the urinals. His eyes concentrated on the front wheels of the great diesel engines. If he could get out onto the tracks undetected, he could slip by his pursuers without incident. But what good would that do? If the police boarded the train, rode to St. Paul, he'd be trapped, on a moving train–with no place to run or hide.

Unless. He smiled. As always, he invented an alternative, that would allow him to arrive safely in the Twin Cities, just in time for his visit with Mr. Field.

It took nearly thirty minutes for the boarding to be completed. Slater, Swanson and the uniformed officers carefully stopped and eyeballed each passenger moving through the turnstiles. Jack Johnson, Jack Kobe, was not one of the hundreds of souls that walked by. They did not see him board the train. They were certain, after touring the restrooms and other areas of the station that Kobe was not in hiding. He did not leave the main building, which would have required him to walk right past McCray.

Slater looked at her watch. The train was already twenty-five minutes late because of their interference.

"Gotta let 'em go, deputies. Can't delay these folks any longer," McCray said in an apologetic tone.

"Just a few more minutes, detective. He's got to be here. In the station. I can feel it in my bones."

Slater's voice wasn't pleading. She was simply asking for some additional consideration.

"I can't. Once it's boarded, without something more, we gotta let it go. Hell, his car's impounded, all the airports and depots are covered, he can't get far. And if he's on this train, there's only one way to find that out and that's to get on it with him."

Swanson's voice brought her back to their present circumstance:

"Deb, we might as well toss our bags on and go back to the Cities. If he's on the train, we'll see him. If not, he's probably on his way back to Belgrade," the detective said in a low, tired tone.

"I guess you guys are right," Slater agreed. "I'd feel a hell of a lot better if we had found him in the station. Let's get on. Maybe he's not as smart as we think he is."

Swanson thanked McCray and lead Slater by the arm onto the train. Slater didn't resist her partner's direction, though she still had doubts as to where Kobe was. She thought it was more likely Kobe enticed his pursuers to the station, only to vanish again, leaving a cold and disappointingly stale trail to follow. His being on the train seemed too damn easy.

The train suddenly surged forward. They were underway. The gentle sway of the cars undisturbed by the slow, deliberate power of the diesels. The rhythmic phrasing of the ties passed beneath them as they accelerated away from St. Charles. Three hundred and eighty souls were listed on the manifest. Some would disembark in St. Paul and Minneapolis. Others were traveling further west, to Fargo or Seattle.

In the confines of the cabin of the lead engine, fireman Tim Stressan evaluated a cluster of gauges on the locomotive's control panel as he kept his right hand on the throttle. Near Stressan's feet, the train's Engineer lay inert, sprawled across the hard metal of the floor. The man was out cold. A nasty bruise obscured the right side of the Engineer's forehead, the result of trying to fight with the intruder. The stranger stood four feet away from the prostrate form of the Engineer, holding a cocked .38 to the base of Stressan's skull.

The locomotive's radio, smashed into pieces, littered the floor around the fallen man. The fireman tried to think, tried to reason why someone would hijack a train full of business passengers. It made no sense. The train was headed west on the same single track their route originated on. They were headed for the same destination they started out for. There was no reason to hijack a train to force it to go in the direction it was already going.

Stressan glanced nervously at the man with the gun. He watched a trace of a smile spread across the intruder's face. The stranger's lips parted as he spoke perfect English with a slight accent:

"Relax, Mr. Fireman, I paid for my fare," Kobe said. Pulling a one-way ticket to St. Paul out of his pocket, the UDBA Agent handed the document to his hostage.

Chapter 23

December 3, 1991

Marvin Field knew it would come out in the end. He was seventy years old, face to face with a giant American Indian in his office. The Indian claimed to be from the FBI. The man waiting patiently for Field was full of questions. The Agent's telephone call suggested that the questions would be about men, dead men whose names Marvin Field believed the world had forgotten.

Herb Whitefeather's red-haired friend and Agent Fuqua gave the FBI Agent enough information in separate bits and pieces for him to understand the secrecy behind the immigration of Tomich and Essen. It was the brainchild of Marvin Field. Field's name appeared on the memo requesting that the files be classified as "secret." The former OSS Agent had invoked confidential protection for routine INS documents, documents that would otherwise be publicly accessible. An FBI background check on Field revealed he left the CIA in 1960 after serving as Assistant Director under Eisenhower.

In addition, financial documents from the IRS showed a remarkable accumulation of wealth on Field's behalf, beginning with his return to Washington from Italy after World War II. Field's investment ledgers recorded numerous profitable financial transactions in stocks and bonds. Lots of trading, buying and selling in precious metals, particularly gold.

By 1978, when Field moved from Arlington, Virginia to Minnesota, he had already made in excess of twenty million dollars playing the futures and stock markets.

Minnesota was an even bigger financial playground for the old man. Using his portfolio as collateral, Field purchased an unwanted subsidiary of Control Data, Olinka Computer Programming. Mired in the aging technology of the mainframe computer, Olinka was nevertheless on the verge of breaking into the then–blossoming personal computer software market. Using his ties to the military engineering pool to recruit computer-programming experts away from the armed forces, he launched Olinka into the computer spreadsheet market. Overnight, the Olinka name became synonymous with low–cost, high usability financial software. A sleepy, low–earning cash drain became a veritable font of income.

The Legacy

Al Pagotti added a final piece of information to the Marvin Field story. Father Sanjina had studied the photo of the two young officers, the medals, the tale of the gold bars in the safety deposit box. According to the priest, Tito's Partisans were known to carry large amounts of silver and gold bullion with them during the war. Tito being a firm believer that, whenever bullets could not win your escape, the greed of your enemy might. It was the priest's deduction that the gold that Tomich and Essen had hidden away in their safety deposit boxes was likely the spoils of World War II. The gold, or so the priest believed, was war booty, booty stolen from the Partisans during the occupation of Yugoslavia by the Nazis.

It also stood to reason, and this was Whitefeather's own belief, his own hunch, that since OSS Captain Marvin Field had been the one to seal the INS files of the two dead men and had come home from the war a rich man, Field's wealth was tied to the two dead men. Their immigration, safe and free of any retribution from the Yugoslav Security apparatus, was a direct result of a deal the two men made with Field. In a nutshell, reasoned Whitefeather, the two war criminals used stolen gold to buy their lives. All this Herb Whitefeather surmised before he decided to pay Mr. Field a visit.

Field's office was opulent. The suite was furnished with custom-made mahogany and teak furniture and had broad windows unencumbered by draperies. Field's office offered exhilerating vistas of the Mississippi. From the former OSS Officer's office, one could follow the great river as it made its way through the Twin Cities. One could watch barges and tugs wrestle with the river's currents.

Herb Whitefeather stood near a window, reflecting on the view, thankful he wasn't permanently assigned to deal with the complexities of urban crime and violence that were part of the Twin Cities. He was glad to be officed in Duluth. Blue lake water, not swirling river sludge, suited him.

He watched the play of man and river for a moment. From behind the desk a heavy wooden door opened. A distinguished-looking, gray–haired gentleman of military bearing entered the office. The millionaire wore a smile on his face. Whitefeather knew it to be an expression of limited gentility; he perceived a feigned pleasantness in the man displayed strictly for Whitefeather's benefit.

"Agent Whitefeather, I'm Marv Field. How can I help you?"

Field extended his hand and motioned for the bigger man to take a seat.

"I see you admire the view. It's the one reason I stay downtown. This can't be duplicated in the suburbs."

Field's thin face looked out across the river bluffs, his thoughts obviously elsewhere. Turning from the view, the tycoon sat down in a tan leather chair behind his desk. The writing surface was oval shaped and uncluttered. Definitely not the desk of a man who left details for others to handle.

"Let me be frank, Mr. Field. I've been working with the St. Louis County Sheriff's Department, Deputies Slater and Swanson, and Agent Chen of the BCA, on two murders up near Duluth. I've done some checking. It seems you knew both men. From when you were in Italy with the OSS."

The FBI Agent stopped his remarks at that point. It was obvious that Field wasn't happy to have Whitefeather in his office in the first place. FBI agents rarely showed up bearing good news. It served no productive purpose to have a FBI man digging up forty year–old skeletons; skeletons Field thought had long since decayed. Field's eyes betrayed his feelings. Whitefeather went on:

"Their names were Franz Essen and Damos Tomich. From what I've heard from D.C., you met them sometime after they escaped from Yugoslavia, on the heels of the Soviet expulsion of the Germans. Apparently those two were wanted by the Yugoslavian Partisans, Tito's communists, for some sort of atrocity that took place along the Sava River."

The agent took a breath. Field's back muscles arched defensively. Whitefeather thought the old man was beginning to look an awful lot like a rabbit caught against a fence by a fox.

"Some hundred or so defenseless old men, women, children were executed by the Nazis and the Croatian Ustashi. Your acquaintances were the commanders of the involved units."

Whitefeather paused. He let the history he learned from the priest sink in. Field's body became less rigid. The look of concern passed from the old man's face. Field appeared to be back in control:

"That's classified. Confidential. How in the world did you dig that old story up?" Field said in a voice filled with false annoyance.

Field was trying to be flippant. He wasn't convincing.

The Agent remained silent. Field spoke again, compelled to do so by his nervousness:

"I knew them. I arranged for their passage to Brazil. It was authorized, cleared by the brass in the States. They gave us invaluable information. Stuff we couldn't obtain elsewhere. For that, I arranged their transport to Brazil. I was the officer who finalized the deal."

"And one hell of a deal it was," Whitefeather thought. "Essen and Tomich escape a firing squad with thousands in gold. With new identities, new lives.

The army gets intelligence it can't get anywhere else. And Marvin Field gets rich. Everyone's happy except the Yugoslavian government. Time to put the cards on the table."

"Look sir, I know about the gold. So does a guy named Kobe. He's a Yugoslav Security Agent with UDBA. He tracked down your two buddies in Northeastern Minnesota and shot 'em both stone cold dead. One shot each. 9mm German Mauser. Some sort of perverse revenge angle, I guess. Anyway, your name was found in his stuff. He's on the run after assaulting a guy in Chicago. Two deputies are on his tail now. They think he's coming here next. For you."

The agent left the confines of his chair. He leaned his big frame over the edge of the desk. His voice was low, down to a whisper, for emphasis.

Field gracefully pushed his chair away from his desk revealing no hint of urgency in his movement. Whitefeather guessed the old man played tennis because the man's reflexes seemed spry, his torso remained trim. A quick glance at Field's midsection revealed no paunch. His face sported a little Clark Gable mustache dyed deep black. His hair was not visibly dyed, despite his age. The former CIA man glared indignantly at the Indian, rising to his feet as he spoke:

"I don't know what the hell you're talking about. I traded safety for information. That's all I did. That's all I know. I didn't even know those two were in the United States, much less in Minnesota. As for the Yugoslavs, I never did have much respect for their security forces, OZNA. UDBA. Never did. More terrorists than counter–intelligence experts. Ragged, unprofessional. So even if one of their operatives is after me, and I can't believe that one is, but even if that's true, I'll handle him."

The old man opened the top drawer of his desk, pulled out a pearl handled, brass-plated Colt .45, and brandished the handgun in the air like a geriatric Wyatt Earp. Whitefeather knew the old man was serious, knew there'd be no convincing him to come clean, to fill in the blanks about the gold.

Marvin Field smiled as he began to speak again, his voice cocky and strong; his earlier fears apparently having been vanquished by his own bravado:

"And if this doesn't deter the bastard, I've got four armed security guards in this building he's got to elude as well. You see, in the intelligence business, you learn that old enemies mean festered hate. They always come back to haunt you. You always have to expect it, be ready. Now, Agent Whitefeather, if there's nothing more I can do for you, I'm due at the Governor's Mansion in fifteen minutes."

Field carefully placed the automatic back in its resting-place. Closing the drawer, the old man extended his right hand the FBI agent. Whitefeather produced a business card with a Minneapolis phone number penciled in, just in case Field needed it.

"Thanks for your time," the agent said, his tone of voice obviously tainted with insincerity.

Marvin Field walked with the agent to the threshold of the suite and opened the door. As Whitefeather departed, the former intelligence officer's face erupted in an ingenious smile:

"I think your UDBA agent will probably realize that I'm not the man he's looking for," Field explained. "He'll come to his senses and head for home, if the damn Serbs and Croats haven't destroyed his home already. Nasty business this civil war, eh?"

Whitefeather nodded and tried to return a smile. He could not. He knew that, somehow, some way, Kobe would pay Mr. Field a visit. Powerful spring hinges forced the great weight of the walnut door to close, ending their dialogue.

Despite the thick protection of the door, the agent heard Marvin Field call for his secretary. To the Indian, the old man's voice seemed anything but calm.

The Legacy

Chapter 24

December 3, 1991

Outside of Redwing, Minnesota, the Amtrak train slowed to a halt. High above the Mississippi River valley, steam rose from the exhausts of the locomotives while the train remained motionless, perched on a narrow trestle some two hundred feet above swirling water.

Deb Slater was completing her fifth slow walk through the passenger cars when the train stopped. Swanson was checking the baggage car. They found no trace of Jack Kobe though Swanson had finally convinced his partner that the UDBA agent was on the train. She was now certain that Kobe was using the train to get back to the Twin Cities, to Field. Slater returned to her seat and resumed observing the intricacies of the winter landscape through a small Plexiglas window in her aisle. Waiting for Swanson to return, she concentrated her attention upon the distant details of the river gorge below. Movement down the car regained her interest. Swanson was walking towards her, shaking his head as he caught her stare. Her partner sat down dejectedly. Slater noted that his suit was completely crumpled and soiled from his inspection of the baggage car.

"Zilch. A big fat zero," Swanson proclaimed wearily.

Slater silently sipped a glass of root beer through a straw. She offered a half-eaten bag of corn chips to Swanson.

"No thanks," he demurred through a yawn.

He reclined his seat to take a nap. Slater returned her gaze to the dismal December landscape. The hardwood trees were long devoid of leaves, the ground was bare, allowing Slater to surmise that the rolling hills of Southeastern Wisconsin had missed the early snows experienced by Northern Minnesota.

Contemplating the riverbed, it occurred to her that the train had not moved, that they had been immobile on the narrow bridge over the river gorge for an inordinate period of time. The realization made her uneasy.

Outside, walking gingerly above the river's froth, Kobe directed the fireman to disconnect the engines from the cars. Kobe's revolver was trained on the fireman's temple as the railroader did his job, uncoupling the diesels, releasing their burden. The two men walked back to the locomotives with quiet determination so as to avoid the frequent holes perforating the bed of the aging bridge. As they came in close proximity to the lead engine, Kobe gestured for his companion to climb the ladder into the locomotive. Kobe joined Stressan in the frigid cabin of the diesel, careful to avoid stepping on the form of the still-unconscious engineer.

Silently, instinctively knowing what was required of him by the foreigner, the fireman opened the throttle and engaged the drives. Kobe grinned as he felt the weight of the train disconnect from its source of power. In a few seconds, the diesels were churning relentlessly towards St. Paul, leaving the cars and the passengers, including two persistent police officers from Duluth, behind.

The departure of the locomotives caused the disconnection of the train's electrical system. When the lights went out without warning, Slater grabbed her partner's arm, waking him. It was still daylight but the loss of power to the car was immediate and noticeable. Porters tried to contact the Engineer over the intercom. There was no response. Swanson staggered out of his seat, still groggy from his nap, and confronted the nearest porter. Displaying his badge, the Deputy and the porter walked to the exit platform at the rear of the car and disappeared.

Standing on the wooden decking of the trestle, Swanson made the mistake of looking down. His eyes followed the rolling brown water, its white foam and debris boiling relentlessly south at breath–taking speed, beneath the slender trusses of the bridge. Swanson watched the water for only an instant. He looked up, feeling queasy.

Stomach acid rose to his throat. He saw the porter continue to advance ahead of him. Suddenly, the man broke into a run, dodging the occasional hole in the bed as he scampered down the tracks, yelling at the top of his lungs. Swanson started to jog, trying to keep up, his stomach convulsing with every step.

"Wait up," Swanson urged in a weak voice.

Swanson's request had no affect on the porter.

"Wait up. You deaf or somethin'?" Swanson pleaded in a louder tone of voice.

Swanson's words finally reached the railroad employee, causing the younger man to wait. The Deputy attempted to weave his way, avoiding holes in the decking. There were no handrails along the trestle for him to rely upon to steady his gait.

The two men stood at the front of what was left of the train, at the head end of the first passenger car.

"Kobe," Swanson muttered with venomous inflection.

Off to the West, Swanson spotted the escaping profiles of the locomotives skirting a line of oak trees defining the Minnesota shore. The porter finally broke the silence, pointing out the obvious:

"The damn problem, Deputy, is that some asshole disconnected the engines from the train. That's the damn problem."

The man pointed towards the far riverbank, where the engines were just clearing the end of the trestle.

"Can't figure out why our crew would pull such a stunt, leave us up here. Wonder if he's coming back," the man remarked.

"Your men were forced to disconnect the cars by a guy we've been chasing for a long time. They're not coming back," Swanson whispered, trying to restore some semblance of control over his innards, as he fought the continuing urge to vomit. Holding his stomach, the Deputy spoke again:

"Now the question is, how the hell are we gonna get off this bridge?"

The porter shrugged his shoulders and looked back, towards the Wisconsin side:

"As long as the tracks are clear, we've got three choices, Deputy. We can walk east to Wisconsin. We can walk west to Minnesota. Or we can stay up here without lights or power, without heat, and probably freeze to death, before dispatch can send a unit to either push us or pull us across. I can call dispatch on the portable but it'll take hours to find an engine."

The men surveyed the distances.

"I'd say our best bet is to walk towards Minnesota," the porter continued. "We're better than half way there now. And we're only a few blocks out of Redwing. You and the others can get transportation out of there to the Twin Cities. I'll call dispatch, tell them the problem. Keep the trains off this line until we're safely across."

Swanson nodded, unable to respond vocally in the midst of the dizziness that had overcome him. The height of the bridge, the water rushing below, seeing it again as he bent his head between his knees toppled him to the tracks. He threw up. Great streams of yesterday's lunch and supper trickled between the ties and the wooden cross members of the bridge; down, down into the Father of Waters where it splashed and became lost in the millions of gallons of water surging downstream to New Orleans.

After a few minutes of retching, Dave Swanson stood up, placing a hand on the porter's shoulder for balance before beginning their walk back to the passenger cars.

In the relative security of the unheated train, Swanson took stock of the situation, assured himself of his composure, before he spoke to his partner:

"Deb, you're not gonna believe this. I was right all along. That son–of–a–bitch was on the train. He uncoupled us from the engines and left us stuck up here in the middle of the air. Kobe took the Fireman and the Engineer with him."

Slater pondered what she'd been told.

"He was probably in the engine from the moment we left," she theorized.

Swanson, still fighting residual nausea, nodded weakly. His partner noticed his condition.

"Dave, what's wrong? You look terrible," the woman asked, her voice edged in concern.

Slater watched droplets of sweat dance across her partner's forehead. The man looked feverish despite the cold air of the unheated car.

"Are you sick, Swanny?" she asked.

She used a paper napkin to dab the salty moisture. He shook his head.

"No, just dizzy from being stuck up here. Never did like heights. Looked down too long. I'll be O.K."

His breath smelled of stomach acid. Slater felt sorry for the guy. She knew how much he hated being even a few feet above the ground, knew how many Dramamine he took to fly into O'Hare. She tried to change the subject, to get her partner thinking logically instead of being caught up in irrational fear.

"What'll we do?" she asked.

She knew they couldn't stay where they were. The cars were rapidly becoming cold. She also knew it would likely take hours to get another engine to move them. By that time, the older passengers, or the kids, might become sick from the winter's chill.

"I guess we get everybody out and hoof it over to the Minnesota side. Hopefully we've got enough able bodied between the porters and the adult passengers to help those who need it. Make sure no one slips and falls in the drink. Christ, Prescott would have a bird if he knew we were going to play Moses to a bunch of Amtrak passengers two hundred feet above the Mississippi River. He'd be reading the fine print in the County's liability policy for sure," Swanson said.

It took several minutes with the porters to organize the passengers. Starting from the last car moving forward, they climbed down the stairs onto the uneven hardwood of the trestle. The passengers formed into a column of twos and began their slow, dangerous escape across the bridge with the deputies at the head of the march. The group crossed over into Minnesota without incident, arriving safely at the end of the span. Once again on solid ground, the column left the tracks and followed a gravel maintenance road into the city of Red Wing.

In town, the Deputies located the chief of police and explained their situation.

Chief Knutson of the Red Wing Municipal Police made a squad and an officer available to give the Slater and Swanson a ride to St. Paul. Before they left, Slater placed a call to the Minneapolis office of the FBI. It was unnerving to hear a familiar voice answer her call. Unexpectedly, the agent on the other end of the telephone was Herb Whitefeather.

"Deb, where the hell are you?" the big man asked.

"Herb, you won't believe it. It's a long story. We're in Red Wing. I'll tell you the details later. What are you doing about Field?"

"Don't worry, Deb. It's covered. St. Paul PD will have an escort for him wherever he goes. His office and his home will be protected. It's all set. The old man tried to feign that he wasn't rattled when I paid him a visit, but he was. He's scared, Deb, damn scared."

"I would be too. Kobe's no amateur. Just ask our two dead war criminals up North."

"No question, the man knows his business. But Field will be all right. He's still, for all his fear, a tough old bastard."

"Just keep him alive, Herb. Swanny and I should be up there in an hour or so. We'll be staying at the Midway Sheraton. I'll give you a call when we get in."

"How did you end up in Red Wing, anyway, Deb?"

"Later Herb. Later."

She put down the phone and walked out of the Red Wing police station. Absently noting the old stone buildings of the quiet little river town, Slater mused that it was unlikely that they'd catch up with Jack Kobe. His cover was blown; his weapon of choice was in the hands of the police. It would be sure suicide for the Yugoslav to attempt to get to the old man now. Deputy Slater hoped that she was wrong, she hoped that Kobe would make a move to take out the ex–CIA man despite logic, odds and common sense. She had a burning desire to catch up with the man, to meet him because Jack Kobe was really starting to piss her off.

The Legacy

Chapter 25

December 4, 1991

Kobe left the engines on a little–used spur south of Stillwater. Mr. Stressan joined the Engineer unconscious on the floor.

To the Yugoslavian, Stillwater wasn't much of a town. Its narrow downtown streets were crammed with antique stores and Yuppie restaurants. Quiet quickly enveloped the town's neighborhoods once the tourists went back to the Twin Cities after shopping. Plenty of automobiles remained behind. Kobe knew at least one had to have its keys left in the ignition. He hung around until the mercury vapor lights suspended over the streets began to brighten, casting shadows over the renovated brick buildings of the City. It wasn't long before Kobe found transportation. A brand new fire engine red Mustang. Coated with the dust and salt of new winter, the car possessed plenty of muscle to outrun most anything else on the road.

The driver's door was unlocked. Kobe found the keys under the seat. He hopped in, fired up the car's V-8 and pulled out onto the empty roadway. The twenty-five mile ride west to the Twin Cities brightened his attitude. As the car crested the bluffs of East St. Paul, lights, thousands of lights, illuminating the bronze and glass of the downtown, struck his eyes. Ahead of him along the interstate scores of concrete and steel office buildings, smoked–glass skeletons, carcasses of corporate wealth, monoliths to American business, defined the city's bosom. The City, perched over the industrialized river bottom, paid homage to the major financial institutions, the manufacturers and the insurers that called St. Paul home. Each tower's thin, metal skin housed the offices of some of the state's wealthiest corporate citizens.

"And this," Kobe reflected as he drove into the City, "is but a minor player among the cities of America."

To see such wealth, such power in the most modest of the nation's backwaters, made Jack Kobe envious.

He'd never been dogmatic in his adherence to Marxism. It seemed to him that his affiliation was like a membership in a boys club. Those who yelled the loudest, who were the most vocal, ran the show, like bossy little kids.

It never really seemed to matter what they planned or did. Yugoslavia's economy had never been as depressed as the former Eastern block satellites of the USSR, or the USSR itself, for that matter. On the other hand, the country never saw its economy blossom, never saw the nation's growth equal the potential of its people. Sadly, any chance for the Yugoslav nation to realize its economic potential vanished with the advent of another civil war.

No, communism had not been the godsend it was supposed to be. He'd not joined the party out of a sense of political altruism. He'd joined solely to enhance his chances of promotion within the army. He stayed a member out of loyalty, not to his country, but to his mother. She had remained, throughout the years, a firebrand of communism, a consummate Partisan and Tito communist. He had stayed in the party mostly to please her.

Pulling off I–94 onto the narrow streets of downtown St. Paul, Kobe parked the Mustang along Kellogg Boulevard. He abandoned the coupe, its engine steaming in the cold from the high speed run, in a loading zone. He did not bother to wipe his prints from the steering wheel. There was no need to be careful anymore. All he had left to accomplish, the only task left on his agenda, was to find Marvin Field. He would confront the man, learn whatever secrets he could from Field about the Sava, about the murders, about the gold.

If the old man still had any of the gold, he'd take it. If not, Kobe determined he'd either kill the man or disable him. Maybe leave him paralyzed. He'd decide how it would be, how it would play out. Tomorrow.

Tonight. Tonight, Jack Kobe was going to find someone to hold. He needed to touch the soft skin and hair of a woman. He needed to laugh, to smell perfume. It had been months since he'd been with anyone.

"Far too long," he murmured to himself as he walked down the snow covered sidewalk along Kellogg Boulevard, its roadbed cut into a sandstone bluff far above the silent barge docks and gray–green ice of the river.

He wasn't incapable of love. No, that wasn't it. He'd fallen in love many times; not simply lust, but deep affection. It was just that his job demanded too much. It claimed one's true self, one's identity, one's soul. Each personal relationship had to be based upon lies, a false name, the need to keep moving. The job prevented any commitment based upon trust and honesty. And though there had been times when he was ready for a normal domestic life, he'd always known that it was not possible. Not while he hunted the Nazis and the Ustashi.

A change in the wind's velocity made his mind cease wandering. He stopped to look out over a wrought iron railing. The draught's icy fingers stung his cheeks. The discomfort of the wind's touch alerted him to the brevity of time that was left to him. He vowed to displace the melancholy of the moment with an evening of laughter. He hailed a nearby Yellow Taxi and climbed in.

"Where can I find a beer, some interesting American ladies and music?"

"What kind of tunes you after, bud?" the cabby asked, his ruddy complexion exaggerated by the meager illumination provided by the car's dome light.

"Rock and roll," Kobe responded.

"Live music?"

"Yes, but only if the band's good."

"You want Stephanie's. Best house band in the Cities. It's only a few blocks."

"Stephanie's it is."

After a few twists and turns through the decaying warehouse district of the old City, the cab came to a stop.

"That'll be three fifty", the cabbie observed.

"Here's five. Keep the change."

"Thanks. Hope you enjoy the music. They are one hell of a band."

Kobe stepped from the warm confines of the taxi into a tidal wave of cold air. The zephyr buffeted his body, the wind having gathered power on its course between the Rocky Mountains and the City. Swirling in from the West, first through Minneapolis, then into St. Paul, the weather attacked the office towers. Careening down deserted streets and alleys, the gale assaulted the exposed flesh of anyone tempting its touch. There was snow in the air. Kobe could sense it: snow on the way in St. Paul, Minnesota felt no different than snow on the way in Yugoslavia.

Stephanie's name flashed blue and orange. The saloon was located on a side-street in the railroad district of the city where the streetlights were set a block apart. Antique cast iron standards projected faint spheres of light directly beneath the fixtures but no further. The nightclub occupied most of an old sandstone fortress containing few windows. The black soot of a hundred year's of coal dust coated the building's skin. An old machine shop had occupied the building for seven decades but the lathes and presses had been auctioned off long ago. The men who'd earned their daily bread in the searing heat of the unventilated shop were long dead; their ghosts exorcised from the building by the din of electric music.

Kobe paid a muscular bouncer the two-dollar cover charge. It wasn't hard to determine that the man's strength, his chiseled biceps, were the product of steroids.

Inside, it was dark. The smell of stale cigarette smoke and spilled beer greeted Kobe as he opened a well–worn door. A blast of feedback and dissonant chords split his ears. It was a big place. A couple hundred people were milling around, standing at the bars, sitting in groups at round tables and in leatherette booths. At least a hundred more were crowded onto a tiny dance floor gyrating to Springsteen's "Born to Run." Kobe smiled. It was an omen: his favorite American song greeting him as he entered.

There were three bars, each tended by female bartenders, ten or so in number. Each bartender appeared to be perfect. Each was tall, well tanned, blond, their uniform yellow tresses tied up in ponytails or buns.

None of the women was a natural blond by the look of the color of their roots but they were all nearly identical, as if cut from the same paper doll book.

One of them, Kobe judged her to be about twenty-five, stepped towards him, pouring a drink for another customer as she moved, bobbing her head to the song.

"What'll it be sir?" she asked politely, with no hint of personality disclosed by her voice's coarse texture.

"Too many smokes," Kobe observed to himself.

He felt like a scotch, his favorite drink away from home, away from the brandy of Yugoslavia. But he knew it would make him drink too much. Its warmth, its soft, velvet glow would ensnare his attention, dragging him stupidly into the dim nether world of the liquor's potency.

"A beer. Molson Dark if you have it."

He said it with as thick an accent as he could and still speak English. It was a trick that always worked with American women. Always emphasize that you are foreign. They go nuts over foreigners. It was a lesson Kobe learned early in his travels.

"You're a foreigner, aren't you?"

The Legacy

The bartender's voice betrayed a surge of curiosity. She was not his type. She was too large chested. Her large, bouncing breasts were likely the products of some American laboratory. No, she was not his type. Still, he tried to be friendly:

"Yes, that's right. German. From what used to be East Germany. Soccer coach with the national team. Hans Neidrich is my name. What's yours?"

He wiped his hand on his jacket and extended it to the girl. It was always better to be from somewhere else. You never knew whether your audience knew anything about Yugoslavia. But Germany. Everyone knew about Germany. It was a good choice. Especially East Germany. Women felt sorry for you when they realized your country had recently broken free of communism.

She smiled, showing the same perfectly formed white teeth all of the other bartenders displayed.

"My name's Helen. Stick around, Hans. I'll be right back with your beer."

His eyes followed her as she went to the cooler. Her tight Lees stretched to the breaking point as she leaned into the cold to pull out a Molson. Maybe he had judged her too harshly. Kobe smiled back.

Around him, couples were talking. Kissing. Fondling. Some discreetly. Others more obviously. The band went on break, emptying the dance floor, funneling the dancers to the johns or to the bars. Bob Seger tapes piped over the bar's PA spelled the loud frenzy of live music.

To his left, three young Americans in their twenties were engaged in a heated debate. Two women. One man. He recognized the two women as singers from the band. One of the women caught his eye.

She was short and small chested. He could see she wore no bra. Her nipples were obvious against the teal blue fabric of her cotton Beneton T-shirt. Even in the poor light of the bar, he could see that the blue of her shirt reflected the blue in her eyes. Her hair was raven black, long, luxurious and thick. She wore it pulled up off her shoulders, which exposed the sensuous curve of her neck. Despite the distance between them, he was enthralled by her round, full lips, starkly red and noticeable despite the absence of lipstick. High, fragile cheekbones accented her mouth. She had an exquisite face, an intelligent face.

"Without question," Kobe thought, "she is beautiful."

He wanted to see her up close, to talk to her. If it didn't work out, he could always try to charm Helen. Helen wouldn't be nearly as difficult, nearly as complex. Petrich always told him to have an alternative plan: he was simply following orders.

He slid his stool closer to the conversation. Helen brought him the Molson. Taking his ten off the bar, she smiled again. He caught the gleam of her white teeth out of the corner of one eye. Kobe allowed a subtle grin to spread across his face.

"Maybe Helen isn't such a bad alternative," Kobe thought.

He riveted his attention on the bartender, watching her lean over the till. Helen's blouse fell away from her shoulders, revealing the delicate lace of her bra, the garment gently cradling the curve of each breast. She pulled change out of the cash register, handed him the money, deliberately delaying the retraction of her hand, allowing her moist, sensuous palm to linger against his hand. Kobe placed a five-dollar bill on the counter between them. Helen-with-no-last-name smiled again, her sandy-brown eyes sparkling in the glow of the neon canopy above the bar.

"I'll be back to talk. Pretty busy right now. Don't leave without talking to me." As she picked up the currency, she squeezed his arm playfully.

The argument grew louder. Both women were pointing at the man, screaming at him. He was tall and thin. He looked Italian. Blue Eyes was standing beside a lanky black woman. Both of the women sounded angry. In a blink of an eye, the black one reached across and slapped the Italian in the face:

"Crack."

The noise was loud enough to be heard around the bar.

"You bastard faggot. You promised me I could stay with the band through next week. I've been sleeping with your sorry ass for three months. Now you tell me I'm all through? Bullshit. Either I walk and you pay me the five hundred bucks you owe me for the week or I sing and you pay me anyway. One way or the other, asshole."

Blue Eyes supported the black woman's statement by nodding affirmatively. Kobe noted that her T-shirt was tucked neatly into a miniskirt. The skirt was short, barely longer than the T-shirt itself and revealed strong, well-formed calves and thighs.

"Dancer's legs," Kobe guessed.

The Legacy

The voices grew angrier.

"That's right, Freddy, you slime. Gina is singing with us or she's not the only one leaving," Blue Eyes declared.

The woman was definitely no wallflower. She spat out the word "slime" with such venom that it was clear she had nothing but utter disdain for the man.

Freddy, massaging the welt on his right cheek caused by Gina's blow, stepped back from the women. Without warning, he lunged forward, grabbed Blue Eyes around the throat and pushed the black woman to the floor with his other hand. The man was stronger than he looked.

"You damn little bitch, I'll kill you. You little whore, I'll fucking strangle you."

His bony hands tightened around the woman's throat, causing her to gasp for air, causing her body to spasm. Freddy's arms bulged beneath his expensive sportcoat as his wrists tightened. No one moved to help the girl. It was obvious that this Freddy was a man of importance.

Kobe put down his beer and waded wordlessly through the crowd. In the background, Helen saw him leave the bar and called to him:

"Hans, don't get involved. You don't know Freddy. He's not gonna like it."

Kobe heard the admonition her but did not look back. Pressing through the patrons, he came to the black woman's side. She was bleeding from the mouth, unconscious from the fall. Blue Eyes was struggling to breathe. No one made a move to break the thin man's stranglehold on her. Kobe stepped out from the crowd and confronted Freddy. He spoke in his best German accent:

"Why don't you let go of the Fraulein? Pick on someone your own size."

Freddy's pockmarked face turned to greet the intruder. His grip tightened. Kobe could see Blue Eyes was beginning to fail, to pass out. Her face was white.

"Who the fuck are you, Mr. Nazi? Get the hell out of my bar. I own this damn place and this little bitch. Get out of here before you're sorry you poked your nose where it don't belong."

Kobe looked the man over. He was taller than the Yugoslav had first thought. Not too broad but a good six three anyway. Kobe determined time was of the essence. One never knew if an opponent had a weapon. Or friends.

The UDBA agent's right forearm came down upon Freddy's wrists, breaking the chokehold. With his other hand, Kobe pulled Blue Eyes free and tossed her towards the bar, out of the zone of danger. Freddy wasn't slow. Before Kobe could plant himself and ready for it, the bigger man landed a left to the Yugoslav's stomach. It was a solid punch and it sent pain into Kobe's chest and legs. He crumpled backwards, towards the prostrate black woman.

"Get 'em Freddy, get the little asshole."

The bar's bouncers were not shy about backing their boss in a fight. A crowd formed around the two men, the bouncers taking time out from their boredom to sit at the bar and sip tap beer while the two men fought. Freddy moved forward as Kobe caught himself on a chair, slowing his downward momentum.

The bar owner pressed him, forcing Kobe back against a jukebox. Freddy threw another right. There was power in the punch, much like the first one. But Freddy's initial success made the thin man cocky. Kobe timed the next punch, an uppercut, and dodged to the left. Avoiding the wild swing, the Yugoslav struck out with a roundhouse kick. The blow caught the bar owner in the groin. The move was a brutal load of force originating high behind Kobe's back. Kobe delivered a second blow, a sidekick, into the collapsing man's back, directly above the kidneys, causing the bar owner to emit a groan. The noise was the sound of air involuntarily escaping the man's lungs. Freddy landed in a heap on the hardwood. He'd had enough. His goons had not.

Two of the bouncers who'd been sitting at the bar stepped into the circle. Kobe calculated their advance. He could not let the larger men corner him or allow them to use their strength against his speed. He moved away from the solid background of the bar. Out of the corner of his eye he saw Helen dabbing the corner of Blue Eyes' mouth, soaking up blood.

Movement caught his eye. One of the bouncers was rushing him. His mind was called back to the room, to the fight.

As the bulk of the big man surged towards him, Kobe saw the other bouncer attempting to circle behind, trying to flank him. A huge paw reached out from the on–rushing enemy. Kobe ducked and rolled into the attacker with his shoulder. Before the bouncer realized he had an opportunity to use his size and weight to crush the foreigner, Kobe struck upwards into the man's jaw with a closed fist, breaking the unprotected bone into splinters. The man collapsed on top of the crowd, pinning two customers beneath his unconscious form.

The second of the bouncers watched Freddy and the other man fall.

Determined to avoid a similar fate, he reached behind the bar and pulled out a baseball bat. Advancing on Kobe, the bouncer, whose entrance into the fray had been met with cheers, now heard boos and catcalls thrown at him as he brandished his weapon. A fair fight was one thing. It was entertainment, a break from the cabin fever of winter. An attack with a baseball bat on an unarmed man defending the honor of two women was quite another. The crowd, for what it was worth, was now on Kobe's side:

"Come'on Joey, fight fair. Put the bat down and box the guy."

Joey turned and grimaced at the disparaging voice in the throng. The moment was enough of a distraction. Without warning, Jack Kobe picked up a barstool and rotated the chairs' full weight into the back of the bouncer's head. The force of the blow forced the man to drop the bat. Unarmed, the bouncer turned, fists held at the ready to face his enemy. Kobe was gone but he had not run. Before the man could see the punch to his ribs coming and block it, the UDBA Agent landed a blow and two or three more to the man's head, the last jab closing the man's eye and sending him spinning to the floor.

The remaining bouncers slid off their stools and approached the foreigner. There were three more. Kobe knew he was spent, that they'd be able to take him. He also knew the blow landed by Freddy had done much more damage to his ribs than he let on.

Blue Eyes stepped in front of them. Crimson streaks criss–crossed her neck, where only moments before, the bar owner's emaciated, bony hands had been.

"Don't bother, assholes. We're leaving. Tell Freddy he can get somebody else to sing in his fucking bar."

She grabbed Kobe's arm and led him to where her black friend lay. She looked up at the stranger, the cool blue of her eyes refreshing and honest.

"You're a lifesaver. Thanks for stepping in," Blue Eyes said in a soft, pleasant voice.

Kobe remained silent. He nodded, looking intently into the young woman's eyes.

"Can you help me get Gina to her place? I've got her key."

Her eyes stared back at him. Unlocking the door to his heart like she'd been there before, like she'd always known him. He had never seen anyone look at him that way before. He couldn't refuse. He wouldn't refuse.

"Surely. But tell me, Miss, what is your name?"

He stayed with the German accent. Despite the feelings he had for her, he couldn't let her know the real Jack Kobe, not with the task that lay before him tomorrow.

"It's funny as hell."

She was smiling as they lifted Gina up to her feet, the black woman still groggy but slowly coming to.

"It's Stephanie. Stephanie Delaney. That creep Freddy named this damn place after me. But that was a long time ago."

They grabbed the dazed woman under each arm and helped her through the door, out into the quiet stillness of the St. Paul night. The wind had died, leaving only the muffled sounds of Freddy's rage echoing inside the bar. It was not exactly how Jack Kobe had hoped to meet someone he could fall in love with. With Marvin Field's fate at hand at first light, his mind told him to forget her, to help her bring her friend home and disappear. Common sense told him to fade away into the anonymity of his profession.

But then, as they slid Gina's limp form into the back seat of the black woman's Celica, Stephanie Delaney studied him through deep, resilient pools of silver blue. And Jack Kobe knew that forgetting her was something he could not do.

Chapter 26

December 4, 1991

It was well after midnight when the two deputies checked into the Sheraton Midway in St. Paul. As she walked into her room, Debra Slater felt the need to take a shower. She was exhausted. Perspiration stained the underarms of her blouse. The walk on the trestle hadn't been physically demanding. But psychologically, it had been traumatic. Trying to keep Swanson from looking down, from getting sick; guiding a bunch of citizens over an aging railroad bridge high above a raging torrent; knowing that their quarry was still on the loose and likely to kill again; had taken its toll.

"A shower'll cleanse away the disappointments of the day, not to mention the dirt," she thought.

Swanson took a room two doors down. He called Pagotti and filled the supervisor in:

"We think Kobe is in St. Paul. Local police found a Mustang stolen from Stillwater, stolen about the time Kobe hopped off the train. The prints match Kobe's. The guy's either getting more careless or more confident."

Swanson let the import of his words sink in over the phone lines.

"Hang tough, Dave. You gotta find him."

The fat detective's labored breath forced Pagotti to pause for an inordinate amount of time before he continued.

"Whitefeather visited Marvin Field. Yesterday. While you and Slater were on your vacation train ride from Chicago. Couldn't break him. Couldn't get the old man to admit he'd profited from his involvement with the two dead men. The old man was shut up tight as a clam. Brushed Herb off. Be careful around Marv Field, will you Dave? He carries a .45. No telling what the crazy old fool will do if Kobe shows up."

Swanson did not have the heart to tell the Pagotti that they already knew most of what he was confiding.

"Thanks for the update, Al. We'll keep in touch. I'll pass along your concerns to Deb."

Swanson hung up the phone.

For her part, Deb Slater was happy to be in the shower. Hot water beat down on her head, shoulders and back, flushing the sweat and dirt of the day out of her pores, making her skin shiny and clean. She felt alive again, pure, whole. Cupping a bar of hotel soap in her hand, she gently cleaned the most private reaches of her body. She felt a sudden rush of adrenaline.

Gently, she washed the curve beneath each bosom, ignoring the feeling of pleasure, of arousal, knowing that Rick was waiting for her back in Duluth. The thought of her husband's touch brought a warm rush over her body.

Standing in front of the mirror, she pulled a hairbrush from her bag and admired her naked silhouette. Spurred by a sudden sense of modesty, she covered herself with a satin robe retrieved from the same valise and began to comb the kinks out of her hair, its red tints highlighted by the glow across her cheeks, with kind, deliberate strokes of the brush. Her clothes were being laundered. The valet said it would take half an hour or so. She tuned in a pay per view channel on the television. "Silence of the Lambs" came on. She'd seen it. Switching to the public television channel, she came across "It's a Wonderful Life." She turned the channel again. George Bailey's story always made her cry. It was too early to be crying Christmas tears.

On another premium channel she found "Mad Max." Something about watching Mel Gibson when she was nearly naked intrigued her. She was on her stomach, a pillow under her chin, her head facing the television as she settled for Mel Gibson.

The phone rang.

"Deb. It's Swanny. You naked or you got your clothes back?"

He giggled. She wasn't amused. His attempt at humor hit too close to the heart.

"Stuff it, Dave. I'm watching Mel Gibson. Why in the hell would I want to talk to you?"

She could tell her abrupt reprimand stung her partner. She thought it best that she jump in, before her remark festered into real hurt.

"Tell you what, Dave. Soon as my clothes come back, let's go get a pizza. I'm starved."

At the mention of food, Swanson's spirits seemed to lift.

"I talked to Pagotti. And the St. Paul PD. I set up an appointment for us to meet the locals at Field's office building at 7:30 a.m. tomorrow. How's that sound?"

"From what Herb told me when I called from Redwing, the locals will have the Field Tower covered from top to bottom. It sounds pretty good to me. Let's hope he shows. Christ, how I want to catch this guy, find out what makes him tick," Slater replied.

"Me too, Debra. Me too. There's no way Kobe can beat us to the punch. He can't take Field tonight, at home. The old man's in Omaha on business. Won't be in town until 6:30 tomorrow morning. Kobe will have to wait until morning. And by then, we'll be ready for him, won't we Deputy?"

"Damn right, partner. Damn right. See you for pizza in five."

"Sounds good."

Placing the phone back on its base, Deb Slater wasn't so sure they were a step ahead of the man this late in the game.

Across town, Gina Brown came away from Freddy's assault with only a minor cut in her scalp and a terrific headache. Stephanie Delaney put the black woman to bed after cleaning the wound. It was all Blue Eyes and Jack Kobe could do to assist the woman the three flights up to her apartment. She wasn't small, definitely not petite.

Once Gina was in bed, they found themselves walking down Lexington Avenue, alone in the Minnesota night. The stars were blocked by clouds that earlier seemed certain to snow. No snow arrived. Remnants of the potential storm remained behind, floating high above the city, blocking out whatever moon there was. A faint golden light crept around the cloud's wispy edges, serving as a reminder that the moon was a reality.

Stephanie Delaney put her arm around Jack Kobe's waist as they walked. There was something delicate yet strong about her way, something infinitely interesting and challenging to Jack Kobe. Her voice, the same voice that could belt out the best of Rock and Roll, seemed small and distant, like the soft whisper of a hummingbird's wings in flight. It was a calming, honest voice, the first such voice Kobe had heard in years.

"So, Mr. Neidrich, what'll we do now for excitement?"

The pools of blue stared directly at Kobe as she spoke. He found no hint, no trace of guarding or hesitation in her eyes.

"What do you do over there in Europe for late night entertainment?" she asked, her eyebrows raise in playful anticipation.

"Ah Fraulein Stephanie. In my country, it is customary for the young lady who has been saved from the dragon to reward the knight. But the choice of reward is hers alone."

He stopped their progress down the sidewalk. He found himself returning her intense look. He was enthralled by her openness, her self-assured manner, her certainty of her own destiny. She returned his gaze with a look of mock horror.

"You don't mean something like a gift of my charms, do you, kind sir?"

She portrayed the role of a rescued damsel without pause, batting her long lashes at him like a Southern belle. But the accent was more St. Paul Irish than Virginia socialite.

"Like I said, Fraulein, the choice belongs to you."

As he said the word "you," he kissed her heavily on the lips. His kiss denied her air and left her starving to catch her breath. She knew she couldn't refuse the gift even if he had made the choice, even if the rules of chivalry had been broken.

Her apartment was on the top floor of an old brownstone mansion off Summit Avenue, perched high atop Crocus Hill. The Hill's great stone mansions had been built by the timber, iron ore, railroad and grain entrepreneurs whose greed trampled the State's natural resources into the dust of Minnesota's soil, allowing the owners of the mansions to amass huge fortunes at the dawn of the twentieth century.

"My apartment is on the top floor of that."

She pointed to a large, slightly sinister-looking complex. Even in the slim light of evening, Kobe could see the building had seen better days.

"It's the B.A. Lancaster House. Fairly historic, for St. Paul, though nothing compared to the buildings you're familiar with in Europe, I'm sure."

As they climbed the narrow stairway, she told him of the home's sordid history:

"The house was built in 1879 by the founder of Lancaster Flour and Grains, B.A. Lancaster. He was found shot to death. His wife Sara discovered his body. The police always considered her to be the prime suspect. It was alleged that she had an affair with her gardener, was making love to the man the very night of her husband's murder, in the bed they shared."

Her eyes shown brightly as she continued the story, a story of little consequence to the moment.

"Anyway, not long after B.A.'s death, she married the gardener, Mr. Burton. Had four children by him. She raised them well. She was the sole heir to the money B.A. left behind. Though accused and convicted of the crime by the newspapers, Sara Lancaster Burton never stood indicted or charged with her husband's death."

Stephanie smiled sweetly in the sparse light of the entry. Jack Kobe smiled back. He was a patient man. He was willing to wait for her to complete the story. Knowing that she felt it important enough to share with him, he showed interest, though his thoughts were elsewhere.

"She died in this house in her nineties, a recluse, ostracized by St. Paul's aristocracy. Her contemporaries apparently put much stock in rumors. My apartment is what used to be the ball room."

A highly polished oak floor and stark white walls defined the landing where they stood. A single leaded glass light fixture hung over the doorway. She fumbled in her purse and pulled out a key. Kobe touched her lightly around her waist, entranced, not wanting to let her go, fearful that the night might vanish, might evaporate into another dream, another nightmare. She shifted his arm from around her hips, holding his hand tightly. She turned the doorknob, pushing the door open. They walked into her home; hands still clenched together in an anxious grip.

Inside the flat there wasn't much in the way of furniture. Old fish crates full of books, a stereo, and a black and white television were stacked on top of one and other to the ceiling. Stephanie Delaney dropped her coat on a wicker chair and disappeared into the kitchen. Kobe stood in the living room, surveying the books. Law books. History books. Contemporary novels. English literature. Some volumes sat open on the floor; lengthy notes scribbled across a variety of legal pads. Some sat closed, with more legal pads protruding from their pages. Each notepad was covered with perfectly formed script. He guessed from the precise nature of the script that they were her notes.

The remaining living room furniture consisted of two wicker chairs and a beat up old couch. Another fish crate served as an end table. The only light in the room came from a single bulb in an antique floor lamp. The lamp's water-stained satin shade was connected to its stem by intricate spider webs. Dust clung thickly to the spider's handiwork.

Stephanie stepped back into the room, her cheekbones shadowed by the light. She held a Guinness in each hand.

"She's got taste," Kobe said to himself. "She's educated. Beautiful. A perfect partner for tonight. Perhaps beyond."

"No," he told himself, discarding the thought. "Kobe, you're absurd."

There was no room in his life for such foolishness. He could be tied to no foundations, follow no set road or path. Not as a member of UDBA. He tried to keep his smile as honest as he could despite his knowledge that there could be nothing between himself and Stephanie Delaney beyond the moment.

He accepted the beer. The cold bottle chilled his palm. He liked his Guinness cold, not merely cool like they served it in Dublin.

"May I use your telephone?"

He was still using a heavy German accent. He had discarded the formality of calling her "Fraulein".

"Sure, go ahead."

She pointed to the phone and sat down in one of the chairs. The well–worn wicker creaked as she stretched out her legs, kicking off one of her ankle high cowboy boots, then the other.

Kobe picked up the receiver and used his calling card to dial Petrich's number. He knew it by heart. It took a few seconds to make the connection to Ottawa. Kobe let it ring. Petrich was doubtlessly fast asleep.

"Hello."

Petrich's voice was gravely, sounding like he'd been dragged from a deep sleep. Jack Kobe spoke softly in their shared dialect.

"George. It's Jack. I'm in deep shit. Those two you wanted me to bring in? Tomich and Essen? I shot'em both. Dead as Croatian lumber."

He paused to let his boss wake up. He could sense the fury build across the void that separated them.

"I'm not stupid Jack. I already know you shot them. Why? Did they resist you? Give you a fight? Why'd you shoot them? They were two old men, for

Chrissake."

Petrich's voice could be heard across the room as it bellowed out of the speaker. Stephanie's eyes grew wide.

"I should have told you George."

"Jack, Mendevich, the Consul already called me. I thought it was your doing. What the hell are you up to? I didn't authorize this. You were supposed to find the old men, not kill them."

"George, do you Remember my father, Eli?"

"Of course I do. How could you ask such a question?"

Petrich remembered. Petrich knew it was the reason Jack Kobe was an UDBA agent. Kobe had been selected to join the organization based upon Petrich's friendship for Kobe's long–dead father. A bond forged in the war. Kobe knew Petrich remembered. He simply wanted to hear it from the old man. The agent wanted to establish some common ground. Of course the old Partisan would remember. Kobe went on.

"My father's family, two brothers and two sisters, all children, were executed on the Sava. November 1, 1942. You remember. By the Ustashi. Those two sons–of–bitches, Essen and Tomich, they did it. They were there."

Kobe paused, realizing his voice had risen to the same level Petrich's had. He glanced at the woman. Her eyes were riveted upon him. He turned away, lowering his voice.

"I'd planned all along to kill those bastards if I ever got the chance. If I ever found them. Except you found them for me, George. You sent me to bring them in. I should have told you it was personal with these two. But you wouldn't have given me the assignment. I'm sorry I didn't tell you. But I'm not sorry I sent their souls to the devil."

Petrich sighed. He turned on his side, trying to keep the conversation from his wife. He knew he should have sensed that the assignment was too close to home for Kobe to handle. He should have remembered that Kobe had a personal stake in those two. He'd known it once, known about Eli Kobe's brothers and sisters. But it happened years ago. A life time ago, before a united Yugoslavia emerged from the ashes of the war. Now, with the new civil war, everything was once again turning to ash, ash to be blown away by the storm.

It was the kind of thing that he would not have forgotten ten years ago. But now, now he was old. And he had forgotten. George Petrich tried to rationalize it, tried to justify his lapse. He could not. All that was left for him to do was try and help the man. Find some way to get Kobe out of the country. Back to Belgrade. Kobe's voice interrupted.

"One more thing. I'm still in Minnesota. St. Paul. Had to blow my cover. Knocked my boss in Chicago on his ass. Took off. There are two Duluth cops on my back. Some locals as well, I think. But I'm still going to visit our friend, Marvin Field. See if I can recover the rest of the gold, if there's any left. You know that I found some of what the old men had hoarded?" Kobe inquired.

"I know. Mendevich told me he has it."

The tone of Petrich's voice once again became hard-edged. Kobe braced for a second blast from his boss. He dug into his jacket, searching for the .38 in his pocket to reassure himself he could handle the job.

Petrich's breathing stopped. His voice came across the telephone line in a reserved tone. He no longer sounded angry. His voice was fatherly:

"Jack, you can't be serious. Field isn't one of our objectives. Yes, he shared in the stolen gold. Partisan gold. That's documented. It's the reason he gave those two refuge, protected them. That's no basis to risk your life. It's stupidity. Bull–headed stupidity. After forty some years, its unlikely he has any of the gold left anyway. He's a rich man in his own right. Not like Essen or Tomich. Old fools hoarding the stuff for who knows what reasons. You can't accomplish a thing by visiting Field. I'm ordering you to stay away from him. Stay the hell away from him. I'll get you out of there somehow. But I can't help you if you kill Field. I can't save your skin then. Do you understand that, Jack? He's ex–CIA. If you kill him, all hell will break loose. I'll have no power to undo that."

Petrich's tone changed again. He was lecturing.

Stephanie Delaney walked over and picked up Kobe's empty Guinness bottle and disappeared into the kitchen. Before he could respond to Petrich, she came back into the room with another cold Stout. Placing the bottle in his free hand, she stroked his hair. He smiled up at her, kissed her wrist. She sat down in her chair and lit a Virginia Slim. Or was it an Eve? So she did have a fault. Kobe found himself momentarily concentrating on the woman once again. Petrich's voice called him back to reality.

"Look George, I appreciate the concern. I want to see this guy. I need to meet him face to face. I thought I'd kill him. For saving Essen and Tomich. That's passed. I won't kill the old man. But I must look into his eyes, tell him what those two did in terms only one of us can relate. Tell him about the four children whose blood was spilled into the Sava. Tell him about my father, my grandfather. What they fought and died for. I want him to hear the truth. Not some Ustashi or Nazi lies. And he must hear it from me."

Kobe took a big swig of the beer. The liquor's pleasant euphoria was beginning to assert itself.

"I'll go see him tomorrow. Then you can get me the hell out of here. With the gold. You know, the stuff I got back from the Ustashi whore and his Nazi friend. It's at the Consulate. Tomorrow, George. Get me out of here tomorrow. Before noon. Can you do that?"

Petrich pulled himself up in bed. His ribbed T-shirt fell loose over his arms. Once his torso had been firm and hard; now, his shoulders slumped, his muscles having lost the resilience of youth. He was too thin. He ran five miles a day. He'd have to forget about his five miles tomorrow.

"Damn it Jack, I don't want you near the man. He's not stupid. He knows you're coming. He's a professional, or at least he was, just like you. He'll probably shoot you before you can even tell him why you're there."

He tried one last attempt to plead with Kobe. He knew it wouldn't work.

"Sorry George, I gotta see him. I've got to tell him. See his eyes. Make him sweat a little. That's all. Twenty minutes and I'm out of there. That's all I need."

Petrich knew it was hopeless. His voice became a whisper. He didn't want anyone, not even his wife, to overhear his words.

"All right Jack. I've got a favor or two due me from the CIA. Some of the stuff we got for them on the Gorbachev coup. And that information we provided them on the status of the Albanians. I'll cash those chips in. I don't know if that's enough or if they'll even bite. But given the two men you killed were war criminals condemned to hang, I'll do what I can to convince them to let you go. It's got to be done tonight. Let me see what I can do. Give me a number where you can be reached."

Kobe looked at the number taped to the telephone and recited it to his superior. Petrich took down the number to Blue Eyes' apartment and hung up.

"What was that all that about? That wasn't German you were talking," the woman observed.

The young law student placed her Guinness on the oak floor. Sitting cross-legged in front of Kobe, she studied the UDBA agent with a hint of skepticism on her face.

"Business. I needed to take care of some business. Had to do with a soccer match coming up in Europe. I was speaking Serbian—I'm Yugoslavian, not German. I just pretend to be German because its easier. No one knows where the hell Yugoslavia is."

He smiled. His discussion with Petrich put him in a fragile mood. The woman's face melted the tension away. Reaching out he touched her black hair, relishing its softness. Caressing her hair released emotions that had been building within him for too long.

Kobe slowly slid out of the chair. His head came to rest in her lap, where her legs crossed. The UDBA Agent noted that his companion had firm, sculptured legs, slender but strong, their strength built from years of dance. He anticipated their seductive power through the rough texture of her hose.

She bent her head down, kissing his cheeks, his forehead, nibbling at his chin. He slid up the bottom of her T-shirt, staring at her tight belly, the lovely curve of her stomach, her delicately shaped navel. Her waist was narrow, it's skin tight and firm. She stroked his hair. He could feel her thighs begin to tense, to anticipate his next touch.

One hand slid slowly beneath her shirt. His fingers encountered no obstacles. He gently touched the smooth flesh of her breastbone. His hand lay between her small breasts, his fingers slowly massaging the cleft where they lay against her. Her nipples strained and pressed against the fabric of the T-shirt. His thumb and forefinger moved in unison, gently circling the aureoles. He refrained from touching the nipples themselves, his fingers delicately dancing around them, avoiding them. His touch was nearly indiscernible; a touch of restrained passion.

With one motion, as if cast in a dance that she'd practiced for all her life, Stephanie Delaney pulled her shirt over her head. He sat upright. She tossed the garment into a dark corner of the room. Her hair fell about her shoulders in disarray. She stood up, her body directly over him, her form blocking out the solitary light of the floor lamp. As she moved, her shadow crept across his face, darkening its features. With one hand, she held his neck, tilting it towards her swaying form. Her free hand loosening the hooks of her skirt, sliding it down, to the floor. With equal deftness, she stepped out of the miniskirt and pushed it away with her toes.

Kobe could see that she wore nothing but nylons. Her dark mound pressed against the mesh of the material. He reached up and slowly rolled the hose down around her ankles. Her legs were indeed those of a dancer, their every curve defined by strength. Her buttocks and thighs, her sinewy calves; each muscle stretched as she stood up. Reaching out to him, her soft, supple hands pulled him up to where she stood.

Wordlessly, she undid his jeans, sliding the zipper down slowly, deliberately. He let go of her, pulling his sweatshirt over his head, wincing as the fabric brushed against the ribs injured in the fight. She touched his skin; white, well-muscled from martial arts. Her soft hands tip–tapped their way down his chest, onto his stomach.

She placed her hand in his and led him towards the bedroom. Her hair trailed behind her. The heavily perfumed strands touched the skin of his neck, tickling him. As they passed a dilapidated dresser, she stopped and pulled a small wooden box out of one of the drawers. The sparse light of room reflected off of the small foil packet she retrieved. A condom. She handed it to him in silence. There was no need for words. He was not about to endanger himself or her for the mere sake of spontaneity.

After, he lay with her, talking, finding out about her childhood in St. Paul. She'd gone to Derham Hall, a private academy for girls, then to St. Catherine's College. She'd also taken thousands of hours of dance and voice lessons.

"There's really nothing special about me. I'm just another Irish Catholic girl from the East Side."

Her faith, her ethnic heritage, she explained, were the major attributes of those who held power in St. Paul for the past hundred years.

"Just being Irish makes you a success in this town."

"I think there's much more to you than mere happenstance, Stephanie. Anyway, how did you come to know this 'Freddy'?"

He was curious how a woman like Stephanie Delaney became embroiled with a man clearly her inferior.

"I met Freddy singing for a garage band. I was in college. He was a bigshot local booking agent. He saw me at a dance, singing, said I had talent. Put me in a band on the rise as the lead singer. He promised the moon and the stars. The band took off like he'd promised. I felt I owed him. So did Freddie. But I was naive, didn't know what he was really like. One night after a great show at the World Theater, he got me drunk. I passed out. When I woke up, I was in his bed. He'd stolen my virginity and I hadn't even been there to witness it. I guess he briefly stole my self respect as well."

Kobe reached out, touched her arm, lightly, innocently. As a friend.

"Just my luck. I got pregnant. He paid for the abortion. He promised to marry me. I should've known better. He was simply keeping me happy, so I wouldn't go to the police. Anyway, I didn't know what to do. My old friends told me he was a creep, a user. I wouldn't listen to them. I should have. I moved in with him, I didn't know what else to do. We were together for a year. He inherited some money, or so he said, bought the old machine shop, and opened the bar."

Jack Kobe continued to listen intently, enthralled by the soft, golden tones of the woman's voice, the words tinged with a trace of Irish lilt, though her family was more than a generation removed from County Cork.

"He named it after me. Thought it would be enough to make me forget. But it wasn't enough to keep me there. You see, I found out he had a nasty coke habit. He never did the stuff at home or around me. He knew I'd lost my brother Tom to drugs, that I wouldn't put up with it. I figured it out when he became violent, when his temper took control of our relationship.

His anger left too many scars for one act of love to wash away. And then I found out he'd started seeing other women. With AIDS and all the rest, he never protected me. Never thought that sleeping around could kill me."

Her eyes glanced to the used condom lying on the nightstand beside the bed.

"He wasn't as considerate as some," she whispered.

Kobe smiled in remembrance of their union, the earlier melding of their bodies. Being cautious had not diminished the sensations of their lovemaking. It had given them the peace of mind to be unrestrained in expressing their passion.

"As soon as I found out that he had other women, I left him. My old friends, my family, thank God, stood by me. Dad helped me get into law school, William Mitchell, where he'd gone. I joined another band. But Freddy wouldn't leave me alone. He fell in love with Gina, at least for a while, and begged me to give her a job with my band. In return, he kept my name on the bar. He said it had fan recognition. I fell right into his trap, working his bar. Tuition is high; dad can only help so much. I should have known better. Now he's done the same thing to Gina. Next month, it'll be somebody new. But I'm through with him, through with his bar. I've got too much invested in law school. Someday I'll be somebody on my own, without Freddy's hand in it."

"I think you're already somebody."

"Maybe. But when I become a lawyer, I can tell the Freddy's of the world to kiss my ass."

Kobe chuckled to himself listening to her talk about becoming a lawyer.

"I wonder if you'll defend me," he mumbled half beneath his breath.

"What did you say?"

"Nothing, forget it Stephanie, forget it. It was just stupid talk."

He told her as much about himself as he could sticking to the cover. He told her little about the real Jack Kobe, though bits and pieces of reality managed to slip through. Things about his mother, his stepfather, his half brothers and sisters. About soccer, coaching. Against his better judgment, he even told her his real name.

"It's not Hans. It's Jack. Jack Kobe."

She listened to it all intently. He could not tell if she believed him or not. But he was convinced she was indeed a remarkable young woman, the first American he'd ever met who actually listened.

After they'd talked long into the night, he left her bed to retrieve another condom. They made love again.

This time their embrace was slower, more deliberate, a gentle exploration of each other's souls. He felt it was love, elusive, mature, unqualified.

As she lay asleep, he stared at the graceful form of her bare back. He wished she'd have told him it was love as well for her. Or perhaps, for her, he was but a momentary diversion, a conquest. Exhausted, he turned away from her and fell fast asleep.

Mark Munger

A trace of sunlight entered the kitchen as Kobe stared out the cracked, frosted glass of the room's only window. Water dripped from a gap caused by a fissure in the glass. Though the beads of moisture distorted the view, the apartment had a fine overlook of the Mississippi. Below, the lowlands, the marshes, the docks and factories were all visible from Stephanie Delaney's kitchen. A slight breeze pushed the haze of the city away, leaving the impression of a fresh morning, a new beginning. The beauty of the morning was made all the brighter, more vivid, by the memories of the emotive evening.

A shuffling sound came from the bedroom. Stephanie walked into the room, her eyes moist. She wore only a long sweatshirt which covered her to just above the knees. "University of Minnesota–Duluth Bulldogs" was printed in maroon letters across the white fabric. She smiled, wiping the moisture away from her cheek with a sleeve. He smiled back and poured her a cup of coffee. A cloud of steam rose from the cup, pushed upward, towards the ceiling, by a cool draft from the old window. Blue Eyes sat down next to Jack Kobe and put her hand on his forearm. She squeezed the skin tenderly, but with firmness. Her voice sounded tiny, small, like a little girl's.

"Jack, I think you've made me fall in love with you."

His eyes moistened. He wanted to tell her he was in love with her, with every part of her, with every fiber of her being. But there was no time for love today. Today was the day he would meet Marvin Field. Today was not his to give her.

Chapter 27

December 5, 1991

Deb Slater and Dave Swanson ate a quick breakfast, caught a Taxi and rode to Field's office where Agent Herb Whitefeather was to meet them. Outside the Field Tower twenty of St. Paul's finest formed a thin blue perimeter around the building. Every entrance, every stairwell, every elevator was controlled and appeared safe. Slater wasn't so sure. Not with Kobe. The guy, whatever he was, whoever he was, was good, too good.

"Morn'en Deb."

Herb's big face grinned. He gave his friend a hug. She didn't resist. She might have, so early in the morning, had it been anyone but Herb.

"Field's up in his office. 43rd floor. Wait'll you see his desk. About a year's salary might buy the furniture polish for it. The guy is loaded."

He nodded to Swanson, stuck out his right hand. A mit. A claw. Swanson grimaced as Herb's grip tightened. A show of macho. Always trying to feel the other man's strength. Usually gauging it to be far inferior. That was just how Herb was. Swanson had long ago given up trying to retaliate. It proved less painful to simply acknowledge that the big man's grip was stronger.

The three officers walked by two St. Paul uniforms guarding the main elevators. A plain-clothes detective stood to one side, studying the front page of yesterday's newspaper. He was obviously disinterested in their presence. An elevator car stopped on the main floor. Its glimmering bronze door opened with a quiet "swhoosh." A short balding man looking to be about forty stepped out of the yellow light of the car. Ample paunch and pink cheeks, the man appeared to be out of breath from walking the few steps that separated them. He held a Marlboro in his left hand. Smoke curled slowly upward, disguising the man's fat face in a thick cloud of cigarette haze.

The detective's right hand was shoved deep within the pocket of his rain coat, a coat stained with spots of grease from too many nights at the Greenmill, nights spent devouring the best deep dish pizza in St. Paul. From his look, his demeanor, it was obvious to Slater that the St. Paul officer wore the twin badges of cigarette burns and pizza stains with pride.

Mark Munger

"Bill Harris, St. Paul PD"

He held out his right hand. Thick. Short fingers. Pudgy. Slater reached for it. He withdrew it and turned to Swanson. The female deputy muttered to herself. Something about Harris' manners fitting his physical appearance. Slater's anger, her pain showed in her face. As much as she tried to hide her emotions from the others, she could not. The pain was too real. It was a pain she'd felt hundreds of times in dealing with male peace officers. Swanson saw it and moved quickly to put it behind them.

"Dave Swanson, St. Louis County Sheriff's Office. My partner, Debra Slater. Best damn cop in the Department."

Swanson put his arm loosely on her shoulder in an embrace of brotherly reassurance. The gesture calmed Slater, as it had countless times before. She managed a smile, forced, beauty pageant style. It killed her to do it. She wanted to knee the fat bastard in the crotch. Make him feel the pain she felt. Another place, maybe. Another time.

"And this big guy, I'm sure you know. Herb Whitefeather, FBI. Duluth office."

Dave Swanson nodded in the agent's direction, still maintaining a calming arm around his partner, waiting for the tension to evaporate. Harris reached across Slater, as if she wasn't there, and shook Whitefeather's hand.

"Christ, go easy with the grip, will you Herb? You nearly broke my bowling hand."

Harris dropped his burning cigarette to the tile. With his left heel, the detective crushed the hot ember against the flooring, ignoring an ashtray that was well within his reach.

Harris continued to caress his numb right hand. He scrutinized Slater with obvious distrust before rendering his views on women in police work. His voice, high and tinny, sounded like a mouse suffocating under the cruel metal of a spring trap:

"No offense, Missy, but this ain't no damn place for a woman. This Kobe is one mean, calculating bastard. From everything we've put together, the man is as hard as nails and a pro known throughout the International espionage community. No, this here's no damn place for a lady.

Wouldn't let my wife get involved in this work. Dirty, foul. Like a sewer. No way I'd allow that."

His eyes narrowed, ferret–like in their slits. He tried to stare her down, to show her he meant business.

Slater broke free of her partner's gentle restraint. She stood eye to eye with the detective. She could smell last night's gin on his breath. Stale and pungent. Gin and pizza. It nearly gagged her. Her voice was soft, but edged with venom, the poison having built up from years of sexist confrontations.

The comment was but one more frustrating battle for her within the profession, a solitary battle that commenced the first day she put on the tan uniform of the Sheriff's Department.

"Listen you fat little toad. I'm a cop, just like you. I put my life on the line every day. I put my badge on, holster my gun every morning I go to work. I'm twenty-eight years old. Not some high school bimbo you can bully or push around. You bite me–I bite back. And if you don't understand where I'm coming from, I'll wrap those sorry little walnuts you call balls around your neck like pearls. You got me?"

Her voice remained soft, feminine, despite the message she conveyed. Harris looked blankly into her eyes, his swagger and bravado gone. From his prolonged silence, it seemed clear Harris thought she was nuts. Maybe she was. But he understood. He cast his eyes to the floor, embarrassed.

"Hey, don't get me wrong Deputy. It ain't personal. You gotta understand that I'm just talken generalities. Didn't mean to make it personal."

She nodded and stepped back next alongside Swanson. She had made her point. She knew that wouldn't change the way Harris looked at woman cops. But she had gained a small moment of self–respect. For now, that would have to be enough.

"So what's the setup, Harris?"

Whitefeather was chewing on a toothpick, looking down at the little man. His shadow engulfed the detective's pudgy form.

"What's the plan?" the Agent repeated.

Harris ushered the officers over to an information desk where an uniformed patrolman sat observing a bank of video monitors. The monitors covered the basement parking ramp and every other entrance to the building. Harris pulled out a set of blueprints for the Field Tower and detailed the locations of the twenty officers and detectives assigned to him. Slater guessed Harris had no women assigned to this duty, even though the St. Paul Department had long promoted their hiring. She was right. She turned away and looked out into the new light of morning, holding her tongue.

"We've got all the entrances and exits covered. Uniformed patrolman at every door. Field has four armed security people in the building as well. Two are stationed on the 43rd floor with him. Two others man the fourth elevator, this one here," the fat detective related as he pointed behind him. "It's the only one that reaches the penthouse office. Others end at the 42nd floor. I've got men posted at the top and down here, in the lobby. Every officer has a portable so they'll be in constant communication with me. There's no way in hell one man can ever get through them all to the 43rd floor."

Slater looked at the blueprints spread out in front of her. She noted there were two sets of stairs leading as high as the 42nd floor. One set lead to the 43rd.

"What about the stairs?"

Harris grinned. His bad breath found its way to Deb Slater's nostrils, forcing her to feign a cough to turn her head from the stench. Harris obviously relished a woman asking questions. He wanted to show her he was prepared with answers, answers to prove he had anticipated every possible contingency.

"Of course we've put a man in that stairwell at the top. And one on the 42nd landing. So we'll have two men in that area."

He was pointing to the single set of stairs that lead to the penthouse.

"And the doors are locked down here. No access. Only the officer here at the information desk has the keys; only I can give authorization for the doors to be unlocked. "

It seemed like a foolproof plan to Slater. She looked at Whitefeather and Swanson. Their nods confirmed her viewpoint. She had to reluctantly agree with Harris that his proposal made sense. One elevator to the top covered top and bottom by police. One stairwell to the top, locked at the bottom, locked at the 42nd floor, covered at the 42nd stairwell and the landing by two men.

As the detective in charge, Harris made the call as to where Slater and her companions were deployed. Given the open nature of the grounds surrounding the Field Tower, each of them were deployed with an uniformed St. Paul officer outside the building near one of the main entrances. It was Harris' belief that the best way to protect the millionaire from harm was to intercept the source of the potential harm before it entered the building. Slater drew Patrolman Tom Maloney, a square-jawed young rookie from South St. Paul as her partner. She was relieved to find out, from talking to Maloney, that the young officer did not share Harris' negative views regarding females in law enforcement. The two officers found a protected alcove and watched pedestrians struggle against the early morning traffic.

Jack Kobe departed Stephanie Delaney's apartment with mixed emotions. He knew by leaving her that morning he was likely leaving her for life. And there was no question in his heart that she was the one, that she could not be replaced.

But his heart also told him that he had a mission to fulfill; an obligation to complete. Fate would not allow otherwise. His melancholy continued as he walked, feeling the sting of the cold wind off the valley. The weather's brutal touch burned his unprotected face as he negotiated the frost heaves pockmarking the sidewalk down Crocus Hill. There was no comparing the pain of the winter's cold with the pain caused by the sorrow in his heart.

Before he left Stephanie's apartment, Petrich had called back, from an airplane, from somewhere over Ohio. The old Partisan had it all arranged. They had CIA clearance, the chance for a rapid exit. No customs, no questions. All Kobe had to do was make it to the Consulate in Minneapolis. Without killing Field. Then Petrich and the two CIA agents with him would get Kobe out of the country. Petrich had tried a second time to talk the younger man out of meeting Field. Kobe had smiled to himself as Petrich listed the reasons it was foolhardy to challenge the old American. He hadn't smiled because the reasons weren't logical; he'd smiled because of the fire he saw in the eyes of the young American woman sitting across from him. Even after the call had ended, her eyes continued to bore into his soul. She sat there, her curves hidden under the folds of a ragged sweatshirt, hot coffee steaming from the cup held by her soft, delicate hands.

In the end, he convinced Petrich he couldn't be persuaded. They were to meet at the Consulate at ten the next morning. He wouldn't kill the old man. He promised. He left Stephanie Delaney with a kiss on her forehead. She had wanted more; her lips had yearned for his to part. But his fear of what lie ahead left him unable to respond. All that his tortured soul could muster was a long hug of goodbye.

A single tear dropped from his eye as he walked unfamiliar streets. The tear landed on the wet asphalt, desolate and alone.

Not since his wife Resta died of ovarian cancer had he felt whole, complete, with another woman. Resta's family had watched him clutch at their daughter's corpse for an entire day after she'd died. They'd had to pry them apart. That had been along time ago, before UDBA took over his life. He knew that, if he stayed with the Irish girl, it would happen again. It could not, not with the cries of the Sava undiminished. So he had pulled away, perhaps too roughly. His mind forced him to see, even now as he shuffled through the dirty snow of the city toward Marvin Field, Stephanie Delaney's pain. Try as he might, he could not escape from her pain, from the hurt he'd seen flash across her face as the door to her apartment shut behind him. He could still hear her crying. The sound of her sobs could not be locked away.

St. Paul's neighborhoods were just coming to life as Jack Kobe quickened his pace towards downtown. A thin copper–tinged haze gathered, hanging low in the sky. The wind slowed, allowing the smog of the factories to accumulate. Across the river, he noted the bluffs of West St. Paul, dark against the pastel orange of early morning. Dawn was coming to the City.

He heard the cars of the city coughing loudly, their starters churning in the thin morning air. Here and there, an engine would ignite and roar under the pressure of its accelerator; the pedal pushed to the floor in an urgent, frustrated attempt to get the stubborn vehicle moving. Kobe's bare hands remained tense, concealed within the warmth of his jacket sleeves; the ends of the fingers tucked into his jacket pockets. As he walked, his right hand recoiled from time to time, its uncovered flesh singed by the frigid steel of the gun. The sting of the frosted weapon reminded him who he was, of what he had come to do.

His left hand reached into his pants pocket and pulled out a well–worn black and white photograph. The picture was old, having turned brown with age. He could not resist one last look at the faces of his long–dead relatives. Two young girls and two baby boys murdered long before his birth, their souls sent to the Creator, if one believed in such things, by the hands of the Ustashi.

The Legacy

Such innocence. Their eyes stared starkly at the photographer. Slight smiles pursed their lips. The girls were dressed in simple white peasant gowns, their budding womanhood hinted at but not confirmed in the fit of their garments. The boys wore matching sailor suits, black buckled shoes, and stood close, their arms wrapped around each other. He returned the picture to his pocket. His hands tingled. Jack Kobe looked down the street. Just ahead, he could see the sunrise reflected in the metal skin of the Field Tower.

He'd promised Petrich one thing. And he'd meant it, at least until he'd looked at the photograph of the children again. Now he wasn't at all sure that his promise to Petrich was one that he could keep. It seemed far more likely that Mr. Marvin Field was going to have to die.

Chapter 28

December 5, 1991

She really didn't know why she followed him. He wasn't the first lover she'd taken since she left Freddy. There were more than a few in the years she'd been on her own. Some of them looked far more promising than the foreigner. But there was something compelling about his sadness, about the strength, both physical and intellectual, she sensed within him.

One or all of these things made Stephanie Delaney pull on her faded jeans, cover her shoulders with a battered navy blue coat hanging in the hallway. Something more than mere curiosity tugged at her; compelled her, to break her cardinal rule of dating: Never run after a man.

"Well," she thought to herself, "I'm not really running. I'm walking."

It wasn't difficult to follow him down Crocus Hill. He stayed on Summit Avenue, the main drag. Her hands were cold. She'd forgotten her gloves. But her heart, her heart was warm. It was awake after several years of slumber, after several years of going through the motions.

Jack Kobe realized he really hadn't formulated a plan. He knew Field would be protected by the police, garrisoned in his office tower and well armed. Field was ex–CIA, ex–Army. It would take some doing to make it into the building, much less to the top. Yes, it would be difficult. Maybe impossible, now that they were ready for him. Surprise, he'd lost the element of surprise.

A block away from the Field Tower, Kobe ducked into Morris' Cafe, away from the bustle of another weekday of business in the State's capital. A bright winter's light illuminated the city. The sun reflected off thousands of frost-covered evergreens and the bare–boned limbs of leafless shade trees. In turn, the brightness was snared, intensified and released as it reflected off the red tile roofs of stately old mansions and the artificial exteriors of modern office buildings.

Outside, tightly bundled pedestrians lumbered by each other on the sidewalks. Cars lurched through the gridlock of the downtown rush hour. Drivers, still half asleep and in poor humor, cursed under their breath as vagabonds, with no sense of courtesy, careened their vehicles in and out of traffic in bold attempts to steal parking spaces.

The Legacy

Morris' coffee was strong. It brought Kobe back to the task at hand, took him away from the unfolding routine of another day in downtown St. Paul. He turned from the window in thought.

An uniformed police officer sat across the room in a ragged booth. The man was about twenty-five, the Yugoslav guessed, slender, with a slight mustache, sandy brown hair and glasses. He was engrossed in the morning paper, the sports page. Kobe smiled.

Jerry Abrams had been the first Jewish cop to patrol the downtown business district in the history of the St. Paul Police. Until he put in for the beat, the downtown foot patrol had been the exclusive province of the Irish. Jerry Abrams changed all that.

It hadn't been easy. It'd taken four years of quietly doing his job. Four years of making arrests, counseling shopkeepers, being a friend. Ed Morris had been one of the first to warm to Abrams. The café owner respected the diligence, the sincerity that the cop put into his work. In return, as a reward for the effort, Morris provided Abrams with free coffee every morning. Double stacks of pancakes. Extra fries or rings with his burgers. Morris showed his appreciation as only a cook could. He took a real liking to the Jewish cop, tried to make him feel at home among the Gentiles. For his part, Abrams made sure he spent the first break of every shift at the cafe, amidst the smell of fried food and the peeling paint, usually with his face buried in the dismal tales of the Vikings or the Twins in the *Pioneer Press*.

This morning was no exception. Between sips of coffee the cop contented himself with reading another blistering attack on the lack of fan support for the Twins.

"Hell," Abrams thought to himself, "If the damn Twins scored more than one run a night, maybe I'd take the wife and see a game or two. Naw. At twenty-two bucks a pop, they'll have to play a hell of a lot better to drag Jerry Abrams out to the Dome. A hell of a lot better."

"Shit, Eddie, I don't know what you put in this coffee of yours. Two cups and I gotta run to the john."

"What's a matter, officer? Stuff too strong for you? Maybe we can water it down next time, or maybe serve you some herb tea or some other Yuppie piss water."

"Yeah, yeah. I hear you. So maybe I got weak kidneys. Is that a sin? I mean, even a camel's gotta take a leak once in a while, eh Eddie?"

"With camels like you Abrams, the Arabs would perish in the desert. They'd pee away their water supply in a day's time."

The cop smiled, left the table and opened the door to the men's room. Morris' urinals had a chemical smell. The smell emanated from the little white air fresheners Eddie stuck over the drains. Jerry Abrams tried to ignore the strong disinfectant odor as he stood spread eagle over the cracked porcelain of a urinal.

He'd had more than enough coffee to make relief instant. It felt good to release the pressure that had been building up over the last two cups. Finished, he zipped up his fly and walked across the damp cement floor to a sink. Placing his hands under the slow, steady flow of the faucet, he carefully avoided the brown tarnished stains under the stream of hot water. He didn't hear the door open behind him. He never noticed the small foreigner in the harsh fluorescent light of the lavatory, never saw the upraised arm, the brutal blow to the back of his neck. The motions of the attacker were all framed in the starkness of the flickering light but by the time Abrams realized what was happening, realized it was his head that was the target of the attack, it was too late. A black veil of unconsciousness fell over him, engulfed him, in the instant before he collapsed.

Abram's black storm coat was too small in the shoulders. It bound the Yugoslavian's powerful upper arms, reminding him of the lack of planning on his part with each movement of his upper body. It was the best he could do.

Pulling the unconscious patrolman into a toilet booth, he propped the slumping body up on the seat. Kobe let himself out the restaurant's back door. He followed Minnesota Avenue until it intersected with Field Place, stopping only yards from the main entrance to the Field Tower. He stood alone in front of the building, searching the base of the millionaire's corporate headquarters for an opening.

It was obvious the place was crawling with cops. Kobe pulled the collar of the coat up under his chin and found a stone wall near the complex to lean against as he observed the building's security. Two policemen stood twenty or so feet from him guarding the front entrance. One was in uniform. He was of average build and height. The other, a huge Native American, was in plain clothes. He presented a big problem. Too big to risk a direct attack. He'd fight hard, take time to bring down. Couldn't risk using his thirty-eight. If he killed a cop, Petrich's efforts with the CIA wouldn't be worth spit. No, he'd have to use guile to get by the big man. It'd take some doing. Some planning. Some time. Time, something he did not have much of.

As he sat contemplating his options, a Greyhound bus pulled up to the curb across from him, its yellow flashers blinking in the morning. The vehicle's doors opened with a loud hiss. The silver beast disgorged its passengers; Japanese tourists, dozens of them, on some kind of tour of the Twin Cities, stopping to visit Marvin Field, the quintessential American success story. They walked slowly across the avenue. Young, old, and every age in between, chattering in Japanese, a language Kobe had never taken the time to learn.

In their lead walked two American women, smartly dressed, appropriately clad in tan overcoats, blue business suits and black leather pumps. They wore their coats pulled tightly around them. Their hair, a uniform mousy brown, was tied back. The effect was entirely conservative, entirely proper. The women motioned for the tourists to follow them across the street.

As the tourists passed Kobe, he saw an elderly Japanese woman falter and stumble her heel caught a small patch of ice on the cement. She screamed, and took a crazy tumble to the ground. A loud "crack" resounded across the plaza as her hip caught the full brunt of the accident. Landing upon the cold cement, she let out a tremendous cry of agony recognizable in any language. Kobe sprang from the wall and moved to the woman's side. The two cops from the entrance heard the cry and came on at a dead run. The tourists and the tour guides formed an informal circle around the stricken woman. The big Indian and his companion pushed their way through the crowd.

"What's up, officer?"

It was the big man. He spoke to Kobe as he bent down on one knee beside the Yugoslavian. The Indian's dark eyes were fixed on the old woman. He did not look at the man tending to her. A big, weathered paw reached out to the stricken tourist, grasping the Japanese woman's hand in a symbol of compassion, universal in its meaning.

"Looks like the old girl took a Minnesota header and cracked a hip."

It was the smaller cop talking. Kobe looked up at him and shook his head affirmatively. He didn't have much of an opening.

"Take it now", he thought, "while you can."

"You guys any good at this first aid stuff? I'm not. Too damn rusty. Haven't used it in years. O.K. if I make the call for the ambulance? You guys take care of the old lady?"

He tried to conceal his accent and make his plea sound convincing, like blood and trauma made him queasy.

"Stan, you stay here with the lady. Make her comfortable. Me and the officer, we'll go make the call."

"Shit," thought the foreigner, "why couldn't the big one stay put?"

But it was too late. The plainclothes cop was already walking across the commons to the doorway. Kobe pushed himself up with one hand and followed, trying to catch up to the Indian. Stan and the Japanese remained huddled over the fallen woman, the tour leaders looking on; not knowing exactly what to do while they waited.

"Hey, what's the name? Mine's Herb. Herb Whitefeather. FBI."

Kobe looked up at the face of the man walking next to him, trying to keep pace with Whitefeather's big strides. The pace matched the man's physique. He had big hands and broad, square shoulders. He appeared to be a block of granite. Suppressing his anxiety at the other man's physical size, Kobe smiled.

"Abrams. Downtown."

He was taking a chance, hoped the agent couldn't possibly know all the beat cops in St. Paul. From the lack of any change in the man's expression, it seemed clear he didn't know Abrams. And if he'd seen Kobe's picture, he hadn't made the connection. It was tough to do so with Abram's cap pulled down low to the brow and the coat's collar pulled up high. They shook hands as they walked. Kobe returned the Indian's grasp with a handshake of nearly equal strength.

"Not a bad grip, there, officer."

"Thanks. I work out quite a bit."

Whitefeather nodded, spoke again.

"Damn winters are tough on the older folks."

"You got that right."

They walked to the building's main entrance. Whitefeather pulled open the door. Inside the vestibule, Kobe discerned that there was one set of revolving doors and a second set of swinging doors. The UDBA agent glanced inside. One uniformed officer sat behind a desk. No one else was immediately in sight. It was now or never.

"After you."

Kobe smiled and took the door handle from the Agent's grasp. He held the door open.

"Thanks."

Whitefeather grinned and stepped into the revolving cylinder. With one motion, the Yugoslav reached towards his waist, underneath the storm coat, and pulled out Abram's nightstick. Wordlessly, he brought the solid barrel of the baton down atop the big man's skull. Whitefeather staggered forward into the glass cage, coming to rest against the far pane of glass. The UDBA Agent spun the door shut, jamming the handle of the nightstick between the door and its frame. The stricken FBI agent slid down the plate glass wall until his knees hit the floor. He was dazed, but not completely out, momentarily locked in a prison of glass.

Kobe walked calmly through another set of doors. Only a few preoccupied tenants of the Tower were inside the lobby. All were too busy to notice Whitefeather's collapse, too busy reading their Wall Street Journals to see what had taken place.

"How you doing, officer?"

It took the deskman a second to finish the line of the crossword puzzle he'd been working on. He glanced up. Smiled. His nametag said "R. Talbot". Another St. Paul uniform. Another big man. But paunchy. Near retirement. Talbot put the paper away.

"What's up?"

Talbot's brows crossed. He was looking Kobe over. A hint of recognition. Kobe couldn't be sure, didn't want to give him time to ponder.

"An old Japanese lady just slipped and fell on some ice outside. Broke her hip. Stan is out there right now. You know, with Herb from the FBI. Told me to call an ambulance."

As he spoke, Kobe glanced around the confines of the lobby. The public had cleared out. There was only one man within sight. A plain clothed detective stood near the elevators. The officer was obviously preoccupied, watching the rear end of a female janitor bending over, watering a planter. Kobe's gaze returned to the top of the desk, looking for something, anything to give him an advantage. His eyes focused on a set of keys laying half hidden under the newspaper. Next to the keys-a rolled up set of blueprints.

"Jackpot. No time for niceties now," the Yugoslav thought.

As Talbot turned to reach for the phone, a right cross tore into the man's jaw, catching him full on the chin. The punch sent the policeman spinning off his chair. Talbot landed face down on the soft wool of the carpeting behind the desk. He was out cold.

With one motion, the Yugoslav braced his right arm on the top of the desk and vaulted it, picking up the keys and the building plans with his free hand. He pulled the .38 from his waistband and pointed the weapon's muzzle towards the main entrance. Terrific noise emanated from that direction. The disturbance caused Kobe concern.

Behind the plate glass doors, the FBI Agent was raising holy hell. The big man was slowly coming to. It was obvious he was in a rage.

"Soon," thought Kobe, "he'll be kicking in the door, dislodging the night stick. Once he's free, I'll have no choice but to kill the man. There's no other way to stop that one."

A quick glance towards the elevators confirmed that the detective was still making small talk with the young cleaning lady. Kobe stepped around Talbot's body, using the profile of the desk to remain out of sight. Spreading the blueprints out on the floor, he noted blue dots spaced out around the building.

"Police," he murmured to himself. "Twenty or so."

The Elevators appeared to be covered top to bottom. They were out of the question unless he wanted a bloodbath, which he did not. If he killed again, especially a cop, he would never leave the country. There would be nothing Petrich could do for him.

The stairwell to the 43rd, to Field's office, looked to be covered, but not at the bottom; only at the top. The UDBA Operative tossed the blueprints and sprinted to the door leading into the stairwell, the stairwell leading to the 43rd floor. As he rushed by the prostrate Talbot, the blueprints came to rest atop the slumbering officer like a thin paper blanket. He discarded Abrams' storm coat as he moved. The garment fell off Kobe, covering Talbot's face.

As the Yugoslavian approached the stairwell, he fumbled with the keys on the ring. After several false starts, he found the right key, inserted it, and opened the door. Casting one last glance about the lobby, it was obvious to the Yugoslav that the detective by the elevators did not suspect a thing.

Kobe made the fortieth floor before Whitefeather escaped from his glass prison. The FBI agent tried to shoot his way out but the discharge from his handgun nearly broke his eardrums. Finally, bracing himself on the stationary portion of the glass, he kicked at the revolving door with enough force to bend the frame and dislodge Abrams' baton. The effort twisted his ankle, causing a painful sprain. Like a maddened bull seeking the matador tormenting him, the big Indian lumbered into the lobby.

From a distance, Whitefeather saw Talbot out cold on the floor. The FBI agent could also see the remaining detective engaged in conversation with the female janitor as the Indian studied Talbot's prostrate form.

"Kobe. Goddamn the sonofabitch. He got through. Shit, the old man is in for it now."

Whitefeather grabbed for his portable radio. It was not on his belt. Looking back towards the mezzanine, he saw that the device had been crushed and thrown to the floor.

"Damn, the man is quick. How'd he get that off of me without me knowing it?"

The big man removed the blueprints from the unconscious man's face and noted he was still alive:

"Looks like a nasty bruise, nothing more."

"Hey, detective, you got a man down over here," Whitefeather called out to the man near the elevators. "Kobe got through. Stop BS'ing and give me a hand."

The detective sprinted towards Whitefeather, the tail of his sportcoat flapping loosely as he ran.

"No way, sir. No way he got through here. I haven't even taken a piss since I came on duty."

Talbot was starting to moan. The detective stopped beside the stricken man and knelt.

"Holy shit. I guess he did get in."

"Stay here. I'm going after Kobe. Call Harris on your portable and tell him the guy is on his way up."

"Sure thing, sir. You bet."

The detective raised his portable radio to his ear. There was nothing but static:

"Battery's low. Can't get through."

"Shit. Some help you are."

"Hey, take it easy, fella. I'm doing the best I can."

The FBI agent knew better than to respond. He had nothing but disgust for officers who did not do their job, who did not remain diligent at their post. Pointing out the man's ineptitude would not save Marvin Field. The Agent held his tongue. He stood up and moved as quickly as he could.

It was clear that Kobe hadn't used the elevators. The only way to Field was up the stairwell. Kobe had a head start. Whitefeather picked up the telephone to dial Field's office in hopes of alerting the old man. There was no dial tone. He cursed the Yugoslav's thoroughness. The telephone cord had been ripped from the wall.

Chapter 29

December 5, 1991

"Where's your badge, officer?"

Detective Bill Harris ran his hand through his bald spot. He was standing in the vestibule of Marvin Field's penthouse officc, contemplating a cop who had just entered the lobby on the 43rd floor. Harris' eyes tried to pry underneath the rim of the cap, tried to look around the fabric of the shirt collar pulled high around the new man's neck.

A floor below, two more St. Paul policemen lay at rest. Both had made the foolish mistake of turning their backs as Jack Kobe noiselessly stalked his way up the stairwell. A slash of the flat of a hand to each officers' neck, another pair of sleeping patrolmen.

"Sorry. I must've left it in the squad. Should have kept it on so those jokers'd know who I was. I mean, being I'm from the East Side and all. Didn't know as they'd believe me."

Kobe grinned. Not too broadly so as to be conspicuous.

Harris studied the face. Thinking. Analyzing. Two big boned security guards sat in over–stuffed chairs near the door to Field's inner sanctum. Both were fidgeting with the trigger guards of their automatics. The polished ebony handles of the guards' weapons protruded from beneath their sportcoats. Neither paid much attention to Harris or the new arrival on the 43rd floor.

Harris nodded slowly as the new man finished talking. It was a nod that told Kobe he was in trouble. Harris raised his radio.

"Talbot. Come in Talbot. This is Harris in the Eagle's Nest."

Silence. There was nothing but silence. Harris' head began to turn away from the mouthpiece, ready to ask the stranger who the hell he really was. His eyes never made contact with those of Jack Kobe.

With a whirl of his legs, the Yugoslavian collapsed Harris with a kick into the inside of the detective's left knee. Writhing in pain, the cop reached for his service revolver only to watch it spin away crazily across the tile, kicked out of his hand before he could cock the hammer.

"It's Kobe. Get the SOB," Harris screamed in agony, clutching his torn knee.

Field's men moved in unison and reached for their weapons. Sensing danger from another quarter, the UDBA agent threw his body across the floor, away from Harris and into the stomach of the closest guard. His shoulder impacted with the thick muscle of the man's midsection as he threw an elbow into the man's throat. Another heap of flesh fell to the floor.

A glimmer of polished steel flashed to his left alerting Kobe to renewed danger. Kobe's eyes caught sight of the muzzle of a 9-mm Ruger pointed at his head. Diving crazily behind the fallen guard, rolling into a tight ball, he formed his torso into a human battering ram. One well–placed heel into the second guard's groin and the man's automatic slipped to the floor, followed by its owner.

Holding his own .38 at the ready, Jack Kobe sprang towards the door. Before he could enter Field's office, a shot rang out from behind him. A slug slammed into the thick wood paneling to his right, showering Kobe with splinters. The tiny missiles of wood stung his forehead, nearly blinding his eyes.

"Where the hell did that come from?" the UDBA Agent muttered.

He looked around the room. From behind the fallen men, he could see the open door of the 43rd floor elevator.

A female police officer stepped out of the shadows. She was confident, poised; her feet were solidly spaced in a classic police stance. Her hands steadied her weapon. Though the handgun looked heavy in her grasp, it's barrel did not waver.

"Don't move Kobe. I won't miss a second time."

Nervous. From the slight tremor in her voice, he could sense she was nervous, unsure. Kobe calculated his chances. Surrender was unthinkable. Shooting the officer wouldn't avenge the Sava, wouldn't cleanse the blackness from his heart. Only looking into Field's eyes, looking into the man's soul, making Field see fear, could do that.

In the milliseconds he stood crouched by the door, his only chance to survive loomed clear. He stood up and raised his hands.

"I said don't move, damn it. I don't want to kill you, but I will. I saw what you did downstairs. This is it. It's over. Lower your weapon to the ground. Slowly. Grip first. One finger through the trigger guard."

Deb Slater didn't feel threatened. But she was having a hell of a time keeping a bead on the man, steadying her aim. She found it difficult to keep the weapon's business end centered on his chest. Her heart was pounding, making her aim difficult. Kobe's right hand slowly lowered his revolver to the floor. He kicked it across the floor. It stopped near one of the stricken guards. The gun came to rest against the man's boot, scuffing its finely polished surface.

Using the far wall for support, Harris made an attempt to stand on his injured knee. The Detective's groans distracted Slater.

Her second bullet struck the doorframe, piercing the air where the Yugoslav's chest had been only a moment before. A mere instant before impact, Kobe vaulted away from harm, crashing through the door into Field's office, breaking it off the hinges. His entrance was so explosive; it caught the ex–CIA operative off guard.

Field had heard the commotion outside his office. Behind the thick walls, the old man readied himself for Kobe. But when he heard Deputy Slater's voice, his guard was lowered. The hammer on the big .45 had been placed back to its neutral position when Kobe's shoulders crashed through the door.

In a single, uninterrupted tumbling motion, the intruder covered the distance from the door to Field's desk in less than a second's time. Again, the .45's hammer cocked. His attention concentrated on the twirling form of the UDBA devil, Field attempted to squeeze off a round and dispatch the enemy. Before his muscles could carry out his mind's command, a bright flash of silver split the air. Its course caught Field's eye. Then, a searing, burning pain erupted in the old man's shoulder. A knife buried itself to the hilt in the old man's flesh. Field's right arm sagged in shock as he strained to pull the trigger. In response, the big .45 coughed, but its slug tore a hole through the Oriental rug covering the hardwood floor.

Before the stricken millionaire could transfer the weapon to his left hand, Kobe was beside him. Field gasped in pain. He was in shock, paralyzed by the horror of watching his own blood flow from the wound, spoiling his freshly pressed Christian Dior shirt. Field's rich, deep red lifeblood dripped onto the crisp linen fabric.

The ex-OSS Agent clutched the wound, trying to stop the bleeding. Kobe forced Field's right arm up. The old man to cried in pain.

Outside St. Paul was beginning to warm in the winter's sun. Jagged chunks of river ice spun slowly in the river current, bumping together, drifting apart. Nature's patterned ballet seemed lost amidst the bustle of the city.

Kobe's eyes were drawn to the poetry of ice and water visible through the office windows. The scene called him back to the Sava and reminded him of the winters of his youth. His attention was distracted for but a second, a lapse covered by the sobs of the wounded millionaire.

Kobe wrestled the gun away from the old man. The .45 fell to the desk, marring the exquisite mahogany. In one motion, without loosening his grip on Field, Kobe picked up the automatic. The ex-CIA Agent trembled in his hands. No longer the soldier, he was simply a frightened old man.

Jack Kobe pressed the muzzle of the heavy weapon to Field's cheek. A small spot of crimson appeared from the corner of the old man's mouth. It dripped onto the desk, mingling with the other blood. Debra Slater's form remained visible outside the broken door. The Deputy stayed low. The barrel of her pistol caught the glint of the sun. Kobe looked at Slater and spoke to her in perfect English.

"Officer, it seems we have a bit of a standoff. As you can see, Mr. Field here is quite preoccupied. His weapon seems to have acquired a new owner. And I'm not certain the new owner's hand is steady."

Kobe cocked the hammer for emphasis. Field's body began to tremble. The foreigner kept his eyes leveled at the young woman. She didn't move.

"So what'll it be, Mr. Kobe? You've got him. I've got you. And I'm sure you're sharp enough to realize we can't let you out of this building. Under any conditions. Seems like your adventure in America is at an end. Why don't you give it up before someone else gets hurt?"

Harris limped up to the doorway, his sidearm pointed in Kobe's general direction.

"Unlikely the bald one can come close to hitting me," the UDBA agent thought. "But the woman. She has me. Given the smallest opportunity, she will kill me."

His voice broke the tense silence hanging between them.

"Look, officer. All I want to do is talk to Mr. Field. Give him a history lesson or two. Nothing more. He's not worth any more of my time than that. I've no reason to kill him."

The Legacy

Kobe wasn't sure if he meant the words he spoke or not. He hadn't thought it through that far.

"Let me have five minutes with the man. He's in a good position to listen to what I have to say. Right, Mr. Field?"

The muzzle of the handgun dug into the old man's cheek tissue, causing Field's eyes to bulge.

"Tell her, Mr. Field. Tell her to give me five minutes."

"I think he's serious," Field whispered dryly.

Millionaire Marvin Field was having difficulty forming words. His mouth was parched. There was no moisture in his throat.

"Give him the five minutes or I believe he will pull the trigger."

The Yugoslav's eyes continued to stare at the Deputy's shadowy form. He saw her lean over to converse with the one called Harris. There was a nod of affirmation from the wounded detective.

"O.K. Kobe. You've got your five minutes. We'll pull back some. But when the time is up, we want Field out of there. Agreed?"

"We'll see, officer. When the time is up, we'll see. It all depends on how fast Mr. Field catches on to the history lesson I'm going to give him."

Deputy Deb Slater's voice grew harsh:

"Not acceptable, Mr. Kobe. I can't just leave it up to you. No, I can't do that."

Her pistol was again leveled at the foreign agent's temple.

"For God's sake, let him talk to me. I don't think we're in a position to negotiate."

Field's voice cracked as he pleaded with the officer. Hearing the man's terror, she relented and backed into the reception area. Harris shuffled along beside her. Lowering his weapon, his round body merged with the shadows beyond the door. Behind them, coming out of the elevator, Kobe saw the form of the big Indian he'd coldcocked in the revolving door. Several other officers followed. They all remained in the shadows, allowing Kobe to have his time with the old man.

"Now, Mr. Field, I want you to listen closely. I know you are the man responsible for bringing Damos Tomich and Franz Essen to this country. For allowing them to escape the Partisans. I also know that you extracted a handsome fee for the freedom of those two men. Enough gold to make you a rich and powerful man."

Kobe's gaze bore down upon Marvin Field's face. His grip tightened on the .45, pushing it forcefully into the hollow of the old man's jaw.

"What you may not know nor understand is that I am here because the two men you saved from the gallows killed my family. Butchered them on the banks of the Sava River. When they were only children. This isn't duty. This is personal."

Field's eyes widened in the sudden realization that his life was imminently in danger. A tear formed and remained suspended from the man's left eye. Field tried to speak. The muzzle of the gun was pressed too tight.

"So you see, Mr. Field, I had to kill those two bastards.

For my family. Wherever they hid. Wherever they were. They escaped justice in my country. I could not let them escape it here. As for you, I came here thinking it might be enough to see you. Make you fear me. However, it seems I am in a bit of a predicament here. It seems the police aren't about to let me walk away from this place."

He paused, glancing through the doorway. There had been no movement by the police.

"So then, what are we to do? What am I to do with you? A man who protects butchers of women and babies? A man whose fortune was born of my family's blood?"

Kobe felt the old man going limp. He let the muzzle of the .45 slip downward until it was resting against the jugular, cutting off Field's airway. The ex–OSS operative shook as a spasm came over him.

"Time's up, Kobe."

Kobe recognized the voice to be that of the big Indian. Herb Whitefeather stood next to the woman, nursing his head bruise, obviously annoyed at having been brought to his knees by the much smaller Yugoslavian. Kobe thought he saw the hint of a smile cross the FBI Agent's lips, as Whitefeather brought his weapon up and aimed it at Kobe's head. The big man's words filtered out slowly, without any hint of emotion.

"So what's it gonna be?"

Before the UDBA agent could respond, another figure appeared from the shadows. Words drifted to him, as if frozen in time, from somewhere behind the crowd of police. They were spoken by a familiar voice, a voice seemingly out of place for the circumstance, for the situation. His eyes strained to verify the improbable. The impossible. Then, out of the corner of his eye, he saw her. It was Stephanie Delaney.

Chapter 30

December 5, 1991

Petrich's charter landed at St. Paul Airport. The airplane touched down beneath shadows cast by smooth sandstone cliffs. As the jet came to rest, a thick mist curled upward, created by the River water's warmth mixing with the cold air of winter. The temperature inversion formed a ground fog that blocked the diplomat's view of the landing strip.

He opted to land in St. Paul rather than at the International Airport out in Bloomington. Quietly in. Quietly out. Petrich knew that was how it would have to be done. It was the only way Petrich could save Kobe from his foolishness.

Two high ranking, stone-faced CIA operatives sat next to Petrich in the plane. Both agents had worked with Bush before he'd won the oval office. It hadn't been easy to cash the chip. They hadn't bitten on the Soviet and Albanian information as readily as Petrich had thought. To get their attention, he had to give them some highly sensitive data on the internal situation in Yugoslavia. Sensitive enough to get him hung as a traitor if leaked. He thought about that possibility as the plane bounced along the runway.

Time seemed to churn backwards since Tito's death. Power had emanated from the hero of the liberation. Unity had been wielded from that power, that persona. Now it was all coming to an end, coming unglued.

Petrich was a Serb and a communist. The Serbs still held the reins of power. Through the Yugoslav military, they held the reins. But the horses, the Croats, the Bosnians, the Slovenes, even the Serbs living outside of Serbia itself, had escaped the reins, were running wild, destroying the unity, the strength.

Petrich's confidences to the CIA detailed the probable plans and reaction of the Federal Military if the horses continued to run away from the barn. The answer was simple. All out civil war was inevitable. Petrich was certain that even the Federal military would find it impossible to stop the resettlement process initiated by the Serbians in Bosnia. He was not blind; he could see that the brutality of the militant Serbs had reached levels equal to, if not greater, than the Nazis and Ustashi during World War II. Yet still he hoped for a reunion of the country, for preservation of the Yugoslav nation. But he knew it was a naive ideal.

All this rushed through Petrich's mind as the plane screeched to a halt. His hand reached upward. Petrich lifted his hat off of the luggage rack. The garment was very European; brown felt with a wide brim and a faded red leather band. He carried it loosely in one hand, turning it nervously by the brim, a brim as old and worn as the hand that grasped it, as he walked down the aisle.

Dallas Thomas watched the Yugoslavian closely. Fifteen years in the CIA, ten spent in the Company's Southern European office, Thomas was intimately familiar with the fragile balance within Yugoslavia that allowed its nationalities and religions to remain united. Petrich's details had simply confirmed suspicions. Confirmed the inevitability of the war. But the information on the Soviet coup had been astounding, far more revealing and vital than Petrich suspected.

Thomas' small green eyes studied the floor as he waited for the door to open. It was time to worry about Petrich's boy in St. Paul, to concentrate on the moment. Behind him, he heard his partner, Agent Irene Simon, speak.

"Look's like a cold day in Minnesota" she observed.

The female agent's teeth, stained from a constant supply of cigarettes, clicked together lightly as she spoke. Her hoarse, raspy voice, made the Yugoslavian wince. She had interrupted his daydream. He smiled, bowing to the female agent in mock affirmation. She obviously had other things on her mind. He wished she'd get to them.

"We've got the police commissioner meeting us as soon as we get off. Seems like your man has attracted quite a crowd. Cops upon cops surrounding Field's office building. Tried to get word to the man in charge, a detective Harris. Can't be reached. Communications are down. Your boy might be in custody already. That will complicate things. Tremendously. Once he's under arrest. Don't know if these locals will give us any slack. Worse yet, some cowboy might take him out."

Simon stood up, smoothed her wrinkled skirt, and followed Thomas behind Petrich. An unbuttoned wool overcoat hung loose from her shoulders. The open coat revealed a .44 magnum holstered to her hip. Petrich thought her manner impersonal.

"No, cold. That's what she is," he thought, correcting himself. "That's what she is trained to be."

Petrich forced a smile as they stepped down the stairs and onto the asphalt.

"Agent Simon, I doubt that the local police have, as you say, 'taken out' Jack Kobe. He's very resourceful. I doubt you will find him under arrest. Or dead."

Petrich continued to smile at the woman as he spoke. His voice, his words, were softly formed but said with confidence, the confidence of knowing a man, his family, over a fifty-year span.

Outside the plane, Commissioner Ian McCabe stood alongside a Lincoln Town Car. Silhouetted in the finely polished black finish of the limousine, the commissioner watched the foreigner and the CIA agents descend from the jet. Two young patrolmen stood at rigid attention on either side of McCabe, oblivious to the weather.

"Commissioner McCabe, Agent Thomas, CIA. This here's Agent Simon and Col. George Petrich, Special Yugoslavian Diplomatic Officer."

Thomas extended his hand. McCabe didn't make a move to accept the gesture.

"Cut the crap, Thomas. You're in my jurisdiction now. I know you've got friends in high places. Christ, I've heard from the mayor. The governor. The White House. That doesn't mean squat to me. This is my town. These are my people. And Petrich's boy is running around like some B–Movie bandit playing avenger. It isn't all right. I'm not a happy man. And the phone calls just piss me off even more."

McCabe's fat belly shook as he spoke. His face turned a deep hue of red. The sparse wisps of scarlet hair, all that was left of what had once been a proud, crimson mane, tossed madly back and forth in the wind. He was a short, fat Irish sea of upset waiting to explode. His two adjutants displayed discernible smirks upon their faces as they enjoyed their boss' dressing down of the CIA.

"Look, McCabe. I know how we're walking on eggshells here. We blow into your state, your town. We ask you to give us some slack. There's an international agent running around knocking down cops. Killed two of your citizens. Men of long-standing virtue. So it seems. And we ask you to let us waltz in, take the guy and whisk him away for interrogation in Washington. With no promise that he'll ever be back for trial. Doesn't sound fair but that's how its gotta be. You're out of your league here, McCabe. Way out," Thomas stated respectfully, almost apologetically.

Listening to the lecture, McCabe's face turned a shade of blue that Thomas never thought possible for human flesh.

"Bullshit, Thomas. Bullshit. That's what this whole damn situation is," the Commissioner roared. "We've got a double murder. A hostage. Half a dozen assaults on police officers. Assaults on security guards. Not to mention kidnapping. Violation of federal law for pirating a trainload of people, leaving them stranded on a trestle. And you want me to let you wander out of town with this guy? I can't understand who's behind this. I can't understand it at all."

McCabe's head kept shaking violently from side to side. Petrich stared at the man; convinced that McCabe's head would simply pop off.

"Sir, I know this is unusual. I know we're being indelicate. The fact is Mr. Kobe is my subordinate. He has diplomatic immunity. Even if you arrest him, even if you try him, ultimately he must be released. That is international law."

Petrich spoke quietly, calmly. He was attempting to defuse the Commissioner's wrath. Of course it was a lie. Kobe was not a diplomat. He was outside the protection of international law. McCabe may or may not know that. It was worth the gamble. The CIA agents weren't about to correct him.

"So you see, Commissioner, it's senseless to stand here in the cold and argue these points. While we do, Mr. Kobe may well shoot one of your officers if they try something foolish. One of your, how did you say it Ms. Simon, your 'cowboys', might end up dead. That would be unfortunate."

Petrich turned to the female agent, a wry smile on his face. Leaning against the ebony shine of the limousine's hood, he steadied himself against the buffeting wind.

"Of course I was speaking generically, Mr. McCabe. No reflection upon St. Paul's finest," Simon said sheepishly.

She tried to utilize her most deferential demeanor. A delicate apology for using the term "cowboy." McCabe didn't buy any of it.

The little man turned on the balls of his feet and motioned for his assistants to open the doors of the Lincoln. With his other hand, he gestured to the visitors to get in.

Within the warmth of the car, a huge black patrolman sat behind the wheel.

A police radio crackled in the background. The driver turned to McCabe:

"Bad news Commissioner. Just came over the line. Reports of gunfire in Field's office. Yugoslav was hit in the chest. Looks bad. Also seems to be a female civilian involved. Nothing specific on her. Sounds like a war up there. No word on Field or our people."

The black officer was surprised to see a grin cross his boss' mouth. The driver turned to the three passengers in the back seat when McCabe began to laugh.

Commissioner McCabe's sudden mood change seemed to cast a pall over his guests.

Chapter 31

December 5, 1991

Stephanie Delaney managed to enter the stairwell and follow the foreigner after she witnessed his dismantling of the Indian and the others. His actions shocked her. Once again, as it happened regularly in her life, things were not as they seemed. He was not as he seemed. At first, it made her angry; realizing that Jack Kobe wasn't who he said he was. Then she felt determined, damned determined to try and understand what it was all about.

Stephanie Delaney's appearance on the 43rd floor of the Field Tower had not been to the UDBA agent's advantage. It surprised him, caught him off guard. The last thing he needed to happen as he held a gun to Marvin Field's throat was to be distracted. When he heard her voice, when he saw her, a flood of emotions assailed him. Love, tenderness, regret; all cascaded into his mind. They occupied his attention for a brief instant. An instant he could ill afford.

Deputy Slater stood at the forefront of the officers maintaining her pose, holding a steady bead upon the man's chest after the five minutes had passed. When Kobe looked up from Field to the girl, it was the only opportunity the officer needed.

He saw Stephanie Delaney's small form, her face, the face he'd stared into the night before. Not since his youth had he felt such love. Before he became dedicated to UDBA. Before he'd become a killer. He'd thought his capacity to experience romantic love had been destroyed, replaced with mechanical lust, mere biological satisfaction.

He thought of all these things as he saw her emerge from behind the blue line of uniforms. She struggled to break free, to come to him. Kobe could not stop staring at her. In the confusion, he let the .45 slide down Field's throat until the gun's barrel pointed harmlessly at the ground.

Instantly he knew his mistake. It was too late. Out of the corner of his eye, Jack Kobe saw the female officer's index finger squeeze, slowly, like the motion was being frozen in time. A last memory to carry with him on his journey to death.

The muzzle of Slater's handgun jumped. Simultaneously, he felt the impact of the slug thunder into his chest, sending Kobe crashing into a window, lights spinning wildly, Field falling to the floor, out of his grasp. No breath. Darkness. He heard Stephanie's screams from across the room. Pain gripped his torso.

Then there was only silence.

"No. Goddamn it, no. You've shot him. Oh God," Stephanie screamed as she exploded across the floor in unrestrained urgency.

Just as the woman reached the side of her slain lover, Marvin Field's .45 erupted in blue smoke, discharging a bullet aimed at Kobe's brain, launched by Field as the old man staggered to his feet, his eyes wide with fear.

Field's bullet missed its target. His eyes moist with sweat and tears, the old man squeezed off the round too early. Instead of entering Kobe's brain, the hollow point exploded into Stephanie Delaney's right leg, boring into her flesh, tearing through the muscle that she'd built through years of dance. The bullet exited and came to rest in the dark wood of a paneled wall with a loud "thud." A visible wave of pain descended over the dancer's body as she cried out. Shock blessedly silenced her before she could scream again.

Slater was the first to realize what had happened. In two strides she was at Field's side to slap the pistol out of the millionaire's hand. Her blow prevented the old man from firing again.

"Damn fool. You shot the girl. What the hell's wrong with you?" the Deputy shouted at the cowering tycoon. "Kobe was down. Not a threat. Probably dead. What the hell's wrong with you?"

Debra Slater grabbed the ex-CIA Operative by the collar and lifted him off of the floor, oblivious to the fact that Field was bleeding from the knife wound to his shoulder, as she screamed at him.

Pulling more violently with each word, Slater ignored the fear contorting the wounded man's face.

"Come on Deb, calm down," Swanson instructed.

Her partner was there, his hand placed gently on her shoulder.

"Take care of the girl. She looks pretty bad. Herb's got Kobe. I'll deal with Field. It's over, Deb. It's over."

Slater looked at her partner and released her grip on Field's collar. She stood over the wounded man, suddenly nauseated by the stench of Field sitting in his own offal. The old man was crying.

Released from her partner's grasp, Slater turned and tended to the young woman. The victim was small and delicate. There was blood spurting out of the obvious leg wound. It looked bad, a main artery, probably the femoral, appeared to be severed. Slater pulled off her insulated vest, tightly wrapped the wound and elevated the leg. Blood soaked through the fabric in a matter of seconds. In the background, Slater heard Harris on the radio, calling for EMTs, an Ambulance, the Paramedics. She felt the fallen woman's wrist. The skin was soft but cool. The pulse was erratic. Shock had set in.

Slater looked at the face. The woman's thick black hair lay gently across the stomach of the fallen foreigner. Herb Whitefeather carefully pushed the woman's hair aside, off Kobe's abdomen. He opened the UDBA agent's shirt; St. Paul Police Department issue. The garment's cotton fabric was disturbed by the course of Slater's round but the entry wound was not bleeding.

"Shit. He's wearing a vest," the FBI man muttered.

"A vest? What kind of vest?" Slater asked.

"Kevlar, Deb. Goddamn Kevlar. Look at the dent your round put in it."

Whitefeather pulled the man's shirttails out and unbuttoned the shirt. A .357 slug had burrowed itself nearly all the way through the Kevlar and rested near a stamped label. The label read:

"Property of St. Paul Police Department, Officer J. Abrams."

The "P" and "O" in "Police" were nearly obliterated by the slug.

Slater maintained pressure on the woman's leg as she studied the features of the fallen foreigner. After a moment of contemplating the UDBA Agent, the Deputy bit her lip and turned her attention back to the stricken civilian, unsure of why the woman lying next to her had come to Jack Kobe's side.

For the sake of the two dead men in St. Louis County, she hoped the son of a bitch was dead. But what would that do to the woman? She might die while the assassin lived. Slater couldn't make logical sense of it all. She looked back at the woman's face. It was losing color. Her breathing was irregular. Where were those damn paramedics?"

"This guy's got a couple of broken ribs" Whitefeather decided. "Maybe a punctured lung. But he'll make it. Pulse is strong. He'll thank you for a hell of a sore chest though. Shit, Deb, I thought you killed Mr. Ninja with that round. Nice shooting anyway."

The Indian covered the vest with the uniform shirt and stood up. Within minutes, the ambulance and medical personal arrived. IV bottles were hung; a monitor was attached to Stephanie Delaney to measure her rapidly fading heartbeat and her rapid, shallow respirations. One of the EMTs applied a pressure bandage to control the bleeding. Stretchers were loaded onto the elevators and carried safely to the ground. Outside, the red lights of the emergency vehicles churned in the crisp air causing flashes of scarlet to splash across the glass walls of the Field Tower mezzanine.

A crowd gathered near the entrance soon after the gunfire erupted. In the middle of the mass stood the Japanese tourists. They remained silent, staring blankly as the stretchers and the bodies were carried out of the building.

Behind the paramedics walked an assortment of law enforcement officers. A big Indian in a rumpled and blood stained suit, his tie long since lost, supported a very tired-looking old man. The old man's shirt appeared to be stained by fresh blood. A large bandage was wrapped around his right shoulder. His Clark Gable mustache dripped with perspiration. His trousers were stained, like he'd messed himself. The old man hid his face in his hands.

A tour guide stepped out from the crowd and approached the injured man. Marvin Field stopped and looked up at the woman. Her voice was edged with concern as she spoke to him:

"My God, Mr. Field. What happened to you?"

The only response to her innocent question was the sound of millionaire Marvin Field crying. A gust of wind stirred. It was an east wind, a wind that defied the natural patterns of weather, a wind that was born of long forgotten sorrows, sorrows buried alongside the waters of the Sava River.

Marvin Field cowered in the shadow of his office building, the bricks, metal and mortar a lasting monument to himself, to his greed. Tired, exhausted by the weight of living a lie for over forty years, Marvin Field turned his face away from the woman and entered a waiting police car. Outside, the wind continued to swirl, gathering strength and speed as it carried the old man's sobs upward, up into the bright blue sky of the Minnesota winter.

The Legacy

Chapter 32

December 9, 1991

Sheriff Dan Prescott drove South on the freeway four days after Kobe had been taken. A gentle snow fell. A slight breeze from the Northwest kicked up and forced the white powder into compact hedgerows, two to three feet deep along I–35. Prescott's bronze Suburban churned along. Locked in four-wheel drive, it smashed through the drifts like an icebreaker on the Big Lake.

Slater and Swanson had done well. He smiled when he thought of the two of them, two backwoods deputies in a gun battle with an international assassin, terrorist, whatever. They tracked the man across the state, across the Midwest, and nailed him.

Patti Loveless' "Timber, I'm Falling in Love" blared out over the am radio. The County was too cheap to spring for am/fm. It was dark when Prescott pulled the rig into the Ramsey County Medical Center in St. Paul.

He told Slater and Swanson to meet him there. The Deputies had stayed in St. Paul to make sure the paper work cleared the Ramsey County Attorney's Office. They were available to help transfer Kobe back to Duluth for his grand jury appearance. It was murder one for sure. At least two counts, along with kidnapping, assault, other assorted state felony charges. After the State got done with Kobe, the Feds would get a piece of him.

Train hijacking, assault. The list went on and on.

The first trial would be held in Duluth. Kobe would have a public defender, a good one. But public defenders had limited resources. It was likely to be a quick conviction once the indictments came in.

Ramsey County Medical was almost deserted as Prescott walked in the emergency entrance. The Sheriff asked for directions to Custodial Intensive Care, where criminal offenders and suspects in need of medical attention were kept in a locked, secured unit. McCabe had assured him there'd be at least two officers from the St. Paul Police Department on Kobe. Round the Clock. No slip ups. The guy was like an eel. They couldn't afford to take any chances. McCabe promised; no rookies, only experienced cops. Prescott was convinced; he rested more easily after he talked to the Commissioner.

Custodial patients were held on the fourth floor. There was only one secure elevator up, one secure elevator down. Prescott showed his credentials to the on–duty officer at the elevator station. He was buzzed through. He punched the "up" button.

Somewhere above him, he heard a motor start. Gears whined from within the shaft. Stepping into the small car he pushed "4". The car began to move with an uneasy jolt. A slow ascent. Impatiently, Prescott scrutinized the walls. The surfaces were covered with peeling brown paint. Vandals' initials and vulgarities, carved into the smooth paint or applied with thick permanent marker, were everywhere. An attempt had been made to conceal the obscenities with paint. The intent of the messages remained readable. Most of the phrases relied heavily upon variations of the word "fuck" for effect.

Dim recessed lights in ceiling panels greeted the Sheriff as he exited the elevator on the fourth floor. Another door, another officer; another buzzer. Prescott stepped into the secured area. Two nurses sat behind a station, busily working on patient charts. A doctor stood at the counter talking on the phone. The physician was animated. He appeared angry and unhappy with someone. As the Sheriff walked up to the station, he smiled at the nurses. They didn't seem to notice or care. Behind them, looking down the hall into the ward, he could see two uniformed St. Paul officers talking to Swanson and Slater.

"Dan Prescott, St. Louis County Sheriff's Department."

He looked at the nurses. Again no smiles. The doctor ignored him as well, exiting the ward without a word.

"I see my two deputies are already here. Mind if I talk to them?"

The older nurse nodded affirmatively. Prescott walked towards the deputies. He didn't like what he heard.

"What the hell do you mean we can't go in Kobe's room?"

Dave Swanson was hot. His hormones were surging. He was obviously poised for a fight, postured like a linebacker ready to make a tackle. Deb Slater stood by his side. Listening. She allowed no emotion to show.

"That's right. Those are my orders, Deputy. No one but no one other than Commissioner McCabe and the medical people are allowed in."

The cop doing the talking was a skinny puke of a guy. Maybe twenty-two, obviously a rookie. The man smelled of regulation from shoeshine to attitude.

It was clear he was fresh out of the two year Vo Tech training program. His partner looked even younger, but more muscular. The partner displayed a thick neck and a wide, angular jaw.

"What's the problem?"

Prescott stepped up to the discussion.

"I'm Sheriff Prescott, St. Louis County. I've got an order here to transport Mr. Kobe back to Duluth for an appearance before the grand jury. Doctor says he can travel. Your County Attorney's approved it all. What's the beef?"

Prescott placed himself directly in front of the larger of the two young officers. Hands on his hips, establishing authority.

"Sorry, Sheriff. We didn't know. Didn't mean to play hard ass with your deputies but the Commissioner made it clear not to let anyone in."

The skinny ones' name was J. Smith. That's what his nameplate said.

"Listen, Officer Smith, what I've got here is a lawful order of the court. Kobe's going with us. Tonight. If I have to personally knock the shit out of both of you to do it."

He moved in on the larger one. The officer's nameplate said "Fogarty". Prescott pressed his chest into Fogarty's space. Fogarty's facade faded. It was obvious he was uncomfortable. Prescott held his position for an instant, for affect, then backed away.

"Do we have an understanding, Officers Smith and Fogarty?"

Fogarty stepped back. Smith stepped aside as well. Fogarty motioned for the officers to enter Kobe's room.

"Yes sir, go ahead. We can't stop you from executing your duty. Not in the face of a court order. Not even if McCabe wants us to."

Swanson's frown turned into a broad grin. He smiled at Fogarty. Fogarty grinned back as the deputies and Prescott entered Jack Kobe's room.

"Just remember, Sheriff, things aren't always as they appear."

Prescott turned his head to ask Fogarty what he meant by the remark. But Slater's hand tightened around her supervisor's forearm, calling Prescott's attention back into the room.

The hospital room was empty. The bed was freshly made. There was no sign of Jack Kobe, no indication whatsoever that the man had been there.

"Yugoslav's dead, sheriff. So's the girl."

Dan Prescott turned to identify the voice. A round, red–haired man stepped into the room displaying an ample belly bound in an expensive tweed suit. The stranger extended his hand, the skin of the appendage thick, pink and blotchy.

"Commissioner Ian McCabe. Call me Ian."

Prescott looked stunned. Still, as a reflex, he shook the man's hand. The skin was soft, dry and warm, like that of a child.

"You're crazy, McCabe. We saw him. He took a slug, all right, but the Kevlar stopped it," Debra Slater blurted out defensively. "Herb Whitefeather thought he'd come out of it with a few broken ribs. Maybe a collapsed lung. Nothing fatal. The information we got from the doctors last night was that he was ready to travel."

Slater stood next to the Commissioner, glaring at the little man. Behind McCabe stood two cops she'd never seen before. They defined the Commissioner's space like two identical bookends.

"Nice that you and Whitefeather can shoot 'em and doctor 'em. Where'd you two go to medical school, Deputy?"

McCabe chuckled at his own joke. No one else cracked a smile.

"Unfortunately, Mr. Kobe took a turn for the worse overnight. Morning rounds found him stiff as a board. Same with the girl. We were going to keep the bodies after the autopsies but the Yugoslav Consulate pulled some strings, got the bodies out of here. Apparently the two of them were lovers. The bodies are on their way to Belgrade as we speak."

Prescott turned away from the Commissioner, trying to breathe, trying to keep from exploding. His expression did not deter the Commissioner from continuing.

"Another thing, Sheriff. Seems the guys Kobe shot were war criminals. Executed Kobe's family during World War II. Children, women. Mass grave and all that sort of shit. So Kobe's going home a hero. For taking those two out. Tracked them for years. Don't know how Field fits in. He's somehow connected to the dead men. But the CIA took him off my hands. Can't tell you anymore."

The Sheriff pressed closer to the fat man. Eyes lowered. Voice barely audible.

"Listen, you son–of–a–bitch. If Slater says it can't be, it can't be. What the hell is going on?"

McCabe pulled out a manila envelope from inside his coat. Without a word, he handed it to Prescott. McCabe's disingenuous smile was gone.

"I assure you Sheriff, the man called Jack Kobe is dead. Quite dead," the Commissioner related. "I've gone to the trouble of providing you with certified copies of the death certificates, for both Kobe and Ms. Delaney. And the autopsies. You'll see that Kobe did indeed have broken ribs. In fact, a fragment of rib, only the size of a splinter, apparently nicked his aorta, causing him to slowly bleed to death. Should have caught it but what can you do?"

McCabe took another breath, looking at the two deputies with an air of superiority as he inhaled.

"And poor Ms. Delaney, you'll see that she survived the operation to save her right leg only to develop a blood clot. The clot was thought to be under control until yesterday when it broke free and caused a massive stroke."

The fat man paused again and wiped his brow with a red handkerchief he pulled gingerly from shirt pocket. There was a notable change in the man's demeanor as he expressed what seemed to be genuine grief over the loss of the girl:

"Damn asshole Field. Had to play hero. Shoots an innocent girl and eventually kills her. A beautiful young woman dies for no reason other than an old fool's stupidity. There's no justice in that, is there Prescott?"

McCabe motioned for his men to follow, leaving the Sheriff and his deputies alone in the room. Prescott stood open–mouthed; trying to call the man back, still unsure that what he'd been told was accurate.

But Ian McCabe was already gone, having vanished down the corridors of St. Paul Ramsey Medical Center.

Dan Prescott looked at Swanson and Slater. He handed Slater the folder. She shook her head as she read the medical details of why Jack Kobe and Stephanie Delaney had died. Her partner wouldn't read the report. His attention was diverted out the window.

Somewhere in the distance Dave Swanson heard a police siren wail. The stark sound brought him back into the room, back to the present and told him it was time to go home.

Chapter 33

Epilague

St. Paul Pioneer Press (AP)
December 12, 1991

St. Paul Police Commissioner Ian McCabe confirmed today that St. Paul resident Ms. Stephanie Delaney, died as a result of wounds sustained during the recent hostage incident at the Field Tower. A Yugoslavian National, John Kobe, of rural Belgrade, Yugoslavia, believed to be the assailant, also died as a result of wounds sustained in the gun battle. Well–known financier Marvin Field was rescued during the struggle and was treated and released for wounds as well.

Ms. Delaney, daughter of retired St. Paul attorney Thomas Delaney and his wife Margaret, now living in Sun City, Arizona, was the namesake of the popular bar and restaurant in the renovated warehouse district of St. Paul. She was also a third year student at William Mitchell College of Law. Mr. Kobe is reputed to have been an agent of the Yugoslavian government charged with hunting down Nazi and Ustashi (Croatian Fascist) war criminals. Attempts to verify a motive for the assault upon the Field Tower and Mr. Field have proven unsuccessful. Telephone calls to the Yugoslavian Consulate in Minneapolis have not been returned.

In related news, Serbian officers in charge of the Yugoslavian military have denied accusations by the break away republics of Croatia and Bosnia that the federal army fired upon unarmed minority demonstrators in the Bosnian capital of Sarajevo. There are also unconfirmed reports from Zagreb that Croatian farmers living within the Republic of Serbia have been attacked by irregular units of the Serbian militia. Croatian sources indicate there have been an estimated three hundred civilian deaths in the past week. The same sources indicate a number of women and children are included in this total.

UN observation forces assigned to the region have been unable to verify the report but are searching for any evidence of such atrocities. Washington experts predict that the dismemberment of the former Yugoslavian Nation will likely cause long term instability in the Balkans. Long–standing wounds from the violent civil war that scarred the nation during World War II will likely prevent any national unity from being established in the region now that the federal state has disintegrated.

The Legacy

Near Old Fort William, Ontario, a blue Ford Taurus station wagon entered a gravel drive in front of a small house. Five men exited the vehicle after it came to rest. The engine was left idling.

The home was white with yellow trim. There was a matching picket fence. Behind the white spars of the fence, a flower garden lay dormant beneath loose snow.

The ride from Duluth, along Lake Superior's North Shore, had been a maze of turns, hills and curves. The pavement of Highway 61 cut through high cliffs overlooking the black ice of the lake. Overcast skies formed a low ceiling across to the Wisconsin shore.

It hadn't gone exactly right. He thought he would fall in love with the Irish Dancer, perhaps whisk her off her feet, take her away to the river valley of his youth, where he would return to farm his family's land in seclusion. Jack Kobe had fallen in love, true enough, with the Irish Dancer. And he had swept her off her feet. But Petrich and the CIA had made it plain that there would be no welcome for him at home amidst the turmoil of the unrest sweeping through Yugoslavia. There was no quiet farm for them to seek shelter on. His stepfather had boarded up the buildings, sold the livestock and moved with Marta to Belgrade, to the safety of the Federal Capital.

Across the Atlantic, the country of his birth was seething with the talk and acts of war. Regardless of which side Jack Kobe chose to cast his lot with, he would not escape the killing, the blood. Petrich saw it in the way the man looked at him through tired eyes: Jack Kobe had seen enough death, enough killing, for one lifetime. Petrich suggested Canada, a land of promise, unlimited spaces, mountains, valleys and rivers; the perfect place for a new beginning.

The aging diplomat opened the door to the house. Jack Kobe's ribs were still painful, making it difficult for him to use his right arm. The two friends walked into the tiled foyer, leaving the others, two members of the CIA and an officer of the Royal Canadian Mounted Police, outside.

The house was simple and unassuming. Petrich stood beneath the arch of the front entry. A faint odor of new paint, applied to cover the lingering odor of mildew, greeted them as they entered the house.

The dwelling had been vacant for over a decade before Petrich purchased it. Petrich bought the furniture and the house with gold. A few less gold ingots returned to Belgrade. The old Partisan said they would not be missed.

"Look, Jack," Petrich said in Serbo-Croatian. "I know this isn't what you want. It's only temporary. When we're sure you aren't watched anymore, I mean by anyone, including UDBA, the Canadians will move you to Calgary or Banff, somewhere out West, within driving distance of the mountains, rivers, forests for thousands of miles, heaven. But for now, you must be careful. For now, you must stay here."

Petrich placed his arm around the younger man's shoulders and leaned over to kiss the UDBA Agent, like a father kissing a son. Their embrace complete, Petrich backed away. In a barely discernible voice, Petrich spoke once more in their native tongue:

"My debt to your father is repaid. Live in peace."

Before Kobe could offer his thanks, his hand, the old Partisan retreated and was gone.

Jack Kobe walked down an unlit hallway. Turning a tarnished brass knob on the last door in the corridor, he entered a bedroom.

In the solitude of the home's only bedroom, he reclined next to her and gave her his hand. The woman rested uneasily between freshly starched sheets, her right leg hidden by cool linen.

She remained perfectly still in the dark, silently watching him, her gentle respirations the only movement in the room. He knew, even without light, that she was radiant, beautiful. In his mind's eye, he recalled her face. Her eyes, like her soul, were always dancing, as she herself had danced. Before, before she lost her leg to the surgeon's knife.

He had been there when she woke up, far from St. Paul, in the Royal Orthopedic Hospital in Thunder Bay, Ontario. At first she screamed at him to leave. And he did. But he kept coming back. Every time she woke up he was there, patiently waiting for her eyes to open.

Finally, she let him stay. They talked. He told her the truth. About the Sava. About Anna and the rest. He made her understand how it was he came to Minnesota, why he killed Damos Tomich, Franz Essen, why he needed to look into Marvin Field's eyes.

After awhile she said she understood. And they cried. For the children lost so many years ago. For the dancer who would never dance again.

The Legacy

He took her last name. With Petrich's help, they were married in a Catholic Church. With the CIA's assistance, they obtained Canadian citizenship. That was how it came to be that Mr. and Mrs. Jack Delaney found themselves alone in the stillness of their new home in Old Fort William, Ontario.

Everything that he had ever known was changed. His family, his homeland, his few friends had all been swept away by the unrest of civil war. And his quest, his personal pilgrimage, was over. The years of searching, seeking out the murderers of his family, had come to an end, as had his search for love.

It would have been easy for her to push him away. After all, they had only been together for one brief night. She could have blamed Jack Kobe for her misfortune, for the cruel twist of fate that cost her the leg. She did not. Her smile told him that she did not.

With a sigh, a sigh Stephanie Delaney took to mean relief, her husband touched the black velvet of her hair. His fingers absently twisting and untwisting the soft, silky fibers, his hand moved slowly towards the base of her neck. His thumb massaged the smooth hollow where her head joined her shoulders as he looked intently at her face. He became lost in the beauty of her eyes; eyes so blue that their color was visible even in the sparse light of their bedroom.

He tried to think of something to say. No words came to mind. He placed his head upon her chest. He became drowsy, tranquilized by the pattern of her breathing. His eyes closed. She smiled and kissed his forehead and slowly stroked his face. She whispered into his ear. The words she spoke were not her own, but those of another Irishman:

> The brawling of a sparrow in the eaves,
> The brilliant moon and all the milky sky,
> And all that famous harmony of leaves,
> Had blotted out man's image and his cry.
> A girl arose that had red mournful lips,
> And seemed the greatness of the world in tears,
> Doomed like Odysseus and the laboring ships,
> And proud as Priam murdered with his peers.
> Arose, and on the instant clamorous eaves,
> A climbing moon upon an empty sky,
> And all that lamentation of the leaves,
> Could not compose man's image and his cry.

She urged his face close to her breast as she finished reciting the final passage ofYeats' The Sorrow of Love. It was a poem she learned from her grandmother, a woman old enough to remember Ireland as home.

A lump formed in Stephanie Delaney's throat as she studied the serene face of her husband, while across the Atlantic, along the banks of the Sava, the treads of Serbian tanks began to cross the cold waters of the river, churning relentlessly towards the destiny of civil war.

St. Paul Pioneer Press

Thursday, January 4th, 1992

St. Paul financier Marvin Field, recently in the news as a result of a failed kidnapping attempt and tragic shoot-out at the Field Tower, was found asphyxiated in his Eden Prairie garage this morning by the Eden Prairie Police Department. A squad was dispatched to Mr. Field's home when he failed to report for a 9:00 a.m. board meeting at his office.

According to a spokesperson from the Hennepin County Medical Examiner's Office, Mr. Field's death has been ruled a suicide. No note was found and investigators would not speculate as to the reasons behind the death.

Friends and relatives contacted by the Pioneer Press indicated that Mr. Field had been extremely reclusive and introspective since the kidnapping incident. The Washington Office of the CIA has denied rumors that Mr. Field's death is linked to his service in the CIA, or its predecessor, the OSS.

Other Savage Press Press Books

BUSINESS

SoundBites by Kathy Kerchner

Dare to Kiss the Frog by van Hauen, Kastberg & Soden

LOCAL AND REGIONAL HISTORY, HUMOR, MEMOIR

Beyond the Mine by Peter J. Benzoni

Crocodile Tears and Lipstick Smears by Fran Gabino

Jackpine Savages, or Skinny Dipping for Fun and Profit by Frank Larson

Some Things You Never Forget by Clem Miller

Stop in the Name of the Law by Alex O'Kash

Superior Catholics by Georgeann Cheney and Teddy Meronek

Widow of the Waves by Bev Jamison

ESSAY

A Hint of Frost, Essays on the Earth by Rusty King

OUTDOORS, SPORTS & RECREATION

Cool Fishing for Kids 8 - 85 by Frankie Paull and "Jackpine" Bob Cary

Floating All-Weather Sailboat Log Book, Coast Guard Approved

Floating Outdoor All-Weather Journals, Kayak, Canoe, Generic

The Duluth Tour Book, by Jeff Cornelius

The North Shore Tour Book by Jeff Cornelius

Stop and Smell the Cedars by Tony Jelich

POETRY

Appalachian Mettle by Paul Bennett

In the Heart of the Forest by Diana Randolph

Gleanings from the Hillsides by E. M. Johnson

Moments Beautiful - Moments Bright by Brett Bartholomaus

Pathways by Mary B. Wadzinski

Philosophical Poems by E. M. Johnson

Poems of Faith and Inspiration by E. M. Johnson

Thicker Than Water by Hazel Sangster

Treasured Thoughts by Sierra

Treasures from the Beginning of the World by Jeff Lewis

FICTION

Burn Baby Burn by Mike Savage

Keeper of the Town by Don Cameron

Something in the Water by Mike Savage

The Year of the Buffalo by Marshall J. Cook

Voices From the North Edge by St. Croix Writers

SPIRITUALITY

The Awakening of the Heart by Jill Downs

The Hillside Story by Pastor Thor Sorenson

About the Author

Photograph by Jeff Frey Photography

Mark Munger, a third generation descendant of Slovenian immigrants, is an honors graduate of the University of Minnesota-Duluth and the William Mitchell College of Law in St. Paul. He is a District Court Judge and former trial attorney. He and his wife, René, and their 4 children live in Minnesota, where Mr. Munger tends a farm and coaches youth athletics. He is at work on his second novel.